D1602342

The
Repertory
of Shakespeare's
Company
1594–1613

The

Repertory

of Shakespeare's

Company

1594–1613

ROSLYN LANDER KNUTSON

THE UNIVERSITY OF ARKANSAS PRESS
FAYETTEVILLE • 1991

Copyright © 1991 by Roslyn Lander Knutson

Manufactured in the United States of America

95 94 93 92 91   5 4 3 2 1

Text design: Lisa Heggestad
Typeface: Galliard

The paper used in this publication meets the minimum
requirements of the American National Standard for
Permanence of Paper for Printed Library Materials
Z39.48-1984. ∞

Library of Congress Cataloging-in-Publication Data

Knutson, Roslyn Lander, 1939–
The repertory of Shakespeare's company, 1594–1613 /
Roslyn Lander Knutson.
p. cm.
Includes index.
ISBN 1-55728-191-2 (alk. paper)
1. Shakespeare, William, 1564–1616—Stage history—To
1625. 2. English drama—Early modern and Elizabethan,
1500–1600—History and criticism. 3. English drama—
17th century—History and criticism. 4. Repertory
theater—England—London—History—17th century.
5. Repertory theater—England—London—History—16th
century. 6. Chamberlain's Men (Theater company). 7. King's
Men (Theater company) I. Title.
PR3095.K6 1991
792'.0942'09031—dc20
                                        90–47012
                                        CIP

For my parents

ACKNOWLEDGMENTS

I wish to thank the University of Arkansas at Little Rock for support of my research with stipends from the Faculty Research Fund and the Provost's Discretionary Fund. I wish also to thank colleagues and friends in the English department at UALR, whose scholarship and productivity set a fine example. I owe a particular debt to the Shakespeare Association of America, which, by the design of the seminars at its annual meeting, offers members an opportunity to develop their research in a community of scholars. In the theater history seminar, I benefit from friendships as well as professional guidance. I reserve special thanks for my husband, Brent, who appreciates my work.

CONTENTS

INTRODUCTION

In June 1594 Philip Henslowe, owner of the Rose playhouse, blocked out a section in the diary that he kept of his business activities and made the following entry:

In the name of god Amen begininge at newing
ton my Lord Admeralle men & my Lorde chamberlen
men As ffolowethe   1594

3 of June 1594	Rd at heaster & asheweros	viijs
4 of June 1594	Rd at the Jewe of malta	xs
5 of June 1594	Rd at andronicous	xijs
6 of June 1594	Rd at cvtlacke	xjs
8 of June 1594	ne-Rd at bellendon	vijs
9 of June 1594	Rd at hamlet	viijs
10 of June 1594	Rd at heaster	vs
11 of June 1594	Rd at the tamynge of A shrowe	ixs
12 of June 1594	Rd at andronicous	vijs
13 of June 1594	Rd at th*e* Jewe	iiijs

Theater historians agree that this record of ten performances by the Admiral's and Chamberlain's men at the playhouse in Newington is our earliest evidence that Henry Carey, lord Hunsdon, the Lord Chamberlain, granted his patronage to a new company of players in 1594. This company was formed in the wake of more than a year's disruption of theatrical activity due to official restraints, and it was now prepared to offer plays to the London public on a daily basis.

We know a great deal about the Chamberlain's men. We know, for example, that after the run at Newington they left London to give a performance at Marlborough. We know that in the fall of 1594 their patron attempted to help them procure a stage in the City. On 8 October, he wrote to the lord mayor and asked him to "permitt & suffer" the players to perform at the Cross Keys Inn throughout the winter (*MSC*, I.1, 74). We know that in December, during the Christmas revels at Court, the company entertained the Queen on two occasions, St. Stephen's Day and Holy Innocents' Day, for the Treasurer of the Chamber paid £20 to "Will*i*am Kempe Will*i*am Shakespeare & Richarde Burbage" for the company's appearances (*MSC,* VI, 29). From this set of names, plus a name in a Chamber Account for December 1596 (George Bryan), plus the names in the cast list of *Every Man in His Humor* (Augustine Phillips, Henry Condell, William Sly, John Heminges, Thomas Pope, Christopher Beeston, and John Duke), we know the principal membership of the Chamberlain's men in their early years of business.

Because one of these members was William Shakespeare, who had become preeminent among Elizabethan dramatists long before *Henslowe's Diary* or accounts from the Treasurer of the Chamber were discovered and published, theater historians have treated every scrap of information about the company as priceless treasure. In public records, theatrical documents, contemporary literature, maps, excavations of playhouse sites, letters, and diaries, we have found information on numerous aspects of the company's theatrical enterprise. There is consequently much beyond the few details of activity in 1594 that we can state as fact about the Chamberlain's and King's men in the years subsequent, when Shakespeare was contributing new plays to their daily offerings. Yet there remain gaps in the surviving material; we simply do not have records for every detail of company business.

Furthermore, virtually from the start of historical studies of Elizabethan drama, the perspective of scholars on the activities of the Chamberlain's men for the years of Shakespeare's career has been shaped by certain assumptions about the quality of the various companies and the nature of the competition they carried on. It oversimplifies the mind-set of theater historians at the turn of the twentieth century, but not by much, to say that they believed Shakespeare to have been the consummate dramatist of his age and the company with Shakespeare's plays to have been the most successful. They did not talk much of success in terms of commerce, which for them implied a company debased by a concern only for financial profit. Such were the companies in the records kept by Henslowe over the years from 1592 to 1603. Such in particular was the company of the Lord Admiral's men, putatively the arch rival of the Chamberlain's men. These theater historians meant success to be equated with prestige. They saw the elevation of the Chamberlain's men to be the servants of King James I as testament to the differences between them and all of their competitors, differences obviously manifest in the contrast in artistry between Shakespeare's plays and the hackwork of the dramatists who supplied the other companies.

The question of a company's success, of course, is very complicated. It cries out for evidence that does not exist—for data on attendance, day by day, playhouse to playhouse; for monthly budgets and annual fiscal statements; for the criteria on which companies were assigned to royal patrons in 1603. Yet there is one aspect of the fortunes of the Chamberlain's and King's men that can be addressed, even though valuable records of daily business have been lost. This is the role of the repertory in the company's commercial success, and there are documents that enable us to address this subject. There are, for example, the play texts that the Chamberlain's and King's men offered to the London public year by year. A number of these texts have survived in print. We are indebted to the stationers who saw the texts as marketable and who published quartos frequently in relative conjunction with the initial stage runs of the plays, but we are also indebted to the promoters of collections such as the edition of Shakespeare's plays in 1623 and the edition of Beaumont and Fletcher's plays in 1647. In addition, the titles of company plays have survived in both public and private records, though the texts themselves are lost. In a few cases, the title contains a clue to the subject matter and genre of the play. *Cloth Breeches and Velvet Hose,* for example, probably took its story and perhaps structure from one of the dreams in Robert Greene's *A Quip for an Upstart Courtier.* In other cases, the way that the title was preserved has provided information about the play itself. Thus we know that the play a London astrologer saw and called *Richard the 2* contained a scene in which the duke of Lancaster ordered a wise man to be hanged for giving him an answer he did not want to hear.

In addition to the plays owned by the Chamberlain's and King's men, there are the offerings of companies in business at the same time. The records in *Henslowe's Diary* provide us with nearly complete playlists for the Admiral's men from 1594 to 1603. The diary also provides partial lists for Strange's men in 1592–93, Sussex's men in 1593–94, Sussex's men with the Queen's men in 1594, and Worcester's men in 1602–03. Perhaps as many as two dozen of these plays survive in print. For the repertories of companies not mentioned in the diary and for all companies in the years after 1603, we depend largely on claims on title-pages of quartos to indicate the owners of the playbooks. From the texts of surviving plays and the titles of lost ones, we get a sense of the subjects and styles that were popular with all playgoers. Further, from the patterns of performances in Henslowe's records of daily offerings, we learn the strategy in scheduling that the companies used to market their commodities to advantage day after day, season after season, year after year.

To approach the success of Shakespeare's company by way of its entire repertory, however, requires a shift in perspective that would have been anathema to most theater historians as recently as a generation ago. It requires that we seek out the similarities in the battery of plays offered to the public on a daily basis by the Chamberlain's and King's men and the battery of plays offered by companies at other playhouses. It requires that we look for similarities in the way they appear to have acquired and scheduled those plays and the methods of other companies' activities as indicated in sources such as *Henslowe's Diary*. It requires, in other words, that we remove Shakespeare's company from a privileged status and treat it merely as one of the men's theatrical organizations that formed in the wake of the playhouse closings in London, 1592–94, and that sought to make a living for their players and investors by keeping as busy and attractive a program of dramatic activity as they could muster. I am encouraged to make that change in focus by the entry in *Henslowe's Diary* quoted above, in which the

Chamberlain's men mesh their operation with that of the Admiral's men at the playhouse in Newington.

Scholars have long agreed that entries in *Henslowe's Diary* give the basic features of the Elizabethan repertory system such as the number of plays it called for each year, the mix of new and old materials, and the daily rotation of offerings. However, from F. G. Fleay's *A Chronicle History of the London Stage, 1559–1642* (1890), to W. W. Greg's volume of commentary (1908) for his edition of *Henslowe's Diary* (1904), to E. K. Chambers's discussion of companies at the Rose in *The Elizabethan Stage* (1923), to R. A. Foakes and R. T. Rickert's edition of the diary (1961), to Bernard Beckerman's *Shakespeare at the Globe, 1599–1609* (1962), there is a fundamental disagreement on the employment of the system by various companies and the commercial implications of that employment. Fleay, Greg, and Chambers believed that certain features of the system were unique to those companies at the Rose. In the rapid consumption of potboiler dramas, in the partial payments on works-in-progress, and in the team of collaborators who turned out those potboilers and defaulted on the works-in-progress, these scholars saw the hand of a tyrannical Henslowe, who kept players and dramatists alike living on the edge of financial distress from season to season, perhaps even from play to play. They condemned this style of business, and they imagined that in the Chamberlain's men, where gentle Shakespeare set the level of professionalism among the dramatists and salt-of-the-earth player-administrators such as John Heminges and Henry Condell typified company personnel, the acquisition and scheduling of plays worked differently. First Foakes and Rickert, then Beckerman revolutionized the perception of Henslowe in theater history by debunking the myth of his capitalist exploitation of the players and dramatists. Beckerman even asserted that the repertory practices in *Henslowe's Diary* were analogues for the practices followed by Shakespeare's company.

In the chapter here on the repertory system, I adopt Beckerman's premise that the men's companies acquired and scheduled their offerings by similar techniques of management year to year. I do not intend to prove that Shakespeare's company used these techniques but to make obvious that a men's company could not have competed successfully over the long haul at a London playhouse if it disdained the methods of business employed by its competitors. In this effort, I am hampered somewhat by the fact that some of Henslowe's entries are erroneous or simply unreadable. Greg corrected what he considered mistakes, for example, the scheduling of plays for Sunday performances. Also (often at Fleay's instigation) he reduced the number of puzzling play titles by identifying some of these with one another, for example, the identification of "valy a for" with "antony & vallea" and "seleo & olempo" with "olempeo & hengenyo" (*Diary*, II, 173–74, 175). I follow Greg's identifications of plays, but I do not follow his dates because I believe that there were some Sunday performances and that there would have been more if the players had had a choice. In the discussion of company activities annually, I consider the repertory year to begin in the fall and end the following summer. For the Admiral's men (for example), I refer to the opening day of 27 October 1596 as an event in the fall of 1596–97; similarly, I refer to the change in Henslowe's accounting system on 24 January 1597 as an event in the spring of 1596–97. In using the receipts in the lists of performances, I repeatedly specify that these receipts were payments to Henslowe, by which I mean to emphasize that the receipts were not the company's returns. Even so, I assume that an offering profitable for Henslowe was profitable for the company as well. The expenditures that Henslowe recorded for old and new plays from October 1597 to March 1603 are incomplete. It may be, therefore, that the Admiral's men and Worcester's men spent much more money on revivals and continuations than the entries in *Henslowe's Diary* imply. Nevertheless, I assume that the general pattern of expenditures in these years—more on apparel and properties for new plays than for old—is an accurate one.

In conjunction with the repertory system and its economics, I discuss the commercial strategy that the companies used to take advantage of playgoers' tastes. It may be that the companies created those tastes by the dramas they supplied; however, I am not concerned with the direction of influence but with the tactics that the companies used in making their offerings attractive. These tactics were simple. Regarding story and genre, the companies offered a preponderance of comedies and comical histories and a preponderance of material in long-popular dramatic formulas. But when an innovation by a dramatist captured the attention of playgoers, as did the revenge tragedies of Thomas Kyd and Christopher Marlowe and the humors comedies of Ben Jonson and George Chapman, the companies were quick to acquire similar offerings. One of their means was to have dramatists duplicate the successes in other companies' repertories, both in subject matter and form. If the success was their own to begin with, they serialized the subject into a second, third, or even fourth part.

In chapters II through V, I discuss the business activities of the Chamberlain's men by way of the repertories in 1594–1599 and 1599–1603 and the King's men in 1603–1608 and 1608–1613. In the process of making annual calendars of new and revived plays, I run into two difficulties that scholars have not resolved to everyone's satisfaction. One is the canon of plays owned by the company. There is not a list of the repertory for the Shakespearean years comparable to that for 1616–1642 in *The Jacobean and Caroline Stage* by G. E. Bentley (I, 109–34). In *The Elizabethan Stage* (II, 192–220), E. K. Chambers discusses the repertory year by year, but he identifies some lost plays as versions of extant plays and implies the wholesale migration of playbooks from Strange's (Derby's), Pembroke's, and Sussex's men in 1592–94 to the Chamberlain's men. In *Shakespeare at the Globe, 1599–1609*, Bernard Beckerman restricts the repertory to a ten-year span and to the new plays for which a text survives. In *William Shakespeare: A Textual Companion*, Gary Taylor and Stanley Wells reconsider the case of many plays attributed to the company through attribution to Shakespeare, but they do not address company ownership apart from the question of authorship.

I, however, am interested only in ownership. In the appendix, I list the plays attributable to the Chamberlain's and King's men on evidence in documents from the period as diverse as the title-page of an edition of the play, an entry in the Stationers' Register, an account from Offices of the Revels or Chamber, a cast list, a dedicatory epistle published with a play quarto, a business diary, a commonplace book, personal correspondence, additions to a play, and an anthology in a king's library.[1]

Much of the confusion about ownership has originated in the attribution of plays to Shakespeare and thus to his company. In the cases of those plays that are surely his—and the most recent list is in Wells and Taylor's *William Shakespeare: A Textual Companion* (1987)—we are safe in assuming ownership. But we are not safe with those questionably his in whole or in part. I accept the attribution to his company of plays not in the First Folio where there is corroborative evidence of ownership such as the name of the company on the title-page of the quarto: for example, *The London Prodigal, A Yorkshire Tragedy, Thomas Lord Cromwell, Pericles,* and *Two Noble Kinsmen.* I reject the attributions implied by the ascriptions to Shakespeare for which there is either conflicting evidence from title-pages and play catalogues or no evidence at all. By this decision, I reject the attribution of *The Troublesome Reign of King John, Edward III, 1 Sir John Oldcastle, The Puritan,* the two parts of *Edward IV, The Arraignment of Paris, Hoffman, A Trick to Catch the Old One, The Birth of Merlin, Sir Thomas More,* and *Edmund Ironside.*

There remain a few plays that have been associated with Shakespeare's company but for which there is no real evidence of ownership. For the most part, these plays were written before 1594 (or are so dated), and the main basis of their attribution is a theory of migration, which claims that playbooks moved from one company to another during the chaotic years of 1592–1594. It seems clear that Shakespeare's old plays traveled to the Chamberlain's men, and we have assumed that they did not go alone. The problem is identifying the migrant texts. Which old plays had a stage life after May 1594, and which of these had that life with Shakespeare's company? Some eligible texts are those subsequently published but not identified with a current company through a title-page advertisement or entries in *Henslowe's Diary:* for example, *Orlando Furioso, A Looking Glass for London and England, A Knack to*

Know a Knave, Edward II, Arden of Faversham, Soliman and Perseda, Summer's Last Will and Testament, George a Greene, and *Locrine.* I feel sure that some of these plays migrated to the Chamberlain's men in 1594, but I cannot determine on present evidence which they were.

The chronology of the plays acquired by the Chamberlain's and King's men is as vexed a question as the make-up of the canon, and reliable evidence is as difficult to come by. The art of dating Shakespeare's plays began with an essay by Edmond Malone for the second edition of George Steevens and Samuel Johnson's *The Plays of William Shakespeare* in 1778 entitled "An Attempt to Ascertain the Order in Which the Plays Attributed to Shakespeare Were Written." As he ran across evidence in addition to that in the Stationers' Register and on title-pages of quartos, Malone changed the dates for some plays in versions of the essay in 1790 and 1821. E. K. Chambers readdressed the issue of chronology both in *The Elizabethan Stage* and *William Shakespeare: A Study of Facts and Problems,* and he agreed with most of Malone's final dates, give or take a year. He corrected the others with dates that have held up under the scrutiny of subsequent researchers (again, give or take a year) except in the case of *The Merry Wives of Windsor.* The so-called "early chronologists," most distinguished of whom is E. A. J. Honigmann, assign nearly one-third of the canon to a date of composition before June 1594, but their opinion is still in the minority. For the Oxford *Complete Works,* Stanley Wells and Gary Taylor offer a chronology that differs little from that of Malone and Chambers, and I use Wells and Taylor's dates of composition as a guide in the assignment of plays to a repertory year unless otherwise noted in the appendix.

For some of the plays owned by the company and written by dramatists other than Shakespeare, there is reliable evidence on stage history, but for others there is no evidence of any kind. We can date the plays by Ben Jonson to the year of first performance because of title-pages included in the Folio edition of 1616. We have to guess about most of the plays by Beaumont and Fletcher. The Folio edition of 1679 includes some cast lists, but these often give us merely a range of years and not the date of first performance. For the anonymous plays there is rarely a better clue than the dates of registration at Stationers' Hall and/or publication. We have accepted the stationers' records at face value for plays such as *A Larum for London, Thomas Lord Cromwell,* and *The London Prodigal.* In other cases, however, we have pushed back the date of composition a considerable number of years before the entry of the play into the Stationers' Register or its appearance at London bookstalls. An example is *A Warning for Fair Women,* which is commonly dated 1588–90, even though it was registered and published in 1599.

My method of annual calendars forces me to be specific. In those cases where there is no helpful evidence on the date of entry into the repertory, I assign the play to a year that is about eighteen months before its appearance in the hands of stationers, either to be registered or published. I justify this arbitrary dating on a combination of factors. First, I believe that stationers did not as a rule acquire plays that were still in a maiden production at a London playhouse. A glaring exception is *A Knack to Know an Honest Man,* which was registered at Stationers' Hall on 26 November 1595 and which continued in production at the Rose until November of 1596. But the other plays published out of the Admiral's repertory at the Rose and Fortune were retired (or seem to have been) before they were published. Second, I believe that the stage run of most moderately successful plays lasted for four to six months, and I see no reason to assume that these plays were on the whole more successful than that. Third, I believe that the interest of the stationers indicates a currency of the play. By choosing an eighteen-month spread, I am therefore allowing about six months for the run itself, six months for the play to come into the hands of stationers, and six months for good measure. A couple of plays in the Admiral's repertory are exemplars: *The Blind Beggar of Alexandria,* which ran from February 1596 to April 1597 and was registered and published in 1598; and *The Comedy of Humors,* which ran from May 1597 to some time past October 1597 and was published in 1599.

I realize that my dates may be off by a year or two. I may also call some plays new that were acquired secondhand. However, these possible errors do not undercut the argument that the plays were valuable commercial properties. I base a discussion of their value less on age than on subject matter and dramatic formula. New plays had a special commercial advantage to the company in that they could be offered at doubled admission prices at the opening show; and, after all, they were new. But old plays had advantages too. In some years, as in 1594–95, when the London playhouses had been closed more or less continuously for two years, revivals were as profitable as new plays, according to the receipts in *Henslowe's Diary*. For the Chamberlain's men in 1594–95, I assume that differences in profits between new plays and old had no serious effect on the financial success of the company.

Although my argument does not depend on an exact chronology and a clear distinction between new and secondhand texts, it does depend on evidence that the company filled out the offerings each year with old plays. There is some documentary evidence for both continuations and revivals. *The Tempest, The Winter's Tale, A King and No King, The Twins Tragedy,* and *The Nobleman* were presented at Court during the winter of 1611–12, and all were carried over into the repertory of 1612–13 and presented at Court again, according to surviving accounts from the Offices of the Revels and Chamber. *Every Man in His Humor* and *Every Man out of His Humor,* which were first presented on the public stage in 1598 and 1599, respectively, according to the title-pages printed with the texts in the 1616 Folio, were revived for performances at Court in 1604–05 according to an account from the Office of the Revels. But there is not much evidence of this kind. A few of the continuations and revivals that I propose originate in allusions to the plays in contemporary literature and the dates of second and third editions. This evidence is extraordinarily flimsy. It may not be evidence at all.

Yet some allusions are coincident with stage runs, and this coincidence invites me to see allusions as a sign of a play's currency. An example is allusions to Thomas Kyd's *The Spanish Tragedy* in

1597–98. In a poem published in *Skialetheia* in 1598, Everard Guilpin talks about going to plays at the Rose and Curtain where one may see a comedy by Plautus or "the *Patheticke Spaniards* Tragedies" ("Satire V"). As it happens, *The Spanish Tragedy* was in revival at the Rose at about the time Guilpin was writing the poem. According to *Henslowe's Diary*, the Admiral's men introduced "Joronymo" on 7 January 1597, and they still had it in production in October, when some members from Pembroke's company came over to the Rose. There is also an allusion to it in Ben Jonson's *Every Man in His Humor*, which was written at about the time of Guilpin's poem and played at the Curtain in 1598–99. One of the gulls-in-training, Matheo, raves about a play called *Go By, Hieronimo*. He quotes several lines, thus identifying it to audiences as Kyd's play. Jonson had reason to know the plays at the Rose. He had himself sold a plot to the Admiral's men in December of 1597. To be sure, I cannot say whether Guilpin and Jonson were alluding specifically to a run of *The Spanish Tragedy* in 1597 (which by good fortune we know about) or generally to the popularity of the play in other, earlier runs. By the same measure, I cannot say that allusions to plays in the stock of the Chamberlain's and King's men establish that these plays had recently been or were currently being performed, but I include the allusions to suggest the possibility.

Many of the plays owned by Shakespeare's company were published after having been introduced to the stage, and in general we have assumed that a successful maiden run led to an interest in the text on the part of stationers and to the initial publication. We know very little about the market for these quartos, and even less about a market for subsequent printings. One possibility, though, is that a successful stage revival led to the publication of another edition of the play. There are about a half-dozen instances in which we can document the occurrence of a reprinting of the play within a year or two of a revival: Q1599 and Q1602 of *The Spanish Tragedy*, if the run at the Rose in 1597 lasted into 1598 and if the play was indeed revived in 1601–02 (when Jonson was paid for revisions); Q1604 of *Doctor Faustus*, if the play was indeed revived in 1602–03 when William Bird and Samuel Rowley were paid for additions; Q1606, Q1610, and Q1611 of *Mucedorus,* if the play was revived just after James I came to the throne and again (apparently) in 1609–10; Q1612 of *The Merry Devil of Edmonton,* which was revived in 1612–13 according to the Chamber Accounts; and Q1613 of *1 Henry IV,* if it was the "Hotspurr" in the Chamber Accounts of 1612–13. All of these coordinations may be coincidence. Even if not, this number is too few on which to construct a theory of revival and reprinting. Nevertheless, I take publication as a sign of a commercial market of some kind for the story of the play and as such as an indirect reflection of the value of the play to the company. I therefore include information about the publication of quartos as possible evidence of theatrical currency.

Despite the efforts of scholars over a three-hundred-year search for information about Shakespeare and his company, we have only partial playlists for the Chamberlain's and King's men from 1594–95 to 1612–13. There is not even a year in which we can name half of the plays in production unless it is 1612–13, when a clerk in the Office of the Chamber copied down on a draft of the accounts the titles of eighteen plays given by the King's men at Court. We have only scattered references to the reception of any play with audiences, and these references rarely indicate the criteria on which playgoers applauded or hissed. Nevertheless, we have come to think of the company to which Shakespeare belonged as the most successful and of the quality of his plays as the most important factor in that success. I do not want to deny these conclusions, but I do want to redesign part of the foundation on which they rest. In place of the premise that the success of the company depended on a unique style of repertory management, I suggest that the success depended on a provident management of the system in use by the men's companies at London playhouses. In place of the premise that the company relied most heavily on Shakespeare's plays and filled in occasionally with the best of Jonson or Marston or Dekker but usually with the work of hacks now understandably forgotten, I suggest that those very fillers were valuable items in the company repertory—if only because of their number, conventionality, and appeal to a spectrum of tastes. I do not wish to denigrate the role of Shakespeare; indeed, I promote it by arguing that his contributions were not only his mastery of theatrical literature but also his understanding of the playhouse as a marketplace.

Much of the latest work in theater history provides an economic and sociological context for the daily activities of the Elizabethan playing companies, including the one that Shakespeare joined in 1594. We have learned new facts about the boom in playhouse construction, starting with the erection of the Red Lion in Stepney and including the Theatre in Shoreditch, the Swan in Paris Garden, the Boar's Head in Whitechapel, and the second Globe in Southwark. We have learned more about such shadowy investors in the theatrical industry as John Brayne, Francis Langley, Oliver Woodliffe, and Richard Samwell. We have even learned more about such prominent men as Philip Henslowe, Edward Alleyn, and James Burbage. We are beginning to understand something of the finances of the companies, the engineering and design of a playhouse, the cost of building, the economic place of touring in the annual life of the London-based company, the preparation of playscripts for staging, the level of interest among stationers in playbooks, the position of the companies in the households of their patrons, and their place in the political dynamics of the community. I believe it is high time that we provide these companies with repertories and consider the implications of their choices in subject matter and kinds of plays. For the Chamberlain's men, it is with *Henslowe's Diary* and entries for the Newington run in June 1594 that their repertory takes the stage and begins its commercial life.

I

The Repertory System
and Commercial Tactics

In the years between 1780 and 1790, Edmond Malone was busy preparing an edition of Shakespeare's works that was to be a summation of the editorial efforts begun with Nicholas Rowe's *The Works of Mr. William Shakespeare* (1709). Malone gathered material from these editions—Rowe's "Life," Pope's "Preface," Johnson's "Preface," and revisions of his own "An Attempt to Ascertain the Order in Which the Plays of Shakespeare Were Written" and "An Historical Account of the Rise and Progress of the English Stage"—to accompany the texts from the First Folio plus *Pericles* plus the poems in *The Plays and Poems of William Shakespeare in Ten Volumes.* But "as this work was issuing from the press," he was contacted by the Master of Dulwich College and the Reverend Mr. Smith, librarian, and shown a heretofore unexamined set of papers from the collection bequeathed to the Dulwich archives by Edward Alleyn, player and theatrical entrepreneur with Philip Henslowe.[1] Much excited by this new material, Malone appended extracts from it to the essay on theater history in part two of volume one, with an apology that the extracts were made in haste to allow the information to be available to the public as soon as possible. From the folio volume now known as *Henslowe's Diary,* Malone printed lists of the plays in Henslowe's accounts of performances and expenditures, 1592–1603. From loose papers, he printed such items as an inventory taken in 1598, the Fortune contract, and theatrical Plots. The selections were only a partial mining of Henslowe's gold, but they were enough to draw the next generation of theater historians into the rush for information on the business practices of Elizabethan repertory companies.

In 1845 John Payne Collier produced an edition of much of the Henslowe material for the Shakespeare Society, specifically, the theatrical records in the folio volume. Malone had not had time to annotate the extracts beyond the occasional comment, and he did not expand this phase of his research in the working papers that Boswell used for the revised and enlarged posthumous edition of the *Plays and Poems* in 1821. It therefore fell to Collier to suggest an attitude toward *Henslowe's Diary* for the scholarly community. He did so on the one hand by pointing out the value of the information: it "authentically . . . contributes to our knowledge of particulars" in the operation of the theatrical business.[2] But on the other hand, he characterized Henslowe in a way that was guaranteed to prejudice subsequent scholars:

> Henslowe was an ignorant man, even for the time in which he lived, and for the station he occupied: he wrote a bad hand, adopted any orthography that suited his notions of the sound of words, especially of proper names . . . , and he kept his book, as respects dates in particular, in the most disorderly, negligent, and confused, manner (xv).

Moreover, Collier pointed out that the name of Shakespeare did not appear in Henslowe's accounts and that the dramatists whose names did appear differed from Shakespeare in that they worked for more than one company at a time. Thus separating the diary and its methods of business from Shakespeare, Collier implied that Henslowe's information was at odds with business as it was practiced by Shakespeare and his company.

Although he did not edit the diary, F. G. Fleay abstracted material from it in *A Chronicle History of the London Stage, 1559–1642* (1890), making table on table of playlists, dates of performances, expenditures, and sales by dramatists to companies. Like Collier he opened the discussion by speaking of the "extreme importance" and "general utility" of the diary, but in the same sentence he called it "the old, pawnbroking, stage-managing, bear-baiting usurer's MS."[3] He then proceeded to make explicit what

Collier had implied. He attacked the idea that the practices of the companies in the diary were typical. He characterized Henslowe as a shrewd manager who kept "his actors in subservience and his poets in constant need . . . by lending them money and never allowing their debts to be fully paid off" (117–18). His peroration was a comparison of Henslowe's style of management to the style he imagined to have been in place with the Chamberlain's men:

> Managed by the housekeepers or principal sharers, whose interest was that of the whole company, and not by an independent employer whose object was to fill his own pocket, they [the Chamberlain's men] sought to produce plays of lasting interest, which would bear revival and be a perennial source of income. They employed few poets, and paid them well. I have not been able to trace more than three poets at one time in their employment during Elizabeth's reign—Henslow usually occupied twelve—nor more than four new plays produced by them in any one year (say one in two months). Henslow's playwrights averaged one every two weeks. The subsequent history confirms this view. Hardly ever do we find a play passing out of the possession of these men, and if we do it is invariably by some surreptitious procedure; while the plays produced for Henslow were continually rewritten, renamed, and resold to other companies (118).

The value of *Henslowe's Diary* to Fleay, then, was not "in its showing us what the inner arrangement of Shakespeare's company must also have been, but in setting before us the selfish hand-to-mouth policy on which its principal rivals were guided, and consequently an explanation of their ultimate failure, in spite of the excellence of many of their plays and the genius of their authors" (118).

W. W. Greg brought out an edition of the diary in 1904 with a volume of commentary in 1908. He followed the tradition of identification and interpretation that had begun (if sparsely) with Malone; in fact, much of his commentary was an attempt to sort out fact from fancy in the previous analyses of data in the diary. He looked at the relationship between Henslowe and the companies in the accounts with particular care, and he decided that Henslowe did not manage the company in the full sense of that word but rather served as accountant and banker. But Greg continued to perceive the practices as destructive and the employment of those practices as an idiosyncratic feature of companies associated with Henslowe:

> I quite agree with Fleay that Henslowe's methods were not those best adapted to the free development of the dramatic energies of the company, being such as were forced upon them by their want of capital, and I believe his comparison to be in the main a true one. What it is important to bear in mind is that the financial arrangements which we find obtaining in the groups of companies under Henslowe's control were the exception rather than the rule (*Diary*, II, 113).

In *The Elizabethan Stage*, E. K. Chambers did not embrace Fleay's paradigm as explicitly as this, but he did confine a discussion of repertory practices to the essays on the Admiral's men and Worcester's men. Moreover, he spoke disparagingly of "the extremely out-at-elbows men of letters who hung about the Rose" (II, 162) and sympathetically of "the disadvantages under which a company in the hands of a capitalist lay" (I, 368). Clearly Chambers too believed that Shakespeare's company did not run its business as the companies in Henslowe's records did.

In 1961, R. A. Foakes and R. T. Rickert produced the third scholarly edition of the Henslowe material. We are in their debt, and in Bernard Beckerman's, for rehabilitating Henslowe and enabling us to read the diary for what it implies about the practices of Elizabethan theatrical companies in general, including the Chamberlain's and King's men. Foakes and Rickert challenge Greg's assertion that practices at the Rose were not observed throughout the theatrical industry. They point out that Henslowe "had dealings with all the principal companies of his time; from 1594 until 1602 he financed one of the two main companies, and in 1602–03 two (Admiral's and Worcester's) of the three officially recognized companies" (*HD*, xxxii). They also challenge the excoriation of Henslowe because he was interested in making a profit; they point out that theatrical investors including the Burbages were "all capitalists" (*HD*, xxxiii). In an essay on Henslowe as manager

at the Rose, Beckerman demolishes the image of him as an ignorant, usurious tyrant and substitutes the characterization of a
benevolent banker who loaned out money without interest to
acquire financial stability: "He was guaranteeing continuous use of
his playhouse through his loans."[4] Considering the language of the
entries in 1597–1603, Beckerman determines that Henslowe did
not expend the company's money without authority: "to write of
him as a hard taskmaster who maintained ruthless control over a
stable of writers, forcing them to turn out hack script after hack
script, simply does not fit the facts" (46–47). These conclusions justify retroactively a premise on which Beckerman had built a study
of staging at the Globe nearly ten years before. In that work, he
contends that records of practices at the Globe are principally valuable "in their agreement with the conditions reflected in
Henslowe's *Diary,* and it is to this source that we must turn to
secure a picture of how plays were produced in the Elizabethan
age."[5] Most theater historians now accept Beckerman's premise. In
A Companion to Henslowe's Diary (1988), Neil Carson declares that
a study of the diary is "indispensable" to an understanding of the
"original theatrical context" of Shakespeare's plays.[6]

As these scholars have done in varying detail before me, I
would like now to discuss those features of performance in
Henslowe's Diary that indicate the existence of a system of management in regard to the company repertory. The management of the
repertory was a dimension of a company's commerce, its means of
marketing plays. I therefore discuss also the economics of the
repertory system—the features that were expensive but necessary
to the financial success of a company as well as the features that
enabled a company to husband monetary resources over hard
times. In addition, there are commercial tactics implicit in the lists
of plays and schedule of performances in *Henslowe's Diary.* These
tactics are simple and familiar but nonetheless important to the
economic health of a company. They include the proportion of
comedies and histories to tragedies in the seasonal offerings, the
inclusion of popular old formulas along with the latest in dramatic
fashions, and the use in new plays and serials of the story materials

that Elizabethan playgoers seemed never to tire of. *Henslowe's Diary* is the richest document we have in evidence of the Elizabethan repertory system and its economics, and I will therefore focus on it. However, it is not the only document. The plays offered by the companies in and outside of Henslowe's records (or titles, when only those survive) and the chronology of those plays as they came to the various stages in and around London show us the old and new favorites in narrative matter and style. The Chamberlain's and King's men contribute both plays and titles to this body of evidence, and, as I hope to show in the chapters on their repertories specifically, these contributions indicate that the tactics of management evident in the activities of other companies were a strategy of their business also.

The Repertory System: Practices and Economics

Most students of Elizabethan drama know the format of the theatrical records in *Henslowe's Diary*. The entries that pertain to the repertory come in two basic patterns: the first is a list of performances; the second a series of expenditures. The lists of performances begin on 19 February 1592 and continue through 5 November 1597. The expenditures overlap these performance lists somewhat, beginning with purchases of playbooks and apparel in October 1597 and running into March of 1603. The lists of performances give us information on the calendar of playing years, seasons, and weeks; on the titles of plays a company owned; on the order in which those plays were presented; on the dates when new plays were introduced; and on the length and pattern of a stage run. Sums accompany all of the performances. The entries of expenditures give us information on the titles of new and old plays purchased by the company, the dates on which these plays were purchased, the apparel and properties bought for these productions, payments for additions, the selection of a play for performance at Court, the person who authorized the expenditure for the company, and the person to whom the money was paid. Sums accompany all of the expenditures.

Henslowe's Diary is not a flawless and unambiguous document. Every user of the information has to decide how to read some aspects of the entries. Before I discuss specific practices in the management of batteries of plays from these records and deduce from these practices an impact on the finances of a company, I would like to review some of the hazards that the data present on the subjects of repertory management and economics. To illustrate the major problems, I will use a set of entries concerning performances by the Admiral's men in the fall of 1594. The sequence begins on 25 August with the entry of "the venesyon comodey," marked with "ne" and followed by the sum of 50s. 6d. The same title occurs subsequently on 5, 15, and 22 September. Then, on 24 September, the word "venesyon" (again preceded by "ne") appears with the title, "the love of & Ingleshelady" and the sum of 47s. In the playlists of the next several months, the following entries occur:

4 october	1594	Rd at the love of a gresyan lady	xxvjs
11 october	1594	Rd at venesyon comodey	xvjs
24 october	1594	Rd at love of & Ingleshe ladey	xxiijs
11 november	1594	Rd at the venesyon comodey	xxjs
13 november	1594	Rd at the gresyan ladye	xvs
23 november	1594	Rd at the greasyon comody	xs

After 23 November, there are four more entries of *The Venetian Comedy,* nine of *The Grecian Comedy,* and none of the other titles.

The first problem in this sample is the number of offerings: how many playbooks do these titles represent? If we read the entries literally, we will decide that there are five: *The Venetian Comedy, The Love of an English Lady, The Love of a Grecian Lady, The Grecian Lady,* and *The Grecian Comedy.* However, the scholars who have interpreted the diary for us have not been so literal. They consider *The Love of a Grecian Lady* and *The Grecian Lady* to be the same text because Henslowe habitually shortened titles, as illustrated by the abbreviation of "the Jewe of mallta" (20 May 1592) to "the Jewe" (18 January 1593) and "the knacke to knowe A knave" (22 June 1592) to "the knacke" (24 January 1593). The abbreviation of *The Love of a Grecian Lady* to *The Grecian Lady* appears to be an analogous instance of abbreviation.

But are there even fewer plays than four? Starting with Malone, theater historians have tended to read similarly worded titles as variants of one another. The best-known example is probably the variety of titles for *The Spanish Comedy* in the playlists for Strange's men in the spring of 1592: "spanes comodye donne oracioe," "the comodey of doneoracio," "doneoracio," and "the comodey of Jeronymo." Fleay, then Greg, concluded by analogous logic that *The Love of a Grecian Lady/Grecian Lady* and *The Grecian Comedy* were the same play (*Diary*, II, 169). Greg made a further suggestion: that *The Love of an English Lady* is a variant title for *The Love of a Grecian Lady/Grecian Lady/Grecian Comedy* (*Diary*, II, 170). I find Greg's suggestion an attractive one. I think it reasonable either that Henslowe wrote "English" when he meant "Grecian" or that he thought the play was about an Englishwoman when he made the entry. In counting the number of playbooks represented by the entries, I will therefore say that there are two: *The Venetian Comedy* and the play that Henslowe at first called *The Love of an English/Grecian Lady* but came to call *The Grecian Comedy*.[7]

The second problem in the set of entries is the meaning of "ne." Each editor of the diary has offered an interpretation: "ne" as an abbreviation of "new enterlude" (Malone); "ne" as a shortened form of "new" (Collier); "ne" as an indicator of an initial performance, a first performance by a particular company, or a revival with revisions (Greg); "ne" as a sign of a newly licensed play (Foakes and Rickert). The one common element in these readings is that the "ne" indicated the newness of the play so marked. I believe that these scholars would also agree with Foakes and Rickert that Henslowe's flagging plays with a "ne" had something to do with the extra-large sums of money recorded (as a rule) at "ne" performances. I do not know what that something was, but I suggest that it pertained to the commercial treatment of the play as a new offering. In discussion of the diary, therefore, I take "ne" to mean the first performance of a play that was to be marketed as new.

I assume that plays not so marked were old, either because they were being continued in production from the previous season, or because they were in revival. An example of a play in continuation from one season to the next is *Seven Days of the Week*. Henslowe marked it "ne" at its initial show in 1594–95 (3 June). The play was still in the offerings of the Admiral's men after the summer break in 1595, and it appears among the performances of 1595–96 without a "ne." It also survived the summer break of 1596, and it appears in the performance lists of 1596–97 without a "ne." An example of a play in revival is *The Massacre at Paris*. When the play was first introduced by Strange's men on 30 January 1593, Henslowe marked it with "ne." When it was returned to the stage on 19 June 1594 (now with the Admiral's men), he did not mark it with "ne." Exceptions to this rule are the first performances of *1* and *2 Tamar Cham* and *Jeronimo* (*The Spanish Tragedy*) by the Admiral's men in 1595–96 and 1596–97, respectively. Greg said that these plays, which had previously been owned by Strange's men, had been revised for revival. That may be so, and I believe it to be so for *The Spanish Tragedy*. But I believe that even in these instances the "ne" was a commercial marker, not a textual one.

The significance of the "ne" becomes apparent when I apply the guidelines above to the 1594 sample. Only two of the titles are marked as new: *The Venetian Comedy*, "ne" on 25 August; and *The Love of an English Lady*, "ne" on 24 September (I read "venesyon" in this entry as a false start). Because there is not a "ne" marking the first performances of *The Love of a Grecian Lady* (also, "gresyan ladye") and *The Grecian Comedy*, I may assume either that both were old plays in revival or that they were in continuation. If they were discrete texts from *The Love of an English Lady*, I must choose the interpretation that they were in revival. If, however, they were the same play that Henslowe meant by *The Love of an English Lady*, I may read these entries as continuations of the run of that "ne" play.

The third problem raised by the sample entries is the significance of the sum that Henslowe recorded in the right-hand column of the performance lists. The meaning of the sums in the entries from 19 February 1592 through 22 January 1597 seems not to be at issue. Malone suggested that the sums were Henslowe's share of the daily receipts, in other words, his share as playhouse owner of one-half the moneys from the galleries.[8] Subsequent scholars have agreed. On 24 January 1597 Henslowe changed the format of the accounts to a five-column entry, and no one has satisfactorily explained the new system. There is tacit agreement that Henslowe continued to enter the pounds and shillings received for half of the galleries in the first two columns. It seems logical that he would use the other columns for daily income also, perhaps for the players' share of the galleries. The five columns seem to be a total of some kind, for Henslowe began to use the abbreviation "tt" ("ttottalis") in place of "Rd" (literally, "R*es*" for "received") on 26 January. But beyond the guess that the new format reflects company receipts in some way, theater historians have been stumped by the five-column entries.[9]

This conundrum notwithstanding, the sums that Henslowe recorded are significant in that they appear to indicate the size of the audience at a given show and therefore to indicate both the popularity of particular plays and the financial success of the company. Indeed, the sums do give us some ideas on these subjects, but they do not give a full answer. The sums reflect the income of the gallery but not (as far as we know) that of other places to stand or sit in the playhouse: for example, the yard, a stool on the stage, and the private rooms. It complicates matters further that some playgoers paid one penny to enter the galleries and some paid two.[10] Therefore, from Henslowe's single figure on 25 August for *The Venetian Comedy* (606d.), I cannot tell how many customers were in the yard, how many paid more than an additional penny on entering the galleries, or how many were in other viewing areas. It does seem, though, that the maximum number of playgoers possible in the galleries on that afternoon was 1212 (Henslowe's half plus the company's half of gallery receipts).

Two factors make it hazardous for us to translate the sums directly into popularity and financial success. One is the influence of a "ne" performance on receipts. Contemporary witnesses report that opening days were popular times for playgoing and that the admission price was doubled to two pence for these debuts. It might appear, therefore, that Henslowe's receipts for "ne" performances reflect the doubled prices. But they should not. It was the fee at the playhouse door that was doubled, not the fee at the gallery entrance from which Henslowe's receipts were drawn.[11] Possibly the company, which received all of the door receipts, gave Henslowe an extra sum at the "ne" performance. Foakes and Rickert imply a kind of compensation by suggesting that "ne" marks the payment of the seven-shilling fee for a license from the Master of Revels (*HD*, xxx–xxxi). However, even after this amount is subtracted, the "ne" receipts are usually much larger than the receipts at subsequent performances. The "ne" return of *The Venetian Comedy* (50s. 6d.) minus the licensing (7s.) yields a profit to Henslowe of 43s. 6d., which is still appreciably larger than the next highest return of the play (36s. 6d.).

A second factor is the influence of a holiday on receipts. Henslowe's sums are remarkably high for certain holidays: during Christmastide (St. Stephen's Day, St. John's Day, Holy Innocents' Day, New Year's Day, Epiphany); during Easter Week; during Whitsun Week; and for a day around Midsummer. On these holidays, the Admiral's men usually scheduled plays that had been in performance for some time, yet the receipts are often comparable to those of a "ne" performance. The run of *The Grecian Comedy* illustrates the situation: after having brought Henslowe 4s. on 1 December 1594, the play brought him 46s. when it was scheduled on St. Stephen's Day. The receipts averaged less than half of this over the next four shows (28s., 15s., 28s., 20s.), but they rose to 51s. when it was scheduled on Easter Wednesday, 1595.

Obviously, we must use Henslowe's sums for one play in the context of the receipts for other plays and in the context of other factors that indicate popularity and success such as the pattern of the play's stage run and the play's continuation from one year to the next. By these criteria, *The Venetian Comedy* and the play Henslowe came to call *The Grecian Comedy* seem to have had about the same market value. For the year of 1594–95, both brought in a good return to Henslowe at the "ne" performance (50s. 6d.; 47s.), both received about the same number of performances (eleven; thirteen), and both were in production for about nine months bringing in average receipts per performance to Henslowe within a shilling (26s., 27s.). The only distinction seems to be that *The Grecian Comedy* was carried over for one performance into the offerings for the fall of 1595–96 (on that afternoon Henslowe's receipts were quite low [10s., 9 October]). In relation to the other "ne" plays in 1594–96, we may say that the returns of *The Venetian Comedy* and *The Grecian Comedy* indicate an average success. Neither was as long-running or as profitable as the most lucrative new plays of the year, *A Knack to Know an Honest Man* and *The Wise Man of West Chester*, but both received more performances than ten of the company's other new offerings.

The sample entries raise at least one more question: do the data imply that a company could have administered the repertory system in such a way as to increase its profits? If *The Love of an English Lady*, *The Love of a Grecian Lady*, and *The Grecian Comedy* were discrete playtexts, we may reasonably conclude that the Admiral's men used the repertory system inefficiently and prodigally. They spent rehearsal time and incurred production expenses that they then wasted by retiring two of the plays (one of which was to be marketed as new) after two performances each. They then revived the third, *The Grecian Comedy*, and kept it in production for ten performances even though its receipts to Henslowe at the first two of these shows were the comparatively miserable returns of 10s. and 4s. However, if the three titles belonged to the same playbook, we may argue that the Admiral's men handled the repertory system efficiently and profitably. By this reading, they spent one block of rehearsal time and put together one set of properties and apparel on a single playbook that combined the lucrative occasions of a "ne" performance and two holiday appearances with eleven additional peformances for a run of thirteen months.

Perhaps the greatest hazard of working with *Henslowe's Diary* is that we may forget that the accounts are partial and that some of the entries are puzzling or hopelessly garbled. We are therefore tempted to ignore the items that produce ragged or illogical answers or to alter the data to conform to our expectations of play-house practice. Greg felt reasonably free to correct what he perceived as Henslowe's errors (especially respecting dates), but Foakes and Rickert recommend that we leave the entries as they are: "Henslowe certainly made some mistakes, but it is . . . better to assume that he is right unless he can be proved wrong" (*HD*, xxxi). As I discuss aspects of the repertory system, I cannot offer interpretations and calculations that every user of the diary will accept because of Henslowe's omissions and confusions. Nevertheless, I believe that the cumulative evidence on the calendar, offerings, performance schedules, and receipts gives us the elements of that system. It is the general design and the ways in which a company could exploit that design to protect itself against bankruptcy when times were hard and to make money when times were good that I am most concerned to show.

The Playing Year: Judging by the dates of performances that Henslowe recorded from 19 February 1592 to 5 November 1597, we might reasonably conclude that the playing companies would have scheduled performances seven days a week, twelve months a year, year after year, if they had been permitted to do so. However, several realities took the chronology of the playing year out of their hands.

One of these realities was the plague. The Privy Council, which regularly ignored requests from the lord mayor of London and local churchmen to shut down the playhouses on grounds of public disorder and immorality, respected the virulence of the plague. The councilors knew that the infection spread quickly through crowded areas, and when there was the threat of an epidemic they ordered places of public recreation to be closed. Usually the danger was greatest during the heat of July, August, and September. As a result, the London playhouses were sometimes officially closed for part of the summer. On 22 July 1596, for example, the Privy Council ordered the playhouses to be shut down because of plague; Henslowe's records show that the Admiral's men gave what became their last performance of the summer on the eighteenth and that they did not resume playing at the Rose until 27 October.

Another reality was the observance of holy days. Year after year, in petitions to the Privy Council to suppress playing entirely, the lord mayor and London clergy asked in particular that the playhouses be closed on Sundays and holidays. Entries in *Henslowe's Diary* indicate that the companies seldom if ever played on certain of these days (Christmas, Allhallows Eve, Queen Elizabeth's Accession Day [17 November], Lady Day, and the Sundays of Shrovetide, Easter, Whitsun, and Trinity) but nearly always played on others (the days of Simon and Jude's [also the date of the Lord Mayor's Show], Allhallows, St. Stephen's, St. John's, Holy Innocents', New Year's, Epiphany, Candlemas, Shrove Monday and Tuesday, Ash Wednesday, Easter Week, Whitsun Week, and the Nativity of John the Baptist [Midsummer]). The records on Sunday playing are more equivocal. Henslowe entered over fifty Sunday performances: eight by Strange's men, 1592–93; three by Sussex's men, 1593–94; one by Sussex's men with the Queen's men, 1594; one by the Admiral's men with the Chamberlain's men in 1594 (at Newington); and at least thirty by the Admiral's men, 1594–1597. Although there are records of Privy Council orders such as the one in 1600 stating that the companies "shall refrayne to play on the Sabbath day upon paine of imprisonment" (*APC*, XXX, 397), we cannot assume that the order was strictly enforced, for there continue to be complaints about violations. As late as May 1603, a royal proclamation cites the "great neglect in this Kingdome of keeping the Sabbath day" and declares "that no Beare-bayting, Bul-bayting, Enterludes, common Playes, or other like disordered or unlawful Exercises or Pastimes be frequented, kept or used, at any time hereafter upon any Sabbath day."[12]

If the playing companies respected the wishes of officials about holy days at all, it was during Lent. Strange's men began their run at the Rose in 1592 in the second week of Lent, and they played almost daily throughout the season (including one Sunday, Maundy Thursday, and Easter Even). I suggest that the schedule of the Admiral's men is more representative, however. In 1594–95 they played for about a week into Lent, then broke until Easter Monday. In 1595–96 they played for only a couple of days after Ash Wednesday. In 1596–97 they stopped playing on the Saturday after Ash Wednesday but resumed two and a half weeks later, giving performances almost daily for the remainder of Lent except for the holy days of Passion Week. Henslowe even acknowledges the resumption with a marginal note: "begynyng in leant marche 1597" (*HD*, 56). In the years after 1597 we cannot see the pattern of Lenten performances as clearly. In the spring of 1601 Henslowe made only nine payments for playbooks and none for apparel between 4 March (Ash Wednesday) and 13 April (Easter Monday). In 1602 he made no payments at all in February, March, and April. We may thus infer a slackening if not a suspension of business during Lent in 1601 and 1602. In 1603 the playhouses were closed by the Privy Council three days after Ash Wednesday in deference to the illness of the Queen.

Repertory: The plays that a company owned were its commercial products. The number of those holdings, the age, the schedule by which they were offered to playgoers, and the length and pattern of their stage runs were aspects in their marketing that contributed to the company's financial success.

Size: From 3 June 1594 through 18 July 1596, the Admiral's men played continually in the London area, taking breaks only during Lent and midsummer 1595. Henslowe's records of these years give us the best data available on the number of plays performed by a company over a lengthy period of commercial activity. In 1594–95 the Admiral's men scheduled offerings in about fifty weeks (3 June–26 June, minus about five weeks at Lent); during that time they performed about thirty-five plays, which is a ratio of seven plays per ten weeks.[13] In 1595–96 they gave performances of thirty-seven plays in about forty-one weeks (25 August–18 July, minus five weeks at Lent), which is a ratio of nine plays per ten weeks.[14] From these figures, we may develop a formula for calculating the number of plays in the repertory in terms of the number of weeks of performances: seven to nine plays per ten weeks, or twenty-eight to thirty-six plays in forty weeks (allowing for normal suspensions during Lent and the summer). Because there are no performance lists for 1597–1603, we cannot be sure that the size of the repertory remained a function of the number of playing weeks (and a function at the same rate), but expenditures for the Admiral's men and Worcester's men in 1602–03 suggest that it did. Henslowe's entries show that both companies were making payments on about the same number of works-in-progress (seventeen) between mid-August 1602 and mid-March 1603. Even if these projects were not equivalent to the number of plays each company had in production during these months, it appears that the players considered their needs in terms of new offerings in comparable numbers.[15]

Composition: The records in *Henslowe's Diary* show that the companies at the Rose maintained repertories composed of both new and old plays. The list of plays daily in 1592 shows that Strange's men introduced their first "ne" play (*Henry VI*) two weeks into the run, and they bought four more new plays before they left Henslowe's playhouse on 22 June. Sussex's men introduced one new play after five weeks of playing. The Admiral's men introduced one new play during their opening week at Newington Butts with the Chamberlain's men, and at the Rose thereafter they brought new plays into production regularly. The accounts for 1597–1603 do not indicate the exact number of new plays added each year, but they do make clear that new plays continued to be a basic feature of the company's commerce. Worcester's men, newly arrived at the Rose in August 1602, began to buy new plays and within six weeks had three already paid for.

Because Henslowe recorded performances by the Admiral's men in consecutive years, 1594–1597, we are able to distinguish two categories of old plays in the company repertory: revivals and continuations. Literally, all of the company's old plays in 1594–95 were revivals, for the company itself was new and not all of the members had performed its plays together previously. However, in the playlists of 1595–96 we see the mix of revivals and continuations. The incidence of continuations to revivals is very high, not only in 1595–96 but also in 1596–97. Of the twenty old plays in the playlists for 1595–96, fifteen were being carried over from 1594–95. Five had been retired previously and were now in revival. Two of these, *The Jew of Malta* and *Belin Dun,* had been played in 1594–95.[16] Another of the revivals, *Fortunatus,* was new to the Admiral's playlists. Another two, *1* and *2 Tamar Cham,* were new to the Admiral's lists but were marked "ne." Yet we know that they were in revival because both plays appeared in Henslowe's lists for Strange's men in 1592. Eleven of the titles in the Admiral's lists for 1596–97 had appeared as offerings in 1595–96. Three of these, *Long Meg of Westminster, Belin Dun,* and *The Wise Man of West Chester,* may here be in revival, since their last performance had been months before. Three plays obviously in revival were *Osric, Time's Triumph and Fortune's,* and *The Witch of Islington,* all of which were new to the Admiral's playlists but not marked "ne." Another revival, *Jeronimo,* was marked "ne." Like *1* and *2 Tamar Cham* in 1595–96, it had formerly been owned and played by Strange's men.

There is evidence in Henslowe's records for 1597–1603 that companies continued to carry over the production of plays from year to year and to bring plays out of retirement. The two-part *Robin Hood,* which the Admiral's men bought in February and licensed in March of 1597–98, appears to have remained in production through the winter season of 1598–99, for the Admiral's men paid Chettle to revise one or both plays "for the corte" (*HD,* 102). *Tasso's Melancholy,* which was revived sometime around January 1602, was apparently still in production in the fall and winter of 1602–03 when the company paid for more revisions. In almost every year from 1597 to 1603, the titles of plays from the Admiral's offerings in 1594–1597 turned up in Henslowe's expenditures as revivals: for example, *Hercules*, in 1597–98; *Alexander and Lodowick*, in 1598–99; and *The Jew of Malta*, in 1600–01. Undoubtedly, there were more continuations and revivals in these years than are recorded, but the titles were not entered in Henslowe's payments unless the continuation or revival required an expenditure.

Schedule of Performances: The central feature of the daily schedule of performances in the Elizabethan repertory system appears to have been the rotation of offerings. Strange's men gave eight performances in February 1592 before they repeated one of their plays. Sussex's men gave five plays in 1593–94 before repeating one. The Admiral's men and Chamberlain's men gave six before repeating an offering at Newington Butts. In the fall of 1595–96 the Admiral's men were in their second full week of performances before they repeated a play. Judging by the practice of the Admiral's men, 1594–1597, companies opened a new season with continuations from the previous season and introduced the first new show within a week or two; in the weeks thereafter, they brought new plays and revivals into production at about the rate of one every two weeks. The first few performances of a new offering were often scheduled within a week of one another, but by the fourth show the performances were more widely spaced. For example, *Tasso's Melancholy* was introduced "ne" on 11 August 1594 and scheduled a second time a week later (18 August); over the next nine months, it appeared twice in September, twice in October, once in November, once in December, twice in January, once in February, and once in May, at which time it was retired. *The Jew of Malta* was revived on 9 January 1596 and performed again nine days later on the eighteenth. It received another performance in January and three in February. After Easter it received one performance in May and one in June.

I see no evidence in *Henslowe's Diary* that companies attempted to organize offerings around subject matter or kinds of plays. One exception is the treatment of serials. Often the companies at the Rose scheduled the second part of a play on the afternoon following the performance of the first part. Strange's men, after having introduced *Jeronimo,* scheduled it as the next offering after *The Spanish Comedy* four times (13, 14 March; 30, 31 March; 22, 24 April; 21, 22 May). However, they never did play the two parts of *Tamar Cham* consecutively. The Admiral's men gave consecutive performances to the two parts of *Tamburlaine, Caesar and Pompey, Hercules,* and *Tamar Cham,* but none to the two parts of *Godfrey of Bulloigne* and *Seven Days of the Week.* In one particularly interesting week of performances in May 1595, the Admiral's men scheduled *1 Hercules* on Tuesday, *1 Tamburlaine* on Wednesday, *2 Tamburlaine* on Thursday, and *2 Hercules* ("ne") on Friday. In a few cases, the parts of a serial were retired at the same time, as were *1* and *2 Tamburlaine* in the fall of 1595–96.

Stage Runs: Theater historians have described the length of a stage run in different terms. Chambers used the number of performances, specifying "six to seventeen" as an average run (*ES,* II, 148). In fact, in the three years of 1594–1597, the Admiral's men gave only thirteen of their fifty-two new plays more than a dozen performances.[17] Beckerman used the length of time in production, considering "a year or a year and a half" standard.[18] Yet the Admiral's men kept only five of their fifty-two new plays in production longer than twelve calendar months.[19] They treated revivals similarly. Only four of their twenty-six revivals in 1594–1597 received more than twelve performances, and only four had runs longer than twelve months.[20]

I suggest that a more accurate description of a typical run is one in which the play was given eight to twelve performances over four to six months. This combination of numbers allows us to identify a play that was treated as the majority in the repertory were treated, whether new or in revival: for example, *2 Hercules,* eight performances in seven months (23 May to 25 November 1595); *Cutlack,* ten performances over four months (16 May to 26 September 1594); *The Jew of Malta,* eight performances over five months (9 January to 21 June 1596 [revival]); *A Woman Hard to Please,* eleven performances over six months (27 January to 27 May

1597); and *Pythagoras,* twelve performances over seven months (27 January to 14 July 1596). I suggest further that a company would have considered the production of a play worth the investment if its stage run met the criterion either of eight to twelve performances or of four to six months of production. Thus I assume that the Admiral's men were satisfied with such plays as *Warlamchester* (seven performances over eight months), *The Massacre at Paris* (ten performances over four months [revival]), *Barnardo and Fiametta* (seven performances over seven months) and *Nebuchadnezzer* (eight performances over four months) but disappointed by the reception of such plays as *Disguises* (six performances over two months) and *Fortunatus* (six performances over three months [revival]).

Economics: Even though the sums that Henslowe entered after every performance from February 1592 to November 1597 do not tell us the exact number of playgoers at the Rose each day, and even though the average return of a given play may be distorted by its having been marked "ne" and/or its having been scheduled on one or more holidays, the sums do give us a measure of success to combine with the number of performances that the play received and the number of months that it was in performance. And even though the payments that Henslowe recorded for plays and playing gear from October 1597 to March 1603 do not tell us about the stage runs or receipts of a given play, the expenditures do give us a sense of the company's operating costs. Taken together, the receipts from 1592 to 1597 and the expenditures from 1597 to 1603 imply the economic advantages to the company of new plays, revivals, and continuations. With some understanding of the role of new and old plays in the company's business, we are able to recognize periods of financial success as well as distress by the company's management of its holdings.

New Plays: New plays were potentially the most lucrative members of a company's repertory. By all report, playgoers flocked to the opening performances of new offerings. At these premieres, the company could double the price of admission and not have to share the profits with the playhouse owner. But of course the owner probably made money at a debut also. The sums recorded by Henslowe at "ne" performances were often 50s. to 70s. The company could expect attendance—and therefore receipts—to remain high for several performances after the premiere. Henslowe was receiving well over 60s. at the fourth performance of such offerings as *The Wise Man of West Chester*, part one of *Seven Days of the Week, 1 Hercules, Crack Me This Nut*, and *The Comedy of Humors*.

However, new plays were comparatively expensive to acquire and produce. Occasionally the Admiral's men paid for parts of a script that for one reason or another was not completed. For example, they paid Ben Jonson £1 on a plot that he did not turn into a play; Chapman did, for an additional £4 or more.[21] According to Henslowe's accounts, the Admiral's men and Worcester's men paid £6 for a new playbook, as a rule, and another 7s. to the Master of Revels for a license. The companies had new plays in rehearsal for about three weeks. Many of the new offerings apparently were fitted with apparel and properties out of the tiring house, but some required special costumes. Henslowe recorded expenditures of over £35 specifically for apparel and "diuers thinges" for one part of *Cardinal Wolsey* and another £11. 6s. when the Admiral's men brought an additional part to the stage nine months later. The black satin suit that Henslowe purchased for Worcester's men for *2 Black Dog of Newgate* at £5. 2s. was not reusable for *A Woman Killed with Kindness*, for which Worcester's men bought not only a new black satin suit (10s.) but also a woman's gown of black velvet (£6. 13s.). After the expenses of the playbook, license, rehearsal time, and playing gear, the companies might take the new play out of production almost immediately. The Admiral's men dropped *The Merchant of Emden* from the repertory after one performance, *Diocletian* after two, and *Julian the Apostate* after three.

Revivals: When the Admiral's men acquired old plays from defunct companies in the late spring of 1594, they presumably paid

40s. per playbook for the texts. This is the sum that they paid Martin Slater in 1598 when they bought back some of their recent offerings from him, and the sum that they paid Edward Alleyn for each of ten playbooks in 1601–02. Old plays were therefore less expensive to acquire than new ones. There is even some evidence that a company sometimes had the use of a secondhand text without the expense. The Admiral's men revived *Mahomet* (1594–95), *The Massacre at Paris* (1594–95), *The French Doctor* (1594–95), and both parts of *Tamar Cham* (1595–96), but they did not buy the playbooks from Alleyn until a second revival. They had *Vayvode* in production for nearly five months before Henslowe recorded a payment to Alleyn for the text. Theater historians have thought that old scripts carried an automatic expense of revisions; however, Henslowe's records do not support that belief.[22] A few plays were revised for revival, and those revisions were costly: *Jeronimo*, at least 120s.; *Doctor Faustus*, 80s.; *Tasso's Melancholy*, 80s. Other old scripts were returned to the stage with expenses but not with the expense of mending: for example, *The Blind Beggar of Alexandria*, *The Jew of Malta*, *Hercules*, *Crack Me This Nut*, *Mahomet*, *The Massacre at Paris*, and *Alexander and Lodowick*.

Like many new plays, many of the Admiral's revivals appear to have been fitted with apparel and properties out of the tiring house. There were no payments for playing gear for the revival of *Tasso's Melancholy* in 1601–02, though there were for revisions, and none for the play of *Bacon* in 1602–03, though there were for a prologue and epilogue for the Court. Similarly, though the Admiral's men paid out huge fees for textual changes to *Jeronimo* and *Doctor Faustus* for revival, Henslowe did not record the purchase of new apparel or properties specifically for either play. Some of the revivals had minimal expenses: for example, *Crack Me This Nut*, 5s. for a buckram suit, and *Hercules*, 40s. for a robe. Others appear to have been more costly: *The Jew of Malta*, £5. 10s.; *The Blind Beggar of Alexandria*, £9. 3s. 4d. The production costs of an old play new to the company appear particularly high. The Admiral's men acquired *Vayvode* secondhand in 1598–99, and the revival cost them in apparel what they might have spent to produce a new play (£17. 5s.). *Sir John Oldcastle* had been staged by the Admiral's men in 1599–1600, but that did not save Worcester's men the expense of revisions (50s.) and new apparel (£15. 10s.) when they acquired it in 1602–03. These figures suggest that the first year at the Rose must have been expensive for the Admiral's men (likewise for any company operating at a similar commercial level). Not only were they buying two new plays a month on the average and paying for whatever special apparel and properties these needed, but they were also buying divers things for the revivals: for example, a cauldron for Barabas; a wheel and frame for *The Siege of London;* a coat with copper lace, a bridle, and crimson velvet breeches for Tamburlaine; and a dragon, hell mouth, and city of Rome for *Doctor Faustus.*

The receipts that Henslowe recorded at daily performances of the revivals in 1594–95 indicate that most of the old scripts were as profitable for Henslowe—and thus presumably for the Admiral's men—as the new plays brought into production that year. Receipts at the opening shows of *Doctor Faustus, 1 Tamburlaine, Long Meg of Westminster, Mahomet,* and *The Siege of London* ranged from 63s. to 72s. Over the long term, these plays continued to be profitable. *Mahomet,* for example, averaged receipts to Henslowe of 31s. over eight performances in seven months of production. *Doctor Faustus* ran for nearly two and a half years, received twenty-four performances, and averaged about 20s. per showing to Henslowe. Of course, not all revivals were so successful. In 1596–97 the Admiral's men revived *Osric* in February and *Time's Triumph and Fortune's* in April; *Osric* lasted for two performances, *Time's Triumph* for one. Nevertheless, I find an endorsement of revivals in the fact that the Admiral's men returned a number of old plays to the stage in 1600–01 and 1601–02, their first two years at the Fortune. No doubt they meant for these plays to advertise the return to the stage of Edward Alleyn, who had made the leading roles famous before his retirement in 1597; but they must also have expected these offerings to be profitable.

Continuations: On the basis of Henslowe's receipts, the plays being continued from the previous year's repertory produced the least revenue for the company. *A Knack to Know an Honest Man,* for example, averaged 32s. per show to Henslowe over its maiden year, 1594–95. When it was continued for four performances in 1595–96, it averaged 16s. a show. When it was continued for one final performance in 1596–97, it returned 15s. to Henslowe. Yet plays being continued offered the company several advantages. For one, they required no new expenditures. Only rarely do plays being carried over from one year to the next turn up in Henslowe's accounts from 1597 to 1603 and never then for the expense of playing gear. For a second, the continuing plays could fill out weekly schedules while the company rehearsed new offerings. This function is obvious in the early months of a fall season. In 1595–96 the Admiral's men gave performances of four continuations while they were preparing to introduce *Longshanks,* four more before the debut of *Crack Me This Nut,* and four more before the debut of *The New World's Tragedy.* In 1596–97 the Admiral's men played nothing but continuations for more than a month while they rehearsed new plays, which they then introduced into the schedule at the unusual speed of about one per week.

The receipts of plays nearing the end of a run serve as a measure of commercial exhaustion. In the discussion above, I imply that receipts of 50s. to 70s. were a common return to Henslowe at the opening performance of new plays. A few offerings maintained receipts at or near this level for several performances, but most dropped down quickly to sums of 25s. to 35s., which they maintained through the middle portion of their run. The receipts of aging plays show that the range for retirement was 5s. to 22s. (I exclude receipts of plays with fewer than four performances and with the last performance on a holiday.) The range applies both for plays in a maiden run and in revival. It applies also for plays that the company was to revive in years to come. At its last performance on 23 June 1596, *Crack Me This Nut* returned 12s. to Henslowe, yet the Admiral's men revived it during the winter of 1601–02. *Alexander and Lodowick* returned only 8s. to Henslowe at its final performance on 15 July 1597, yet the Admiral's men revived it in the spring of 1598–99. *Doctor Faustus* slipped to a 5s. return to Henslowe at its final performance on 5 January 1597. Nevertheless, the Admiral's men revived it almost immediately (in October 1597), and they revived it again in the winter of 1602–03, though with 80s. worth of revisions.

From the perspective of economics, the old plays were important to the company repertory. Most cost almost nothing to bring to stage, yet they gave the players something to offer until new productions were ready. During holiday seasons, the old plays might bring in receipts equal to those of a new show. *Alexander and Lodowick,* for example, was offered for the twelfth time on Whit Tuesday, and it returned 60s. to Henslowe, its highest receipts since its second "ne" performance four months earlier. Part one of *Seven Days of the Week,* at its sixteenth performance and in its second year of repertory, returned 42s. to Henslowe on New Year's Day, 1596. When the company needed to produce a set of offerings in a hurry, old plays could be brought out of retirement possibly without expense, as in the revivals of *Long Meg of Westminster* in the fall of 1596–97, *Belin Dun* and *The Wise Man of West Chester* in the spring and summer of 1596–97, and *Doctor Faustus* in the fall of 1597.

New plays, however, were the commercial fuel of the repertory. Each had the potential to attract new customers and to draw back old ones who had begun to frequent the playhouses of competitors. The companies took the risk that playwrights would not complete a given script or that the play when staged would have to be withdrawn from production because any one of them might be as satisfactory as *Philipo and Hippolito, The New World's Tragedy, Chinon of England,* and *Stewtley.* These plays were not dazzling successes. They were not even to be revived, insofar as we know. But they stayed in production from four to eight months and averaged receipts in the range of 28s.–30s. to Henslowe and thus to the company for its share of the galleries. If these offerings fulfilled the expectations of the Admiral's men when they paid the dramatists for the texts and set aside rehearsal time to bring the plays to the stage, and I assume that they did, they exemplify the commercial norms of a new repertory piece.

Commercial Tactics

The Elizabethan theatrical companies appear to have been able to control their finances to some extent by controlling the number and expense of their acquisitions and revivals. However, provident management went for naught if the companies did not respond to playgoers' tastes. Several kinds of information in *Henslowe's Diary*, plus the plays that have survived in print from the repertories of companies contemporary with the activities recorded by Henslowe, suggest that they did respond, and suggest further a few of the commercial tactics that they used to generate business. Apparently the essential feature of competition was diversity. The companies in the diary as well as those for which we have partial playlists from the title-page claims on quartos varied their offerings by presenting comedies, tragedies, and histories made out not only of long-familiar narratives but also out of newly fashionable matter. Although the offerings of the companies were therefore a mix of story materials and dramatic kinds, the repertories of a company year after year and of that company in comparison with others had certain similarities. These similarities arose from a principle of duplication. Companies repeated the subjects and formulas that had been successful in their own offerings and in the repertories of their competitors. This principle accounts for the proliferation of offerings on a popular hero; the growth of species of plays within the framework of each genre; the multiplication of a play into two, three, or even four parts; and the emergence of a minor character from one play to become the star in a sequel. Companies using these tactics in combination had large and varied repertories of old and new favorites in story and genre and sets of multi-part plays and spin-offs with which to compete with one another for playgoers.

Comedies: The playlists in *Henslowe's Diary* demonstrate the popularity of comedies and the variety of comedic formulas in the company repertories. Nearly half of the twenty-seven plays offered by Strange's men in 1592–93 were some kind of comedy (or seem to have been one from the title). Of the fifty-two new plays that the Admiral's men brought into production from June 1594 to July 1597, at least thirty-three were comedies (or seem to have been). Due to the percentage in production in any one season, the Admiral's men were offering two or three comedies per week for every tragical history or tragedy. The percentage of comedies appears to drop slightly in the repertories in the diary after 1597. In 1599–1600, for example, the Admiral's men made payments on thirty-six projects. At least seventeen of these appear to have been comedies. It may be that not all of the thirty-six projects reached the stage; one comedy, in fact, was cancelled (*The Devil and His Dame*). However, two of the comedies not only reached the stage of the Rose but were shown at Court. According to the advertisement on the title-pages of their quartos, *Fortunatus* was played before the Queen at "Christmas" and *The Shoemaker's Holiday* (*The Gentle Craft* in Henslowe's entries) was played "on New-yeares day at night."

These playlists, as well as the quartos published in the period, give us a sense of the many kinds of comedies at the London playhouses season after season. One of the most ubiquitous was the romance. Strange's men had *Orlando Furioso*, Sussex's men had *Huon of Bordeaux*, and the Admiral's men had such pieces as the two-part *Godfrey of Bulloigne, Palamon and Arcite, Utherpendragon*, and *Tristram of Lyons*. *Clyomon and Clamydes* was published in 1599 out of the holdings of the Queen's men. Although *The Knight of the Burning Pestle* allegedly did not please audiences of the children's company at Blackfriars in about 1607, that unpopularity may not have stemmed from its use—or misuse—of motifs from the heroic romance. Certainly the fate of the play did not discourage Francis Beaumont and John Fletcher from risking their fledgling careers on dramas of romance or the King's men from acquiring some of their work, as evidenced by the authorship of *Philaster, Cardenio*, and *Two Noble Kinsmen*. Closely related to the romance was the pastoral. Such titles as *Chloris and Ergasto*

(Strange's men) and *Barnardo and Fiametta* (Admiral's men) indi-cate an interest in pastoral materials before the appearance of plays influenced by the popularity of Sidney's *Arcadia* and Spenser's *The Faerie Queene*. In the years after the 1590s, the pastoral remained a repertory item in such plays as *Mucedorus* (Chamberlain's and King's men), *The Arcadian Virgin* (Admiral's men), and *The Faithful Shepherdess* (Children of Blackfriars).

Another category of comedy present in the repertories of companies generally was the folk play. One variety dramatized stereotypes such as the shrew: *The Taming of a Shrew* (Pembroke's men), *Medicine for a Curst Wife* (Worcester's men). Another treated folk tales: *Old Wives Tale* (Queen's men), *Robin Hood's Pennyworths* (Admiral's men). Another treated superstition: *The Witch of Islington* (Admiral's men), *Two Brothers* (Worcester's men), *The Merry Devil of Edmonton* (King's men). A common ploy in the naming of plays was the use of a folk expression, saying, or proverb: *God Speed the Plough* (Sussex's men), *Chance Medley* (Admiral's men), *All Is Not Gold That Glisters* (Admiral's men), *Like unto Like* (Pembroke's men), *The Weakest Goeth to the Wall* (Oxford's men), *The Blind Eats Many a Fly* (Worcester's men), *As You Like It* (Chamberlain's men), *Give a Man Luck and Throw Him into the Sea* (company unknown). Some of these plays may have been updated medieval moral interludes, as was *A Knack to Know a Knave* (Strange's men). Elizabethan moral plays turn up on stage and/or in print throughout the years of *Henslowe's Diary*. Strange's men, for example, performed *A Looking Glass for London and England* in 1592, and the play was printed in 1594, 1598, and 1602. The Admiral's men had the two-part *Seven Days of the Week* and *Fortunatus*. *Summer's Last Will and Testament*, first produced in 1593, had enough market value in 1600 to warrant publication. A children's company presented *The Contention of Liberality and Prodigality* at Court before 1602.

A substantial number of the comedies were love plays. Many do not give away by their titles any special focus on courtship, mar-riage, or what are now gender issues, but a few in the playlists of the Admiral's men indicate that comedies often treated the social evils of domestic life. In *Two Angry Women of Abington* (1598–99), that evil is quarrelsome women. In *Joan as Good as My Lady* (1598–99) the evil appears to be social mobility; in *Triplicity of Cuckolds* (1597–98), adultery; in *The Widow's Charm* (1601–02), fortune hunting. The titles of one or two plays advertise vulgar behavior and bawdry: *Crack Me This Nut* (Admiral's men) and *A Toy to Please Chaste Ladies* (Admiral's men). A popular stereotype was the female brawler, as evidenced by *Long Meg of Westminster* (Admiral's men) and *The Roaring Girl* (Prince Charles's men). But the most popular seems to have been the patient wife. The Admiral's men had a play on each of the model stories: *Patient Grissil*, in which the wife responds passively to her husband's testing, and *The Golden Ass & Cupid and Psyche*, in which the wife assertively reclaims her husband. Worcester's-Queen Anne's men had several such plays: *How a Man May Choose a Good Wife from a Bad* and *The Wise Woman of Hogsden*. The Chamberlain's and King's men had at least *All's Well That Ends Well*, *The Fair Maid of Bristow*, *The London Prodigal*, and *The Miseries of Enforced Marriage*.

Several new formulas in the comedy seem to have become popular in the years of *Henslowe's Diary*. One is the gild or citizen's play. An early example may have been *The Tanner of Denmark* (Strange's men), but a set of Admiral's plays illustrates the variety in the type: *The Tinker of Totnes* (1595–96), *Mother Redcap* (1597–98), *The Gentle Craft* (1599–1600), and the two-part *Six Clothiers* (1601–02). A second is the disguise play. In the Admiral's playlists, there is a sequence of such, beginning with *Disguises* in 1595–96 and including at least *The Blind Beggar of Alexandria* in 1596–97 and the first part of *The Blind Beggar of Bednal Green* in 1599–1600. A third is the humors play. In 1596–97 several companies had plays any one of which might have been the seminal offering. The Admiral's men had *The Comedy of Humors*, Pembroke's men had *The Case Is Altered*, and the Chamberlain's men had *The Merry Wives of Windsor*. Over the next several years, the Chamberlain's men acquired Jonson's *Every Man in His Humor* and *Every Man out of His Humor*, and the Admiral's men acquired *The Fount of New Fashions* and *The London Florentine* (in two parts).

Subsequent London city comedies were influenced by these humors plays. A fourth new formula is the comical satire. From all report, the infamous *Isle of Dogs* in Pembroke's repertory in July 1597 was a satire, perhaps comical in intent though not in consequence, as it caused three of its players to be thrown in jail (one of whom was one of its dramatists). Some company had *Histriomastix* on stage in 1599, perhaps the boys' company at Blackfriars, which played Jonson's *Poetaster*. The Chamberlain's men responded to Jonson's play with Dekker's *Satiromastix*, which, according to its title-page, was also played by the boys' company at St. Paul's. Even the universities joined in with the two-part *Return from Parnassus*.

Tragedies: There are far fewer tragedies in the Admiral's playlists than comedies, but on the basis of time in production those few were excellent commercial properties. The stage runs and revivals of two tragedies by Christopher Marlowe illustrate the durability and profitability of these works on stage. *The Jew of Malta* appeared in the repertory of each of the companies at the Rose from February 1592 to April 1594, and it was in revival at each run. The Admiral's men acquired it in 1594–95, and they revived it immediately. They revived it again the next year (1595–96) and yet again in their first full year at the Fortune (1600–01). The Admiral's men revived *Doctor Faustus* in September of 1594–95, and they kept it in production over three years despite a drop in receipts to Henslowe. When some players from Pembroke's men came over from the Swan to join them at the Rose in October 1597, the Admiral's men revived it at once, an action I take as a sign of its ability to generate revenue. The company revived it again in 1602–03 with expensive revisions. I take this as another sign of value, for the company would not have spent the 80s. unless the play were likely to return the investment.

By including revenge plays in their offerings, Elizabethan companies were responding to a fashion that seems to have begun with the maiden run of Thomas Kyd's *The Spanish Tragedy* (ca. 1587). There is evidence from the playlists of most of the companies that

London playgoers could have seen some revenge tragedy at one of the playhouses during any given season. Henslowe's records suggest that the Admiral's men ran the following sequence: *The Jew of Malta* in 1594–95 and 1595–96; *Jeronimo* in 1596–97; *The Spanish Moor's Tragedy* in 1599–1600; *The Jew of Malta* again in 1600–01; *Jeronimo* again in 1601–02. Furthermore, the companies seem to have relied on revenge plays to get their seasons underway. *The Jew of Malta* was the first offering by the Admiral's men at the Rose in May 1594; it, *Titus Andronicus,* and *Hamlet* were offered by the combined companies in their first week at Newington in June. One of the first acquisitions of the boys' company at St. Paul's in 1599–1600, apparently, was a revenge play by Marston, *Antonio's Revenge,* and its forepiece, *Antonio and Mellida.* If the tragedy that Chettle sold to Worcester's men in August and September 1602 was *Hoffman* (as Fleay guessed), that company also started its run at the Rose with a revenge tragedy in its offerings. The play that the Children of Blackfriars took from the Chamberlain's holdings was a revenge play (*Jeronimo*); when the King's men retaliated, they did so with one of the boys' revenge plays (*The Malcontent*).

It is not always possible to tell what kind of tragedy the plays in Henslowe's lists are. Greg could make nothing out of the titles of *The New World's Tragedy, The Stepmother's Tragedy,* and *Felmelanco,* for example. The titles of others, however, give away the subject matter. Thus we can identify a continuing interest in contemporary crime. In the one year of 1599–1600, the Admiral's men made payments in full on three such plays: *Page of Plymouth, Cox of Collumpton,* and *The Tragedy of Thomas Merry.* At this time, the Chamberlain's men had apparently just retired *A Warning for Fair Women,* for it was registered at Stationers' Hall on 5 November 1599. Stationers apparently recognized some market value in the type by printing not only the Chamberlain's play but also a new edition of *Arden of Faversham* in 1599. Heywood's play, *A Woman Killed with Kindness* (Worcester's men) pretends in some ways to be similarly a domestic tragedy, and the presence of *A Yorkshire Tragedy* in the repertory of the King's men as late as 1605–06 shows that the formula remained popular for some time.

Histories: Elizabethan playgoers seem not to have made subtle generic distinctions between plays like *Richard II,* which we would call historical tragedies, and plays like *Woodstock,* which we would call history plays with tragical plot lines. When Simon Forman saw a play about Richard II at the Globe in April 1611, he responded to the narrative as a series of moral lessons in treachery, if his notes on the play are to be trusted. Because most of the texts for which we have titles have not survived, we cannot tell which among the historical plays are in fact tragedies (even with the texts, scholars disagree in the assignment of generic labels). I think it best, therefore, to describe the variety of histories without attempting to identify the tragedies and comedies among them. I leave it to readers to make distinctions as they choose from the subject matter implied by the titles. However confusing the issue of genre, it is clear that the schedules of every company for which we have complete or partial repertory lists are full of offerings based on historical materials and that stories of the past and present were equally in demand.

In the categories of ancient history and pseudo-history, we see the variety of popular matter from the titles of plays in the repertory of the Admiral's men which name philosophers (*Pythagoras*), lovers (*Aeneas and Dido* [by way of Pembroke's men]; *Troilus and Cressida*), friends (*Damon and Pythias*), conquerors (*1, 2 Caesar and Pompey, Jugurtha, Hannibal and Scipio*), and politicians (*Julian the Apostate*). Complementary offerings are to be found in the repertories of Strange's men (*Titus and Vespasian, Constantine, Jerusalem*), Sussex's men (*Titus Andronicus*), the Chamberlain's and King's men (*Troilus and Cressida, Sejanus, Antony and Cleopatra, Catiline*), and Queen Anne's men (*The Rape of Lucrece*). Akin to these histories were the dramatizations of myths, as illustrated by the following plays from the offerings of the Admiral's men: for example, the two-part *Hercules, Troy, Phaeton,* and *Polyphemus.* Also taken from ancient story materials were the plays on biblical heroes and villains. Sussex's men played *Abraham and Lot,* the Chamberlain's men offered *Hester and Ahasuerus,* and in a ten-month period starting in December 1601, the Admiral's men made payments on all of the following: *Judas, Jephthah, Tobias, Pontius*

Pilate, Samson, and *Joshua.* Henslowe's accounts for Worcester's men show that they had a play in 1602–03 that required "poleyes & worckmanshipp for to hange absolome" (*HD,* 217).

In addition, there were dozens of offerings on the contemporary wars and political intrigues of various European countries. Plays such as *The Battle of Alcazar, Philip of Spain,* and *The Massacre at Paris* had well-known casts of heroes and villains with connections to British history. Some of these heroes turned up in plays of their own: for example, *King Sebastian of Portugal.* The appeal of others such as *Strange News out of Poland, Stuhlweissenburg, The Conquest of the West Indies,* and *Albere Galles* is harder to explain except as a reflection of an Elizabethan taste for adventure. *Tasso's Melancholy* may be a psychological drama on the artistic personality. It was a very successful play, enjoying a run of twelve performances over ten months in 1594–95 and a revival in 1601–02. Easily the favorite of all of the foreign histories, however, was the two-part *Tamburlaine.* The Admiral's men played it during their first year at the Rose in 1594–95 (and it was old then), and the company had Tamburlaine's coat with copper lace, bridle, and breeches of crimson velvet in inventory in 1598 awaiting a revival.

British history, both ancient and modern, was as popular as any of the historical matters, if the number of texts in the Admiral's repertory is a measure. A sample of their plays includes *Cutlack, Longshanks, Henry I, Hardicanute,* the two-part *Earl Godwin,* the two-part *Brute, Connan Prince of Cornwall, Mulmutius Dunwallow, Ferrex and Porrex, 2 Henry Richmond,* the two-part *Sir John Oldcastle, Malcolm King of Scots,* the two-part *Cardinal Wolsey, Richard Crookback,* and *Mortimer.* No doubt much of the historical material is hidden from view by titles such as *The Blind Beggar of Bednal Green,* which in fact dramatizes the loyalty of some nobles and the treachery of others during the reign of King Henry VI. There are at least four British histories in the repertory of Sussex's men at the Rose in 1593–94, and the first new play that Strange's men introduced into their repertory in the spring run of 1592 was *Henry VI.* Kings were not the only heroes of English history plays. A fair number treated the escapades of thieves, highwaymen, and various other scoundrels and low-lifes: for example, *Belin Dun* and the two-part *Black Bateman of the North* in the Admiral's repertory; *Cutting Dick* and the two-part *Black Dog of Newgate* in Worcester's.

Duplicate Plays: The Elizabethan companies recognized that certain famous personalities and historical periods had extraordinary appeal for playgoers. One of their responses to this condition of the theatrical marketplace was to revive old plays. The fact that the Admiral's men revived *The Massacre at Paris* in 1594–95 and 1601–02 no doubt indicates that Marlowe's tragical-historical plays were good commercial properties and that this piece had a good role for Alleyn. But it also indicates that the French Civil Wars made popular drama whoever the dramatist and lead player. Companies responded also by acquiring one or more additional plays on popular subject matter. Evidence of this imitation is the series of plays bought by the Admiral's men in 1598–99: beginning with part one of *The Civil Wars of France,* the story grew to a second, third, and fourth part ("The Introduction").

We see the principle of duplication in operation in a set of plays on the Wars of the Roses, which were played in the years of 1590–94. The Queen's men had *The True Tragedy of Richard the Third.* Strange's men had *Henry VI.* Pembroke's men had the first part of *The Contention between York and Lancaster* and its sequel, *The True Tragedy of Richard Duke of York,* as well as (perhaps) the third play in the sequence, *Richard III.* Sussex's men had *Buckingham* (which I take to be about the Buckingham in *Richard III*). In the middle years of the decade, the Chamberlain's men gathered the serial parts that Pembroke's men had had into their repertory, adding the original play from the repertory of Strange's men (*Henry VI*). At the end of the 1590s, three companies in competition with the Chamberlain's men also acquired plays on the subject. Admiral's men had *2 Henry Richmond* (1599–1600), as well as the three parts of *The Blind Beggar of Bednal Green* (1601–02).

Derby's men had the two-part *Edward IV.* Worcester's men made payments on a play called *Shore's Wife.*

A series of plays on the North African campaign that culminated in a battle at Alcazar illustrates how frequently one company drew on the same body of subject matter. Prior to May 1594, two plays on this material were in circulation. One was *The Battle of Alcazar,* which was probably written around 1589; it was published in 1594 with a title-page that advertised ownership by the Admiral's men. A second was a play Henslowe recorded for Strange's men in 1592–93 called "mvlo mvllocco," or *Muly Mollocco* (not marked "ne"). Greg (*Diary*, II, 149) and Chambers (*ES*, III, 460) mention an alleged connection between these two plays, but another possibility is that *The Battle of Alcazar* was the text that Henslowe called "mahomett" (also not marked "ne"), which the Admiral's men introduced in August 1594. *Mahomet* ran for eight performances, closing on 5 February 1595. In December 1596 the company began to show a play that Henslowe called "stewtley," and it ran through June 1597. Among these plays were probably the offering or offerings for which the company kept "The Mores lymes," "iiij Turckes hedes," and "owld Mahemetes head" in inventory (*HD*, 318, 319). In August 1601 the Admiral's men revived *Mahomet* and bought the text from Alleyn. Just a few months before (April, May 1601), the Admiral's men had bought a new play on Stukeley's commander for the invasion in the North African war, *King Sebastian of Portugal.*

Henslowe's records show, further, that in a single year a company might have more than one play with similar characters or with similar titles. In 1592–93, for example, Strange's men had a play called *Machiavel* as well as one in which Machiavelli was a character (*The Jew of Malta*). In 1594–95 the Admiral's men revived a play called *The French Doctor* on 18 October, and four months later they introduced a new play, *The French Comedy.* The pair, *The Venetian Comedy* and *The Grecian Comedy,* have the same formulaic title as *The French Comedy* and were played in the same year. The offerings in other years illustrate different kinds of duplication. In 1596–97 the Admiral's men had *Five Plays in One,* perhaps a set of short works related by theme, as the parts of 2 *Seven Deadly Sins* allegedly were, or by sensibility, as are *Two Lamentable Tragedies* (Q1601). In a year's time, as we have seen, the Admiral's men made payments on six different biblical plays, two of which treated the crucifixion story (*Judas, Pontius Pilate*). From 1597–98 to 1600–01 the company had a Robin Hood play on stage nearly continuously: *The Downfall of Robert Earl of Huntington* (*1 Robin Hood*), *The Death of Robert Earl of Huntington* (*2 Robin Hood*), and *The Funeral of Richard Coeur de Lion*, 1597–99; and *Robin Hood's Pennyworths*, 1600–01.

Theater history as it was written by F. G. Fleay treats duplicate plays as mistakes in the diary for one seminal text and/or versions, revisions, or thefts of a single text. Even Greg, in commentary on a play called *The French Comedy* in the Admiral's repertory for 1596–97, refers us back to *The French Comedy* of 1594–95, though he does consider that the plays may have been separate texts (*Diary*, II, 174). Certainly, the management of the Admiral's repertory looks more streamlined if some of these duplicates were identical, but the frequency with which plays on similar subjects, with similarly formulaic titles, or merely with titles echoing other works in the repertory occur in Henslowe's playlists forces us to recognize that what may be a standard of efficiency for us does not necessarily define the way companies did business. Furthermore, although we have been asked to believe that players watched the shelves of bookstalls hoping to buy a quarto of a rival company's popular success, the principle of duplication implies that it was the subject matter and genre of popular offerings that companies coveted. We may think that they could benefit from the theft of a successful text or save themselves rehearsal time and production costs by having only one play about the French Civil Wars, but the companies apparently believed that several similar plays of unremarkable quality were potentially more profitable than a singular masterpiece.

Serials: By 1592 multi-part plays were an established feature of the Elizabethan repertory. Strange's men had two pairs in production in 1592: *The Comedy of Don Horatio* with *Jeronimo*, and the two-part *Tamar Cham*. If the entry on 3 March 1592 is for Shakespeare's *Henry VI*, the company had acquired the first of what was to be at least a three-part serial. In 1594–95 the Admiral's men revived both parts of *Tamburlaine*. They acquired a second part of *Godfrey of Bulloigne* to play along with a revival of the first part. In May they put on both parts of a *Hercules* play, introducing the sequel in the third week after part one. Regularly thereafter they had some kind of serial in production. For example, in 1597–98, they put on *1* and *2 Robin Hood;* the two parts of *Earl Godwin and His Sons; 1* and *2 Black Bateman of the North*, and *Hannibal and Hermes*, for which Greg thinks they acquired a sequel (*Diary*, II, 194–95). The lists for Worcester's men show an equal interest in serials. When the company first moved to the Rose in August 1602, the players acquired an *Oldcastle* text, presumably one or both of the texts staged by the Admiral's men in 1599–1600. Worcester's men also made payments on a two-part *Lady Jane* and a two-part *Black Dog of Newgate*.

The sample of even these few plays indicates that serials had different narrative relationships. Perhaps the most common formula was that of the *Tamburlaine* texts, which depict the beginnings of the hero's career to *"[w]her death cuts off the progres of his pomp, / And murdrous Fates throwes al his triumphs down"* (Prologue, *2 Tamburlaine*).[23] The performance lists in *Henslowe's Diary* show that the Admiral's men exploited the narrative dependency of part two by scheduling six of its seven shows to follow part one. The company scheduled the first and second parts of *Hercules, Tamar Cham* (1595–96), and *Caesar and Pompey* similarly. Other sequels, for example, the second parts of *Godfrey of Bulloigne* and *Seven Days of the Week*, appear in alternation with their first parts. It may be that these pairs, like *Friar Bacon and Friar Bungay* and *John of Bordeaux*, shared a central character but not a chronological narrative. In a few cases, one play served as the forepiece, as in the apparent relationship of *The Spanish Comedy* to *The Spanish Tragedy*. Strange's men scheduled the tragedy more often without the forepiece than with it, perhaps an indication that the narratives were theatrically and commercially independent. The two parts of *Robin*

Hood serve to caution us not to assume conventional narrative links. In fact, *2 Robin Hood* is itself two short narratives. The first treats Robin Hood's death, and thus closes *1 Robin Hood,* but the second, King John's cruel wooing of Matilda, is related to the adventures of Robin Hood only by shared characters. Other plays intentionally similar in title have no narrative relationship whatsoever: for example, *A Knack to Know a Knave* and *A Knack to Know an Honest Man; Every Man in His Humor* and *Every Man out of His Humor.*

The initial impetus for serials was popular demand, as Marlowe claims in the prologue of *2 Tamburlaine:* "*The generall welcomes* Tamburlain *receiv'd, / When he arrived last upon our stage, / Hath made our Poet pen his second part.*" Selected entries in *Henslowe's Diary* illustrate the procreativity of this success. The stage history of *Seven Days of the Week* and its second part is an example. The initial play, introduced "ne" on 3 June 1595, was immediately popular. It received five performances that month, averaging a stunning 63s. return to Henslowe. When the fall season of 1595–96 began, it continued to attract large crowds. Not until its sixth performance of the fall (14 October) did receipts fall to anything like normal levels. At about this time, the Admiral's men were acquiring the second part, which they introduced "ne" on 22 January 1596. Curiously, the sequel was taken out of production after its second show without harm to the run of the first play, which continued into the fall of 1596–97 for a total of twenty-two performances. Henslowe's accounts for 1597–1603 show a chronology of payments for plays and their subsequent parts. When those payments for sequels are separated by several months, it appears that the company determined the popularity of part one before putting down money in earnest for part two. Thus the spread of eight months between the purchase of *The Blind Beggar of Bednal Green* (26 May 1600) and part two (29 January 1601) suggests that over the fall of 1600 the Admiral's men saw in the receipts the potential success of a sequel. Their judgment seems confirmed by the fact that they extended the sequence to a third part, for which they paid in full on 30 July 1601.

However, not all multiple-part dramas awaited the general welcome of playgoers. Some, it seems, were conceived as serials. Parts one and two of *Hercules* were introduced just over two weeks apart (7, 23 May 1595). The earnest money for *2 Black Bateman of the North* (26 June 1598) followed soon after the purchase of the initial play (22 May). The timing is similar for the two parts of *Black Dog of Newgate* (20 December 1602, 29 January 1603). All four of the plays called *The Civil Wars of France* were acquired between 29 September 1598 and 20 January 1599. Furthermore, by calling *Hercules, Robin Hood,* and *Sir John Oldcastle* "the firste parte" from their first entry in the diary (*HD,* 28, 86, 125), Henslowe indicated that a second part already existed or was in the making. A couple of entries suggest that the Admiral's men occasionally ordered a new second part to accompany the old first part into revival, as in the expenditure of £7 for *2 Two Angry Women of Abington,* apparently to accompany a revival of *Two Angry Women of Abington* (for which there is a payment for apparel but not for a text).

Spin-offs: Another commercial dimension of serial plays was the spin-off. On 26 May 1600, the Admiral's men paid Henry Chettle and John Day 110s. for "the blynd begger of bednall greene." On 29 January 1601, in duplicate entries, Day and William Haughton acknowledged payment to them of 40s. for "the second parte of the blind begger of Bednall Greene" (*HD,* 163) and Henslowe recorded the payment for "the second parte of the blinde beager of bednowle grene with thomme strowde" (*HD,* 166). Subsequently, he entered payments for the text or apparel five times, always calling the play the second part of *Tom Strowd* (*HD,* 166–69). Following these entries are those for a *3 Tom Strowd* (*HD,* 170 ff.). The text of the initial play (Q1659) shows that Tom Strowd is a hearty, somewhat clownish Norfolk yeoman incidental to the story of Momford and Bess, the title character and his marriageable daughter. The play comes to a full close: Momford is reconciled with King Henry VI, and Bess is suitably matched. The second part, now lost, seems to have spun off with the character of Tom Strowd, whose adventures apparently continued into the third part, also lost. I find it reasonable to see such plays as *Sir Thomas Stukeley, Shore's Wife,* and *Mortimer* as spin-offs from plays more obviously at the narrative center of the great battle story or political struggle to which these characters belonged. Likewise, the relationship between *1 Robin Hood* and its sequel may be explained by calling the play-piece treating King John's assault on Matilda a plot that has not spun away from the story complex to which it is tangentially related.

◆

The disdain that Collier felt for Henslowe, whom he believed to have been an ignorant man with disorderly accounts, and the confidence that Fleay maintained in Shakespeare's company, which he believed had run its business by a better system of management and a higher standard of excellence than those implicit in *Henslowe's Diary,* have so permeated our thinking about theatrical commerce that we have found support in what is really an absence of evidence. Because Henry Herbert licensed only four new plays for the King's men in 1623–24, we have inferred that in Shakespeare's time the company achieved greatness on very few plays per year. Because texts of plays that were made of such material as knightly adventures, Bible stories, and Tamburlaine-like heroes have not survived with evidence of ownership by Shakespeare's company, we have persuaded ourselves that there were none. We have even bolstered that belief by imagining an audience that would not have patronized the Globe if it had offered such low fare.[24]

These attitudes, as Beckerman observes, have grown out of "an idolatrous love of Shakespeare."[25] But there is an irony here, for we can trace the elitism back to Ben Jonson, not Shakespeare. In *Timber: or, Discoveries,* Jonson lamented the shallow preferences of ordinary men: "*Expectation* of the *Vulgar* is more drawne, and held with newnesse, then goodnesse; wee see it in *Fencers,* in *Players,* in *Poets,* in *Preachers,* in all, where *Fame* promiseth any thing; so it be new, though never so naught, and depraved, they run to it, and are taken" (*H&S,* VIII, 576). The work of a genuine artist, a "true Artificer," Jonson continued, was not to be classed "with the *Tamerlanes,* and *Tamer-Chams* of the late Age, which had nothing in them but the *scenicall* strutting, and furious vociferation, to warrant them to the ignorant gapers" (587). It is an obvious point, but nonetheless one that needs to be made, that we do not have to separate Shakespeare's company from the others in order to understand why that company succeeded financially, and we do not have to demonstrate Shakespeare's artistic superiority over contemporary playwrights in order to understand his role in that financial success. As I will argue in the chapters to come, the prosperity of the Chamberlain's and King's men was a function of their skill in exploiting commercial dimensions of a repertory system in general use at the time among the men's companies in London.

II

The Repertory of the Chamberlain's Men, 1594–1599

The men who performed at the Newington playhouse in June 1594 under the patronage of the Lord Chamberlain were experienced players. Most of them had been in companies since the 1580s, and they were well acquainted with such conditions of the theatrical profession as pressure from civic authorities, the sudden closure of London playhouses, invitations to play at Court, and touring. Through their experience in earlier companies, they had established contacts with dramatists, some of whom were still writing plays (or probably were): for example, Robert Wilson, Thomas Nashe, Thomas Lodge, John Lyly, Anthony Munday, and George Peele. In addition, the Chamberlain's men had established contacts with players who were now in other organizations. Those who had been members of Strange's men had been fellows with Edward Alleyn and others in the newly formed Admiral's men as well as with Philip Henslowe, owner of the Rose playhouse. Those who had been members of Pembroke's men in 1592–93 had been fellows with Gabriel Spencer and others in the company of Pembroke's men who turned up in London in 1597 and subsequently joined with the Admiral's men. John Heminges, and possibly other Chamberlain's men, had formerly been associated with the Queen's men and thus with any players from that old company who might have become members of the Queen's men that Francis Henslowe joined in 1594.

Through the acquisition of the player, Richard Burbage, the Chamberlain's men presumably found it easy to lease the Theatre (owned by James Burbage, Richard's father, along with a second playhouse in Shoreditch, the Curtain) and thus to acquire a stage comparable in surety to the Admiral's hold on the Rose. Other companies were not as fortunate. Coming to London in 1595–96 from a year-long provincial tour, the Queen's men apparently leased the newly constructed Swan playhouse from Francis Langley, but they did not remain there for much more than a year, if that long. Pembroke's men, ending a stint of touring, acquired the lease in February 1597. After the *Isle of Dogs* affray in August, senior members of Pembroke's left the Swan and joined the Admiral's men. For a time in the fall of 1597, this company of Admiral's and Pembroke's men at the Rose was the major one performing in London along with the Chamberlain's men. But Francis Langley later testified that a company had kept the Swan open after players from Pembroke's men departed, and a company leased the new Boar's Head playhouse from Oliver Woodliffe and Richard Samwell in 1598–99.[1] The Chamberlain's men were themselves without a playhouse sometime in 1596–97 because the Burbages' ground-lease on the Theatre was to expire in the spring of 1597. Presumably, the company moved to the Curtain until the Globe was ready for occupancy in early summer 1599.

The availability of a suitable playhouse, as well as experience in the business and connections with other professionals, would have been of little value if the Chamberlain's men had not developed a sense of playgoers' tastes and a skill in managing their corporate assets profitably. Although we know very few of the playbooks that they brought with them from other company repertories and few of those purchased as new over the next five years, we nonetheless see evidence in the playlists for 1594–95 through 1598–99 that they managed their repertory in terms of the system illustrated most fully in *Henslowe's Diary*. Specifically, they appear to have obtained new plays regularly, extended the runs of those continuing to draw audiences, and revived old favorites. In this combination of offerings, they provided a mix of story materials and dramatic formulas, including those newly in fashion. Sometimes based on the popularity of one of these plays and sometimes based on an anticipation of that popularity, they acquired serials, sequels, and spin-offs.

58

We know from *Henslowe's Diary* that the Chamberlain's men opened for business in June 1594 with four secondhand plays: *Hester and Ahasuerus, Titus Andronicus, Hamlet,* and *The Taming of the Shrew.* We may be reasonably sure that they soon acquired the rest of Shakespeare's old texts, including *1 Henry VI, 2 Henry VI, 3 Henry VI, Richard III,* and *Two Gentlemen of Verona.* We may be reasonably sure also that they acquired other used play-books at this time. Logical candidates are plays that (a) were formerly owned by companies in which current Chamberlain's men had been, and (b) were to be printed in subsequent years: for example, *Fair Em, Arden of Faversham, George a Greene, A Looking Glass for London and England, Orlando Furioso, Edward II, Soliman and Perseda, King Leir, Locrine, A Knack to Know a Knave,* and *Summer's Last Will and Testament.*

For one of these plays—*Fair Em*—there is evidence of ownership by the Chamberlain's men. *Fair Em* turned up in the eighteenth century in a volume bound with *The Merry Devil of Edmonton* and *Mucedorus,* both of which were published in quartos with advertisements of the Chamberlain's or King's men on the title-page. The anthology of plays is marked "Shakespeare. Vol. I," and it is thought to have come to David Garrick from the library of Charles II. From this coincidence of publication, we may infer that *Fair Em* came to be bound with two Chamberlain's plays because it was itself a Chamberlain's play. F. G. Fleay traces its migration to Sussex's men by way of Edward Alleyn, a player in Strange's men in 1592 and therefore in the company advertised on the title-page of an undated edition and a second quarto in 1631.[2] Fleay reads the entry in *Henslowe's Diary* of "william th*e* conkerer" on 4 January 1594 as an indication that Sussex's men played *Fair Em* under its subtitle ("With the loue of William the Conqueror"). From Sussex's men, the play could have traveled along with *Titus Andronicus* to the Chamberlain's men.

In this period of business, 1594–1599, the Chamberlain's men probably acquired about twenty new plays a year, given that there were not season-long closures of the playhouses. At best, though, we can identify a mere three or four of these per year: in 1594–95,

The Comedy of Errors (which was played at Gray's Inn on 28 December 1594), *Love's Labor's Lost,* and *Romeo and Juliet;* in 1595–96, *A Midsummer Night's Dream, Richard II,* and *Love's Labor's Won;* in 1596–97, *The Merchant of Venice, 1 Henry IV, King John* (which may have been in revival), and the anonymous *Mucedorus;* in 1597–98, *2 Henry IV, The Merry Wives of Windsor,* and the anonymous *A Warning for Fair Women;* in 1598–99, *Much Ado about Nothing, Henry V,* and Ben Jonson's *Every Man in His Humor.*

There is not much to indicate the length of stage runs for these plays except in the instances of *Hamlet* and *Titus Andronicus.* In *Wits Miserie and the Worlds Madnesse* (1596), Thomas Lodge alludes to *Hamlet* at the Theatre and therefore implies that the play continued in production until the Chamberlain's men moved to that playhouse in the spring of 1595, perhaps even into the fall season of 1595–96. Describing a devil named Hate-Vertue, the first-born son of Beelzebub, Lodge says "he walks for the most part in black vnder colour of grauity, & looks as pale as the Visard of ye ghost which cried so miserally at ye Theator like an oisterwife, *Hamlet, reuenge.*"[3] Lodge may be recalling a performance at the Theatre when the play was new, in 1589 or earlier, but an allusion to a current play would seem to have been more effective. It appears that *Titus Andronicus* was also in production in 1595–96. In a letter to Anthony Bacon in January 1596, Jacques Petit noted that *"commediens de Londres"* had performed "la tragedie de Titus Andronicus" on New Year's Day at the country manor of Sir John Harington, Burley-on-the-Hill, Rutland. Gustav Ungerer, who discovered Petit's letter among Bacon's papers at Lambeth Palace, hesitates to credit the Chamberlain's men with the performance, but no other London company is as likely to have owned the text.[4]

There are serial plays among those newly acquired, and we may speculate that, like the Admiral's men, the Chamberlain's men continued parts one in a sequence in production to coincide with the runs of subsequent parts. Possibly, then, *Love's Labor's Lost* was carried over into 1595–96 and scheduled in coordination with *Love's Labor's Won.* Part one of *Henry IV* probably remained in production long enough to play in the same repertory with *The Merry Wives of Windsor*, which chronologists consider the second of the Henriad to have been brought to the stage. There are many signs of the popularity of *1 Henry IV*. It generated quartos in 1598 and 1599, sequels to itself, and spin-offs (of a sort) about Sir John Oldcastle, various of which were played by the Chamberlain's, Admiral's, and Worcester's men, 1599–1603. Lines from the play became a source of witticism. In a letter to Dudley Carleton, 20 September 1598, Tobie Matthew alludes to a speech of Falstaff. Commenting on the dubious glory of military service in Ireland and the Low Countries, Matthew mocks several of the noblemen-soldiers, saying "Honour pricks them on, and the world thinks that honour will quickly prick them off again" (*CSP, Dom*, V, 97). If the allusion is current, part one of *Henry IV* may have remained on stage beyond 1597–98, and thus into and beyond the season when *2 Henry IV* was introduced (1597–98). From the entry of *2 Henry IV* into the Stationers' Register in August 1600 and its printing in two issues that year, we may infer that it too remained on stage beyond its maiden year, thus being available to anticipate or even accompany the new production of *Henry V* to the stage in the spring of 1599. It is not unthinkable, therefore, that runs of both parts of *Henry IV* overlapped the debut of *Henry V*.

For the company's revivals in 1594–1599, we have the example of the Admiral's men, hints from advertisements provided by stationers, and allusions in contemporary literature to suggest stage runs. There is one year in which revivals were certain: 1594–95. We deduce that the four plays named in *Henslowe's Diary* were revivals because Henslowe's signatory "ne" is missing from the entries. But what of the other old plays supplied by incoming players? Surely companies did not acquire a playbook, new or used, unless it had commercial value to them, and that value was in its production. The Admiral's men appear to have revived the plays acquired from players in the first two to three years of their run at the Rose. Therefore I assume that the Chamberlain's men staged each of the secondhand plays acquired in June 1594 within a few years. The *Henry VI* plays may have been revived in rapid succession, in which case their runs would allow performances on consecutive after-noons, as in the runs of *1* and *2 Tamburlaine* in *Henslowe's Diary*. The quarto of *Richard III* provides supporting evidence for its revival. When published in 1597, the text carried an advertisement of the Chamberlain's men on the title-page of the quarto. The revival of *Richard III*, in conjunction with an anecdote in the diary of John Manningham, suggests the tantalizing possibility that the Chamberlain's men also revived *Fair Em* in 1594–95. Manningham, a student at the Middle Temple (1602–03), tells the following story about Richard Burbage and William Shakespeare:

> Upon a tyme when Burbidge played Rich[ard] 3. there was a Citizen grewe soe farr in liking with him, that before shee went from the play shee appointed him to come that night unto hir by the name of Ri[chard] the 3. Shakespeare, overhearing their conclu-sion, went before, was intertained, and at his game ere Burbidge came. Then message being brought that Richard the 3^d. was at the dore, Shakespeare caused returne to be made that William the Conquerour was before Rich[ard] the 3. Shakespeare's name William.[5]

If Shakespeare's joke traded on his having played William the Conqueror while Burbage was playing Richard III, that role may have been as the king in *Fair Em,* possibly in 1594–96.

I take allusions in 1598 as evidence that *The Comedy of Errors* and *Romeo and Juliet* were revived in 1597–98. A poem by Everard Guilpin, satirist and epigrammatist, appears to allude to *The Comedy of Errors*. In "Satire V" of *Skialetheia* (S.R. 15 September 1598), Guilpin presents a satyr-figure who imagines the attractions of London, were he to be tempted out of the sanctuary of his rooms. One of those temptations is the playhouse:

> Perswade me to a play, I'le to the *Rose,*
> Or *Curtaine,* one of *Plautus* Comedies,
> Or the *Patheticke Spaniards* Tragedies
> (ll. 28–30).[6]

From *Henslowe's Diary,* we know that the Admiral's men revived *The Spanish Tragedy* at the Rose in January 1597. After the fall season of 1597–98 got underway in October, "Jøroneymo" was one of the offerings that the company continued. If Guilpin's allusion is as neatly structured as it seems, the Plautine comedy would be the play at the Curtain. Shakespeare's *The Comedy of Errors* carried an association with the Roman dramatist in its own time, as evidenced by the language used by the writer of *Gesta Grayorum* in 1594–95. Guilpin may have been thinking of plays in performance at any time between January 1597 and the summer of 1598, but an allusion to the "*Burgonians* tragedy" (l. 56) points to the later date. Guilpin seems to be referring to John Barrose, a Burgonian fencer who was hanged in July 1598 for murder.

An allusion in a poem by John Marston, satirist and dramatist, is evidence that *Romeo and Juliet* was revived. In *The Scourge of Villanie* (S.R. 8 September 1598), "Satire X" presents a satyr-figure who scoffs at Luscus, a humorous playgoer ("Satire XI" in the edition of 1599). An aspect of Luscus's humor is that he copies plays into a commonplace book and memorizes the lines to brighten up his conversation. One of his spiels, laughs the satirist, is "pure *Juliat* and *Romio*" (l. 39).[7] Marston grants that Luscus has good taste in his cobbling, for his lines are "warranted by Curtaine *plaudeties*" (l. 45). The speaker also mentions the Burgonian (l. 63), thus giving the dramatic allusions in *The Scourge of Villanie* the same time frame as those in *Skialetheia* (that is, 1597–98).

These new and old plays gave the Chamberlain's men much variety in story materials and dramatic formulas, as the comedies collectively illustrate. The dozen plays surviving in this genre represent nearly as many different narrative sources and comedic styles. *The Taming of the Shrew,* for example, treats a folk stereotype, popular in the dramatic tradition as early as the character of Noah's wife in Corpus Christi drama. *Fair Em,* like its contemporary, *Friar Bacon and Friar Bungay,* is a peculiarly Elizabethan form of a village girl's betrothal complicated by royals at play. In *The Comedy of Errors,* the company acquired a play in a line of descent from Plautus, one of two most revered practitioners of comic art in Roman literature. We may infer that Shakespeare's play relied on its classical parentage for commercial appeal because of references to

Plautus in *Gesta Grayorum* and Guilpin's "Satire V" of *Skialetheia*. We know that *Love's Labor's Lost* imitates the courtly mode of John Lyly's plays, and *Love's Labor's Won* may have also.

Several of the company's comedies drew on the ancient tradition of pastoral modified in a characteristically Elizabethan way. The most imitative of these seems to be *Mucedorus,* imitative in the sense that it repeats with little variation the motifs of the Elizabethan prose romance from which its story is taken. It therefore remains close to its source of literary inspiration. *Two Gentlemen of Verona* is also a rendering of continental and English prose pastorals; we cannot tell how closely it may follow its dramatic antecedent because the alleged model, *Felix and Philiomena,* has not survived (Queen's men, 1585). A third play, *A Midsummer Night's Dream,* seems from our perspective nearly four hundred years later to be an innovative treatment of pastoral materials. Yet we can imagine that the comedy showed Elizabethan audiences its links to classical and contemporary romances, if only in such simple details as the setting in Greece and the presence in the woods of a vile monster. A fourth, *The Merchant of Venice,* combines its pastoral story with a very urban and tragical story of revenge, and thus is not only a hybrid pastoral but a hybrid comedy.

A new fashion in the Chamberlain's repertory is the set of comedies that treat some aspect of the psychology of humors. Henslowe's entries for the Admiral's men in 1596–97 appear to document the onset of that fashion in the receipts generated in May 1597 by *The Comedy of Humors* (putatively George Chapman's *Humorous Day's Mirth*). After a mediocre return to Henslowe of 43s. on its opening day (11 May), the play brought in higher receipts at each show, peaking at 70s. at the sixth performance (7 June). These figures are all the more astonishing when we consider that only five other plays out of more than seventy in the Admiral's playlists from 1594 to 1597 brought in higher receipts to Henslowe than these at any performance after the opening show unless the date of the performance was a holiday. Nearly 40 percent of the new plays in the diary were retired without even reaching a seventh performance. Until scholars revised the date of *The Merry Wives of*

Windsor, it appeared that the Chamberlain's men did not respond to the success of *The Comedy of Humors* for more than a year, at which time they brought out *Every Man in His Humor* and *Much Ado about Nothing.* Now, with the assignment of *The Merry Wives of Windsor* to the repertory of 1597–98, we see that the Chamberlain's men acquired a play with humorous characters within six months of the show at the Rose.

In comparison with the many varieties of comedy, the history plays in the Chamberlain's repertory look remarkably homogeneous: all but one take their subject matter from the English chronicles. Yet the plays do not treat that matter similarly. The three parts of *Henry VI* and *King John* have an episodic structure, dramatizing the linear progress of struggles for power among feudal lords. In this design (or lack thereof) the plays recall such contemporary history plays as George Peele's *Edward I,* which dramatizes random events in the history of the king. In the three plays about Henry V, there are other antecedents: for example, in Falstaff, the figure of Riot from the moral interlude (*Interlude of Youth*); in Hal, the prince at play in the countryside with his nobles (*Friar Bacon and Friar Bungay*); and in Henry V on the battlefield at Agincourt, the disguised king of the romance tradition (*George a Greene*).[8] *Richard III* blends motifs from the revenge play, in particular the villainous revenger, and from the moral play, in the characterization of Richard as Vice. *Richard II* is built on the design of a *de casibus* tragedy, with Richard's sycophants cast in the role of Vice characters.

The exception to the subject matter of the chronicles is the play on a story from the Old Testament, *Hester and Ahasuerus.* An analogue is *Godly Queene Hester* (Q1561), a moral interlude in which Queen Hester reveals to the king the treachery of his ambitious counselor, Aman, and thereby saves the Jews from further persecution. *Hester and Ahasuerus* is the only drama based on Bible stories known to have been performed by the Chamberlain's men. There are, however, biblical plays in the drama at about this time: for example, *Abraham and Lot* (Sussex's men, 1593–94) and *David and Bathsabe* (S.R. 14 May 1594, Q1599). The Admiral's men obtained perhaps as many as seven, starting with *Nebuchadnezzar* in 1596–97 and continuing in 1601–1603 with *Judas, Jephthah, Tobias, Samson, Joshua,* and *Pontius Pilate*. R. B. Sharpe uses the fact that "we never hear" of a biblical play in the Chamberlain's holdings after 1594 as proof that their offerings differed significantly from those of competitors.[9] However, given the number of plays lost from the Chamberlain's stock, I am not willing to assume that none of these took its story from the Bible.

The four tragedies in the Chamberlain's repertory illustrate three kinds of tragical material. Two are revenge plays. According to scholarly tradition, this kind of tragedy became the rage in the late 1580s with the advent on stage of *The Spanish Tragedy* by Thomas Kyd. In Henslowe's playlists for 1592–1597, we see that every company had at least one revenge tragedy in production (*The Jew of Malta*), and most had at least two (*The Jew of Malta* plus either *The Spanish Tragedy* or *Titus Andronicus*). Thus the presence of two in the offerings of the Chamberlain's men in 1594 is consistent with the practice of companies at the time. Because the old school of theater and textual historians believed that *Titus Andronicus* was merely a revision made for Sussex's men of a play originally written for Strange's men, we have been invited to underestimate the market value of the play in 1594. But if we trust Henslowe that it was genuinely new in January of that year (or new to London) and that it received only three showings (each with receipts to Henslowe of 40s. or better), we can recognize that in June it was still a new play, from a commercial point of view. Furthermore, if we have no interest in protecting the literary reputation of Shakespeare, we are free to admit that the bombastic rhetoric, sentimentality, mutilations, villainous revengers, and outrageous stratagems for murder were features that audiences loved.

I imagine that the anonymous *Hamlet* appealed to audiences for similar reasons, though it lacked the mutilations. Nashe makes fun of its rhetoric in the preface to *Menaphon* with the reference to "whole Hamlets, I should say handfuls of Tragicall speeches."[10] The ghost lived on in the mocking cry of *"Vindicta,"* which echoes through plays in the repertories of various companies including the

Chamberlain's men as ridicule of the convention of vengeful spirits. Between the description provided by Lodge of old Hamlet with a pale vizard, crying miserably like an oyster wife, and the description provided by Comedy in the induction of *A Warning for Fair Women* of "a filthie whining ghost, / Lapt in some fowle sheete, or a leather pelch" that screams "like a pigge halfe stickt," we get some idea of the stage business and costuming of these ghosts.[11] We also get an idea of the costuming of Hamlet. Lodge, in the same allusion that likens Hate-Vertue to the ghost, refers to the devil's black suit. Guilpin implies in "Satire V" that black apparel had become so fashionable for melancholic poseurs as to be "out of fashion" (l. 89).

Romeo and Juliet is a sentimental love tragedy. It therefore would have had some of the same appeal as *Soliman and Perseda,* which was registered at Stationers' Hall in 1592 and printed within a year or two. But though it was old in 1594–95 when *Romeo and Juliet* was new, *Soliman and Perseda* had currency of a kind through revivals of *The Spanish Tragedy,* for the love story of Soliman and Perseda was the subject of the play that Bel-Imperia and Hieronimo performed for the Kings of Spain and Portugal. According to *Henslowe's Diary,* the Admiral's men revived *The Spanish Tragedy* ("Joronymo") in January 1597, and they kept the play in production when the playhouses reopened in October 1597. At every performance, playgoers watched Perseda kill herself after murdering Soliman for having had her beloved killed. In 1599 *Soliman and Perseda* was reprinted, as were *The Spanish Tragedy* and *Romeo and Juliet.* The story of Shakespeare's star-crossed lovers has little in common with that of Soliman and Perseda, but in both plays the dramatists use Love, Death, and Fortune to emphasize the sadness of the deaths. On the basis of similar plot, *Romeo and Juliet* invites comparison with the romantic comedy. Shakespeare himself provides the most excellent pairing in *A Midsummer Night's Dream*: the tragical match of the young Veronese lovers is seen through "A Tedious Brief Scene of Young Pyramus and His Love Thisby; Very Tragical Mirth," and it is in turn complementary to the successful matches of the young Athenian lovers.

The fourth tragedy, *A Warning for Fair Women,* is the dramatization of a murder that took place in London in 1573. Therefore, like *Arden of Faversham,* which was republished in 1599, and probably like the set of crime dramas that the Admiral's men bought for production in 1599–1600 (*Page of Plymouth, Cox of Collumpton,* and *The Tragedy of Thomas Merry*), *A Warning for Fair Women* teaches domestic morality by exploiting the sensationalism of an actual murder. In the play, George Browne enlists the aid of the widow Drurie and her servant Roger to woo Anne Sanders, a young wife with two small children. Anne seems reasonably content with Sanders until she is beseiged by marital vices. First, he is late for dinner, and the meat is ruined. Second, he refuses to buy her some finery. Third, the widow Drurie reads her palm and foretells the coming of a gentleman lover, whom Anne takes to be Browne. Presumably, she encourages Browne with at least one love letter, but by the time he kills her husband, she is sufficiently remorseful to refuse his advances (he, too, instantly repents the crime). She does, however, give him some money to escape. In the play proper, the dramatist does not explore the psychology of adultery (either for Anne or Browne), but he makes clear its consequences: Browne, Anne, the widow Drurie, and Roger are condemned to death. Kneeling at her children's feet, Anne delivers a litany of contrite prayers:

> Mercy I aske of God, of him [Sanders], and you,
> And of his kinred which I have abusde,
> Of my friends and kinred wheresoever, . . .
> And of al men and women in the world,
> Whome by my foule example I have griev'd.
>   (ll. 2675–80)

She gives each child a book of meditations with instructions to "learne by [their] mothers fall / To follow vertue, and beware of sinne" (ll. 2686–87).

Although clumsy in the handling of plot and characterization, the author of *A Warning for Fair Women* understands stagecraft. The induction itself is an energetic play. History, equipped with a

68

drum and ensign, and Tragedy, with a whip in one hand and a knife in the other, enter by separate doors. Comedy enters soon after, and the three quarrel over who will govern the performance. Tragedy whips the two contenders from the stage, which now is "hung with blacke" (l. 82). She reappears periodically to present and explicate the dumb shows. Each of these is a Freudian nightmare of the progress of an adulterous courtship. The first parodies a wedding ceremony: Lust leads in the bride, who wears a black veil; the cele-brants *"march about, and then sit to the table: the Furies fill wine, Lust drinckes to* Browne, *he to Mistris* Sanders, *she pledgeth him: Lust imbraceth her, . . . the Furies leape and imbrace one another"* (ll. 809–15). Tragedy concludes the festivities by bathing the hands of Browne, Drurie, and Roger in blood; demonstrating the relative cul-pability of the participants, Tragedy bathes only the finger of Anne. In the second dumb show, George and Anne meet secretly, but when they embrace, there "suddenly riseth up a great tree betweene them" (l. 1266). Lust offers Anne an ax to cut the tree down; when she refuses, Browne does the job. The crime itself is accented with omens, blood, and violence. Browne's attempts are aborted twice, and on the day of the murder the sweetheart of the servant to be killed has bad dreams and a nose bleed. George dips his handkerchief in Sanders's blood and sends the token to Anne (she refuses it). The wounds of the servant bleed afresh on sight of Browne. In the final scenes of George and Anne, the dramatist achieves contrasting effects of death and pathos. George is hanged on stage. Anne is taken away to be executed, but not before she bids her children a tearful farewell.

A few tragedies acquired by the Chamberlain's men in 1594–1599 have been lost, and we have no way of knowing what these plays were unless they are alluded to in some kind of record or literary work. In the postscript to *Kemps Nine Daies Wonder,* William Kempe comments on several popular tragical subjects. He addresses a writer whom he advises to "leaue writing these beastly ballets," and he recommends that the balladeer take up another kind of writing instead:

Call vp thy olde Melpomene, whose straubery quill may write the bloody lines of the blew Lady, and the Prince of the burning crowne, a better subiect, I can tell ye, than your Knight of the Red Crosse.[12]

The reference to Melpomene, muse of tragedy, identifies the kind of writing Kempe has in mind. Because Kempe had been a player for so long, and a player with the Chamberlain's men, it is tempting to infer that he is recommending subjects for tragical plays. One of these subjects was to be used for a play in 1602–03, when Henry Chettle started to write *Hoffman* (Q1631). The play tells the story of Hoffman, who uses a burning crown as a murder weapon in revenge of his father's death. I do not know the story of the Blue Lady.

In addition to showing a variety of genres, narratives, and formulas, the partial repertory for 1594–1599 shows that the Chamberlain's plays duplicated some of the popular subject matter in the holdings of other companies in the way that *Edward I* and *Longshanks* duplicate one another. When Shakespeare wrote *Richard III*, he was appropriating elements of the story that the Queen's men had dramatized in *The True Tragedy of Richard the Third* (S.R. 19 June 1594, Q1594). His play seems to have been in production at the same time that Sussex's men were performing a possible spin-off called *Buckingham* at the Rose (Christmastide, 1593–94). When he began to compose *The Merchant of Venice*, *The Jew of Malta* was in revival at the Rose. It had been in production there almost continuously since February 1592 (and at another London playhouse before that). At the debut of *The Merchant of Venice*, therefore, the revenge of Barabas was familiar to all regular playgoers and freshly familiar to some.[13] From the title, it appears that *The Jew of Venice* (date unknown), which has been ascribed to Thomas Dekker, portrayed a character analogous to Marlowe's and Shakespeare's Jews.

When Shakespeare began the trilogy about Prince Hal, later Henry V, there had been at least three plays on stage previously that had used the subject matter. One, *The Famous Victories of Henry V*, was registered at Stationers' Hall on 14 May 1594 and published in 1598 naming the Queen's men as owners on the title-page. In *Pierce Pennilesse* (1592), Thomas Nashe alludes to a play in which "*Henrie* the fifth [was] represented on the Stage, leading the French King prisoner, and forcing both him and the Dolphin to sweare fealty" (I, 213). As Gary Taylor points out, this play cannot be *The Famous Victories*, which has no similar episode.[14] The reference is too early to be the *Henry V* that the Admiral's men introduced as a new play on 28 November 1595 and continued to 15 July 1596. Therefore, when *1 Henry IV* was introduced into the Chamberlain's 1596–97 offerings, it was also following plays to the stage that its audience would have recognized as similar. *1 Henry IV*, which apparently created a market for itself among readers (as evidenced by its three editions in two years, 1598–99), may have led a stationer to expect a market for *The Famous Victories of Henry V* in 1598, unless that market had already been created by the play's revival.

There are two plays in this collective repertory with close analogues in the anonymous drama of the period—so close, in fact, that more than one scholar has believed that Shakespeare rewrote the old plays into his own new ones, or (at the very least) used them as sources. There is still not agreement on the amount of influence and the direction of that influence between *The Taming of a Shrew* and Shakespeare's *The Taming of the Shrew* and *The Troublesome Reign of King John* and Shakespeare's *King John*. But whatever a comparative study of the texts may say about abridgments, Ur-sources, revisions, memorial reconstructions, and the like, the existence of more than one play on the same narrative is thoroughly consistent with the commercial strategy of the companies to duplicate the popular offerings of their competitors. In fact, pieces of the stage histories of Shakespeare's *King John* and *The Troublesome Reign of King John* appear to come together in 1595–97 to demonstrate the commercial relationship of plays with the same subject matter. According to the title-page of the first quarto of *The Troublesome Reign of King John*, the Queen's men owned the playbook in 1590–91. If the players with the company by that name in 1595–96 had retained a copy, if they leased the Swan when Francis Langley opened it in the late summer of 1595, and if they revived the play at that time, the Chamberlain's men may well have had a special interest in acquiring (or reviving) a text of their own on the same subject.

Another commercial practice in evidence in the Chamberlain's repertory is the extension of popular narratives into sequels, serials, and spin-offs. The paradigm had been provided by *Tamburlaine,* which audiences liked so much that Marlowe wrote a second part. Shakespeare's play of *Henry VI* appears to have been extraordinarily popular, perhaps even as popular as *Tamburlaine.* On 3 March 1592 Strange's men introduced a play called "harey the vj." Its receipts to Henslowe at that opening show were £3. 16s. 8d. Strange's men continued the play for another fourteen performances through June. When they returned to the Rose at Christmas, 1592–93, they presented *Henry VI* twice more. Over the seventeen performances, the play returned an average over 41s. to Henslowe. Its opening-day receipts were to be the highest that Henslowe recorded for any play through 1597. Thomas Nashe appears to confirm the extraordinary success of *Henry VI.* In a passage of *Pierce Pennilesse* that defends stage plays (1592), he cites Talbot as a hero who has received his proper honor by being represented in a play. Nashe sees

> braue *Talbot* (the terror of the French) [pleased] to thinke that after he had lyne two hundred yeares in his Tombe, hee should triumphe againe on the Stage, and haue his bones newe embalmed with the teares of ten thousand spectators at least (at seuerall times), who, in the Tragedian that represents his person, imagine they behold him fresh bleeding (I, 212).

According to one version of the composition of *2 Henry VI* and *3 Henry VI,* Shakespeare responded to the popularity of his extant *Henry VI* by writing a sequel which became the two parts subsequently published as *The First Part of the Contention betwixt the Two Famous Houses of Yorke and Lancaster* and *The True Tragedie of Richard Duke of Yorke.*[15] In a normal year, presumably, these plays would have been acquired by Strange's men and presented in serial performances with *Henry VI.* However, 1592 was not a normal year. The playhouses were shut down in June. After opening at Christmastime, 1592–93, they were shut for the rest of 1593 because of the plague. One of the sequels, *The True Tragedy,* was published in 1595 with a title-page that names Pembroke's men as owners of the text. From this evidence, we have theorized that Pembroke's company had owned *The First Part of the Contention* also, which had been published in 1594 without the name of a company. In fact, we have theorized that the texts originally acquired by Pembroke's men were the texts we know as *2 Henry VI* and *3 Henry VI*. Separated from the seminal play of *1 Henry VI*, the second and third parts acquired titles that do not advertise themselves as sequels to that original play. The titles do, however, advertise their serial relationship to each other, in that *The True Tragedy* has as part of its subtitle the phrase "with the whole contention betweene the two Houses Lancaster and Yorke." This pairing accompanied the plays when the texts were sold to another stationer. According to the Stationers' Register on 19 April 1602, Thomas Millington (publisher of the texts in 1594, 1595, and 1600) sold "the first and Second parte of henry the vj^t" to Thomas Pavier, who subsequently published both texts with a joint title (*BEPD*, I, 18).

Shakespeare's plays on Prince Hal and Falstaff illustrate not only the serialization of *1 Henry IV* into *2 Henry IV* and *Henry V* but also the spin-off of *The Merry Wives of Windsor* from matter in parts one and two. Most editors of the plays believe that Shakespeare began work on *2 Henry IV* soon after he finished *1 Henry IV*. Whether he made the second and third parts to capitalize on the success of the first or whether he was a shrewd enough forecaster of audience taste to have planned sequels all along is less important here than the fact that he did serialize the narrative. Apparently, *2 Henry IV* was known in its own day as a sequel. In the Stationers' Register it is called "the second parte of the history of kinge henry the iiijth" (*BEPD,* I, 16), and on the title-page of its quarto it is called "THE Second part of Henrie the fourth."

Shakespeare suspended work on *2 Henry IV* at some point to begin a new but related project: *The Merry Wives of Windsor.* Two legends have grown up around the composition of this play. One is of a recent and scholarly origin. Reading through the Controlment

Rolls for 1596, Leslie Hotson discovered an entry that subsequently led him to a network of documents about Shakespeare, Francis Langley, William Wayte, and Justice William Gardiner. He decided that the character of Justice Shallow in *2 Henry IV* and *The Merry Wives of Windsor* was a lampoon of this Justice Gardiner, and he revised the dating of the latter play to precede Gardiner's death in November 1597. Finding that the Chamberlain's patron, George Carey, was initiated into the Order of the Garter on 23 April 1597, Hotson chose that occasion of the ceremony at Windsor as the impetus for Shakespeare's writing of *The Merry Wives of Windsor*.[16] The second legend belongs to the tradition of Shakespeare biography. As John Dennis told the story (in the epistle to *The Comical Gallant*, 1702), Queen Elizabeth commanded Shakespeare to write *The Merry Wives of Windsor* and to do so in fourteen days because she was eager to see the play. Nicholas Rowe embellished Dennis's version, adding that the Queen "was so well pleas'd with that admirable Character of Falstaff, in the two Parts of Henry the Fourth, that she commanded him to continue it for one Play more, and to shew him in Love."[17] Hotson's story may have more truth in it than Rowe's embellishment of Dennis's, but Rowe's conveys splendidly the commercial logic of the spin-off in which a character in one play becomes so popular that he turns up next in a play of his own. The language both of the entry in the Stationers' Register (18 January 1602) and of the advertisement on the title-page of the quarto (1602) indicates that the play was meant to be called *A . . . Comedy of Sir John Falstaff.*

No doubt the most curious instance of sequels in the Chamberlain's repertory for any of the years is the one made a mystery by a lost text. Francis Meres attributed a play called *Love's Labor's Won* to Shakespeare in *Palladis Tamia* (1598), but most Shakespeareans refused to believe that a play with that name—now lost—had ever existed. Instead they assumed that one of the plays not named by Meres had once carried the title. In 1957 T. W. Baldwin published a bookseller's inventory dating from 1603 that listed, consecutively, "loves labor lost" and "loves labor won."[18] This evidence may not convince some scholars, for the use of the titles by the bookseller does not establish that the plays were what they seem to be or that the now-lost play was by Shakespeare. However, the currency of the title *Love's Labor's Won*—regardless of the narrative that title serves—makes a commercial point: someone meant to promote the play by advertising it as a sequel to *Love's Labor's Lost*.[19]

But what if Shakespeare did write a play called *Love's Labor's Won* that ended with nuptial celebrations for the King of Navarre and the Princess of France along with the pairs of their attendant lords and ladies? Some playgoers, I assume, would have realized the novelty in turning a comedy into two parts. In the drama before 1595–96 (the date assigned to *Love's Labor's Won*), there are serialized histories, and there is a revenge tragedy with a romantic forepiece, but there is not an instance on record in which a love story is suspended over two plays. The commercial appeal of Shakespeare's pair, therefore, goes beyond the advertising in the titles to an experiment in comedic form. Judging by the titles in *Henslowe's Diary*, the next dramatist to write a sequel for a comedy was Henry Porter, who sold the Admiral's men *2 Two Angry Women of Abington* to accompany the original play to the stage. He began a third part, *Two Merry Women of Abington*, but seems not to have finished it (he was killed in a duel with a fellow dramatist, John Day, in June 1599). The three-part *Blind Beggar of Bednal Green* (1600–01) was apparently a sequence of comedies (if the second and third parts were consistent with the extant first part). The two parts of *The London Florentine* (1602–03) sound like satires of fashion, and the two-part *Honest Whore* treats the themes of patience and prodigality in a comedic structure. If Shakespeare did try a serial comedy in *Love's Labor's Lost* and *Love's Labor's Won*, it seems he developed a standard commercial tactic in a way that other dramatists would subsequently imitate.

By way of exemplifying commercial aspects of the repertory acquired and performed by the Chamberlain's men during their first five years of business, I offer the marketable features of *Every Man in His Humor*. For one, the play was new. The Chamberlain's men therefore would have charged an extra penny at the playhouse door at its opening-day performance, and all of the revenue would have gone to the sharers in the company.

For a second, by purchasing this particular play the Chamberlain's men were employing an experienced dramatist. Ben Jonson, though new to their ranks, was not new to the theatrical enterprise. In fact, he had no doubt already acquired some notoriety in the playhouse world because of events growing out of his company membership in the summer of 1597. As a member of Pembroke's men at the Swan, he had recently been imprisoned for several months allegedly because a play on which he had collaborated had offended members of the government (*The Isle of Dogs*). He had gone from jail to the Admiral's men, to whom he promised—but did not complete—a text by Christmas of 1597. He did, however, complete the text of *Hot Anger Soon Cold* for the Admiral's men in collaboration with Henry Porter and Henry Chettle in August of 1598. He must have had *Every Man in His Humor* completed at that time (or nearly so), for Tobie Matthew quipped in a letter dated 20 September that a member of the entourage of a French gentleman had recently lost 300 crowns "at a new play called Every Man's humour" (*CSD, Dom*, V, 97). Two days later, on 22 September, Jonson killed a player, Gabriel Spencer, in a duel, and he escaped hanging "only by claiming right of clergy" (*H&S*, I, 18).[20]

For a third, the play capitalizes on a current fashion in drama: in this case, the psychology of the humors. The main characters, Lorenzo Senior and his son, are not the best examples of an aberrant humor, though the father is a bit over-anxious and fears his son is a bit over-melancholy. Those genuinely afflicted by the "monster bred in a man by selfe loue, and affection, and fed by folly" are the gulls (Q1601; III.i.157–58). Thorello, husband of Biancha, terrorizes himself with jealousy. Bobadilla is the soldier and gallant whose favorite topics are swordsmanship and tobacco. Confiding in Lorenzo Junior, he imagines Falstaff-like that he could secure the state of Florence with the help of nineteen gentlemen whom he had chosen "by an instinct" (IV.ii69–70), trained at fencing, and sent into battle to combat the enemy:

thus would we kill euery man, his twentie a day, thats twentie score; twentie score, thats two hundreth; two hundreth a day, fiue dayes a thousand: fortie thousand; fortie times fiue, fiue times fortie, two hundreth dayes killes them all, by computation (IV.ii80–84).

The lesser gulls, Matheo and Stephano, follow him about like puppies. Matheo is afflicted by the delusion that he is a poet; Stephano, a chameleon, is casting around for the most suitable humor to affect.

For a fourth, *Every Man in His Humor* uses the motif of disguise, which was popular in the drama of the late 1590s. A recent success in this vein on the stage at the Rose had been *The Blind Beggar of Alexandria* by Chapman (1595–97). The center of interest in this play is a character with four identities: a blind beggar, a usurer, a nobleman, and a warrior. The character's intention is to pass the time by mischief-making until in the identity of the warrior he can assume the throne. According to the title-page of the quarto in 1599, *Look about You* was also an Admiral's play. The master of disguise in this comedy is Skinke, who picks up the identities of other characters in the play by donning their discarded apparel. Many of the other characters assume disguises as well, including Robin Hood and Marian. It is reasonable to assume that *Disguises* (Admiral's men 1595–96) relied on mistaken identity also. In *Every Man in His Humor*, if we discount the characters who play roles in the affectation of a humor, the primary masker is Musco, Lorenzo Senior's clever servant. Initially, Musco disguises himself as a veteran soldier now abandoned by the state and reduced to begging. He subsequently switches clothing with Doctor Clement's man; then he pawns a cloak to buy the habit of a serjeant. In one or another of these identities, he manages to make "a fayre mashe" of the gulls (V.ii.74). When he explains these tricks in court, Doctor Clement commends his wit and punishes the humorous fools accordingly.

The Chamberlain's men acquired *Every Man in His Humor* at a problematic time for them commercially. They had been closed out of the Theatre by the expiration of the Burbages' ground-lease, and (we assume) they had moved into the equally old but less commodious Curtain. If Jonson's play was as new as Tobie Matthew thought in late September 1598, it served as one of their drawing cards in the fall repertory. The text called on the talents of ten of their most senior members and most experienced players. The evidence suggests that it was a successful offering: it generated a second play with a title that alluded to its own; it was published within a few years of its maiden run with a title-page that advertises the names of the playwright and the company; it was revived in 1604–05 to be played during the first Christmas when the new king, now their patron, kept the Revels season in London. I assume that it was successful enough in 1598–99 to carry over into their offerings for the first year at the Globe, where it would have been given occasional performances during the opening run of its titular sequel, the new play *Every Man out of His Humor*.

Nicholas Rowe tells the story that Jonson brought the Chamberlain's men a text of *Every Man in His Humor*, and they, "after having turn'd it carelessly and superciliously over, were just upon returning it to him with an ill-natur'd Answer, that it would be of no service to their Company, when *Shakespear* luckily cast his Eye upon it, and found something so well in it as to engage him first to read it through, and afterwards to recommend Mr. *Johnson* and his Writings to the Publick" (I, xii–xiii). Rowe tells the story, of course, because it shows Shakespeare to have been generous enough of mind to encourage a fledgling poet. But we may detect a sharp eye for commercial value behind this generosity. In fact, each of the experienced members of the company would have seen *Every Man in His Humor* as a new play full of the latest fashions in comedy and therefore potentially able to attract not only this year's customers to the old Curtain in Shoreditch but possibly even next year's customers to the large and expensive playhouse soon to be built on the Bankside.

The Repertory of the Chamberlain's Men, 1599–1603

The Chamberlain's men acquired a new playhouse in 1599. When it was clear that the ground-lease on the Shoreditch property would not be renewed, Richard and Cuthbert Burbage took a crew of workmen to the site on 28 December 1598 (by one report), dismantled the Theatre, and had the wood and timber carted across the Thames to a location in Maid Lane in Southwark. Using these materials, the Burbages had the Globe built for £700, which was the same sum that the Theatre had cost in 1576.[1] Senior members of the company must have known about the plans to construct a new playhouse well in advance of its availability for playing. The Burbages had secured the property from Nicholas Brend by Christmas 1598, and by February 1599 they had solicited William Shakespeare, Augustine Phillips, Thomas Pope, John Heminges, and William Kempe to become investors in both the property and building. Presumably, therefore, the Chamberlain's men had the spring of 1599 to anticipate the transfer of business to the Globe and to prepare a suitable repertory.

The Admiral's men were to face a similar situation in 1599–1600 with the construction of the Fortune, and according to the entries in *Henslowe's Diary* for their early years at the new playhouse, there were changes in the size of the repertory and the age of the offerings that have significance in terms of the move. In 1599–1600, when they were still at the Rose, they made payments on thirty-six new playbooks (or new to them), which is a number up to a third larger than the "ne" plays per year, 1594–1597. In

January through June of 1600–01, part of their first year at the Fortune, they made payments on about half as many playbooks as in the same period of the previous year, and they added one revival (*Phaeton*). In 1601–02 and 1602–03, they resumed a more normative level of purchases but added a large number of revivals. We may explain the expansion of the repertory with new plays in 1599–1600 as a response to the arrival of the Chamberlain's men at the Globe across Maid Lane, and no doubt it was to some extent; but the Admiral's men may also have been thinking of the contract Edward Alleyn signed with Peter Street in January 1600 and their imminent relocation to Middlesex. Once moved, they could use the plays from 1599–1600 to fill out the schedule at the Fortune, thus saving themselves the expense of new productions (when their other costs were up) and at the same time extracting whatever fresh commercial value the old plays had accrued by their transfer to a new playhouse and neighborhood. In 1601–02, supposedly, Alleyn returned to playing after a sabbatical of three or four years. We have explained the revivals starting in May 1601 as a tactic to advertise his return, but they serve as well to replace the continuations in 1600–01 with less expensive productions than new plays would require.[2]

The list of plays performed by the Chamberlain's men in the opening years of the Globe is incomplete; therefore, we cannot say with certainty that they used the same tactics to manage the repertory that the Admiral's men appear to have used. Yet we can be sure that their primary concern was to establish their business in the Southwark location and to continue to compete successfully for the growing number of playgoers in the London area. And there are hints from entries of old plays in the Stationers' Register that the Chamberlain's men kept several offerings from 1597–98 and 1598–99 in production into 1599–1600. On 4 August 1600, four plays were entered on the fly leaf of Register C "to be staied" (*BEPD*, I, 15). Three of the four—*Much Ado about Nothing, Every Man in His Humor,* and *Henry V*—were new in 1598–99 but are registered here with a play new in 1599–1600, *As You Like It*. A logical inference is that all four had recently been in production. A little more than two weeks later on 23 August, *2 Henry IV* was registered with *Much Ado about Nothing* as the property of Andrew Wise and William Aspley, who published both texts that year. Perhaps, then, *2 Henry IV* had also been continued into 1599–1600. If so, these old plays joined with the following and other new plays now lost as attractions at the company's new playhouse: *Julius Caesar, Every Man out of His Humor, Cloth Breeches and Velvet Hose, A Larum for London, As You Like It,* and *Oldcastle.*

We know less about the offerings in 1600–1603. It appears that the new plays in 1600–01 were *Hamlet, Thomas Lord Cromwell,* and *The Freeman's Honor;* in 1601–02, *Twelfth Night,* and *Satiromastix;* and in 1602–03, *Troilus and Cressida, The Merry Devil of Edmonton, All's Well That Ends Well, Jeronimo* (old?), and *Stuhlweissenburg.* It is certain that the Chamberlain's men revived one play in 1600–01, but for only one performance on Saturday, 7 February 1601. According to a member of the audience, the play told the story "of King Henry the Fourth, and of the killing of Richard the Second" (*CSP, Dom,* V, 575); according to one of the players, it dramatized "the deposing and killing of King Richard II" (*CSP, Dom,* V, 578).[3] Presumably these descriptions refer to Shakespeare's *Richard II.* I would guess that there were more revivals, if for no other reason than that the Chamberlain's men, like the Admiral's men, were looking for ways to expand their repertory inexpensively. For clues to the identity of these revivals, I would consider the interest of stationers in publishing quartos of plays three or more years old: for example, *George a Greene* in 1599; *A Midsummer Night's Dream, Summer's Last Will and Testament,* and *The Merchant of Venice* in 1600 (the Admiral's men revived *The Jew of Malta* in May 1601); and *The Merry Wives of Windsor* in 1602. Further, I would consider the impetus for new editions of *Titus Andronicus,* the two-part *Contention* (*2, 3 Henry VI*) also in 1600, and *Richard III* in 1602. Several of these plays have star roles for Richard Burbage. He had not retired and revived his career as had Alleyn, but his company would surely have used his talents similarly to advertise their move to the new location.

Entries in *Henslowe's Diary* suggest that, in addition to tinkering with the size and age of the repertory, the Admiral's men acquired several plays in the time around their move that publicize the name of the Fortune. On 10 November 1599 the company laid out 40s. to Thomas Dekker "in earnest of abooke cald the hole hystory of ffortunatus" (*HD*, 126). They completed payment on 30 November, paid for some alterations on 31 November, introduced the play into the offerings at the Rose, and took it to Court during the Revels season. Philip Henslowe and Edward Alleyn did not sign the contract with Peter Street to build the Fortune until 8 January 1600. Thus we cannot say that the purchase in November of a play with the name of their playhouse in the title was anything more than a happy coincidence; but at the very least, the presence of *Fortunatus* in the spring offerings served to announce their upcoming move and, if it were one of the plays continued, the name of their new playhouse. On 6 September 1600, some weeks after the Fortune had opened, the Admiral's men paid Dekker 20s. "for his boocke called the fortewn tenes." Greg and Chambers read this title as *Fortune's Tennis*, and they agree that its occurrence in the repertory at this time indicates the company's awareness of advertising. Both scholars point out a possible connection with the fragment of a Plot called *2 Fortune's Tennis* (*ES*, II, 177–78; *Diary*, II, 215). If there were in fact two parts to the play bought in September 1600, the company received double the advertising out of the choice of titles.

The Chamberlain's men had several interesting options if they decided to publicize the Globe in a similar way. They could commission plays with the word "globe" or "world" in the title or with allusions to the Globe in the texts ("All the world's a stage"; "To melt the world, and mould it new againe"; "Round through the compasse of this earthly ball").[4] One popular dramatic subject is suggested by the sign of the playhouse, which according to theatrical legend was Hercules with the world on his shoulders.[5] The Chamberlain's men must have known that the Admiral's men had introduced a two-part *Hercules* in May of 1594–95, which was popular enough to be carried over into the fall offerings of 1595–96. They must also have known that the Admiral's men had revived one or both parts the previous summer (July 1598). The Admiral's men revived their property yet again, in the winter of 1601–02. Queen Anne's men knew the subject was popular, and Thomas Heywood supplied them with a four-part serial, the third play of which dramatizes the labors of Hercules (*The Brazen Age,* Q1613). If the Chamberlain's men also acquired a play about the mythical strongman, they would have had a more explicit (and less vulgar) advertisement of the new location of their enterprise than the allusion in *Hamlet* to "Hercules and his load" (II.ii.361–62).

And, in 1599–1600 particularly, the Chamberlain's men had an extra incentive to advertise the quality of entertainment at their new house. Suddenly there were companies playing all over London: at the Rose, Boar's Head, St. Paul's, Blackfriars, and the old Curtain. The construction of the Fortune freed the Rose for other occupants, further expanding the number of companies at established playhouses. Theater historians at the turn of the century fixed on the reappearance of the boys' companies after a hiatus of about ten years as the most significant alteration in the commercial dynamics of 1599–1603, but I suggest that the situation was more complex than allegations of stage quarrels or wars between adult and boys' companies imply.

There was, for instance, an expanded market for dramatists. The demand for new plays may have attracted poets to the field of theatrical writing, but even if it did not, it made business excellent for those already supplying companies with plays. Dramatists who had written for one company at a time began to write for several, as did Thomas Heywood, for Admiral's men and Worcester's men; Ben Jonson, for Admiral's men, Chamberlain's men, and the Children of Blackfriars; and Thomas Dekker, for Admiral's men, Worcester's men, Chamberlain's men, and the Children of Paul's. For some reason, too, more stationers in 1600 began to see a market in the acquisition and publication of playtexts. Compared to a relatively typical year such as 1598, during which there were five entries in the Stationers' Register involving a total of five plays and the appearance of seven plays in quarto for the first time, there were in 1600 twenty-four entries in the Stationers' Register involving a total of thirty-six plays and the appearance of fourteen plays in first editions. In regard to the Chamberlain's men, at least a dozen of their plays were registered in 1600; of those appearing in quarto, six carried the name of the company on the title-page of the quarto.

Moreover, there were plays being offered at these houses that were to generate new dramatic formulas and to make some old ones popular again. Much of the credit for these developments has been given to the boys' companies, and fairly so. At St. Paul's, for example, the children's company played John Marston's *Antonio and Mellida* (Q1602) and *Antonio's Revenge* (Q1602), thus reviving an interest in two-part revenge plays. Marston took advantage of this success with *The Malcontent* (Q1604), which the children's company at Blackfriars acquired in 1602–03, and which Shakespeare's company appropriated in 1603–04. Both boys' companies played Lylian pastorals such as *The Maid's Metamorphosis* (Q1601) and *Love's Metamorphosis* (Q1601) and middle-class romantic comedies such as *The Wisdom of Doctor Dodipoll* (Q1600). The Blackfriars company took the nascent dramatic satire to perfection with Jonson's *Poetaster* (Q1602).

But the boys were not the only companies with innovative drama. The Admiral's men had a play celebrating citizens in *The Gentle Craft* [*Shoemaker's Holiday,* Q1600], which they gave at Court in 1599–1600. Derby's men at the Boar's Head had *How a Man May Choose a Good Wife from a Bad* (Q1602), an early member in the class of prodigal husband plays, and *The Weakest Goeth to the Wall,* a link between old-fashioned romances and the heroic tragicomedies to come. Worcester's men at the Rose had *A Woman Killed with Kindness* (Q1607), which meshes the prodigal and crime plays into domestic tragicomedy. These men's companies were also presenting new plays in old formulas: for example, Derby's men with the two-part *Edward IV* (Q1599), which traded on a continuing interest in English historical matter, particularly the Wars of the Roses; Worcester's men with *Medicine for a Curst Wife* (1602–03), which appears to be a shrew play in new guise; and Admiral's men with new crime dramas such as *Page of Plymouth* (1599–1600), biblical dramas such as *Judas* (1601–02), classical histories such as *Hannibal and Scipio* (1600–01), and foreign histories such as *Philip of Spain* (1602–03). Platter does not name the play that he saw at the Curtain in the late summer of 1599, but it sounds like familiar fare too. According to his plot summary, the play began with a tournament in which an Englishman fought a series of contests with foreign warriors "for a maiden," finally losing to the German. However, when the German and his servant got drunk and quarrelled ("and the servant threw his shoe at his master's head"), the Englishman climbed into their tent and carried off the girl; thus he "outwits the German too."[6]

It is in this context—a new playhouse, a burgeoning theatrical industry, and a consequent multiplication of play offerings in new and old dramatic forms—that we can best appreciate the strategy of the Chamberlain's men to distribute their offerings among new plays and old, select a mix of new and old story materials, and obtain plays in the most popular new dramatic formulas while keeping old favorites in the schedule.

Perhaps one of the first new plays to take the stage at the Globe was a comedy that raised expectations of being the sequel to *Every Man in His Humor*, a popular offering at the Curtain the previous year: *Every Man out of His Humor*. Although the two plays have no narrative connection, the implied continuation is not altogether a false advertisement. *Every Man out of His Humor* does sport a gallery of humorous characters. For example, there is the uxorious merchant who, in *Every Man in His Humor*, is obsessed with the fantasy of his wife's infidelity and who, in *Every Man out of His Humor*, is shaken out of his humor by that fantasy's nearly becoming real. There are numerous courtiers and railers. Fastidious Briske, the premier courtier, models the latest in suave wooing to the rhythms of smoking tobacco and playing the viol. When he recounts his success in a recent duel, we find that the new fashion in sword play is to wound the clothes, not the man. Puntarvolo is a dinosaur, a "Vaine-glorious Knight" ("The Character of the Persons"), who invents a quixotic sally to Constantinople with his wife and dog, or, when his wife drops out, with his dog and cat. Reminiscent of the gulls-in-training who follow Bobadilla in *Every Man in His Humor*, various imitators swirl around Briske and Puntarvolo. One of the most pathetic is Fungoso, sick with "the *fluxe* of apparell" (IV.viii.128), who brings along his tailor literally to duplicate Briske's new suit but who is doomed to stay one costume behind. The clever servant multiplies into three characters in *Every Man out of His Humor*: Carlo Buffone, trickster and social parasite; Shift, small-time con-artist; and Macilente, envious satyr.

Every Man out of His Humor* is also justifiably the sequel to *Every Man in His Humor* in terms of genre, leading past the comedy of humors to the dramatic satire. Breaking from the older formula, it sacrifices a love plot in order to present more humorous stereotypes. In *Every Man in His Humor*, the women are minor characters, but we are invited nonetheless to care whether the maiden (Hesperida) finds a husband and whether the matrons (Biancha, Tib) keep the husbands they have. In *Every Man out of His Humor*, Jonson does not make even this slight nuptial gesture toward the romantic comedy. Characters like the farmer, Sordido, are brought into the narrative not because they have domestic relations with others but because their particular humor adds to the variety being dramatized.

A further break with the humors comedy is Jonson's characterization of the humors as vices. Behavior that is merely silly in Stephen, Matheo, and Bobadilla is morally corrosive in Briske and company. The dramatist's role, as Asper tells us, is "to ceaze on vice, and with a gripe / Squeeze out the humour of such spongie natures, / As licke vp euery idle vanitie" (Induction, ll. 144–46). The violence of the language here, as well as the violence of the action (Puntarvolo's dog is poisoned, Briske's lips are sealed), goes far beyond the amused toleration of irrational behavior in the mock trial and its verdicts in *Every Man in His Humor*. Over the next several years, Jonson was to refine this experiment in comedy into the dramatic satire and to sell his product to a boys' company. For offerings of their own in the new genre, the Chamberlain's men turned to Dekker and Shakespeare (and possibly others), who in different ways were to out-Jonson Jonson.

One of the lost plays in the offerings of 1599–1600 is *Cloth Breeches and Velvet Hose*. The title suggests that it dramatized an episode from Robert Greene's *Quip for an Upstart Courtier* (1592), subtitled "A quaint dispute betvveen Veluet breeches and Cloth-breeches—*Wherein is plainely set downe the disorders in all Estates and Trades.*" The play may therefore have been a satire of occupations and occupational morality, as is this probable source. In Greene's story, the narrator dreams about a debate between two monsters, each of whom claims the more ancient lineage. These are "vncouth headlesse thing*es*" with bodies that are all legs (sig. A4ᵛ).⁷ One wears velvet breeches of Spanish satin decorated with gold twist and knots of pearl; his netherstockings are of the finest Granada silk. The other wears simple cloth breeches "of white Kersie" with netherstockings "of the same . . . seamed with a little couentry blewe" (sig. B). To settle the dispute, the monsters summon a jury, and representatives of the various estates and trades cross the stage one by one to be impaneled or excused, according to their moral and commercial virtue. Cloth Breeches objects to some tradesmen because they have corrupted their service to cater to wearers of velvet breeches. Velvet Breeches objects to others on the grounds of their price-gouging and parasitism. When Velvet Breeches recommends a player, calling him a "plaine, honest, humble" man, Cloth Breeches rejects him, saying that players are "too full of selfeliking and selfeloue" and too inclined to make "a plaine country fellow as my selfe . . . clownes and fooles to laugh at in their play" (sig. F3ᵛ). They compromise on the poet as the final juror. The verdict is for Cloth Breeches, because he has an ancient and local ancestry, and against Velvet Breeches, because he is "an vpstart come out of *Italy*" (sig. F4).

About halfway through *Every Man out of His Humor*, Mitis, whom Jonson created to be the student-audience, observes wistfully that the play does not have his favorite kind of plot, one that calls for "a duke to be in loue with a countesse, and that countesse to bee in loue with the dukes sonne, and the sonne to loue the ladies waiting maid: some such crosse wooing, with a clowne to their seruingman" (III.vi.196–99). He and playgoers of his persuasion would have liked the romantic plots of Shakespeare's new comedies in 1599–1603: Orlando's learning from a woman to woo, the substitution of

Helena for Diana in the bed trick, and the love triangle of Orsino, Viola, and Olivia. John Manningham, who saw *Twelfth Night* in performance, specifically remembered with pleasure the cross-wooing that turned a servingman into a clown: "A good practise in it to make the steward beleeve his Lady widdowe was in Love with him, by counterfayting a letter, as from his Lady, in generall termes, telling him what shee liked best in him, and prescribing his gesture in smiling, his apparraile, &c., and then when he came to practise, making him beleeve they tooke him to be mad."[8]

I think it likely that *The Freeman's Honor*, the comedy by Wentworth Smith, had a romantic plot also, although perhaps with the cross-wooing of merchant taylors instead of dukes. I suggest this on the basis of the narrative in a possible analogue, Thomas Dekker's *The Shoemaker's Holiday*, known to Henslowe as *The Gentle Craft*, which the Admiral's men purchased in July 1599 and which was therefore performed at the Rose in the first year of the Chamberlain's men's tenure at the Globe and at the Fortune in the year when *The Freeman's Honor* was new (by my chronology). The only clue to the narrative beyond the title provided by Smith in the dedicatory epistle to Sir John Swinnerton, a merchant taylor and former lord mayor, is that the play was meant "to dignifie" Swinnerton's company. Presumably, therefore, the hero was a freeman of the merchant taylors who defends his honor. Even if that honor were challenged only in a professional sense, I would guess that some of the plot contained romantic tangles.

Perhaps the last comedy that the Chamberlain's men acquired before the playhouses were closed in 1603 was *The Merry Devil of Edmonton*, a romantic comedy also. Sir Arthur Clare and his lady Dorcas, who have promised the hand of their daughter Milliscent in marriage to Raymond Mounchensey, reconsider in expectation of a wealthier son-in-law. But until the new and more suitable match can be made, they sequester Milliscent in a nunnery. Raymond solicits the aid of Peter Fabell, his Cambridge don, who is known also as "the merry Fiend of Edmonton."[9] Fabell devises a stratagem whereby Raymond, in the disguise of a friar, will rescue Milliscent from the nuns. The lovers receive unexpected help from the clown plot. A Falstaffian gang of alehouse keepers and their best customer (Sir John) plan an expedition into the king's forest to hunt deer. The keeper, in search of the poachers, directs the lovers to his inn and stalls the pursuers; meanwhile, the poachers, who have mistaken Milliscent's white gown for a ghost, run up and down the forest, adding to the general confusion. By morning, when Sir Arthur and his party find their way out of the woods, the lovers are married, and the out-maneuvered father accepts the event gracefully: "Deere Sonne, I take thee vp into my hart; / Rise, daughter; this is a kind fathers part" (V.i.261–62).

Playgoers would have found the casting of Fabell as a matchmaker a familiar role for stage magicians. In the analogous *John a Kent and John a Cumber* (ms. 1590), *Friar Bacon and Friar Bungay* (Queen's men, 1594), *John of Bordeaux* (sometimes called *2 Friar Bacon* [Strange's men, 1592]), and perhaps in the lost *Wise Man of West Chester* (Admiral's men, 1594–95), the magicians usually take some part in the sorting out of marriage partners, even though they have more interest in their own magical experiments and in duels with rival magicians. The magic in *The Merry Devil of Edmonton* is equally recreational. Peter Fabell promises disruptions of nature to cover the lovers' elopement:

> Ile make the brinde sea to rise at Ware,
> And drowne the marshes vnto Stratford bridge;
> Ile driue the Deere from Waltham in their walkes,
> And scatter them like sheepe in euery field.
> (I.iii.23–26)

As it turns out, the crowd of poachers are a sufficent distraction. Fabell also plans a diversion at the nunnery:

> Ile send mee fellowes of a handful hie
> Into the Cloysters where the Nuns frequent,
> Shall make them skip like Does about the Dale,
> And with the Lady prioresse of the house
> To play at leape-froge, naked in their smockes,
> Vntill the merry wenches at their masse
> Cry teehee weehee;

And tickling these mad lasses in their flanckes,
They'll sprawle, and squeke, and pinch their fellow Nunnes.
(II.ii.87–95)

But he does not play this trick out either. A subsequent boast that he used "some pretty sleights" in the lovers' interests seems largely fulfilled in his changing the ale-house signs so that the lovers have an uninterrupted wedding night (V.i.247). All the same, at the end of the play he claims the role of marriage god: "And let our toyle to future ages proue, / The deuill of Edmonton did good in Loue" (V.i.258–59).

There were several plays about magicians in performance in 1602–03: in September, the Admiral's men bought Alleyn's copy of *The Wise Man of West Chester,* presumably for imminent revival; and at Christmas, they paid Thomas Middleton 5s. for a prologue and epilogue suitable to accompany to Court a play Henslowe calls simply "bacon" (*HD,* 207). But it is the third of the Admiral's revivals that winter, the one for which the company paid William Bird and Samuel Rowley 80s. for additions, that *The Merry Devil of Edmonton* evoked specifically when it appeared on stage in the spring of 1603. In the induction of the Chamberlain's play, Peter Fabell is not the wise man of West Chester or Friar Bacon but Doctor Faustus. The scene opens in Fabell's chamber at the midnight hour when the devil comes to claim his soul. Fabell awakens, startled: "What meanes the tolling of this fatall chime? / O, what a trembling horror strikes my hart!" (ll. 1–2). Coreb, a messenger from Hell, enters and repeats the conditions of Fabell's damnation:

Didst thou not write thy name in thine owne blood,
And drewst the formall deed twixt thee and mee,
And is it not recorded now in hell?
(ll. 27–29)

But rather than cower and ask the devil's pardon, Fabel tricks Coreb into a magic chair. The devil demands to be released, and Fabell complies after he negotiates an extension of seven years to his contract. Bested, Coreb departs. Thus while a magician at the

Fortune was being dragged from the stage through Hell's mouth, one at the Globe was helping young lovers to the marriage bed.

The tragedies in the holdings of the Chamberlain's men recall other popular dramatic subjects in some common and some not so common ways. *Julius Caesar* reflects the continuing fascination of playgoers with such heroes of ancient Rome as Caesar, Pompey, Cleopatra, Hannibal, Scipio, and Jugurtha. The memorable features of the production to a foreign visitor, though, had nothing to do with narrative treatment but with the skill of the players and the post-performance jig: "very pleasingly performed, with approximately fifteen characters; at the end of the play they danced together admirably and exceedingly gracefully, according to their custom, two in each group dressed in men's and two in women's apparel." Both of the company's revenge plays, *Jeronimo* and *Hamlet,* have problematic links to earlier texts, and as such they raise slippery questions about duplicate texts and the value to the company of the particular texts they had in hand.

If the conversation between Condell and Sly in the induction to *The Malcontent* means what it seems to mean—namely, that the Chamberlain's men owned a playtext called *Jeronimo,* which the Children of Blackfriars took from them and played—we may reasonably conclude that Shakespeare's company acquired a drama featuring Hieronimo sometime after the spring of 1594. We know of two such plays that existed at the time, both of which had been in the repertory of Strange's men in 1592: the "spanes comodye donne oracioe" (Henslowe's title), or *The Spanish Comedy,* which we have called it; and "Jeronymo" (Henslowe's title), or *The Spanish Tragedy,* which is the title of this play in print (or so we assume). *The Spanish Comedy* is lost, unless it survives in some sense in *The First Part of Jeronimo,* Q1605. *The Spanish Tragedy* was published once before 18 December 1592 and again in 1594. It was thus publicly on sale, as well as available through a company or player, when the Admiral's men and Chamberlain's men were being organized in 1594. Because the Admiral's men played "Joronymo" starting on 7 January 1597, we have assumed that they acquired the text owned formerly by Strange's men, perhaps thanks to Alleyn and his instinct for good theatrical property. Yet Alleyn was not the only member of Strange's men with a sense of popular subject matter and profitable texts. Someone acquired *Henry VI* (at least) from the repertory, and it ultimately came to the Chamberlain's men.

There must have been more than one playbook of *The Spanish Tragedy* floating around in December 1592 because Edward White acquired and published one when Abel Jeffes claimed to be the owner himself. Two references to Richard Burbage imply that he was widely associated with the role of Hieronimo. That association could have come in 1592, if he was with Strange's men, but the context of the allusion in the epitaph (with such roles as Hamlet, Lear, and Othello) implies a role of Burbage's maturity, as does the allusion in the second part of *Return from Parnassus,* which is dated 1601–02. Edward Archer, listing "Hieronimo, both parts" in a catalogue of plays, attributed the texts to William Shakespeare, whose name was by 1656 synonymous with that of his company; perhaps Archer was actually thinking of the texts that Burbage had performed for the Chamberlain's men.

We may never find more evidence—and this is purely circumstantial—that the *Jeronimo* owned by the Chamberlain's men was Kyd's *The Spanish Tragedy.* But if we assume for the sake of argument that it was, that ownership raises provocative questions about the nature of commerce in the Elizabethan playhouse. Why, for instance, did the Chamberlain's men make such a fuss when the boys' company stole a text of *The Spanish Tragedy?* The play was very old, and another company (the Admiral's men) had revived it in 1596–97, probably with revisions, and probably again in 1601–02, with more revisions (Jonson's). Since 1594 the text had been printed twice: in 1599; and in 1602, with additions. Were the Chamberlain's men angry over the theft of this *particular* playbook, over the theft of *any* playbook from their offerings, or for some other reason not clear from Condell's quip?

Both of the former alternatives comment on the commercial role of texts. If the anger was over the theft of Kyd's *The Spanish Tragedy,* we may infer that the play continued to have significant market value in performance despite its age, exposure to London audiences, and availability in print. If the anger was over the act of thievery, we may infer that the Children of Blackfriars had broken a rule of decorum observed by the companies generally. They thus compounded one offense (that of attracting customers as a new company) with another (that of taking away business with one of the Chamberlain's men's own offerings). But what if *Jeronimo* was not *The Spanish Tragedy*? What if it was merely a clone of it in the sense that the many plays about King Henry V duplicated one another? This hypothesis is intriguing also, for it leads to the conclusion that the story of old Hieronimo was popular and profitable regardless of its textual form.

The possibility that the story of a given hero drew playgoers to the Globe whatever its text brings us face to face with another mystery in the management of dramatic properties: why did the Chamberlain's men acquire Shakespeare's *Hamlet* when they already had a play by that name? This old *Hamlet* had been very popular, as the allusions by Nashe and Lodge indicate. The Chamberlain's company had played it, evidently successfully, in 1594–95 and possibly into 1595–96. There appears to have been new interest in the revenge play around 1600, as illustrated by *Antonio and Mellida* and *Antonio's Revenge* at St. Paul's and a new edition of *Titus Andronicus* (with the name of the Chamberlain's men added to the list of company owners on the title-page). But why did the Chamberlain's men not simply revive *Hamlet* in 1600–01 if they wished to respond? It is possible, of course, that they had to acquire a new text because the old playbook was lost. It could have been mislaid in one of the moves between playhouses, or it might have been eaten by rats. Perhaps the company had never had an actual playbook. If incoming players in 1594 had been together in a company that had played *Hamlet,* those players might have produced it from memory for the Chamberlain's men.[10]

But whether a copy of the old text did exist in 1600, the decision to replace 1594 *Hamlet* with a new version is a sign of something extraordinary in the theatrical commerce of 1600–01. It is not enough that the company could have offered the new play at the maiden performance at a doubled admission fee, for the profit would have been offset by the time spent in rehearsal of the new script and the cost of new apparel. I suggest that the decision to offer a new play had to do with the way in which the revenge tragedy as genre had developed since the old *Hamlet* had been written. The texts of *The Spanish Tragedy*, before and after revision, show some of these developments. The character of Hieronimo in the text printed in 1602 has four additional mad scenes. He has acquired a sardonic humor. He has become a more bloodthirsty and thus a more villainous revenger, in the Marlovian sense of triumphing in the violence of his revenge. Recognizing these new directions in the genre, the Chamberlain's men had two courses of action: either to update the old *Hamlet* with revisions or to acquire a duplicate play. Facing a similar situation with *The Spanish Tragedy* in 1601–02, the Admiral's men chose to revise. They did not save much money by this choice. They paid Jonson 40s. in September 1601 and 200s. less the cost of *Richard Crookback* in June 1602. The Chamberlain's men, apparently, chose to acquire a duplicate play. For their money, they too got a text that treated the madness, wit, and ethics of the revenge principals in new ways, though it did not make the hero more vicious. In addition, they got a text that had witty allusions to their new playhouse ("Hercules and his load") and to their pipsqueak competition ("little eyases").

If *Thomas Lord Cromwell* and *Oldcastle* are a fair measure, there were also changes taking place around 1600 in the choice of subject matter for English history plays and in the treatment of that subject matter. These changes are reflected in the two-part *Sir John Oldcastle* (Admiral's, 1599–1600), the two-part *Cardinal Wolsey* (Admiral's, 1601–02), the revival of *Oldcastle* (Worcester's, 1602–03), and *Lady Jane* (Worcester's, 1602–03). Like these plays and in contrast to the chronicle plays in production in 1594–1599, *Thomas Lord Cromwell* takes its subject matter from contemporary history; both it and *Oldcastle* are dramas about martyrs rather than kings. *Thomas Lord Cromwell* charts Cromwell's rise to power and fall. In the degree to which it emphasizes the caprice of Fortune, the play is a medieval *de casibus* tragedy:

Now, *Cromwell,* hast thou time to meditate,
And thinke vpon thy state, and of the time.
Thy honours came vnsought, I, and vnlooked for;
Thy fall as sudden, and vnlooked for to. . . .
But now I see, what after ages shall:
The greater men, more sudden is their fall.

(V.v.1–4, 8–9)[11]

A twin theme is the saving grace of charity. The subplot of the money broker (Bagot) and the merchants (the Banisters, Friskiball) dramatizes the survival of the misfortunate through others' generosity, and Cromwell himself is shown to succor the needy. One salient feature of *Thomas Lord Cromwell* is that no reigning monarch would find offense in it. Cromwell speaks in the most general way about the political conspiracies that brought his overthrow. Bishop Gardiner, not the king, is the villain. Walking to the block, Cromwell thinks only on salvation: "My soule is shrinde with heauens celestiall couer" (V.v.132).

The issue of offense makes doubly interesting the identity of the play called "Sir *John Old Castell*" by Rowland Whyte in a letter to Robert Sidney dated 8 March 1599/1600.[12] Whyte was referring to a performance given by the Chamberlain's men at a dinner hosted by their patron for Louis Verreyken, a diplomat from the Spanish Netherlands. E. K. Chambers assumed that Whyte meant "Falstaff" when he called the play "Sir *John Old Castell,*" and he attributed the performance to *1 Henry IV* (*WS,* I, 382). This guess would seem to be a good one, for Shakespeare allegedly changed the name of Sir John at some time early in the maiden run of *1 Henry IV* after the Cobham family objected to the association of their family saint with an old reprobate.[13] We have assumed that the Admiral's men acquired a two-part *Sir John Oldcastle* in the fall of 1599–1600 in an attempt to capitalize on the offense by Shakespeare and the Chamberlain's men. The prologue of part one of the Admiral's play, registered at Stationers' Hall on 11 August 1600 and printed that year, reminds audiences and readers of the incident while it separates its title character from Falstaff, whom it condemns as a *"pamperd* glutton" and "aged Councellor to youthfull sinne" (*MSR*, Prologue, ll. 8–9). However, Chambers's identification requires us to assume that Whyte was familiar with playhouse activity and gossip in 1596–97 as well as 1599–1600. If Whyte did know of the Oldcastle-Falstaff flap, George Carey, the present Lord Chamberlain and host of the dinner at which the play was being presented, must surely have known also. What would his reaction have been to his company's performing a play at a diplomatic function that Court gossips like Whyte still associated with an insult to his predecessor's ancestry? I should think that he would have been embarrassed, if not offended.

However tactless the choice of *1 Henry IV* may seem, that of a play on the life of Sir John Oldcastle seems more tactless still. The guest of honor, Louis Verreyken, was *audiencier* and first secretary of state to Archduke Albert of Austria. By way of marriage to King Philip III's sister, Isabella, the archduke had acquired sovereignty of the Spanish Netherlands. Verreyken was the archduke's ambassador, and his mission was to expedite negotiations in a peace between Philip III and Elizabeth. Given the history of conflict between Catholic Spain and protestant England, we might assume that a play celebrating the martyrdom of a proto-protestant would arouse any hostility Verreyken harbored toward the English. However, the politics of the occasion may have a more subtle texture here. Archduke Albert sent Verreyken to England in one sense as a representative of the Spanish crown, but the archduke was also acting on his own initiative. The peace was a higher priority for him than it was for Philip III, who continued to hope for a Catholic succession in England when Queen Elizabeth died. Verreyken himself was a Fleming, not a Spaniard. His prominent position in the archduke's circle of advisors reminds us that the government of the Spanish Netherlands was Flemings in a coalition with the sovereign designated by the Spanish line of Habsburgs. From the English point of view, Verreyken and the Spanish Netherlands might have seemed approachable on the subject of individual religious freedom. Perhaps, then, the story of Oldcastle's martyrdom was a way of suggesting to Verreyken that he and his host nation had much in common.

Because of problems with the assumption that Rowland Whyte was sufficiently well informed about theatrical controversies to say "Oldcastle" when he meant "Falstaff," I prefer to take the statement in the letter to Robert Sidney literally, that is, as evidence that the Chamberlain's men owned a play named *Oldcastle* in the spring of 1599–1600 and that they performed it at a dinner hosted by their patron for the Flemish ambassador on 6 March. Taken in this way, Whyte's information gives us a multi-layered instance of professional shrewdness on the part of Shakespeare's company. At the level of theatrical commerce, the Chamberlain's men were duplicating a successful two-part drama currently in the repertory of another major London company, the Admiral's men (Worcester's men were to acquire and perform an *Oldcastle* play in 1602–03). At the level of national diplomacy, they were offering an entertainment that implied an area of mutual advantage between the Spanish Netherlands and England (religious freedom). But there is a level of courtesy here in the etiquette of patronage also. By acquiring a play on the martyrdom of Oldcastle, the Chamberlain's men were showing the Cobhams that they could redeem an inadvertent slight with a gesture more far-reaching than the alteration of a character's name. And, by taking the opportunity of presenting *Oldcastle* at the dinner for Verreyken, the Chamberlain's men were showing their patron that they were sensitive to the complex politics of family and office. In the midst of this elaborate conjecture, there is one certainty about the performance by the Chamberlain's men: the guest for whose entertainment a play had been requested watched "to his great Contentment."

Another of the Chamberlain's history plays is interesting in the context of Verreyken's mission in England. *A Larum for London* dramatizes the siege of Antwerp, which George Gascoigne described in a pamphlet called *The Spoyle of Antwerp* (1576), and Antwerp was a bargaining chip in Verreyken's negotiations. Gascoigne's account of the battle is propaganda, and so is the play. Reminiscent of massacres of innocents in the Corpus Christi drama, *A Larum for London* exploits the cruelty of the soldiers and the helplessness of their victims. In a representative sequence, two

Spanish soldiers run on stage in pursuit of a girl and her brother, yelling "Kill, kill, kill" (sig. E2). Helpless, the sister turns and entreats, "Haue you the heart to kill a prettie Girl" (sig. E2ᵛ). Indeed they do—along with the children's mother and blind father. It is clear from their taunts that the soldiers enjoy their work: "Bitch, art thou rayling? take thou this (sig. E3). The dramatist invents a hero, a one-legged Flemish soldier named Stump, who saves citizens from the slaughter, even though they have previously spurned him for his beggary. In one instance, Stump discovers a fat burgher whom the soldiers have hung up by his thumbs. Stump knows the man to be a villain, a "dung-hill" of "carryon flesh," unfit "for any thing but to feede wormes" (sig. F4). Nevertheless, he cuts the burgher down, leaving him to endure the condition he had mocked in others: "Goe liue, if thou canst scape their bloudie hands, / Till want and beggerie cut short thy daies" (sig. F4). In the epilogue, Time delivers a sermon on the fate of Londoners unless, of course, they heed the warning:

> Thus worldings, Time . . . doth wish to see
> No heauy or disastrous chaunce befall
> The Sonnes of men, if they will warned be:
> But when they spurne against my discipline,
> Wasting the treasure of my precious houres:
> No maruaile then, like misery catch holde
> On them, did fasten on this wofull towne. . . .
>   (sig. G2)

Stuhlweissenburg, the story of a battle in 1570 between Turks and Christians for the Hungarian town, was perhaps as nationalistic and moralistic as *A Larum for London,* but it is not likely to have been as topical.

There is a new dramatic formula in the offerings of the Chamberlain's men in the repertories for 1599–1603: the satire. The genre sprang virtually full grown from the injuction of 1 June 1599, which decreed that satires and epigrams (along with other libellous books) were no longer to be printed and that some editions now in print were to be publicly burned. The poets who were also dramatists brought the satyr to the stage. The plays most commonly identified as satires turned up at St. Paul's (*Histriomastix, Jack Drum's Entertainment*), Blackfriars (*Cynthias's Revels, Poetaster*) and the Globe (*Satiromastix*). We may also add *Troilus and Cressida* to the list.[14] We have been hampered in assessing the role of Shakespeare's play in the rise of the dramatic satire because we have been led to believe that it was not performed in its own time (in spite of the claim at its registration that "yt is acted by my lord Chamberlens Men"). But if the Chamberlain's men did not play it when it was new, they wasted a property that not only reflected the latest in dramatic genres but also used popular narrative material. Like the Admiral's plays of *Polyphemus* or *Troy's Revenge* and *The Tragedy of Agamemnon* (1599–1600), Shakespeare's play uses the Matter of Troy. Like the Admiral's play of *Troilus and Cressida* (for which a fragmentary Plot survives [1598–99]) and an offering by the players in *Histriomastix,* Shakespeare's play retells one of the famous tragic love stories in that Matter.

In *Satiromastix,* Dekker exploited current plays somewhat differently. He lifted characters straight out of Jonson's *Poetaster* (Blackfriars, 1601) to create the plot-line to which the title of the play refers. Horace (Jonson) is a poet who seeks recognition at Court, and Asinius Bubo (a joke on the name of Asinius Lupus) is his cohort. Horace has antagonized some of his fellows by his mean-spirited barbs, and two of the poets—Crispinus (Marston) and Demetrius (Dekker)—come "to purge" his "sicke and daungerous minde of her disease" (I.ii.247–48).[15] Horace is conciliatory, but when Tucca (the bombastic soldier) barges in with a tirade of criticism, Horace vows to get even. His weapon is scurrilous epigrams. These set Tucca off on another verbal rampage: "Art thou not famous enough yet, my mad *Horastratus,* for killing a Player, but thou must eate men aliue? thy friends?" (IV.ii.61–62). Horace backs off, excusing himself as having "writ out of hot bloud" and offering to "quaffe downe / The poyson'd Inke" to satisfy friendship (IV.ii.66–68). Tucca accepts the apology warily, knowing Horace's nature: "Thou'lt shoote thy quilles at mee, when my terrible backe's turn'd for all this, wilt not Porcupine?" (IV.ii.97–98). And another fight does erupt at the wedding banquet, a fight that Tucca,

Crispinus, and Demetrius settle in a mock trial staged for the festival ending of the play. Horace and Bubo are *"pul'd in by th'hornes bound, both like Satyres"* (V.ii.156–57 [s.d.]). Horace is stripped of the satyr's hairy skin and crowned with nettles. In addition, he is enjoined to stop calling attention to himself in the playhouse, stop rushing his work into print, and stop whining about the reception of his plays at Court. He swears to abide by the judgment.

In deference to playgoers of Mitis's taste, Dekker coordinated the untrussing of Horace with two romantic plots. The minor of these concerns a widow who is wooed by several comic courtiers. In a surprise move, Tucca claims the widow as his own at the end of the play. The major love story is the marriage of Sir Walter Terrill and Cælestine. During the revelry after the wedding ceremony, the king (William Rufus) insinuates a right to the bride's maidenhead, and he challenges Terrill to bring Cælestine to his bed that night. Fortunately, the bride's father takes the comedy into his own hands at this point. He gives Cælestine a drug that she thinks is poison. When Terrill insists that she go to the king, she drinks the potion. Terrill, grief-stricken by her death, takes up her body and joins the maskers on their way to the king's chambers: "Leade on, and leade her on; if any aske / The mistery, say death presents a maske" (V.i.177–78). When the king sees the consequences of his lust in the maskers' procession, he repents. Cælestine regains consciousness, and her father explains to all that the potion was a trick "to trie / The Bride-groomes loue, and the Brides constancie" (V.ii.102–3). At this moment, Tucca arrives with Horace and Bubo in tow, and the untrussing becomes another entertainment of the wedding night. In a familiar festival close, the king leads Cælestine and the revelers in a dance, saying—without a hint of irony—"But Mistris Bride, one measure shall be led, / In scorne of Mid-nights hast, and then to bed" (V.ii.364–65).

In the epilogue, Tucca apologizes for having railed against "Courtiers, Ladies, and Cittizens" when he was a character in *Poetaster* (l. 7). He acknowledges that some playgoers have come to *Satiromastix* to hiss at the treatment of Horace, but he urges them to reconsider because their hissing will "blowe away *Horaces* reuenge" (l. 20). He suggests that there will be more sport if Horace thinks his untrussing has been popular and writes against it. Tucca promises that he and his poetasters will then "vntrusse him agen, and agen, and agen" (l. 24). I see in this formulaic request for applause a perception of the nature of theatrical commerce in the last years of the Elizabethan period that is consistent with the evidence of a commercial strategy in the repertory of the Chamberlain's men. Tucca takes for granted that audiences are well acquainted with aspects of the playhouse world, and, trading on that knowledge, he invites each audience to play along in an extended jest, this time at Horace's expense. Through his tirades earlier in the play, Tucca has shown playgoers the tactics to be used in the jest. On the one hand, there are biographical allusions: Horace's beginnings as bricklayer, failure as a player, run-in with the authorities over *The Isle of Dogs,* duel with Spencer, vocation as a writer of "strong garlicke Comedies" (I.ii.334–35), and currently self-imposed exile. On the other hand, there is the reprise of theatrical subject matter in the allusions to dozens of plays, from old favorites to recent offerings in the many London playhouses.[16] This particular jest—a serial of revenges and untrussings—assumes the cooperation of the dramatists to write the plays, the companies to produce them, and the audiences to patronize them. It therefore assumes also a commercial perspective in which the jest will become more sporting and profitable as more dramatists, companies, and audiences join in.

IV

The Repertory of the King's Men, 1603–1608

Within two months of his accession on 24 March 1603, James I granted his patronage to the Chamberlain's men, making them the King's players. The royal patent, which was dated 19 May 1603, licensed the company "to vse and exercise the Arte and faculty of playinge Comedies Tragedies histories Enterludes moralls pastoralls Stageplaies and Suche others like . . . aswell for the recreation of our lovinge Subjectes as for our Solace and pleasure when wee shall thincke good to see them" (*MSC*, I.3, 264). At the time, however, the playhouses in London were officially closed by a Privy Council order on 19 March 1603, issued when it became clear that Queen Elizabeth was near death. The restraint would have been lifted by May, but the number of plague deaths rose, and the playhouses did not reopen. The license anticipated an epidemic and authorized the King's men to play not only at "theire nowe vsual howse called the Globe" but also "within anie towne halls or Moute halls or other conveniente places within the liberties and freedome of anie other Cittie vniversitie towne or Boroughe whatsoever within our said Realmes and domynions" (*MSC*, I.3, 264). The plague continued into the autumn. The coronation took place as scheduled on 25 July, but Trinity Term was adjourned and Michaelmas Term was moved to Winchester.[1]

On 21 October Joan Alleyn wrote to her husband, Edward, reporting that "heare is none now sycke neare vs" (*HD*, 297). Part of her news concerned the other play companies: "All the companyes be Come hoame & well for ought we knowe . . . and all of your owne Company ar well at theyr owne houses" (*HD*, 297).

Under these circumstances, the companies may have given performances at various locations around London throughout the winter,
but the government maintained the position that the playhouses
were closed. An entry in the Chamber Accounts makes this clear:
Richard Burbage was paid £30 on 8 February 1604 "for the mayn-
tenaunce and releife of himselfe and the rest of his Company being
prohibited to presente any playes publiquelie in or neere London
by reason of greate perill that might growe throughe the extraordinary Concourse and assemblie of people to a newe increase of the
plague" (*MSC*, VI, 39). Officially, the restraint was not lifted until 9
April 1604 (Easter Monday).

The events of 1603 forced Shakespeare's fellows as well as the
men in other companies to address simultaneously several conditions of business that were familiar to players old in the trade but
that—because of the conjunction and persistence of the conditions
at this time—required immediate, shrewd, and sustained responses.
One is the condition of patronage. By the end of the first year of
the new reign, not only had the Chamberlain's men become the
King's men but the Admiral's men had become Prince Henry's
men, Worcester's men had become Queen Anne's men, and the
boys' company at Blackfriars had become the Children of the
Queen's Revels (the Children of Paul's maintained their affiliation
with the Cathedral school). Due to this royal patronage, the companies committed themselves to being available at the Court's pleasure; and, compared to the Court of Queen Elizabeth, the Court
of King James was to schedule companies for more performances
over a longer holiday season, and these were given before audiences presided over by either the king or the crown prince. The
Prince's men, for example, were paid in the Chamber Accounts for
five performances in 1603–04, eight in 1604–05, six in 1605–06 and
1606–07, and four in 1607–08. The King's men were paid in the
Chamber Accounts for eleven performances in 1603–04, eleven in
1604–05, ten in 1605–06, nine in 1606–07, and thirteen in 1607–08.
Therefore the companies had to be ready with new and suitable
offerings. Fortunately, the members of the Court audience whom
the players were most concerned to please—the royal family—were

not familiar with their old offerings. In at least one year, as we know from the Revels Account of 1604–05, the King's men satisfied much of their obligation with revivals.

A second condition is restraints against playing. The year of 1604–05 seems to have been relatively undisturbed, but based on the numbers of deaths from plague per week, the playhouses may have been open for as few as two months in 1603–04, three in 1605–06, one in 1606–07, and five in 1607–08.[2] Philip Henslowe enables us to feel the uncertainty of these times in entries for May 1603. On the fifth, as though he were concluding a period of business with the Admiral's men, he tallied the balance due him since the change of monarchs in March, but he followed the tally with the payment on a black cloak, presumably apparel for a play. A few days later, he began a set of accounts for Worcester's men, optimistic about their "Begininge to playe Agayne by the kynges licence" (*HD*, 225). He followed this heading with an expenditure of 40s. in earnest for a play, *Shore's Wife*. But then the entries cease, and there are no more for either company until March 1604, when Henslowe noted a payment for *The Honest Whore* and tallied the Admiral's accounts for the final time. The effect on the companies and their management of the repertory must have been severe. At the very least, they would have bought fewer new plays, having fewer weeks in which to introduce them. Their offerings, therefore, may have contained a higher ratio of old plays to new. If they found themselves playing in London one week and closed out the next, they may have kept a play in production for a longer period of calendar time than was the norm before it was commercially exhausted.

A third condition was touring. Because of the playhouse closings, plus perhaps their own habit of touring and the expectation of touring by their patrons, the companies spent much of the five years from 1603 to 1608 in the provinces. In E. K. Chambers's and W. W. Greg's day, theater historians believed that touring was an activity undertaken only under the most desperate of circumstances— namely, near-bankruptcy—and the economics of touring was supposed to have impoverished the companies still further. To counteract the expenses of travel, troupes allegedly reduced the scale of their operations at every level: fewer players, a truncated repertory, minimal productions, and abridged texts. As the records of provincial dramatic activity accumulate in print by way of The Malone Society and Records of Early English Drama (REED), we are finding little support for these beliefs. At present, we still do not have evidence that addresses specifically the effects of touring on adult companies with London playhouses normally available to them. But, clearly, the King's men and the other companies under royal patronage did not go out of business because they divided their seasons between touring and London performances; indeed, despite the poor conditions, the playhouse industry continued to expand and attract new investors.

There is one set of entries in *Henslowe's Diary* that may show the effect of closure and/or a month's-long tour on the offerings of a company for its first few months back in London. On 27 October 1597, the Admiral's men returned to the Rose after having closed the previous July (on the eighteenth). They opened the fall season with a repertory of old plays, both continuations and revivals of very recent productions. They did not introduce a new play until 4 December. But for the next two months thereafter, they introduced a new play (or a play new to them) nearly every week. These entries imply that a company alternating frequently between London and provincial performances might keep a number of old plays in production, both for the tour itself and as filler in the London schedule while the players rehearsed new material. Thus reinforcing each other in effects on the repertory, playhouse closure and touring may have served to reduce the number of new plays needed by a company in a given year and to increase the number of old plays kept at ready.

However distressed from the uncertainties of intermittent outbreaks of plague, 1603–1608, the King's men nonetheless did not manage without some new plays. In 1603–04, they acquired at least the following: *Sejanus*, *The Fair Maid of Bristow*, *Robin Goodfellow*, *The London Prodigal*, and *The Malcontent* (though not new to a London stage, this play was new to the King's men). In

1604–05, when the playing seasons were not interrupted, the company had two new plays from Shakespeare, *Othello* and *Measure for Measure*, and at least two from dramatists unknown, *The Spanish Maze* and *Gowrie*. In 1605–06, although the plague returned, the King's men acquired *The Revenger's Tragedy, Volpone, King Lear, A Yorkshire Tragedy,* and *Macbeth* (plus perhaps others now lost). The plague returned yet again in the summer of 1606, and for the next several years we have no clear sense of when the playhouses were open and, consequently, when new plays were introduced. Possibly, though, the King's men played *The Miseries of Enforced Marriage, The Devil's Charter,* and *Antony and Cleopatra* along with other new offerings in 1606–07 and *Pericles, Coriolanus,* and *Timon of Athens* among others in 1607–08.

The plays kept in production across breaks in the playing schedule year to year are difficult to identify because so little evidence speaks to the length of a stage run. Though it is reasonable to assume, given the conditions of playhouse closure and touring, that the King's men extended the productions of new plays over a longer period than six months or even a year, there is evidence of such extentions only in the case of two plays: *King Lear* and *Volpone. King Lear* appears to have received performances from a date in proximity with the registration of *King Leir* in May 1605 and until at least 26 December 1606, when it was presented at Court according to information in its entry of registration at Stationers' Hall (26 November 1607). It appears therefore to have been continued from the repertory in 1605–06 into that of 1606–07. *Volpone,* which was new in 1605–06 also, was apparently continued into 1607–08. Jonson dedicated the quarto of the play in 1607 (possibly 1608) to the "Two Famovs Vniversities," thereby implying that performances on the tour included the one in the provincial records of Oxford for the fall, 1607 (*H&S,* IX, 196).

Though there is no documentary evidence to support the claim, I suggest that plays introduced new at a time when the playhouses were to be closed unexpectedly for long periods of time would be retained in the active repertory until they were given three months or more of continuous showing in London. An example of a play in this situation is *The Merry Devil of Edmonton*. If the allusion in *The Black Book* locates it correctly in the repertory of the Chamberlain's men in the spring of 1603, it made its debut at a bad time, from a commercial point of view. Given its popularity, as suggested by its revival in 1612–13 and publication in 1608, 1612, and 1617, we may reasonably assume that the King's men held it over into the spring of 1603–04 and possibly even into the fall of 1604–05.

An additional set of circumstances suggests that *The Malcontent* was continued from 1603–04 into 1604–05. The Children of the Chapel Royal at Blackfriars had acquired and performed the play in 1602–03, according to G. K. Hunter.[3] Sometime in 1603, the children's company "acquired" *Jeronimo*, which the King's men considered their property. Outraged, the King's men retaliated by getting their hands on a copy of *The Malcontent*. They then commissioned an induction and additions to the text. The revisions must have been expensive—in a class with the work for which Bird and Rowley were paid £4 on *Doctor Faustus* and Jonson perhaps as much as £6 for *The Spanish Tragedy*—for between them, John Webster (induction) and John Marston (text) provided nearly six hundred new lines.

These revisions were advertisements of the King's players and of the company's power in the playhouse world. The new additions created the role of Passarello and expanded the parts of two characters. According to Hunter, the purpose of these changes was quite simply to give more stage time to popular members of the company, namely Richard Burbage as Malevole and Robert Armin as Passarello (xlviii–xlix). The induction advertised the players by creating roles in which not only Burbage but also William Sly, John Sincler, Henry Condell, and John Lowin appeared in their real-world guises.[4] The rhetorical intent of the induction was to justify the production of *The Malcontent* as an appropriate response to the breach in professional ethics committed by the boys' company at Blackfriars.[5] A continuation of the play into the seasons of 1604–05 would have given the King's men a longer time to advertise their revenge as well as to recoup their expenses in the production.

In comparison with continuations, there is much evidence of revivals from 1603 to 1608, though perhaps not all of the evidence is equally persuasive. One questionable revival is that of *As You Like It* in 1603–04. William Johnson Cory, a nineteenth-century scholar and historian, was a tutor in the household of the Herbert family at Wilton in the summer of 1865. In his diary for 5 August, he recorded a conversation with Lady Herbert in which she mentioned a letter in the family's possession that referred to a performance of *As You Like It* at Wilton House. Cory's diary entry reads as follows:

> The house (Lady Herbert said) is full of interest: above us is Wolsey's room; we have a letter, never printed, from Lady Pembroke to her son, telling him to bring James I from Salisbury to see *As You Like It;* 'we have the man Shakespeare with us.' She wanted to cajole the king in Raleigh's behalf—he came.[6]

According to the Chamber Accounts, the Court was indeed at Wilton in December 1603, and the King's men were paid £30 for going there from Mortlake and "presenting before his majestie one playe on the second of december" (*MSC*, VI, 38). However, there is some doubt about the authenticity and accuracy of the letter to which Lady Herbert referred. Cory did not claim to have seen the letter itself, and he appears to have been quoting Lady Herbert rather than it in the phrase about "the man Shakespeare." E. K. Chambers attempted to track the letter down in 1898, but the Pembroke family did not know its whereabouts (*WS*, II, 329). Nevertheless, he was inclined to credit the revival, partly because he trusted Cory as a reporter and partly because the entry in the Chamber Account corroborates all of the details about the performance except for the title of the play (*WS*, I, 76). Recent editors of *As You Like It* are skeptical.[7]

A number of plays that had been in the repertory of the Chamberlain's men and had come into print at that time were republished at some time between 1603 and 1608: *Mucedorus, The Taming of a Shrew, 1 Henry IV, Richard III,* and *Richard II.* One of these, *Mucedorus,* was apparently published in connection with a revival, and others of the plays may likewise have been. The new edition of *Mucedorus,* which came out in 1606, contains revisions in the epilogue that alter the monarch addressed from a queen to a king, thus implying a performance before King James, perhaps in 1605–06.[8] Malone conjectured that *The Taming of the Shrew* was revived in 1606–07 on the basis of the publication of *The Taming of a Shrew,* which he took to be the text acquired by stationers in place of a copy of Shakespeare's text.[9] It appears to add weight to Malone's guess that Nicholas Ling, who bought the text of *The Taming of a Shrew* along with *Romeo and Juliet* and *Love's Labor's Lost* from Cuthbert Burby on 22 January 1607 and who already owned a text of *Hamlet,* chose to publish only the *Shrew* play before he sold all four texts to John Smethwick ten months later (19 November 1607).

A possible revival of *Richard II* also hinges on a stationer's interest in one play in a mass purchase, specifically, in his providing an accurate, updated title-page for a new edition. On 25 June 1603, Matthew Law purchased *1 Henry IV, Richard III,* and *Richard II* from Andrew Wise. Law put out editions of *1 Henry IV* in 1604 and 1608 and one of *Richard III* in 1605. On the title-pages of these editions, he repeated old information from Wise's title-pages, including apparently false information about changes in the texts. In 1608 he put out an edition of *Richard II* that included the scene in which Richard gives over the crown to Henry Bolingbroke. At some point in the printing, an updated title-page was inserted: the name of the company was changed to the King's men, the name of the Globe was added, and notice of "new additions of the Parliament Sceane, and the deposing of King Richard" was included. Unlike the perfunctory editions of *1 Henry IV* and *Richard III,* therefore, Law's publication of *Richard II* appears to be capitalizing on something very current in a market that stationers and play companies shared. Although Law could have expected his customers to remember an earlier run of the play (and the last might have been seven years before, in a single performance for which the company became involved in the Essex conspiracy), his advertisement of Richard's deposition would have been doubly effective if the play had been performed by the King's men in 1607–08 with the parliament scene intact.

Against the guesswork of these revivals, we have the certainty of the revival of seven plays in the winter of 1604–05. An account from the Office of the Revels for the holiday season indicates that among the performances given at Court by the King's men were showings of the following old plays: *The Merry Wives of Windsor,* on the Sunday following Allhallows (4 November); *The Comedy of Errors,* on the night of Holy Innocents' (29 December); *Love's Labor's Lost,* on a day between New Year's and Twelfth Night; *Henry V,* on 7 January; *Every Man out of His Humor,* on 8 January; *Every Man in His Humor,* on the night of Candlemas (2 February); and *The Merchant of Venice,* on Shrove Sunday (10 February) and also on Shrove Tuesday (12 February).[10] There is corroboration of the revival of *Love's Labor's Lost* in a letter dated 1604 from Walter Cope to Robert Cecil:

> Burbage ys come, & sayes there is no new playe that the quene hath not seene, but they have revyved an olde one, cawled *Loves Labore Lost,* which for wytt and mirthe he sayes will please her excedingly. And thys ys apointed to be playd to morowe night at my Lord of Sowthampton's. . . . Burbage ys my messenger ready attending your pleasure.[11]

In Cope's fortuitous quoting of Burbage, and in this large number of revivals, I believe that we see the combined effects of the change in patronage, playhouse closures, and touring on the repertory of the King's men.

By the old plays that they did retain in production and revive, as well as by their purchases of new plays, the companies collectively determined the currency of story materials and the evolution of dramatic formulas. Since Henslowe stopped keeping the *Diary* with the entry of "the pasyent man & the onest hore" (*HD,* 209), we know only a few plays in the repertory of Prince Henry's men. Stationers' records identify three histories: *The History of Richard Whittington* (S.R. 8 February 1605), Samuel Rowley's *When You See Me, You Know Me* (Q1605) and Thomas Dekker's *The Whore of*

Babylon (Q1607). Queen Anne's men received from Thomas Heywood a mixture of romantic comedies (*The Wise Woman of Hogsden*, ca. 1604, Q1638; *How to Learn from a Woman to Woo* [Revels Account, 1604–05]; and *The Fair Maid of the Exchange*, Q1607), contemporary histories (the two-part *If You Know Not Me, You Know Nobody*, Q1605, Q1606), and classical tragedy (*The Rape of Lucrece*, Q1608). In addition, the company acquired *Nobody and Somebody* (Q1606); John Day's *Travels of Three English Brothers* (Q1607), and Thomas Dekker and John Webster's *Sir Thomas Wyatt* (Q1607). At the boys' playhouses, we find a similar variety including revenge plays (*Bussy D'Ambois*), London comedies (*Eastward Ho!, Westward Ho!,* and *Northward Ho!*), satire (*The Isle of Gulls*), and foreign histories (the two-part *Charles, Duke of Byron*). Interesting plays in the Blackfriars repertory are *The Knight of the Burning Pestle* (Q1613), *The Faithful Shepherdess* (Q1610), and *Cupid's Revenge* (Q1613), which signal the appearance among the London dramatists of Francis Beaumont and John Fletcher, who were writing for the King's men by 1609. At the newly opened playhouse in Whitefriars, at least one of Shakespeare's fellows would have taken note, for the company there performed *The Two Maids of Moreclack* (Q1609) by Robert Armin, who was of course at the time a member of the King's men.

At the Globe, the King's men appear to have used revivals to satisfy the public's taste for old but still popular comedic formulas. Shakespeare's *Love's Labor's Lost* and *The Merchant of Venice*, for example, brought the romantic comedy back into the repertory. The enduring appeal of these plays is indicated by details of their performance at Court. As Walter Cope tells us, Richard Burbage knew that the wit and mirth of *Love's Labor's Lost* would please Queen Anne "excedingly." After the company scheduled *The Merchant of Venice* on Shrove Sunday, the king himself commanded that the play be repeated on Shrove Tuesday, according to a notation in the Revels Account, 1604–05. On the same Court agenda, the company offered the old Plautine favorite, *The Comedy of Errors*, and the trio of humors plays, *The Merry Wives of Windsor, Every Man in His Humor, Every Man out of His Humor.* Either in

1603–04 or 1605–06, the King's men revived the pastoral romance by way of *Mucedorus* and, in 1603–04, possibly *As You Like It*.

In addition to satisfying nostalgia, the revivals of the humors plays and the pastoral romances may have had an influence on the longevity and development of their respective dramatic formulas. Separated from other plays on stage in 1604–05, John Day's *Humor out of Breath* (1607–08) and the anonymous *Every Woman in Her Humor* (1607–09) look like belated additions to a vogue from the late 1590s; but in the context of these revivals, they look like continuations of a still-current style. Back when we believed that *Mucedorus* was revived for the first time in 1610, we took as obvious its generic influence on Shakespeare's romances, especially *The Winter's Tale*. In light of a revival in 1605–06, however, we may project an influence on the early work of Beaumont and Fletcher as well as on the romances of Shakespeare starting with *Pericles* in 1607–08.

If *The Merry Devil of Edmonton* was continued into 1603–04 (as I suppose), it would have been on the stage in the spring with the new play, *Robin Goodfellow*, which according to Dudley Carleton was given at Hampton Court on New Year's night, 1604. I assume the play treated the adventures of Puck, possibly as told either by the ballad, "The Merry Pranks of Robin Good-Fellow" (1628), or the chapbook, *Robin Good-Fellow; His Mad Prankes and Merry Jests* (1628). Neither exists now in an edition contemporary with the play, but the stories of Robin's mischief-making would have been common knowledge. One anecdote in particular recalls the role of Peter Fabell as a love god in *The Merry Devil of Edmonton* and advertises Robin's ability to change shape like Proteus. According to the story, Robin contrived a stratagem to trick an old lecher into blessing the marriage of his niece to the sweetheart of her choice. Sending the lovers to a local inn to "marry or doe what [they] will," Robin changed himself into the shape of the girl, went to the uncle's house, took up the girl's housework, and finished in record time.[12] The old man, suspecting that "she" was hurrying to a tryst, increased "her" chores, but Robin did the new jobs "in a trise, and playd many mad prankes beside ere the day appeared" (14). Then Robin contrived to extract a dowry: "she" promised to lie with the uncle for a reward of £10 and the freedom to choose a husband. But rather than satisfy the old man, Robin "tooke him up in his armes and carried him foorth; first drew him thorow a pond to coole his hot blood, then did he carry him where the young married couple were" (15). The punishment was salutary. In imitation of Sir Arthur Clare in *The Merry Devil of Edmonton* and of outwitted parents and rejected suitors in comedies generally, the uncle realized that he had been "duly punished." Turning "his hatred into love," he "thought afterward as well of them, as if shee had beene his owne" (15).

One of the comedies that the King's men acquired in these years is reminiscent of dramatic styles from the late Elizabethan years, but it combines the familiar patterns in such a way as to be entirely new. *Volpone* is part moral play, part Roman comedy, part humors play, and part satire. The opening tableau of Volpone and his gold recalls that of Barabas and his gold at the start of *The Jew of Malta*. Instead of venturing his wealth upon the seas, though, or multiplying coins by loans to Christians, Volpone has devised a stratagem by which legacy hunters ply him with gifts. The professions of the gulls recall the use of estate satire in moral plays and in Jonson's humors comedies: Voltore, the vulture, is a lawyer; Corbaccio, the raven, is a miser; and Corvino, the crow, is a merchant.[13] In the prostitution of his wife, Celia, Corvino invites comparison with other merchant-husbands such as the over-possessive Thorello (*Every Man in His Humor*) and the over-fond Deliro (*Every Man out of His Humor*). Mosca, Volpone's clever servant, enjoys the role of sidekick to the Vice, and like Ithamore he catalogues his villainies, though in pretended remorse:

> but that I haue done
> Base offices, in rending friends asunder,
> Diuiding families, betraying counsells,
> Whispering false lyes, or mining men with praises,
> Train'd their credulitie with periuries,
> Corrupted chastitie . . .
> Let me here perish, in all hope of goodnesse.
> (III.ii.25–30, 34)

Doubling the opportunity for the gulls to be brought out of their humors and for the vice characters to be exposed, Jonson provides two trials at the end of *Volpone*. Neither is legally satisfactory. In the first the judges are deceived by the lies of the gulls, and the villains slip through the net. Encouraged by this success, Volpone comes up with a new ruse, but this time Mosca determines "To cosen him of all" (V.v.16). At the second trial, when Volpone realizes that Mosca might gain his fortune, he exposes everyone's villainy rather than allow his henchman to win:

> I am VOLPONE, and this my knaue;
> This, his owne knaue; this, auarices foole;
> This, a *Chimæra* of wittall, foole, and knaue. . . .
> (V.xii.89–91)

Thus, through no cleverness or honesty on the part of the judges, the evil of these social predators is made public.

Three comedies and one tragedy in the collective playlist of the King's men belong to a strain of drama new in the early 1600s on the subject of domestic relations. Its antecedents include domestic crime tragedies such as *Arden of Faversham* (company unknown, Q1592, Q1599), mythological stories such as *The Golden Ass & Cupid and Psyche* (Admiral's men, 1599–1600), folk stories such as *Patient Grissil* (Admiral's men, 1599–1600), and prodigal husband plays such as *How a Man May Choose a Good Wife from a Bad* (Worcester's men, Q1602). A variation of these characterizations and motifs occurs in Thomas Heywood's masterful *A Woman Killed with Kindness* (Worcester's men, Q1607). In the period of 1603–1608, the Prince's men were to produce the two-part *Honest Whore* [*and Patient Man*], Queen Anne's men to perform *The Wise Woman of Hogsden*, and the King's men to acquire at least four plays of this kind from dramatists other than Shakespeare: *The Fair Maid of Bristow*, *The London Prodigal*, *A Yorkshire Tragedy*, and *The Miseries of Enforced Marriage*.

Perhaps the earliest of the set was *The Fair Maid of Bristow*, which the King's men had in production before December 1603. The play contains stock devices from comedy: the rescue of the play from tragedy depends on a set of disguised characters, and a king (here, Richard the Lionhearted) turns up to preside over the ending. However, the central issue of the play is how a man may know a good woman from a bad. The plot therefore presents a prodigal who marries a patient wife but who abandons her for a gold digger and "common stall."[14] After the prodigal has been disinherited, rejected by his strumpet-lover, and condemned to death for murder, he faces his waywardness and embraces his punishment. He is saved from death by friends and a forgiving wife.

The character of Anabell endures the tests of obedience and constancy that are hers from traditional story. She loves one suitor, but another, Vallenger, ingratiates himself with her father. Being dutiful, she accepts the husband that her father chooses. Vallenger takes up immediately with Florence, a courtesan, and Anabell is humiliated in a public scene in which he demands that a rebato and gown she is wearing be handed over to Florence on the spot. Anabell complies, saying "All that I haue sweet Vallenger is thine" (III.iii.499). The family is outraged by Vallenger's actions, but Anabell takes the blame on herself: "In mee consists the cause of all this wo" (IV.i.568). At the trial, she asks King Richard to show mercy on the accused prodigal; she claims to have suffered "no iniury" (V.i.853); and she disguises herself as a man and volunteers to die in his place. At his deliverance, she welcomes him as her "blouds deere solace" and "best content" (V.iii.1197). She dismisses his behavior as typical of youth and considers her role as one who waits until her husband is ready "to amend" (V.iii.1204).

Florence is a wicked foil to Anabell. She mesmerizes Sentloe with protestations of love and comparisons of herself to patient and chaste women, but at the first opportunity she encourages the wealthier and now-married suitor, Vallenger. She hires Sentloe's friend, Harbert (disguised as a servant), to kill Sentloe, and when Vallenger loses his inheritance, she has Harbert arrange Sentloe's murder scene so that Vallenger will be incriminated. Confronting death herself for her role in the murder, she impudently challenges her accusers to "hang" her and Vallenger "closely . . . / To kis in death, as we haue kist in life" (V.i.972–73). Disguised as a friar,

Sentloe comes to take her confession, but she answers him instead with saucy boasts:

> All that I couseaned, I defrauded:
> Those I haue slandered, I have defamed,
> When I hated, I loued not
> And this hath been the manner of my life.
> (V.ii.1043–46)

When she witnesses the saintly offers of Anabell and Challener to die for Vallenger, though, she is finally moved to join the circle of penitents: "Heere is a glasse for such as liues by lust, / See what tis to be honest, what tis to be iust" (V.iii.1176–77). King Richard sends her to a nunnery to amend herself as she will.

The men in *The Fair Maid of Bristow* play conventional roles also. Challener, initially the beau of Anabell, protects her from Vallenger's murder scheme and relinquishes both his hatred of Vallenger and his claim on Anabell when he realizes that she will remain a true wife in spite of her husband's sinfulness. Harbert, the sensible friend of Sentloe, protects him from Florence's murder scheme, thus guaranteeing that Vallenger's execution will be prevented. Sentloe, having learned that Florence has beguiled him, delivers a sermon on women's affections:

> A harlots loue is like a chimney smoke,
> Quiuering in the aire betweene two blasts of winde; . . .
> Hate, and dispaire, is painted in their eies,
> Deceit, and treason, in their bossome lies:
> Their promises, are made of brittle glasse,
> Ground like a phillip, to the finest dust. . . .
> (V.ii.1010–11, 1014–17)

Vallenger, by his father's admission a "wild boy" (III.i.289), is tamed by the consequences of his prodigality. Accepting the scaffold as the stage on which he will act his last part, he praises Anabell as the "wonder" of her sex (V.i.982) and repents his crimes against the heart. When Sentloe reveals himself not to have been murdered, Vallenger renews his request for forgiveness. He says that his soul "repents her lewd impyetie," and he begs that Anabell "seale [his] pardon with one balmy kisse" (V.iii.1196, 1195).

In *The London Prodigal,* the father of Young Flowerdale is inclined to dismiss his son's behavior as a humor, one he himself had indulged with impunity in his youth. Nevertheless, he disguises himself as a servant and, as a test, he develops a stratagem by which the son may deceitfully win a rich wife, Luce. When the boy gloats over the dowry he has won, the father is disgusted and sets in motion another ruse by which the son is falsely arrested on his wedding day for reneging on a debt of £3000. When she defends her husband, Luce is disinherited, and even though she has been forced to marry him, she now pleads for his release from arrest, excusing his behavior as "wildnesse" (III.iii.200).[15] In the contemptuous response typical of prodigals, though, Young Flowerdale repays her loyalty by taking money from her, ordering her to bring him her marriage portion, and telling her to "turne whore" to pay his debt (III.iii.295). Even after he is reduced to begging, Young Flowerdale continues to lie about himself, claiming to a Dutch serving girl (Luce in disguise) that his wife has ruined him by the theft of his money. Luce's father, fearing that his daughter is dead, has Young Flowerdale arrested, but she intervenes. She takes off her disguise and declares her "loue . . . dutie and . . . humblenesse" toward her husband (V.i.309). Witnessing her defense of him, Young Flowerdale is at last converted: "wonder among wiues! / Thy chastitie and vertue hath infused / Another soule in mee" (V.i.320–22). At this point, the father reveals his disguise and his role in protecting Luce and joins the family group of the converted prodigal and his patient bride.

In *A Yorkshire Tragedy,* the ending prevented in *The Fair Maid of Bristow* and *The London Prodigal* by patient wives and disguised protectors cannot be averted. The husband commits a real and heinous crime, the murder of two of his sons, and though his wife forgives him, the law does not. The murders follow a succession of prodigal sins: the husband deserts his sweetheart to marry a woman whom he later rejects with the claim that he chose her only "for fashion sake" (ii.78); he mortgages his fortune to the point that his brother goes to debtors' prison; he squanders his cash on riotous living; he calls his wife a whore and his children bastards "begot in tricks" (ii.70).[16] His wife tries to prevent his fall by securing him a place at Court, but he refuses it. Triggered by a sermon about his brother's beggary, the husband goes mad and sets out to murder his family to spare them the humiliation of a similar poverty. He fails to kill them all only because the baby is away at wet-nurse and a servant distracts him before he can finish stabbing his wife to death. When he is arrested, his wife comes to him and forgives him. Stunned by this, he repents; he kisses the wounds on his sons' bodies as he is led past them to await execution: "Ile kisse the bloud I spilt and then I goe: / My soull is bloudied, wel may my lippes be so" (x.54–55). His wife promises to "Sue for his life" and "plead for [his] pardon" (x.72, 73).

In *The Miseries of Enforced Marriage* George Wilkins reimposes a happy ending on the prodigal's story. Like the husband in *A Yorkshire Tragedy*, William Scarborrow marries against his will. His ward controls both his inheritance and his nuptial contract, and Scarborrow must abandon the girl he loves. When she commits suicide, Scarborrow dedicates himself to a life of dissipation. Infuriated by everyone's urging him to reform, he threatens to murder his wife and children. However, before he can lift his hand, his supporters appeal to the bonds of family—"Kinsman," "Brother," "Husband," "Father"—and he is moved to a change of heart (*MSR*, ll. 2811–14). At that very moment, he receives a letter saying that his ward has died and left him a double portion. Now thoroughly overcome that "heauen [is] so gracious to sinners" (l. 2843), he reaches out to his family ("Your hand, yours, yours") and to his wife ("to you my soule, to you a kisse") and confesses that he is "sorry" to have "straid amisse" (ll. 2846–47). In the epilogue, he asks playgoers to witness that he and his wife are now "new wed" (l. 2866) and to initiate the festival ending with applause: "We hope your hands will bring vs to our bed" (l. 2868).

At least three of the tragedies acquired by the King's men in 1603–1608, as well as the play taken over from the boys' company at Blackfriars, were influenced by the formula of revenge. There had been a revival of interest in the genre in 1599–1603, marked by the debuts of *Antonio and Mellida* and *Antonio's Revenge* at St. Paul's, *The Spanish Moor's Tragedy* at the Rose, *The Jew of Malta* and *The Spanish Tragedy* at the Fortune (revivals), *Hamlet* at the Globe, *The Malcontent* and the secondhand *Jeronimo* at Blackfriars, and *Hoffman* at either the Rose or Fortune. The King's men capitalized on this interest with *The Malcontent* (now secondhand, 1603–04), *Othello* (1604–05), *The Revenger's Tragedy* (1605–06), and *The Devil's Charter* (1606–07). Because the title of *The Spanish Maze* implies a play of intrigue, I am tempted to add it to the list of revenge tragedies, but there is no evidence of its subject matter and form.

As a reflection of the state of revenge drama in the early 1600s, the plays acquired by the King's men show how dramatists were experimenting with some elements of the genre. One feature being challenged was the distinction between heroic and villainous revengers. In those plays that we credit with having created a taste for this kind of tragedy in the Elizabethan playhouses of the late 1580s, that is, *The Spanish Tragedy* as it was printed in 1592 and the anonymous *Hamlet* as we suppose it to have been from the version of the story Shakespeare wrote, the revengers come across to audiences as noble figures. They become revengers when there is no other means to bring guilty men to justice. They delay action in part because they are mad with grief but in part because they want to be certain that the evidence they have against the villains is adequate. When they themselves die in consequence of their revenge plot, they confess their cause and receive some form of theatrical absolution. Following the popularity of these seminal dramas, playwrights developed an alternative hero, an evil revenger, beginning with Barabas in *The Jew of Malta* and continuing with Aaron in *Titus Andronicus*. The villain-revenger delights in cruel stratagems and serial murder. He is not concerned with evidence and guilt. When he is caught by his own machinations, he taunts his adversaries with a recital of his evil accomplishments.

The revengers in the plays of the King's men are more kin to the villainous model than to the heroic one. Iago in *Othello* and

Pope Alexander VI in *The Devil's Charter* are in fact very close kin. Alexander so offends that even the devil who comes to claim his soul finds him repugnant: "Thy soule foule beast is like a Menstruous cloath, / Poluted with vnpardonable sinnes" (V.vi.3120).[17] In *The Malcontent* Malevole, who is in reality the disguised Duke Altofronto, appears to be a brother with them in his eagerness to torment Duke Pietro (the usurper), in his reliance on intrigue, and in his extension of the revenge to include others. However, midway through his scheme Altofronto-Malevole has a change of heart: "I find the wind begins to come about; / I'll shift my suit of fortune" (III.iii.17–18). He will now orchestrate stratagems to expose the villains and bring about their repentance. He will do no murder, but will banish the sinners in one kind of exile or another. Vindice in *The Revenger's Tragedy* affects the manner of a Hamlet, but he fails to establish the fraternal bond. He knows who caused his beloved's death, and therefore he need not delay while he tests the evidence against suspects. He is mad with grief and outrage, but not too mad to act. He perceives no moral dilemma in the revenge. His attack on the duke becomes a series of plots against more and more of the corrupt members of the Court: "As fast as they peep up, let's cut 'em down" (III.v.226).[18] When he is arrested at the end of the play, he confesses that he has become as evil as his foes, but the confession does not redeem him. His final line is in the mode of exultation that identifies captured villains: "We die after a nest of dukes" (V.iii.125).

A source of contamination for revengers is their use of disguise. Iago and Pope Alexander follow the example of Claudius and murder while they smile behind the virtuous public identities of honest ancient and Vicar of Christ. However, Vindice and Altofronto take on separate—and villainous—identities. Vindice pretends to be a discontented courtier named Piato, and he agrees to pimp for Lussurioso and the duke. He retains the identity for the scene in which he tricks the duke into kissing a poisoned skull (the dead beloved's, also disguised), discovering himself as the duke dies: "'Tis I, 'tis Vindice, 'tis I" (III.v.168). This revenge accomplished, he abandons the identity of Piato, but as a participant in the

Masque of Revengers, he murders again in costume. Duke Altofronto pretends to be the malcontent, Malevole. But, as he turns away from revenge, he uses the disguise to bring about the conversion of the guilty. He reveals the disguise to Pietro, the usurper, preliminary to Pietro's disguise as a hermit. After hearing his wife's confession, Pietro determines to adopt the life that goes with the costume: "In true contrition I do dedicate / My breath to solitary holiness" (IV.v.125–26). Altofronto masterminds a final test—of his wife's constancy—before he discards the identity of Malevole to resume the dukedom and dispense justice.

The inclination of the revengers to villainy is complemented by a change in the nature of the crime that provokes revenge. In place of Hieronimo's revenge for a son, and Hamlet's revenge for a father, the tragedies of 1603–1608 dramatize the crimes of rape and adultery. In *The Revenger's Tragedy*, for example, the duke is guilty of sexual assault. The duchess's youngest son rapes a nobleman's wife. The duchess commits adultery with the duke's bastard son, Spurio. Lussurioso, the duke's legitimate son, plans to seduce Vindice's sister and enlists Vindice-Piato to pander for him. Vindice's mother approves of her daughter's prostitution. Understandably, Vindice imagines the world teeming with illicit sexual activity:

> Some that were maids
> E'en at sunset are now perhaps i' th' toll-book.
> This woman in immodest thin apparel
> Lets in her friend by water; here a dame,
> Cunning, nails leather hinges to a door,
> To avoid proclamation; now cuckolds are
> A-coining, apace, apace, apace, apace;
> And careful sisters spin that thread i' th' night
> That does maintain them and their bawds i' th' day.
>   (II.ii.137–45)

Typical of these plays, the language in *The Revenger's Tragedy* is crude and violent. After poisoning the duke, Vindice taunts him with the news of his cuckoldry: "Thy bastard, / Thy bastard rides a-hunting in thy brow" (III.v.181–82). To prevent the duke from crying out as he watches an assignation between his illegitimate son and his wife (even as the duke's mouth is being eaten away by the poison), Vindice orders: "Nail down his tongue" (III.v.198). Later Vindice and his brother prepare a ghastly tableau for Lussurioso and his circle—the putrefying corpse of the duke. Gleefully anticipating the villains' surprise, Vindice's brother calls Lussurioso's courtiers "flesh-flies . . . that will buzz against supper-time" (V.i.13–14), and Vindice calls on "the fly-flap of vengeance [to] beat 'em to pieces" (V.i.15).

Although changed in the ethics of the revenger and the nature of the crime he avenges, these tragedies continue at least one feature of earlier plays in the genre: sensational stage business. *The Devil's Charter,* for example, has two outrageous scenes that involve Lucretia Borgia, Pope Alexander's daughter. In the first of these, Lucretia vows revenge against her jealous husband, Gismond di Viselli, for locking her up. When he comes to her room, she lures him into a chair, ties him down, gags him, and threatens to stab him unless he signs a paper attesting to her chastity. He signs, and she unleashes a torrent of abuse: "Thou Ribbauld, Cuckcold, Rascall, Libeller, / Pernicious Lecher . . . / Periurious Coxcombe, Foole" (I.v.659–61). Then she stabs him to death and arranges the corpse to look like a suicide.

Consequently, her villainy goes undetected for some time, but her father learns of her role from his magic glass and sends her poisons disguised as perfumes from her current lover. The gift arrives in the second of these scenes (IV.iii). Lucretia sits at a table with two mirrors as she prepares for a private supper with the cardinal of Capua. Pouring the new perfume into a basin, she admires herself—forehead, eyes, mouth, neck, breasts, body—recalling with the satisfaction of an aging movie queen the caresses and extravagant love tokens she has received from suitors. But there is one wrinkle on her forehead, and she applies the poisoned water to soothe it. Her face begins to burn from the drugs, and she realizes that she is about to die. The poison works slowly, though, and she has time to repent the murder of Gismond and ask God for mercy.

In another shocking pair of scenes, Pope Alexander woos and then murders his coy lover, a young monk named Astor. He sends the boy jewelry and praises his beauty in a blazon as perverse as Lucretia's catalogue of her own beauties:

> Let me behold those bright Stars my ioyes treasure,
> Those glorious well attempred tender cheekes;
> That specious for-head like a lane of Lillies:
> That seemely Nose loues chariot triumphant,
> Breathing *Panchaian* Odors to my sences,
> That gratious mouth, betwixt whose crimosin pillou
> *Venus* and *Cupid* sleeping kisse together.
> That chin, the ball vow'd to the Queene of beauty,
> Now budding ready to bring forth loue blossomes.
> (III.ii.1207–15)

Won by this and other persuasions to love, the boy agrees to a tryst: "After the Celebration of the Masse, / I come my Lord" (III.ii.1283–84). Subsequently, in a scene that allegedly copies the dramaturgy of Cleopatra's suicide in *Antony and Cleopatra,* Alexander drugs the wine of Astor and another young monk (Philippo). As the boys sleep, he lays asps on their breasts, crooning: "Come out here now you *Cleopatraes* birds. / Fed fat and plump with proud *Egiptian* slime" (IV.v.2547–48). The murders accomplished ("What now proud wormes? how tasts yon princes blood" [IV.v.2566]), he returns the snakes to their box.

The frame structure of *The Devil's Charter* evokes the demonic bargain of Faustus. The play opens in the study with a dumb show of the contract by which Roderigo Borgia will become Pope Alexander VI. Borgia bribes two cardinals and enlists devils in his scheme to seize the papacy. Amid *"exhalations of lightning and sulphurous smoke"* (l. 39), the devils arrive. Borgia rejects one *"in most vgly shape"* but welcomes one *"in robes pontificall with a triple Crowne on his head, and Crosse keyes in his hand"* (ll. 44–45). This devil and his companion slit Borgia's vein so that he can sign the contract in blood. The devil dressed as the Pope drinks the remaining blood and dresses Borgia in the papal regalia. Throughout the play, the study is the scene where Pope Alexander plans some murder or conjures up illusions such as "a King, with a red face crowned imperiall riding vpon a Lyon, or dragon" (IV.i.1764–66). And it is to the study that he returns when he has been poisoned by the wine that he had meant for others. As devils dance to the horn pipe in anticipation of his death, Alexander tries to conjure up a physical antidote, then a spiritual one. Crying softly, he seems genuinely astonished that his prayer of mercy has no magic: "stirre stubburne, stonie, stiff indurate heart. not yet, vp. why, what? . . . what am I damn'd?" (V.vi.3190–91, 3196). Too late he understands, and he warns the audience to take example: "Learne wicked worldlings, learne, lcarne, learne by me / To saue your soules, though I condemned be" (V.vi.3246–47). The victory won, the devils *"thrust"* Alexander *"downe"* and leave the stage *"Triumphing"* (V.vi.3278).

The history plays acquired by the King's men in 1603–1608 appear to differ from those acquired in 1594–1603. The repertory of the Chamberlain's men seems to have been dominated by stories of the English kings from the Norman Conquest through the Wars of the Roses. In comparison, the repertory of the King's men draws on the matter of ancient Britain (*King Lear*), Scotland (*Gowrie, Macbeth*), and Rome (*Sejanus, Antony and Cleopatra, Timon of Athens*, and *Coriolanus*). However, both lists, being partial, are probably misleading. From the years when they were the Chamberlain's men, the King's men had a stock of plays on England's medieval rulers, and they could have revived any number of these whenever they chose. They did, in fact, revive *Henry V* in 1604–05. The editions of *1 Henry IV* in 1604 and 1608, of *Richard III* in 1605, and of *Richard II* in 1608 indicate that these stories continued to have commercial value in bookshops, and we have no reason to think that they did not have commercial value in the playhouse as well. Further, from offerings of Queen Anne's men and the Prince's men, there may be a hint of the history plays lost from the repertory of the King's men. Between 1603 and 1607, the Queen's men played the two-part *If You Know Not Me, You Know Nobody* (Q1605, Q1606) and *Sir Thomas Wyatt* (Q1607); the Prince's men played *When You See Me, You Know Me* (Q1605), *The*

Whore of Babylon (Q1607), and possibly the newly revised *Sir Thomas More*.[19] The King's men had one play on contemporary history that we know of: *Gowrie;* there may have been others.

Gowrie was undoubtedly a dramatization of the incident on 5 August 1600 in which John Ruthven, the third earl of Gowrie, and his brother Alexander allegedly attempted to assassinate James, then king of Scotland. Supposedly, the brothers, who were twenty-one and eighteen at the time, acted to avenge their father's beheading in 1584. According to the official narrative, the king was preparing for a hunt when he was approached by Alexander Ruthven, who whispered to him a muddled story about a hidden pot of gold. The king continued the hunt, but at its conclusion he rode over to Perth to talk to John Ruthven. After he arrived at Gowrie House and dined, he went upstairs with Alexander, and his entourage did not see him again until he cried out from an upstairs window: "'I am murtherit! Treassoun! My Lord of Mar, help! help!'"[20] Some of the nobles rushed to his aid but were unable to break through a locked chamber door. Meanwhile, one rescuer, approaching the upper room from a different direction, broke in and found the king wrestling with Alexander. The rescuer stabbed Alexander in the face and neck, and the king threw his body down the stair. The first party of rescuers found the body when they broke through the door and stabbed him again. John Ruthven now joined the fray and was fatally wounded. The bodies of the Ruthvens were tried for treason, and on 19 November 1600 the corpses were hanged and dismembered at the Cross of Edinburgh.

By 18 December 1604, the King's men had already given two performances of *Gowrie,* according to John Chamberlain, who conjectures in a letter to Ralph Winwood on 18 December 1604 that the play would be "forbidden" because it had offended "some great Councellors."[21] Chamberlain offers alternative reasons for the offense. One was a standard feature of stage decorum: "whether . . . it be thought unfit that Princes should be played on the Stage in their Life-time." This was a disadvantage of contemporary historical subjects generally, and the King's men must have expected it. Chamberlain expresses the other possibility in vague terms:

"whether the matter or the manner be not well handled." He may mean that the play was poorly written, but he may also be hinting that the story of the conspiracy was not carefully told. It seems that the official narrative had met with skepticism in Scotland from the start. Some critics of King James claimed that he set up the confrontation because he wanted to be rid of the Ruthvens, the entire family of whom he considered untrustworthy. The king's story was, frankly, incredible. We may well wonder why the King's men would have chosen a play that risked displeasure not only by its stage part for the king but also by its controversial subject matter. The answer may be in Chamberlain's observation that the play had drawn an "exceeding Concourse of all sorts of People." For good receipts, the King's men were apparently willing to spend the time to rehearse and the money to produce the play, even though they might have to cancel it after just a few shows.[22]

Contemporary witnesses of *Sejanus* on stage, including Jonson himself, attest to the play's failure to please audiences. In an epigram prefixed to the quarto in 1605, "Ev. B" described the reaction of the audience as "beastly rage" (*H&S*, IX, 190). In the dedicatory letter added to the folio edition in 1616, Jonson likened the reception of the play by London playgoers to the dismemberment of Sejanus by the Roman mob: "*It is a poeme, that . . . suffer'd no lesse violence from our people here, then the subiect of it did from the rage of the people of* Rome" (*H&S*, IV, 349). In 1616 William Fennor praised the play, saying that the gentry applauded it; however, "the multitude . . . / . . . screwed their scuruy iawes and look't awry, / Like hissing snakes adiudging it to die" (*H&S*, IX, 191).

What those common playgoers hated, though, is not clear from the witnesses' reports. It probably was not the Roman subject matter, for the Chamberlain's men apparently had success with *Julius Caesar* in 1599–1600 and with *Antony and Cleopatra* in 1606–07. Perhaps it was the dramatic form. Jonson intended the play to be an experiment. After the dramatists whom he satirized in *Poetaster* bit back in *Satiromastix* (and perhaps in other plays now lost), he began to consider an alternative response. In the poem addressed to readers and published with *Poetaster* in 1602, he says that he will relinquish the comic muse, who had proved "so ominous," and "trie / If Tragœdie haue a more kind aspect" (ll. 223–24). He describes a new theory of tragedy in the epistle to readers published with *Sejanus* in 1605: "truth of Argument, dignity of Persons, grauity and height of Elocution, fulnesse and frequencie of Sentence" (ll. 18–20). In *Sejanus* these elements take the form of a tragical-historical satire.

In terms of conventionally commercial motifs, however, the play had several bases of appeal. Sejanus is an impressive machiavel. At the start he declares a hatred for Tiberius and everyone else who stands in his way. No act is too heinous if it forwards his revenge:

> Adultery? it is the lightest ill,
> I will commit. A race of wicked acts
> Shall flow out of my anger, and o'er-spread
> The worlds wide face . . .
>
> (II.ii.150–54)

Stung that Tiberius does not support his ambitions, Sejanus contemptuously plots this Caesar's fall:

> Well, read my charmes,
> And may they lay that hold vpon thy senses,
> As thou had'st snuft vp hemlocke, or tane downe
> The iuice of poppie, and of mandrakes. Sleepe,
> Voluptuous CAESAR, and securitie
> Seize on thy stupide powers, and leaue them dead
> To publique cares, awake but to thy lusts.
>
> (III.ii.595–601)

Sejanus sees no limit to his rise: "I feele my' aduanced head / Knocke out a starre in heau'n" (V.i.8–9). The language of the play is coarse as in the comical satires; for example, Silius sneers at a courtier who fawns over his lordship "if he spit, or but pisse faire, / Haue an indifferent stoole, or breake winde well" (I.i.39–40). There is also a rigged trial of the malcontents, and a showy bit of stage business when the statue of Fortune averts her head from Sejanus. Perhaps Jonson's audiences were disappointed that the dismemberment of Sejanus, the rape of his daughter by the hangman, and his wife's public frenzy of grief were reported rather than staged. Or perhaps they were insulted that Jonson should think them so corrupt that they would genuinely benefit from the moral lesson in Sejanus's fall.

The collective playlist for 1603–1608 implies that the King's men continued to duplicate the narrative materials and motifs of plays in their holdings and those of other companies. Shakespeare's *King Lear,* for example, retells the story of *King Leir* (Q1605). The opening dumb show of *The Devil's Charter* evokes the induction of *The Merry Devil of Edmonton* and the contract scenes of *Doctor Faustus* (Q1604). Being a villain, Pope Alexander has nothing more in common with Peter Fabell, but like Faustus he delivers soliloquies on being resolute and he tries to escape the damnation that that resolution has assured. In regard to serials, we see that the King's men revived *Every Man in His Humor* and *Every Man out of His Humor* in 1604–05 and played both at Court (though in reverse order). However, if they also revived *Love's Labor's Won* with *Love's Labor's Lost,* and the two parts of *Henry IV* with *Henry V,* we do not know of it, for they did not present these companion pieces at Court (one play was paid for in the Chamber Accounts, but the Revels Account claims it was "discharged"). They did revive *The Merry Wives of Windsor,* but it has the least narrative connection with *Henry V* of the four plays concerning Hal and Falstaff.

The one instance of new serialization that has survived in the composite repertory is *All's One.* When *A Yorkshire Tragedy* was published in 1608, the title-page of the quarto read "A YORK-SHIRE Tragedy. Not so New as Lamentable and true." The head-title read "ALL'S ONE, OR, One of the foure Plaies in one, called a York-shire Tragedy." Because the play is short (fewer than eight hundred lines), scholars have conjectured that it was one of four plays that were performed together as a set (as the head-title implies). There have been several suggestions about the narrative relationships of the four plays. F. G. Fleay thought it likely that the set dramatized episodes in the Calverley tragedy and had thus a sequential narrative relationship. Baldwin Maxwell prefers the interpretation that the four plays were related by theme,[23] as is the case with Robert Yarington's *Two Lamentable Tragedies*. In addition, there is the possibility that the parts were related by genre, as is the case of playlets in the plot of *2 Seven Deadly Sins*.

Another dimension of duplication in *A Yorkshire Tragedy* is its putative relationship to *The Miseries of Enforced Marriage*. In *The Athenaeum* in 1879 (4 October), P. A. Daniel claimed that Wilkins had based his play on the Calverley murders, and scholars subsequently have agreed. In the playhouse, however, audiences might easily have missed the narrative connection. Scarborrow is a Yorkshire man who has a brother at Oxford, but otherwise the presence of the historical Calverley is not strong. What audiences would not have missed, I believe, is the manner in which *The Miseries of Enforced Marriage* associates itself with the story of the prodigal and his patient wife on the one hand, and on the other exploits that formula to dramatize the social conditions that encourage not only a life of riot but also the predatory companions of the dissolute young heir.

In most ways, Scarborrow is a conventional prodigal. He is sick with the "Feuer" of self-destruction (*MSR*, l. 1118). He knows the vileness of his actions and his company; nonetheless, he impels himself toward ruin. The traditional pastimes of the prodigal's life—whoring, drinking, and gambling—measure his days: "Weele meet at Miter, where weele sup downe sorrow, / We are drunke to night, and so weele be to morrow" (ll. 1524–25). The character of his wife, Katherine, is also conventional. She has no voice in the scene where Scarborrow refuses to marry her. When he abandons her in Yorkshire and runs to London, she bears her rejection with "loue and true obedience" (l. 1006), patiently waiting "for better dayes when bad be gone" (l. 1010). Even though he offers her to the family servant ("Lie with my wife, and get more Bastards" [l. 2570]) and even though he threatens to kill her and her twin sons, she reaches out to him in forgiveness: "Wee kneele, forget, and say if you but loue vs, / You gaue vs greefe for future happines" (ll. 2829–30).

However, *The Miseries of Enforced Marriage* is singular among the domestic dramas surviving from the repertory of the King's men, including *A Yorkshire Tragedy*, in that Wilkins turns the story of the prodigal into an indictment of Elizabethan practices regarding marriage and inheritance. He gives Scarborrow a stronger motivation to turn prodigal than merely the natural "humor" of youth. He has pledged himself in love and marriage to Clare Harcop; however, he is forced by the conditions of his wardship to take a different bride or lose his fortune. When the guardian learns about Clare but willfully insists on the match he has himself made, Scarborrow is devastated. All he can muster is a piteous one-line plea to his fiancée: *"Forgiue me, I am married"* (l. 798). Clare is doubly victimized: she loses her troth-plight husband; and, though "Young, Fayre, Rich, Honest, Virtuous" (l. 820), she cannot marry without committing adultery. Freeing Scarborrow and his wife from similar taint, she answers his plea of forgiveness with suicide: *"Forgiue me, I am dead"* (l. 851). The prodigal's brothers and sister are also victims of the enforced marriage. As eldest son, Scarborrow inherits their portions, and in his debauchery he spends theirs along with his own. The brothers turn to robbery to set themselves up in London. The sister, avoiding one kind of prostitution, marries a man who has been tricked into thinking her rich.

The man is Sir Francis Ilford, the most zealous of the tavern jackals who fatten on the dissipation of young heirs like Scarborrow. We first see Ilford as a reveler full of cynical advice about women: "Women are the Purgatory of mens Pursses, the Paradice of their bodies, and the Hel of their mindes; Marry none of them. Women are in Churches Saints, abroad Angels, at home Diuels" (ll. 148–51). But he soon reveals an even darker side, boasting of the fellows he has ruined:

> Now let me number how many rooks I haue halfe vndone already this Tearme by the first returne: foure by Dice, six by being bound with me, and ten by queanes, of which some be Courtiers, some Country Gentlemen, and some Cittizins Sonnes. Thou art a good Franke, if thou pergest thus, thou art still a Companion for Gallants, maist keep a Catamite, take Phisick, at the Spring and the fall (ll. 510–16).

He and one of his flatterers, Wentloe, trap Scarborrow into mortgaging his land to free Ilford of a £500 debt. When his father dies,

Ilford decides on a new course of exploitation: marriage to an heiress. Realizing too late that his bride is Scarborrow's penniless sister, he punishes the girl with a torrent of curses: "Whore, I and Iade, Witch, Ilfacst, stinking-breath, crooked-nose, worse then the Deuill, and a plague on thee that euer I saw thee" (ll. 2152–54).[24] That such a man is admitted into the family circle without a chastening proves that the play returns in the final scene to the conventions of the domestic comedy, which prefers a resolution through forgiveness even when the husbands have not expressly repented.

In histories of Shakespeare's company, we are encouraged to declare 19 May 1603 as the day when the playhouse wars ended. On this date, the Chamberlain's men were elevated to the King's men, and rival companies henceforth had to make do with lesser royal patrons and lower-class audiences. Yet this narrative is as much myth as history. We *assume* that Shakespeare's company was chosen to be the King's company because of its excellence. We *assume* that profits and the quality of stage literature declined for the other companies (especially the men's) because the financial records that might tell us otherwise have perished and because it is what we want to believe. In fact, conditions in the years of 1603–1608 put all of the companies under pressure. Recurrences of plague accomplished what no lord mayor had been able to do: close the playhouses for months at a time. The reward of £30 given to the King's men in 1603–04 for their maintenance and relief would not have compensated them for two weeks of revenue lost during the restraints. From the perspective of the repertory, we see that the King's men responded to these stressful conditions by offering a number of plays with characterizations and dramatic formulas popular at the playhouses in general: for example, villainous revengers, merry devils, mischievous fairies, and domestic moral plays.

But there are signs also that the King's men were becoming more assertive in the London theatrical marketplace. One is their acquisition and revision of *The Malcontent*. By way of the customized induction, the King's men declared themselves invulnerable to theatrical sabotage. A second is their production of *Gowrie*.

The players must have known that the play was dangerously political, that it might anger their patron and king however well it was handled; yet they went ahead with the production, and we have only hearsay that it was cancelled. A third is their willingness to experiment with new dramatic materials. One of these experiments, *Sejanus,* seems to have been a commercial nightmare, but the company came back two years later with another, *Volpone,* which was successful enough to remain in production for more than a year. The Prince's men and Queen Anne's men survived into 1608–1613, when at least two new men's companies were to be formed (the Duke of York's men, Lady Elizabeth's men). The Children of Paul's and the Children of Blackfriars were defunct by 1609–10, but the Children of Whitefriars, followed by the Children of the Queen's Revels, occupied the playhouse at Whitefriars. What is remarkable, then, is not the triumph of the King's men over the other companies, but the success of them all in spite of the economic hazards in sudden playhouse closures and extended touring. We may measure the degree of that success for the King's men by the fact that in 1608, when the lease on the Blackfriars property became available, they were ready to assume the expense and professional demands of a second playhouse.

V

The Repertory of the King's Men, 1608–1613

In August 1608, the King's men acquired the lease on the stage at Blackfriars. James Burbage had purchased the property in 1596 and converted it into a playhouse, but he did not lease it to a company at that time, apparently because neighbors filed a petition objecting to its use for playing. Several years after Burbage died in February 1597, his son Richard leased the Blackfriars stage to Henry Evans, who brought in a company of boys. By August 1608, Evans surrendered the lease and Burbage took it up for the King's men. To finance the venture, he assembled a consortium of investors, among whom were his brother (Cuthbert) and four players who were also housekeepers in the Globe: John Heminges, Henry Condell, William Shakespeare, and William Sly.[1]

In 1948, G. E. Bentley addressed the issue of the King's men and their management of the repertory after the acquisition of this second stage at Blackfriars. He argued that the King's men, given the opportunity of a private theater as well as their familiar Globe, made some decisions about what kinds of plays they would buy over the next several years and how they would schedule those plays for the two playhouses. He argued further that the effect of their decisions was a split in the repertory between the plays that would become Blackfriars offerings and those that would be relegated to the Globe. The company would present the new plays acquired from dramatists such as Ben Jonson, Francis Beaumont, John Fletcher, and William Shakespeare on the stage at Blackfriars; but because audiences at public theaters were willing to support a schedule heavy in potboilers such as *The Spanish Tragedy* and *Titus*

Andronicus, the stage at the Globe "could be left to take care of itself with an old repertory" and with new plays by the likes of George Wilkins.[2]

In effect, Bentley was saying that the King's men developed a new commercial strategy as a result of having acquired a second playhouse—or, at the very least, that they set new priorities within their usual strategy. However, the repertory lists for 1608–1613 show that the King's men continued to be concerned in the old way with a mix of new plays, continuations, and revivals. Moreover, they relied as they were used to doing on their own successful plays as well as on those in performance at the other houses as a guide to popular story materials, dramatic formulas, serials, and spin-offs. They looked for new plays as they always had, and at this time those plays came in the formulas of romance, pseudo-historical heroical tragedy, and tragicomedy. But, according to the information we have from playgoers who saw these offerings in performance as well as the information on title-pages of the quartos, the King's men did not reserve their new plays exclusively for Blackfriars; they presented them at the Globe also.

If we knew the titles of the new plays in 1608–09, we could assess the effect of two playhouses on the repertory in more detail, for the King's men must have been planning for the fall season when they acquired the lease. But the plague returned at just that time, and with the plague came an official closure of the playhouses. The King's men spent much of the fall on tour in East Anglia and the Midlands. At Christmas they received a stipend of £40 from the Treasurer of the Chamber specifically for "their private practice in the time of infecc*i*on that thereby they mighte be inhabled to performe their service before his ma*je*stie in Christmas hollidaies 1609" (*MSC,* VI, 47), and they received in addition payment for twelve performances at Court. Perhaps they gave some performances in London through the winter, but by May they were back on tour, spending most of the summer in East Anglia and Kent.

Understandably, scholars have been hesitant to assign new plays to 1608–09 because of the plague and the presumption of year-long closure of the playhouses. Even in these conditions, however, I assume that the King's men did buy some new texts, though far fewer than their norm. I assume further that because of the plague and touring they continued more plays from 1607–08 than they had in years of uninterrupted playing (1607–08 was itself an abbreviated playing year). I would guess that *Pericles* was one of those continuations. The play seems to have been very popular, as evidenced by its publication in 1609 (two editions) and 1611.[3] I assume that the King's men revived several plays also. Two of their old texts, *Troilus and Cressida* and *Romeo and Juliet*, were published in 1609, but neither quarto advertises a revival. The first issue of *Troilus and Cressida* carries a title-page naming the King's men in performance at the Globe, but in the second issue this information is deleted and an epistle added that specifically denies performance ("you haue heere a new play, neuer stal'd with the Stage, neuer clapper-clawd with the palmes of the vulger" [*Riverside*, 492]). The 1609 quarto of *Romeo and Juliet* carries a title-page that updates the name of the company owners to the King's men and adds the name of the playhouse (Globe). Otherwise, the only sign that John Smethwick, the stationer who acquired the play in November 1607, might have had a reason for putting out a new edition is the fact that he chose it at all, when he also owned *Love's Labor's Lost*, *The Taming of a Shrew*, and *Hamlet* but did not publish them at this time.

The number of deaths from plague remained high into the fall of 1609–10, and for the second year in a row the Treasurer of the Chamber paid the King's men for rehearsals in anticipation of the Christmas holidays when the company presented thirteen plays at Court. By Easter Monday (9 April), the mortality rate from plague had declined significantly. For the first time perhaps since the summer of 1608, the King's men were able to offer plays to the London public on a daily basis. As in that summer nearly two years earlier, therefore, they planned their offerings in regard not only to the Globe but also to Blackfriars. Among the offerings new (or reatively new) to London playgoers were *Cymbeline*, *Philaster*, and *The Alchemist*. Among the revivals were *Othello* and (probably)

Mucedorus. We know of the revival of *Othello* because Lewis Frederick of Württemburg visited London in the spring of 1610 and his secretary kept a journal of the visit. Under the date of 30 April 1610 he recorded that the prince attended the Globe (*"alla au Globe"*) and saw a performance of *Othello* (*"l'histoire du More de Venise"*).[4] In 1610 also, *Mucedorus* was reprinted with a title-page that carries new and detailed theatrical information: "as it was acted before the Kings Maiestie at White-hall on Shroue-sunday night. By his Highnes Seruantes vsually playing at the Globe" (*BEPD*, no. 151). The title-page of an edition dated 1611 repeats this information. E. K. Chambers conflated the editions into a single printing and assigned the Shrove Sunday performance tentatively to 3 February 1611 (*ES*, IV, 125). He may be right on both counts. However, the edition of 1611 appears to be a separate printing from the one in 1610, although "a remarkably close" one according to Greg. If so, the title-page of the second of these printings would seem to refer to the performance advertised by the first one, that is, Shrove Sunday 1610 (18 February).[5]

Though the plague returned in the fall of 1610 and the companies went on tour, the playhouses seem to have been open in the winter, during which time the King's men gave fifteen performances at Court. Because Simon Forman, a poor man's wizard, went to the playhouse that spring, we know that in 1610–11 the King's men had in repertory a play he called *Richard the 2* (new) as well as *The Winter's Tale* (new), *Cymbeline* (continued from 1609–10), and *Macbeth* (revived from 1605–06). In addition, they acquired at least *Catiline, The Maid's Tragedy, Bonduca,* and possibly *Valentinian.* Both *The Alchemist* and *Othello* seem to have been continued from 1609–10 into 1610–11, according to remarks in the Latin correspondence of Henry Jackson, a fellow of Corpus Christi College, Oxford, who saw both plays in Oxford in September 1610 (*H&S*, IX, 224).

Five plays owned by the King's men were printed in new editions in 1611: *Mucedorus, Pericles, The Miseries of Enforced Marriage, Hamlet,* and *Titus Andronicus.* In addition, *The Troublesome Reign of King John,* which had belonged to the

Queen's men in 1591, was reprinted. Of these plays, one—
Mucedorus—apparently had been revived recently, as implied by the
advertisement of a Shrovetide performance at Court on the title-
pages of Q1610 and Q1611. I believe it likely that two other of
these quartos—*Titus Andronicus* and *The Troublesome Reign of
King John*—reflect recent revivals. The editions themselves, of
course, indicate that some stationers thought the subject matter to
be marketable at this time, yet the title-pages carry new information (or misinformation) about theatrical provenance, possibly
because that provenance was fresh in the stationers' minds. For the
1611 quarto of *Titus Andronicus,* the name of the King's men was
substituted for the list of Elizabethan companies that had appeared
on quartos in 1594 and 1600. For the 1611 *The Troublesome Reign
of King John,* the information that "W. Sh." was the dramatist was
added to the advertisement of the Queen's men, which was carried
over from the edition in 1591 (in 1622, the initials were expanded
to "W. SHAKESPEARE"). I would guess that *King John* had been
revived recently by the King's men; and the stationer-owners of
The Troublesome Reign of King John, confusing their text with it,
advertised theirs by way of the other play's dramatist, failing to
update the name of the Queen's men to that of the King's.

In 1611–12 and 1612–13, the King's men had the use of both
of their playhouses without the interruption of plague restraints,
though there was an order of closure on 8 November 1612 because
of the death of Prince Henry, King James's eldest son and heir. A
record from the Office of the Revels for 1611–12 and two from the
Office of the Chamber for 1612–13 provide us with the titles of
some of the plays in production for these years. The Revels Account
names the plays that the company gave in five of twenty-two performances at Court in 1611–12. Those apparently new to the repertory
were *The Tempest, A King and No King, The Twins Tragedy,* and
The Nobleman.[6] Another was *The Second Maiden's Tragedy.* We
know that it was new in 1611–12 because the Master of Revels,
George Buc, made a note in the margin of the manuscript when he
approved it for licensing, and his note is dated 31 October 1611.[7]
The Chamber Accounts for 1612–13 give twenty titles, which

appear to represent eighteen plays given by the King's men in twenty appearances at Court between 20 October and 10 March. Four of these are new: *The Knot of Fools*, *A Bad Beginning Makes a Good Ending*, *The Captain*, and *Cardenio*. We learn of a fourth new play because of a disaster that occurred on 29 June: the burning of the Globe. In a letter dated 2 July 1613, Sir Henry Wotton provides the most specific description of the play being performed, allowing us to identify it as Shakespeare's *Henry VIII*. Telling of a fire "this week at the Bank's side," Wotton writes that the "King's players had a new play, called *All Is True*," which dramatized events from "the reign of Henry VIII," including "a masque at the Cardinal Wolsey's house."[8]

Both royal accounts provide also the titles of some of the old plays in the repertory of the King's men in these two years. The Revels Account names *The Winter's Tale* along with the four new plays given at Court in 1611–12; since *The Winter's Tale* was new in 1610–11, it was being continued in 1611–12. It was, in fact, continued another year, for one Chamber Account names it as well as *The Tempest*, *A King and No King*, *The Twins Tragedy*, and *The Nobleman* among the offerings at Court in 1612–13 (these four had been new in 1611–12). Herford and Simpson conjecture that Jonson revised *Every Man in His Humor* "in or about the year 1612" (*H&S*, IX, 334), and most recent chronologists agree.[9] It may be that Jonson reworked the play for reasons of his own, looking ahead perhaps to its publication in the collection of 1616, but it may also be that he was prompted to bring it in line with his latest comedy because the King's men were interested in a revival. We know the names of nine plays revived in 1612–13 from the Chamber Accounts of holiday payments in that year: *Philaster* (also, "Love Lyes a bleedinge"), *The Merry Devil of Edmonton*, *The Alchemist*, *The Maid's Tragedy*, *Othello*, "Caesars Tragedye" (*Julius Caesar*), "The Hotspurr" (*1 Henry IV*), "Sr Iohn Falstafe" (*The Merry Wives of Windsor*), and *Much Ado about Nothing* (also, "Benidicte and Betteris").[10]

In speculating on the relationship between a new edition of a play and its revival, I have restricted myself to instances where the title-page of the new edition advertises new information about the stage history of the play (beyond merely the current name of the company). I have done so in the belief that an updated title-page was a desirable—even necessary—qualification for my putting forth such editions as evidence of booksellers' perceiving a new market for the text because of a stage revival. Applying this cautionary criterion, I would therefore ignore the publications of *The Merry Devil of Edmonton* and *Richard III* in 1612 and those of *Thomas Lord Cromwell* and *Mucedorus* in 1613. However, we know from the Chamber Account of 1612 13 that *The Merry Devil of Edmonton* and *1 Henry IV* ("Hotspurr") were in fact revived in 1612–13. The presence of a new title-page, therefore, seems not to be a criterion at all. Unless these two plays are exceptions, and unless one rejects a relationship between subsequent editions and stage activity entirely, there is no reason not to consider every new edition of a play potential evidence of a revival regardless of the presence of new, expanded, and/or updated information on the title-page.

One feature of the argument that the King's men developed a new commercial strategy with the lease of Blackfriars is the belief that the audiences at the two playhouses differed in social privilege and therefore in dramatic tastes and sensibilities. Recently, scholars have challenged this belief in several ways. In *The Privileged Playgoers of Shakespeare's London* (1981), Ann J. Cook argues that persons of privilege were customers of playhouses such as the Theatre, Rose, Swan, Boar's Head, and Globe; that they were customers throughout the time frame of Shakespeare's career; and that they attended day to day in substantial numbers. In *Playgoing in Shakespeare's London* (1987), Andrew Gurr agrees in the division of audiences according to privilege but not in the consequent division of the repertory: "Before the 1630s, and certainly in the years from 1609 till Richard Burbage died in 1619, the company saw itself as catering for the whole of society, and it offered the same fare at both playhouses."[11]

The evidence on performance venues supports an offering of one repertory, regardless of playhouse. Duke Lewis Frederick saw

Othello at the Globe in April 1610; when the play was published in 1622, the title-page of the quarto advertised performances at the Globe and Blackfriars. Simon Forman saw not only the anonymous *Richard the 2* at the Globe but also Shakespeare's *Macbeth* and *The Winter's Tale;* more than likely, he also saw *Cymbeline* there. Possibly the key here is the season, not the playhouse. Theater historians, including Bentley, have long thought that Blackfriars was used in winter and the Globe in summer.[12] The title-pages of plays published after 1609 with information on place of performance indicate a use of both playhouses. The first quarto of *A King and No King* (1619) advertises performances at the Globe; the title-page of the second quarto (1625) advertises Blackfriars. The title-page of the first quarto of *Philaster* (1620) advertises performances at the Globe; the title-page of the second quarto (1622) advertises the Globe and Blackfriars. Furthermore, the new plays in 1608–1613 do not differ in stagecraft apropos of a change in venue from the Globe to Blackfriars. According to John Astington, a play introduced at Blackfriars could have been staged at the Globe without revisions: "there were no important differences in the stage and stage equipment between the two types of theater, and . . . the stage space was treated in a similar manner by the actors."[13]

Though theater historians would not have said so explicitly, another reason they believed in a separate and superior repertory for Blackfriars has been the assumption that the King's men employed relatively few dramatists. The fact that we could identify five or six of these men, plus the fact that their new plays were in the latest genres, appeared to us to be evidence that the company's new plays were acquired with the audiences at one playhouse in mind. But as I have argued throughout this study, the Chamberlain's and King's men acquired many more plays and thus traded with many more dramatists than we have been encouraged to believe. Furthermore, as they had in previous years, they used revivals as a source of old yet still popular stories and dramatic formulas and with similar results: new currency and influence for those stories and formulas. The revivals of *Mucedorus* are a good example. Knowing as we now do that it was on stage both around 1605–06 and 1610–11, we see that it was in a position to influence the romances and tragicomedies throughout 1607–1613, a period which includes the composition and production of the early pastoral tragicomedies of Beaumont and Fletcher as well as those of Shakespeare (this influence has long been accepted in the case of *The Winter's Tale*).

An instructive perspective on the issue of repertory management in 1608–1613 is the selection of plays presented by the King's men at Court in 1612–13. I suggest that these offerings are a reprise—or microcosm—of the commercial strategy used by the company in 1594 when its hold on the Theatre was tenuous, in 1599 when the Globe was new, in 1603 when the patronage of the king brought an increase in Court performances, and in 1608 when it acquired the indoor playhouse in Blackfriars. Of the plays named in the Chamber Accounts, four were new (as far I know), five were being continued from 1611–12 (at least), and the remaining nine were in revival (unless they too were being continued from a revival in the previous year). As a group these plays are a variety of dramatic formulas, with the emphasis heavily toward the comedic: seven comedies and romances, three tragedies, one tragical history, two histories, and five tragicomedies.

Among the comedies is *The Alchemist,* which looks backward in its use of magic to *Friar Bacon and Friar Bungay* in the repertory of the Queen's men around 1590 and forward to *The Tempest.* Around 1594, there was a flurry of interest in such plays, including *Doctor Faustus* (Admiral's men, 1594–97), *The Wise Man of West Chester* (Admiral's men, 1594–97), and *A Midsummer Night's Dream* (Chamberlain's men, 1594–95). Around 1602–03, there was another such flurry, which saw the revival and revision of *Doctor Faustus* by the Admiral's men, the revival for the Court of "a playe of bacon," and the introduction by the Chamberlain's men of the new play, *The Merry Devil of Edmonton. Doctor Faustus* remained popular at the bookstalls after the revival in 1602–03, being published in 1604, 1609, 1611, and 1616 (this last in a new text). *The Merry Devil of Edmonton,* of course, was another of the revivals in 1612–13 along with *The Alchemist.* The title of *The Knot of Fools* does not give us enough of a clue to its subject matter to do more than consider it a comedy made of intricate confusions, perhaps attributed to bewitchment as in *The Comedy of Errors*.

Although Jonson works an alchemy of his own on this theatrical heritage, the long-time playgoer would have heard echoes of the magical lore in old plays at every turn of the plot. By choosing the Fairy Queen as the ally of Dapper in his wish to be the gamester supreme, for example, Jonson invited the remembrance of Mercutio's description of Queen Mab in *Romeo and Juliet* and Titania's enchantment with Nick Bottom in *A Midsummer Night's Dream*. Just as Bottom carries away memories from fairyland to be preserved in "Bottom's Dream," Dapper carries away from the enchanted house a charm for the gaming tables (a fly in a neck-purse) and a prophecy of imminent good fortune.

The most sustained of these allusions, however, is the transmutation of Doctor Faustus into Sir Epicure Mammon. Like the fabled scholar of Wittenberg, Mammon imagines himself about to possess the means to become a demigod. He speaks dismissively to Surly of the low path to wealth:

> You shall no more deale with the hollow die,
> Or the fraile card. No more be at charge of keeping
> The liuery-punke, for the yong heire, that must
> Seale, at all houres, in his shirt.
>
> (II.i.9–12)

He, with the elixir of the philosopher's stone, will "confer honour, loue, respect, long life, / Giue safety, valure: yea, and victorie, / To whom he will" (II.i.50–52). He will renew old men like eagles, enabling them to "Become stout MARSES, and beget yong CVPIDS" (II.i.61). He will cure "all diseases" and "fright the plague / Out o' the kingdome, in three months" (II.i.64, 69–70). He hardly needs the distraction of a Mephistophilis to abandon legitimate aspirations, for he has already decided on "a list of wiues, and concubines" and "such pictures, as TIBERIVS tooke / From ELEPHANTIS: and dull ARETINE / But coldly imitated" (II.ii.35, 43–45). That these visions lead to the wooing of Dame Pliant is, for the audience, a diminution comparable to Faustus's horning of

144

Benvolio and tricking of the horsecourser. For Mammon, though, the venture promises to fulfill his most exaggerated expectations:

> Now, EPICVRE,
> Heighten thy selfe, talke to her, all in gold;
> Raine her as many showers, as IOVE did drops
> Vnto his DANAE: . . . What? the *stone* will do't.
> Shee shall feele gold, tast gold, heare gold, sleepe gold:
> Nay, we will *concumbere* gold."
> (IV.i.24–30)

In the pairing of Face and Subtle, Jonson recalls not only the servant and master relationships of Mephistophilis with Faustus on the one hand and Lucifer on the other, but also of such sorcerers and their apprentices as Friar Bacon and Miles, Oberon and Puck, and perhaps Puck in the unauthorized mischief possibly dramatized in the company's own *Robin Goodfellow*. Seeing the play in revival in 1612–13, playgoers might have connected Jonson's Subtle and Face with a sorcerer and his familiar in a play that the King's men had given at Court on Allhallows in 1611 and still had in production. One anticipation of that association in *The Alchemist* comes during the opening argument between the two deceivers over roles and importance. Subtle berates Face for his impertinence:

> No, you *scarabe*,
> I'll thunder you, in peeces. I will teach you
> How to beware, to tempt a *furie'* againe
> That carries tempest in his hand, and voice.
> (I.i.59–62)

Subsequently, Face claims to have airy intelligencers of his own—"flies abroad"—who spot new gulls for him (III.iii.65).

In the prologue to *The Alchemist,* Jonson invites playgoers to treat the performance as another in a succession of humors satires, "which haue still beene subiect, for the rage / Or spleene of *comick*-writers" (ll. 10–11). He offers the play as a sweet corrective to the vices of the age. We expect, then, for the magic of the comedy to improve the characters and thus to provide a moral structure like that in *Every Man out of His Humor:* in other words, we expect that the gulls will be humiliated and the cozeners exposed. But Jonson exploits the metaphor of alchemy, not purgative (and therefore restorative) medicine. Dapper may become the gambler of his dreams, but the base metals of Drugger, Mammon, Surly, Ananius, and Wholesome, as well as of Subtle and Dol Common, remain as they are. Face returns to the domestic service of Lovewit and to the plain identity of Jeremy. We in the audience must even adjust our expectations of Lovewit. From the start of the play, Jonson has suspended him in our imaginations as the embodiment of order and justice, or at least of normalcy. But with a guileless admission of indulgence, Lovewit shows the most skillful gamesmanship, winning the fortune of Dame Pliant.

If the playgoer in 1612–13 insisted on a more conventional comedy of humors and was not satisfied with the revival of *Much Ado about Nothing* (or possibly *The Merry Wives of Windsor* and the revised *Every Man in His Humor*), he might have found *The Captain* to his liking. Beaumont and Fletcher claim to be offering a play beyond traditional genres, one that is "nor *Comody,* nor *Tragedy,* / Nor *History*" (Prologue, ll. 6–7), but in fact they cannibalize several varieties of comedy for the personality types here. The title character is Jacamo, a Hotspur in his relish for war, who complains bitterly about the tedium of peace. His humor is for "Men [to] look like men againe, upon a march" (II.i.7). Like Benedick, he is keenly aware of his imperfections, both in figure and in lover's skills. Thus, when he is set up to court a willing young woman named Franck, he muffs the first opportunity out of shyness and the second out of drunkenness. His friends finally have to take the wooing entirely into their own hands. While the men *"drag him to a chaire and hold him downe in't"* (V.iv.6–7 [s.d.]). Franck falls on her knees before him and declares "I do love you more / Then you do your content" (V.iv.23–24). At last, Jacamo takes her up, with something of Benedick's giddiness:

> If I could all this while have been perswaded
> She could have lov'd me, dost thou thinke I had
> Not rather kisse her then another should?
> And yet you may gull me for ought I know,

But if you do, hell take me if I do not
Cutt all your throates sleeping.
                    (V.iv.72–77)

The play ends in multiple marriages. In addition to the pairing of
Franck with Jacamo, there is Clora, a saucy companion to Franck,
with Julio, a romantic youth initially gulled by Lelia, a worldly-wise
widow of dubious reputation; and there is Lelia with Piso, one of
the idle courtiers on the lookout for a rich wife and therefore willingly beguiled into a match.

    The line of plot in which Lelia plays a main role is more an
imitation of a moral play about prodigality than another track of
the romantic comedy. Before we meet Lelia herself, we overhear
Piso and a companion liken her to a plague, a war at sea, or quick-
sand. Her father overhears them as well, and when he asks about
her directly, they take him to be one of her bawds. When he goes
to see her, she treats him as though he were a beggar: "if there be
any cold meate in the Buttery, / Give him some broken bread and
that, and rid him" (I.iii.39–40). Spurning him in the way that
prodigal husbands humiliate their wives, she tells him he should die
and leave her in peace:

              what should you
Or any old man do wearing away
In this world with diseases, and desire
Only to live to make their children scourge-sticks,
And hoord up mill-money?
                    (I.iii.75–79)

Julio, her best chance at marriage, refuses her, and she vows bitterly to win the next man to come through the door. When such a
man comes, she offers food, drink, and wanton pleasure: "mouth
to mouth will we walke up to bed, / And undresse one another as
we goe" (IV.iv.117–18). The man turns out to be her father in disguise, but Lelia is not shamed by this revelation. In fact, her lust is
heightened by the discovery. She renews her proposition but is
interrupted by Angilo, who has dissuaded Julio from marrying her
and who now advises her father to put her away in the hope that

she may amend. The father agrees, and he tells her that he will keep her there until "a well of living teares" from her eyes washes the stain from her body "foul'd with sin" (IV.iv.280, 282–84). He also arranges the marriage with Piso. Fully converted to respectability, Lelia claims at the end of the play to have "a heart / As pure as any womans" (V.v.104–5).

The history plays in the Chamber Accounts for the King's men at Court in 1612–13 are "The Hotspurr" and "Caesars Tragedye" (also "Sr Iohn Falstafe," if it is indeed *2 Henry IV*). If these plays are, as we have guessed, *1 Henry IV* and *Julius Caesar*, they are revivals and show that the company continued to satisfy the long-standing appetite for stories from the English chronicles and Roman history.

One of the new history plays in the repertory for 1610–11—*Richard the 2*—illustrates this responsiveness also. Simon Forman tells enough about *Richard the 2* in the diary he called *Bocke of Plaies* for us to recognize that it depicted episodes early in the reign of Richard II, as do *Jack Straw* and *Woodstock*. Forman does not give much of a clue to themes in the play. He seems to have been single-minded as a playgoer, interested in the stories as guides to behavior. He instructs himself to "Remember" certain incidents from the plot (qtd. in *WS*, II, 339). The first concerns Jack Straw, who was murdered at Smithfield. Forman faults the rebel leader for having had "overmoch boldnes" and not enough suspicion. Forman learns "never [to] admit any party, without a bar betwen, for A man cannot be to wise, nor kepe him selfe to safe" (339). From the incidents in which Thomas of Woodstock defended himself against a night raid by one of the King's favorites only to be betrayed later at a royal banquet, Forman learns that even the king can be treacherous. Forman finds John of Gaunt the most wicked of villains. Not only did he plot to set his son on the throne, but he consulted a wise man and then hanged him to keep his prophecy secret. Forman implies that the play excused this behavior ("This was a pollicie in the common wealthes opinion" [340]), but he is himself outraged: "But I sai yt was a villaines parte, and a Judas kisse to hange the man for telling him the truth"

(340). Since Forman was a professional soothsayer, his reaction is understandable. The proverb that he draws from the death of the wise man characterizes the experience of seeing *Richard the 2*, as far as he is concerned: "Beware by this Example of noble men, and of their fair wordes, & sai lyttell to them, lest they doe the like by thee for thy good will" (340).

By selecting "Caesars Tragedye" to be performed at Court in 1612–13, the King's men were catering to the taste for classical story that led stationers to publish *Troilus and Cressida* in 1609 and *Titus Andronicus* in 1611, but they had discovered with *Sejanus*—and were to discover again with *Catiline*—that playgoers did not like some treatments of these subjects. Apparently *Catiline* failed even more miserably and with more kinds of playgoers than had *Sejanus*, for in *Pleasant Notes upon Don Quixot* (1654), Edmund Gayton said of it that "the judicious part of the Auditory condemn'd it equally with those that did not understand it" (qtd. in *H&S*, IX, 241).

According to Jonson himself in the preliminary address to the reader, Q1611, audiences enjoyed the first two acts, in which he uses theatrical devices that had made many a play a commercial success. Jonson begins *Catiline* with a tactic guaranteed to quiet an unruly audience: a ghost from Hades. Here, Sylla's ghost, like Machiavel in the prologue to *The Jew of Malta* and Guicchiardine in *The Devil's Charter*, introduces the hero of the play and empowers him in an act of world-class villainy. The ghost dismisses the former deeds of Catiline as mere recreation compared to the treason he will now attempt. Catiline relishes the role of Vice, imagining Rome pregnant with his monstrous plot. In the first act, the conspirators gather and pledge their faith in a gruesome covenant in which they will drink the blood of a slave whom Catiline has had murdered for this purpose. They interpret portents of a sudden darkness, subterranean groans, a fiery light, and a bloody arm as divine encouragement in their revenge. In the second act we meet Fulvia. As we watch her use sexual charms to win political advantage, we expect a heady mix of titillation and statecraft in the rest of the drama.

But in the third act, Jonson turns to the mode of undramatic language and action in *Sejanus*: that is, to speechmaking and off-stage violence. Cicero takes over the stage, and Catiline flees. And in the final act, though breaking the unity of place to give Catiline's exhortation to his troops, Jonson banishes us to Rome and the Senate before the decisive battle begins. We therefore do not see the apotheosis of Catiline into Mars. We are told that his "count'nance was a ciuill warre it selfe" (V.vi.644); that with each stroke of his sword "fled a life" (V.vi.650); that the Furies circled the battlefield and "trembled" to see men cause more destruction than they were capable of themselves (V.vi.656). And, finally, we are told that, with the army in ruin around him, Catiline

> Collected all his furie, and ran in
> (Arm'd with a glorie, high as his despaire)
> Into our battaile, like a *Lybian* lyon,
> Vpon his hunters, scornefull of our weapons,
> Carelesse of wounds, plucking downe liues about him,
> Till he had circled in himselfe with death:
> Then he fell too, t'embrace it where it lay.
>   (V.vi.670–76)

Playgoers raised on a diet of *Tamburlaine* and *The Battle of Alcazar* might not be troubled by the transformation from conspirator to warrior, but I suspect that they would have wanted to witness this armageddon for themselves.

By choosing the story of *Bonduca,* Beaumont and Fletcher combine the narrative materials of English and Roman history, as Shakespeare did in *Cymbeline;* and, rather than banish the action behind the tiring house doors, they bring onstage the characters and conflicts that establish the moral parallels and polarities of the drama. The battlefield of Britain is both the physical setting of the play and a metaphor for honor. We assume that the war will demonstrate the virtue of the Iceni versus the barbarity of the Romans, but the dramatists have a different kind of balance in mind: the generals of the opposing armies are equally honorable. They contrast not with each other but with the varieties of martial ethics represented by their soldiers. For the British, Caratach is the standard of excellence. In the opening scene, he lectures Bonduca, the Warrior Queen of the Iceni, on the decorum of victory. She has been jeering at the Romans as they run from the field, and he points out that there is no honor in the defeat of a contemptible foe. Twice in the play Caratach has the opportunity to keep Bonduca's daughters from unworthy behavior: first, when they would hang a clownish pack of Roman soldiers caught foraging for food, and second when they would punish some junior Roman officers tricked into putting down their weapons. At a pre-battle Druid ceremony, Bonduca asks the gods for vengeance, but she fears that they are "deafe and drowsie" (III.i.38). Caratach prays for "good hearts, good enemies, / Good blowes o' both sides" (III.i.64–65), and the fires on the altar flame out in blessing. The only one of the Iceni sufficiently noble of heart to succeed Caratach is the boy, Hengo, who is killed by two Roman knaves.

Among the Romans the moral twin of Caratach is Suetonius. Even though the army has suffered one defeat, he remains eager for the fight and delivers a rousing address to the troops before the next battle. Against the standard of his behavior we measure the malingering of Penius, the lovesickness of Junius, the devil-may-care militarism of Petilius, and the vulgarity of Judas and his pack. At the end of the play, Beaumont and Fletcher emphasize the equivalent honor of Suetonius and Caratach, and thus of the Romans and the British, by having the conqueror extend trust and friendship to the conquered. Setting aside the celebration of his own triumph, Suetonius calls on the Roman troops to "March on, and through the Camp in every tongue, / The Vertues of great *Caratach* be sung" (V.iii.202–3).

In *Bonduca* there is a familiar mix of sentiment and violence. Two of the junior Roman soldiers are also—briefly—in love with Bonduca's daughters. Junius loves the younger girl, and he is mercilessly teased about his feelings by Petilius and his cohorts. Vulnerable because of this love, Junius does not suspect a trick when she arranges a secret meeting at which she captures him and humiliates him with teasing of her own. The betrayal cures him, though; he bids farewell to love: "Puffe, there it flies" (III.v.89). Petilius falls in love with the older daughter when he witnesses the bravery of her suicide, and he comes in for a round of teasing from the now-cynical Junius. There are several scenes of pathos between Caratach and Hengo in the wake of the battle that takes up the middle acts of the play. In one, the old general and the boy are hiding from the Romans and expect momentarily to be discovered and killed. Hengo asks: "Wither must we goe when we are dead?" (IV.ii.6). Caratach answers: "Why, to the blessed'st place Boy: ever sweetnesse / And happinesse dwels there" (IV.ii.7–8). With poignant innocence, the boy asks: "No Romans, Uncle?" (IV.ii.10). Juxtaposed with this sentimentality is a series of onstage deaths: Bonduca's younger daughter stabs herself, the older daughter stabs herself, Bonduca drinks poison, Penius falls on his sword, Judas shoots Hengo, and Caratach smashes Judas's head with a rock.

In earlier years, the King's men had acquired some history plays in serial form. If the "Hotspurr" and "Falstafe" plays were parts of the Hal-Falstaff sequence, they revived two plays in a serial-complex in 1612–13, but there is no evidence that they acquired new sets. Yet the practice of writing serials was not obsolete. In the playlists of other companies, we find the four *Ages* plays by Heywood (Queen Anne's men, ca. 1611–13), the two-part *Knaves* (Duke of York's men, 1612–13), and *The Revenge of Bussy D'Ambois* (Children of Whitefriars, 1609–10), as sequel to *Bussy D'Ambois* (Q1607). I suggest that several characteristics of *Bonduca* are clues to the absence of historical serials in the holdings of the King's men. One is the selection of a tragical formula for the plot. At the end of a tragedy, there are few characters left alive with whom to continue the narrative. A second is the distance of the plot from historical fact. Once Beaumont and Fletcher turn the battle of the Iceni and Romans into fiction, they are under no pressure from the historical events to tell the rest of the story. A third is the replacement of psychologically developed characters with moral abstractions. If Caratach and Suetonius display the nature of honor fully by their behavior in *Bonduca,* the dramatists have no reason to explore the complexities of their personalities in a sequel.

One of the plays in the offerings of the King's men at Court in 1612–13—*The Maid's Tragedy*—represents a new form of duplication being developed in the genre of tragedy. This new kind of imitation is a result, I believe, of the stories, dramatic formulas, and method of characterization in the plays of Beaumont and Fletcher and of dramatists influenced by their work. George Buc, albeit unintentionally, identifies this new mode of the serial by assigning the title, "second Maydens tragedy," to the play that he was licensing on Allhallows Eve, 1611.[14] Humphrey Moseley and John Warburton were to interpret Buc's note according to old principles of serialization and consequently to call their copies of the play the second part of *The Maid's Tragedy*. But the Master of the Revels was nearer the mark.

The Second Maiden's Tragedy is not a sequel to *The Maid's Tragedy*, but it is a tragedy about a second maiden who in some sense is a duplicate of the first. Although the Lady does not have the same story as Aspatia, she has the same morality. On this basis she and Aspatia both are sisters of Lucina, the embodiment of chastity in *Valentinian*. The fallen women—Evadne in *The Maid's Tragedy*, the Wife in *The Second Maiden's Tragedy*—are similarly duplicates. The virtuous men—Amintor and Melantius in *The Maid's Tragedy*, Aecius in *Valentinian*, and Govianus in *The Second Maiden's Tragedy*—are for the most part representatives of romantic and military honor. The villains—the king in *The Maid's Tragedy*, Valentinian, the Tyrant in *The Second Maiden's Tragedy*—are lustful and egocentric to the point of madness. Only a few characters—Maximus in *Valentinian*, Votarius in *The Second Maiden's Tragedy*—act with more psychological complexity than puppets. Without a text of *The Twins Tragedy*, I cannot say whether it was similar in style to the three extant texts, but its very title implies patterns of duplication within the structures of the play.

The plots of *The Maid's Tragedy*, *Valentinian*, and *The Second Maiden's Tragedy* show how characterization and action work against the extension of the narrative into a sequel. In *The Maid's Tragedy*, the story turns on the marriage of Amintor, a courtier and soldier, and Evadne, sister of the warriors Melantius and Diphilus. At the request of the King, and out of loyalty to him, Amintor marries Evadne instead of Aspatia, the woman to whom he has been betrothed. Unbeknown to Amintor, the king has arranged the match because he and Evadne are lovers; they intend to hide their lovemaking and any issue thereby behind the respectability of her marriage. Amintor learns about this perverse and cynical plan from Evadne on his wedding night and, out of shock and revulsion, he pretends the next day that all is well. However, he tells the truth to Melantius, who swears revenge. When Melantius confronts Evadne, she repents, and takes revenge on the King herself. Aspatia, meanwhile, plans to die and to make Amintor strike the fatal blow. She dresses in male clothing and, claiming to be her brother, fights with Amintor, who wounds her. At this moment, Evadne enters, holding a knife covered with the King's blood; she confesses all, and stabs herself. Aspatia reveals her identity and dies. Amintor kills himself. Melantius vows "never [to] eate / Or drinke, or sleepe, or have to doe with that / That may preserve life" (V.iii.288–90). Except for a few walk-ons, the only characters that these actions leave alive are the King's brother, the second of Evadne's brothers, and Aspatia's father.

In *Valentinian*, Lucina, wife of the warrior Maximus, is hounded by bawds to become the emperor's lover. After she refuses repeatedly, Valentinian tricks her into entering his bedchamber, claiming that it is her husband who sends for her. She answers the summons, but when she realizes the fraud, she refuses him again. Therefore, he rapes her. She returns to Maximus, tells him what has happened, and kills herself. On another track of the plot, there is trouble among the soldiers, many of whom are near mutiny in outrage over the prodigal behavior of Valentinian and his neglect of the wars. Aecius, a general with a fierce sense of loyalty to the idea of emperor (and hence undeservedly to this corrupt embodiment of that idea) ironically becomes Valentinian's means of punishing the army. Valentinian suborns a recently cashiered soldier, Pontius, to murder Aecius, but Pontius is so moved by Aecius's courage that he kills himself instead. Aecius in turn is so moved by Pontius's courage that *he* kills *him*self. Now, with the double motivation of Lucina's and Aecius's deaths, Maximus vows to kill Valentinian and then commit suicide. Two soldiers kill the emperor first, however. Maximus rejoices and declares himself revenged. He marries Valentinian's widow, Eudoxa, and tells her that he has engineered all of the preceding events. She believes him (or she says she does), and at the celebration of his election as the new emperor, she poisons him. With the cast of *Valentinian* thus decimated, the few Romans left alive plaintively begin the search for a successor: "*Rome* yet has many noble heires" (V.viii.117).

In *The Second Maiden's Tragedy,* the Tyrant usurps the throne of Govianus, as much to possess the Lady, Govianus's beloved, as to acquire political power. However, the Lady refuses the Tyrant, and she goes into house arrest with Govianus. The Tyrant sends panderers (one of whom is her father) to tempt her to his bed, but she commits suicide rather than be ravished (Govianus would kill her, but he faints as he runs at her and she has to do the deed herself). Undeterred in his desire to have her by the mere fact of her death, the Tyrant steals her body from the tomb, takes it back to Court, and commences his wooing. In a second plot, Anselmus (Govianus's brother) suspects his honest wife of being unfaithful. To test her, he persuades his friend, Votarius, to seduce her. The test backfires when Votarius succeeds. Anselmus learns of the adultery from his wife's maid, who has been encouraged in this betrayal of her mistress by her villainous lover, Bellarius. To throw Anselmus off the track, the Wife and Votarius stage a scene in which he will woo her and she will refuse. But they are double-crossed by the servants, and everyone is killed. Back in the main story, Govianus, disguised as an artist, comes to Court to rescue the Lady's corpse. He paints the Lady's face with poison; the Tyrant kisses her, and dies. Govianus thus regains his throne, but his queen and many of his subjects are dead.

In addition to their similarity in characterization and whole-sale deaths, these tragedies are alike in using revenge as a basis of action. In all three, the impetus for revenge is a sexual crime: adultery, rape, attempted seduction that results in suicide. But despite the flagrance of the crimes, the revengers do not express their motivation clearly. From the perspective of the traditional revenge play, we therefore find it difficult to consider them heroic. In *The Maid's Tragedy,* for example, Melantius declares revenge against the King, but since Evadne has willingly been the King's lover, we cannot be sure whether Melantius defends his sister's honor or his own. Bellarius in *The Second Maiden's Tragedy* never shares with the audience the reason for his hatred of Votarius; he simply exults that he is given the opportunity for "revenge and mischief" (I.ii.328). Maximus has a clear motive for vengeance; and, given the dramatic tradition, his action would be noble, for Valentinian has indeed raped Lucina, Maximus's wife. However, the dramatists give Maximus a peculiar kind of delay; although he knows the crime that has been committed and the perpetrator of the crime, he is too confused to act: "I know not / What to determine certaine, I am so troubled" (III.iii.69–70). He thinks at first that he will retaliate by raping Valentinian's wife. Then he thinks that Lucina may have contrived the crime in order to promote his career. Then he thinks that he should kill Aecius to hide the shame of Lucina's rape and suicide from the world. In traditional terms, this confusion is equal to the heroic revenger's madness, but the dramatists cloud the question of Maximus's nobility further by preventing him from killing Valentinian. Furthermore, they deviate from conventional endings by allowing Maximus to forget about suicide altogether and opt for a career in politics.

The emphasis on sexual crime and the questionable motives of the revengers are reminiscent of the revenge tragedies staged by the King's men after 1600. Veteran playgoers would perhaps have recognized characterizations, language, and dramaturgy from the old plays. Maximus is a reminder of Hamlet, both in his delays and in his self-criticism. Govianus, in imitation of Vindice, tricks the would-be ravisher of his beloved into kissing the poisoned face of her corpse. Commentators point out the similarity between the kings in *The Maid's Tragedy* and *Hamlet*,[15] and there is also a parallel between the jilted maidens. The behavior of Aspatia on her abandonment recalls the suicide of Ophelia:

> when she [Aspatia] sees a bancke
> Stucke full of flowers, she with a sign will tell
> Her servants, what a prittie place it were
> To burie lovers in, and make her maides
> Pluck'em, and strow her over like a corse.

She carries with her an infectious griefe,
That strikes all her beholders, she will sing
The mournfulst things that ever eare hath heard. . . .
(I.i.89–96)

She sings one of those sad songs on Evadne's wedding night. The
words of her stage exit—"Ladies farewell" (II.i.100) and "You'le
come my Lord and see the virgins weepe, / When I am laid in
earth" (II.i.117–18)—recall the mad speeches of Ophelia. Playgoers
of 1612–13, or those who had seen *The Maid's Tragedy* during its
opening run in 1610–11 and *Othello* either at its debut in 1604–05
or revival in 1609–11, might have seen a parallel in staging between
Evadne's revenge against the king and Othello's revenge against
Desdemona. In both plays, the revengers discover their victims in
bed asleep. In both, the victims awaken with the expectation of
lovemaking. The King, finding that Evadne has tied his arms to the
bed, interprets the action as an erotic stratagem, and he teases her
playfully: "Ile be thy *Mars*, to bed my Queene of love, / Let us be
caught together, that the gods may see, / And envie our embraces"
(V.i.50–52). Although Evadne knows that her lover has caused her
ruin, she uses Desdemona's words to excuse him: "Die all our faults
together, I forgive thee" (V.i.112).

Fulfilling playgoers' expectations of revenge plays, these
tragedies are sensational theater. In *The Maid's Tragedy* and
Valentinian, Beaumont and Fletcher exploit a tension peculiar to
drama with protracted scenes of wooing and dying. They pervert
the conventional activities of weddings and banquets to heighten
the feeling of the stage moment. In *The Maid's Tragedy*, for example, the groom's jilted sweetheart decks the bridal bed, singing of
her own death; the bride refuses to lie with the groom; the next
morning, the bride's lover teases the groom about the sexual
prowess of husbands. In *Valentinian*, musicians sing an elegiac lul-
laby to the emperor while he dies; orators and singers who perform
at the banquet celebrating the election of Maximus are unaware
that he drinks a poisoned toast. In *The Second Maiden's Tragedy*,
the secondary plot ends in a play-within-a-play that is more lethal
than the masques at the end of *The Revenger's Tragedy:* the Wife

mistakenly kills Votarius with a sword that she does not know is poisoned; Anselmus stabs the maid for the wrong treachery; the maid's lover then fights Anselmus; the Wife, in despair, kills herself by running between their swords; and the two men kill each other. The main plot turns into a horror show. The Tyrant plays the role of grave robber and necrophiliac. The Lady takes the double part of ghost and corpse. At the tomb, the ghost suddenly appears dressed in white, with jewels, and a crucifix *"in a kind of noise like a wind, the doors clattering, the tombstone flies open, and a great light appears in the midst of the tomb"* (IV.iv.42–43 [s.d.]). At Court, the corpse appears propped up in a chair and dressed in black velvet, with pearls and a crucifix. The ghost, after a costume change to matching black velvet, joins the corpse on stage to witness the Tyrant's death. The ghost attends the corpse, now crowned queen, in a procession back to the tomb.

When proponents of the argument for a select repertory at Blackfriars raise the issue of a new style of drama in the offerings of the King's men, they have in mind primarily the tragicomedies of Beaumont and Fletcher, which are represented in the Court offerings in 1612–13 by a revival of *Philaster* and the maiden run of *Cardenio*. During an apprenticeship with boys' companies, Beaumont and Fletcher had worked on plays separately and collaboratively. Beaumont had written *The Knight of the Burning Pestle*, which he was to call an "unfortunate child" in the dedicatory letter with the quarto in 1613, and which he was to excuse in its unpopularity by blaming audiences for "not understanding the privy marke of *Ironie* about it" (*B&F*, I, 7). Fletcher had written *The Faithful Shepherdess*, which he was to call unpopular in an epistle to readers of the first quarto, and which he excused by blaming the audiences for expecting a pastoral with "country hired Shepheards, . . . whitsun ales, creame, wassel and morris-dances" (*B&F*, III, 497). But the dramatists also had had successes: *The Woman Hater* (primarily Beaumont's) and *Cupid's Revenge*.[16] Out of this apprenticeship, they developed the formula of tragicomedy that, supposedly, made them the hottest dramatists in London.

By the term, though, they did not mean the combination of

tragic and comic plots into a single dramatic design, which is what Sir Philip Sidney called a "mungrell" form in "An Apologie for Poetrie." At about the time that the King's men were introducing *Philaster* to London audiences, Fletcher defined the genre for readers of *The Faithful Shepherdess:* "A tragie-comedie is not so called in respect of mirth and killing, but in respect it wants deaths, which is inough to make it no tragedie, yet brings some neere it, which is inough to make it no comedie" (*B&F*, III, 497). The innovation of this style of comedy, therefore, is the creation of a new dimension of theatrical sensibility that exploited the structures and emotional responses of comedy and tragedy but that was "perfectly neyther" (Prologue, *The Woman Hater* [*B&F*, I, 157]).

All the same, for audiences raised on Elizabethan comedies, there were several familiar characterizations in *Philaster*. Like many a comedic heroine, the princess Arethusa takes the initiative in bringing the love story to a happy ending. When her father betroths her to a foreign prince, she summons Philaster, the rightful heir to the kingdom, and declares her love to him. She remains loyal to him, even though he accuses her of infidelity. One initiative often taken by the aggressive female is to disguise herself and follow her lover. Here, this role is given to Euphrasia, a young noblewoman, who disguises herself as a page named Bellario in order to be near Philaster. Unaware, of course, of the disguise, Philaster sends the page to Arethusa as go-between. Soon Philaster will be told that the princess has taken Bellario as lover, and he will believe it. A familiar clown character is the braggart soldier, represented here by a rebel captain whose spate of epithets and deadpan consideration of his prisoner's dismemberment remind us of Falstaff, Dogberry, and Tucca.

In addition, the play is a pastoral. Philaster, driven mad by his disappointment in love, flees from Arethusa and the Court to find a cave in the wilderness, where he imagines taking

some mountaine girl,
Beaten with winds, chaste as the hardned rocks
Whereon she dwells, that might have strewed my bed
With leaves, and reedes, and with the skins of beasts

Our neighbors: And have borne at her big breasts
My large course issue.
(IV.iii.7–12)

By this choice of settings, Beaumont and Fletcher associate
Philaster with the love story of *Cardenio*. A darker version of the
mad pastoral lover is Bremo, the wild man in *Mucedorus*. As we
now know, this play was revived by the King's men around
1605–06, which is about the time that Beaumont and Fletcher
began to write for the boys' companies. It was revived again in the
maiden year of *Philaster*. If the primitive pastoralism of *Philaster*
and *Mucedorus* was new to some playgoers in 1609–10, it did not
remain so. *Cymbeline* appeared in that year. *The Tempest* appeared
in 1611–12, and it was continued into 1612–13, when *Philaster* was
revived.

Apparently, the feature of tragicomedy that was expected to
take audiences most by surprise was a flirtation with death. Before
Philaster runs from Court to seek a hermit's cave, he has opportu-
nities to kill someone, including himself. In the first, he confronts
Bellario with the charge of a liason with Arethusa, and the boy
begs to be killed rather than to be believed false. In the second,
Philaster confronts Arethusa with her betrayal, but he is too faint
with anguish to do her or himself harm. In the woods, he has
another opportunity, and he is nearly successful. He comes across
Arethusa and orders her to kill him to prevent his revenge against
her. She talks him into killing her instead. But as he positions his
sword, a country fellow wanders by and, sensibly, tries to stop the
execution. Nonetheless, Philaster manages to stab Arethusa, and he
is stabbed himself in a struggle with the country fellow. Faint with
loss of blood, Philaster runs away. He stumbles across Bellario,
whom he stabs and frames as the princess's attacker. The Court
hunting party rescues all of the wounded characters before they
bleed to death. Although Philaster is taken to prison to await execution, we sense the likelihood of a comedic resolution when
Arethusa and Bellario visit Philaster in prison and he begs their forgiveness. However, the dramatists continue to jeopardize the ending by having two characters threatened with torture. As a result of

these dangers, Philaster shows that he can govern and Bellario reveals that she is a girl.

Two tragicomedies new in the offerings of 1611–12 and continued into 1612–13 to be shown again at Court were *The Nobleman* by Cyril Tourneur and *A King and No King* by Beaumont and Fletcher. The text of Tourneur's play is lost, and therefore its generic properties are beyond reach. However, the alternate title recorded in Moseley's entry in the Stationers' Register—"The Great man"—is a reinforcement of the hint in the main title that the protagonist was a duplicate of such potentially heroic and thus potentially tragic noble men as Maximus, Caratach, Suetonius, and Othello. If the play was indeed a tragicomedy, as its initial entry in the Stationers' Register claims, and if it used the new style according to Beaumont and Fletcher's formulation, *The Nobleman* may have shared at least one feature with *A King and No King*: the use of a great man as the hero in a comedy. Fletcher hints at the appropriation of noblemen as protagonists in his justification of *The Faithful Shepherdess* as a proper pastoral. He points out that shepherds in classical and neo-classical pastorals are "the owners of flockes and not hyerlings" (*B&F*, III, 497). He seems also to be hinting at the greatness of protagonists by explaining that the tragicomedy "must be a representation of familiar people, with such kinde of trouble as no life be questiond, so that a God is as lawful in this as in a tragedy, and meane people as in a comedie" (*B&F*, III, 497). The mention of a god here implies the location of the play in the world of courtiers and kings, whose actions are sufficiently significant to cosmic stability to approach the level of tragedy.[17]

Certainly in *A King and No King* Beaumont and Fletcher present the hero, King Arbaces of Iberia, in contexts that emphasize his greatness—but with that greatness, his vulnerability to a tragic hubris. When we first meet him, he is champion of the battlefield, and he triumphs in declamations worthy of Tamburlaine:

> Where lies that foot of ground
> Within [this] whole Realme, that I have not past
> Fighting, and Conquering? . . . I could tell the World

> How I have laid [this] Kingdome desolate
> With this sole arme, propt by Divinity. . . .
> (I.i.121–26)

He has defeated King Tigranes of Armenia in single combat, with such style as is "Fit for a God to doe upon his foe" (I.i.138). As a gesture of his high-mindedness, he plans to free the captive king after matching him in marriage with Panthea, his sister, who "deserves the Empire of the world" (I.i.161).

In *Philaster*, the rhetoric of the genre provides a mixture of signals: for example, the tragic political displacement of Philaster along with the comedic characterization of Arethusa and the pastoral setting. In *A King and No King* the rhetoric operates differently. We receive signal after signal of impending tragedy. Arbaces is quick-tempered. His mother conspires against him. Spaconia, disguised as Panthea's maid, follows Tigranes to Iberia. Arbaces and Tigranes both fall in love with Panthea at first sight. To the danger of cross-wooings, therefore, there is added the taboo of incest. Arbaces knows that his love is forbidden, but he would still ask Panthea "Lasciviouslie, leudlie, incestuouslie, / To doe a sinne that needs must damne [them] both" (III.iii.77–78). If the tragedy is to be averted, Arbaces must control himself and Panthea must deny him. However, she encourages him to kiss her, and she confesses a responding passion: "I feele a sinne growing upon my bloud, / Worse then all these, hotter I feare then yours" (IV.iv.159–60). Soon Arbaces breaks down:

> It is resolv'd, I bore it whilst I could,
> I can no more, Hell open all thy gates,
> And I will thorough them; . . . I must beginne
> With murder of my friend, and so goe on
> To an incestuous ravishing, and end
>
> My life and sinnes with a forbidden blow
> Upon my selfe.
> (V.iv.1–11)

A comedic resolution seems impossible. However, the dramatists have withheld information. The truth about the birth of Arbaces pulls the lovers back from the precipice of tragedy. It seems that the Queen, fearing that the king was too old to beget an heir, feigned pregnancy and pretended that the child of Gobrius was her newborn son. Six years later, she did bear the king a daughter. Arbaces is neither king nor brother, and he and Panthea are free to marry. The rest of the plot falls into place along traditional comedic lines: Tigranes and Spaconia are reunited, and the nuptial pairs go off stage together thankfully and joyfully.

As proponents of a double repertory have believed, the purchase of *Philaster* in 1609 was indeed a significant act by the King's men; but rather than showing a development of two systems of play selection, I suggest that it shows an expansion within the existing system to accommodate the three stages where they would henceforth routinely perform: at the Globe, at Blackfriars, and at Court. In the plays named in the Chamber Accounts for 1612–13, we see the criteria that a large selection of plays was expected to meet. In the purchase of a single play—*Philaster*—we see market value in the offerings from another perspective. *Philaster* was well enough known in its first year of composition to prompt an allusion in non-dramatic literature, specifically Epigram #206 by John Davies of Hereford. It was revived within three years of the maiden run. It was playable on each of the stages where the company regularly performed. Perhaps because of its popularity, the King's men found a new audience for old plays such as *Mucedorus*. If it did not beget a *Philaster II* or a *Euphrasia and Pharamond*, it may nonetheless have shown dramatists that there was a demand for plays with narratives like that of Cardenio's love story.

In June of 1613, the King's men suffered consecutive blows to their fortunes that might have destroyed a company with less experience, expertise, financial structure, and secure patronage. These were the retirement of William Shakespeare and the burning of the Globe. The fire occurred on 29 June during a performance of *Henry VIII* because of a bit of tamping, which was fired during the production from a piece of ordnance and which flew to the roof and lit the thatching. In less than two hours, the fire destroyed the building to the foundations. No one was seriously hurt, though "a few forsaken cloaks" were lost along with the breeches of a man who had the "provident wit" to douse the sparks on his clothing "with bottle ale."[18] For the King's men, however, there were losses in properties and apparel, and irreplaceable losses in playbooks. In the years to come, when the company managers looked through back stock for revivals, they were limited to those with books, actors' parts, and/or Plots that had survived the fire and to those recoverable by way of the memories of veteran players. There were to be no more new scripts from Shakespeare, but luckily nearly all of his playbooks survived the fire, as we know from the manuscripts available to Heminges and Condell in 1623. In the face of these setbacks, though, the King's men retained a powerful ally: that is, a strategy for marketing plays that had served them well for nearly twenty years and had proved itself adaptable to fluctuations in play-goers' tastes and the vicissitudes of competition from other companies. Looking ahead to the fall of 1613–14, with plans already underway to rebuild the Globe and perhaps with *Two Noble Kinsmen* and *The Duchess of Malfi* already in rehearsal, the King's men had reason to be optimistic about their economic future.

CONCLUSION

In the foregoing discussion of repertory practices, I have treated the offerings of the Chamberlain's and King's men in each year without much attention to the contribution of individual dramatists to the success of the company. As coda to this discussion, I would like to address commercial dimensions of the plays by the dramatist who joined the company in 1594 as a player and subsequently became an investor in the Globe and Blackfriars—William Shakespeare. Scholars readily grant Shakespeare preeminence among the company's dramatists because of the quality of his plays. I suggest that we may establish that preeminence tangibly by assessing his plays in terms of the strategy employed by his company for marketing the repertory year after year.

To begin, Shakespeare supplied the company with new plays. When he first joined the Chamberlain's men, he was writing three plays on the average per year. Given that about half of the company's offerings were new (thirty-eight new plays out of seventy-four offerings for the Admiral's men, 1594–1596), he was therefore providing from 15 to 20 percent of the new plays. In addition, in 1594 or soon thereafter, the Chamberlain's men acquired at least six plays by Shakespeare that were new to them, although not new to the stage. Two of these had been staged in London: *1 Henry VI*, in 1592–93, by Strange's men; and *Titus Andronicus*, in 1594, by Sussex's men. However, this prior history did not lower the commercial value of the plays when revived. The Admiral's men were in a similar position in 1594 with the acquisition of the two parts of *Tamburlaine*, which had been played in London (according to the title-page of the second quarto) and which had even been published twice (1590, 1593). Yet the company was able to pay Henslowe excellent receipts of 71s. and 46s. at the opening shows of each play (28 August, 19 December 1594) and an average of 31s. and 40s. in receipts through June 1595. The remaining four of

Shakespeare's secondhand texts—*2 Henry VI, 3 Henry VI, The Taming of the Shrew,* and *Richard III*—apparently had not been performed in London by June 1594. A measure of their value is the run of *Doctor Faustus* at the Rose, starting in the fall of 1594. Although not new, *Doctor Faustus* apparently had not been on stage in London before 30 September. At its opening show, the Admiral's men handed over to Henslowe receipts comparable to those of new plays (72s.). The play earned an average of 31s. per performance for Henslowe in 1594–95, and the Admiral's men kept it in production into 1597–98.

After 1603 Shakespeare did not maintain the pace of writing that he had set in 1594, but he supplied plays to the offerings as continuations and revivals (as he had also in previous years). In 1604–05, for example, in a year when *Othello* and *Measure for Measure* were new, at least five of his old works were also in production: *The Merry Wives of Windsor, The Comedy of Errors, Love's Labor's Lost, Henry V,* and *The Merchant of Venice.* In 1610–11, when *The Winter's Tale* was new, *Cymbeline* and *Othello* were continued from 1609–10 and his *Macbeth* was being revived. In 1611–12, he supplied *The Tempest* to the new offerings and *The Winter's Tale* to the continuations. In 1612–13, he supplied *Cardenio* for the new offerings in the winter and *Henry VIII* in early summer. In addition, he supplied *The Tempest* and *The Winter's Tale* to the continuations; and *Othello, Much Ado about Nothing,* and *Julius Caesar* to the revivals, as well as (apparently) *1 Henry IV* and *The Merry Wives of Windsor.* A bonus from the viewpoint of finances was that the plays did not cost much to revive—at least, they should not have. The company would have paid for the playbook when it was new (or so I assume), and Shakespeare seems not to have revised the texts so substantially that the company had to pay a large sum either for the new parts or for properties and apparel necessitated by the new parts. Therefore, except for rehearsal time, the company could have revived one of Shakespeare's plays virtually for nothing. In some cases even the rehearsal time might have been negligible. When supporters of the earl of Essex asked the Chamberlain's men to perform *Richard II,* they did so with just a day or two's notice.

From 1597 on, many of Shakespeare's plays were printed with the name of the company on the title-page of the quarto. We have believed that the Chamberlain's and King's men guarded their texts against publication, but they would have received free publicity from each new edition all the same. For *Richard III* (as one example), the company benefited from title-page advertisements in 1597, 1598, 1602, 1605, 1612, and 1622. In addition, these advertisements could have generated an interest in the plays during a subsequent revival. Because of the quarto in 1597 with the name of lord Hunsdon's men on the title-page, a customer of the bookseller could have become a customer of the playhouse at the apparent revival of *Romeo and Juliet* at the Curtain in 1597–98. Similarly, because quartos with title-pages carrying the name of the company were printed before *The Merry Wives of Windsor* and *Henry V* were revived in 1604–05 and before the former play (this time as "Falstafe") and *Much Ado about Nothing* were revived in 1612–13, the King's men could have attracted a customer who had read the text but not seen a production. The year 1600 was one of expansion and tension in the playhouse industry. Although the Privy Council ordered in June that the number of playhouses be limited to two (the Fortune and Globe), there were in addition men's companies at the Rose, Boar's Head, and Curtain at some time during the year, as well as boys' companies at St. Paul's and Blackfriars. The Chamberlain's men may therefore have welcomed the publicity provided by the appearance of nine of their plays in quarto, even though not all carried title-page advertisements of the company. Eight of these were by Shakespeare, and six of the Shakespearean quartos named the Chamberlain's men on the title-page: *Titus Andronicus, Henry V, 2 Henry IV, Much Ado about Nothing, A Midsummer Night's Dream,* and *The Merchant of Venice.*

Accounts from the Offices of the Revels and Chamber suggest that Shakespeare's plays were usually a substantial part of the company's presence at Court. Perhaps in ways we have not fully appreciated, companies represented their patrons by these performances.[1] While the servants first of Henry Carey and then of his son George,

Shakespeare's company was an advertisement of the person and office of Lord Chamberlain; and, by their excellence, the players enabled him to entertain the Queen during the winter holidays. Even for the one year that their patron was not the Lord Chamberlain (1596–97), lord Cobham (who was) had the former Chamberlain's men to Court—and only them, in fact.[2] After May 1603, the King's men were performing at Court for their own patron, and their excellence was a representation of his household. The three accounts from the Offices of the Revels and Chamber that give the names of plays performed at Court show that Shakespeare's plays were a prominent part in the offerings of the King's men. In 1604–05, out of eleven performances, eight were of his work. In 1611–12, out of five performances (excluding those with Queen Anne's men), two were of his. In 1612–13, out of twenty performances, nine were of his.

In addition to providing the company with new and old plays in the number needed by the Elizabethan repertory system, Shakespeare supplied the kinds of plays that audiences liked, with stories that they liked, in dramatic formulas that they liked. In the first three years of his membership in the Chamberlain's men, he wrote seven plays based on stories in the British chronicles (counting those of his that migrated to the company). Some of these plays were the duplicates in subject matter of drama in the stock of other companies, both among their old and new plays. It is therefore possible that a play of his was in production at about the time that a play similar in narrative and owned by another company was being produced at another London playhouse. A rather far-fetched but possible instance of duplicate plays sharing the same market involves *Richard III* and *Richard Crookback*. Shakespeare's company revived *Richard III* long before 1602, if the title-page of the quarto in 1597 is accurate, and therefore long before the debut at the Fortune of Ben Jonson's *Richard Crookback* around June in 1602. Yet *Richard III* was reprinted in 1602, which is the same year that Manningham heard an anecdote about Burbage in the role of Richard III; and if it had recently been revived, it could have been on stage at a time near the production of Jonson's version of

Richard III's story by the Admiral's men. A much more plausible instance is one I have suggested previously: the revival of *The Troublesome Reign of King John* by the Queen's men at the Swan in 1595–96, followed by a run of *King John* by the Chamberlain's men in 1596–97.

If the Queen's men were indeed at the Swan in 1595–96, and if they still owned some of that company's old texts, and if they revived some of these for the stint at Francis Langley's new playhouse, I can imagine the involvement of a play by Shakespeare in an even more complicated sequence of plays with overlapping story materials: *The Famous Victories of Henry V,* staged by the Queen's men at the Swan in the fall of 1595–96; *Henry V,* staged by the Admiral's men at the Rose in the winter and spring of 1595–96; and *1 Henry IV,* staged by the Chamberlain's men in the fall of 1596–97. Even if the Queen's men and *The Famous Victories of Henry V* were not a factor in offerings at London playhouses just before the debut of *1 Henry IV,* the Admiral's men and their play were.

After his first few years with the company, Shakespeare continued to choose historical matter that appealed to playgoers. *Julius Caesar, Antony and Cleopatra, Coriolanus,* and *Timon of Athens* benefit from the popularity of Roman history plays generally, as reflected in such offerings in the repertory of the Admiral's men as the two-part *Caesar and Pompey* (1594–95), the *Tragedy of Phocas* (1595–96), and *Jugurtha* (1599–1600). Around 1600, several companies began to offer plays on Tudor history. *Henry VIII,* a late addition to this group, shares characters with the Chamberlain's own *Thomas Lord Cromwell* in 1600–01 (Cromwell, Gardiner), the two-part *Wolsey* owned by the Admiral's men in 1601–02 (Wolsey, at least), the two-part *If You Know Not Me, You Know Nobody* owned by the Queen Anne's men in 1604–05 (Queen Elizabeth), and *When You See Me, You Know Me* owned by the Prince's men in 1604–05 (Henry VIII).

In most years the Admiral's men offered plays on stories from the history of ancient Britain: for example, *Cutlack* in 1594–95, *Valteger* in 1596–97 and 1601–02, the two-part *Brute* in 1598–99, and *Malcolm King of Scots* in 1601–02. The Chamberlain's and King's men may have followed suit, but Shakespeare himself was not the supplier until 1605–06, when he wrote *Macbeth* and *King Lear*. As it happens, the old play of *King Leir*, which the Queen's men had played with Sussex's men at the Rose in April 1594 and which had been registered at Stationers' Hall in May of that year, was registered again in May 1605 and printed with a claim on the title-page that the play had "been diuers and sundry times lately acted" (the language of the entry in the Stationers' Register implies a recent run also). W. W. Greg was unable to believe that *King Leir* had been revived in 1604–05 (for it was old even in 1594), and G. M. Pinciss believes that Shakespeare had been with the Queen's men ca. 1590 and remembered the narrative from performances by that company at that time.[3] But what if the title-page information is correct? In that case, the King's men performed *King Lear* at the Globe within a year of a run of *King Leir* at another playhouse.[4] If the title-page information is wrong, or obsolete, *King Lear* nonetheless shared the market for the story with the publisher and bookseller of *King Leir*.

All but one of the English chronicle plays written by Shakespeare and acquired by the Chamberlain's men through 1599–1600 were part of a serial: the three-part *Henry VI*, plus *Richard III;* and the two-part *Henry IV*, followed by *Henry V*. In the chronological sense that the tragedy of Richard II sets up the rise of Henry IV and the triumph of Henry V, *Richard II* is part one of the latter serial.

But perhaps we may appreciate more fully the commercial value to the Chamberlain's men of a play on King Richard and of serials generally by placing *Richard II* in the context of drama roughly contemporary with it but not owned by the Chamberlain's men (as far as we know).[5] The first of these is *Jack Straw*, which was registered at Stationers' Hall on 23 October 1593 and printed in 1594. In the text that has come down to us, the play is very short; it focuses on an early incident in the reign, the rebellion of Wat Tyler, in which Jack Straw, a fellow rebel, is stabbed by the mayor of London. Except for the implication that the boy-king is not fully in control, the play treats Richard respectfully, giving him a scene at the end in which he pardons the rebels. The second of these is *Woodstock*, putatively 1592–95, which treats incidents that followed on Tyler's rebellion: Richard frees himself of the Protectorate, his favorites maneuver for the titles and influence of the old barons, and Thomas of Woodstock is killed. In *Woodstock*, Richard is not a heroic character. He misuses the power of the monarchy to promote unworthy men, and he condones the murder of "plain Thomas." *Richard II*, which picks up the narrative after this point, is a third and final part to the story. Yet in the depiction of the character of Richard, it is more closely akin to *Edward II*, which was registered at Stationers' Hall in July 1593 and printed in 1594 with the name of Pembroke's men on the title-page of the quarto.[6] In Marlowe's play, there is the tragical pattern of the weak king who chooses the love of a favorite over the administration of the kingdom. For the Chamberlain's men, therefore, *Richard II* came in the wake of the narrative antecedents of *Jack Straw* and *Woodstock*, and the generic antecedent of *Edward II*. Then, within their own offerings, it looked forward to the maturation of the madcap prince into the successful warrior at Agincourt. In 1611, the King's men acquired still another play on the subject of Richard II. This text circled back to the narratives of *Jack Straw* and *Woodstock* in that it treated events early in the reign; as such it served as a forepiece to Shakespeare's *Richard II, 1 Henry IV, 2 Henry IV*, and *Henry V*.

In 1594–1597, in addition to providing the Chamberlain's men with seven histories on popular subjects, many of which were in serial form, Shakespeare supplied seven romantic comedies and one romantic tragedy (again, counting the migrant texts). These plays offer surface differences in the guise of pastoralism, Lylian courtliness, folk stereotypes, medieval Italianate settings, and Plautine mistaken identities, but basically they are love stories. As such, they were both familiar and pleasing to audiences. Among these plays, Shakespeare supplied a comedy that was a duplicate in some sense of *The Taming of a Shrew*, printed in 1594 with a title-page advertisement of Pembroke's men. He also supplied an experimental two-part comedy. I take the ending of *Love's Labor's Lost* to be a signal to playgoers to suspend expectations of a close until the sequel. The four pairings of lovers and even the news of the King's death at the ending of *Love's Labor's Lost* are thus a prelude to the successful wooings of *Love's Labor's Won*. Berowne complains that a wait of twelve months is "too long for a play" (V.i.878), but if Shakespeare had planned the comedy in two plays from the start, the Chamberlain's men could have had the concluding part on stage in a few months. And if the two parts were scheduled consecutively (as sequels often were at the Rose), playgoers would not have had to wait but a day for Love's labors to be won.

In subsequent years, Shakespeare continued to use old comedic formulas as media to accommodate newly popular subject matter and dramatic styles. For example, by associating Duke Senior and his men in *As You Like It* with "old Robin Hood of England" (I.i.116) and Duke Senior's forest with the "golden world" (I.i.118–19), he gestures toward the plays in 1598–1601 that featured the folk wisdom, courtship, downfall, and death of Robin Hood (*Robin Hood's Pennyworths*, *The Downfall of Robert Earl of Huntington*, *The Death of Robert Earl of Huntington*), the funeral of Richard the Lionhearted (*The Funeral of Richard Coeur de Lion*), and the friendship of Robin with such popular characters as a hearty country yeoman (*George a Greene*, Q1599) and a sly boots named Skinke (*Look about You*). In *Twelfth Night*, Shakespeare takes over the satire of personalities in the humors comedies to set off the romanticism of Orsino, the foolishness of Aguecheek, and the vanity of Malvolio, casting all of this up in the familiar narrative structure of the pastoral romance. In *Pericles*, *Cymbeline*, *The Winter's Tale*, *The Tempest*, and *Cardenio*, he updates that structure to complement criteria of a new form, the tragicomedy. We realize the degree to which the genre is plot-driven—and Shakespeare's tragicomedies likewise—by the entry in 1611 that Simon Forman wrote on *Cymbeline* in the part of his diary he called *Bocke of Plaies*. In the attempt to summarize the narrative, Forman disentangles some of the story lines, telling of Cloten's death at the hands of the supposed outlaws before he tells of Iachimo's intrusion into Imogen's bedchamber, but he breaks off the entry at the point where Imogen "was found by Lucius, &c" (*WS*, II, 337). He does not go on to relate any of this matter to the theme of his play-entries, i.e., "Notes hereof & formans for Common pollicie" (that is, how to survive among powerful but fickle men). As audiences may readily appreciate, he seems exhausted simply by the effort of following the turns of the plot.

One of the plays that Shakespeare wrote for the Chamberlain's men—*All's Well That Ends Well*—has been labeled a failure, largely because critics dislike the conventions of the dramatic formula that Shakespeare took as model.[7] These critics assert that the play "in all likelihood . . . [was] given few performances,"[8] and they bolster the assertion by reminding us that the play was not printed in its own time, it was not revived in its own time, and it did not generate allusions to itself in the literature of its own time. However, this kind of evidence could as easily be lost as nonexistent. But even if the play was not printed, revived, or alluded to, these bases of evaluation are not the measures of commercial success used by Shakespeare's company and its competitors. From the weekly schedules in *Henslowe's Diary* we see that a play with some six to a dozen performances, which is just a "few" by modern standards, was a profitable offering. Companies often revived plays with a history of good receipts, but they did not invariably do so. Certainly publication and contemporary references were not criteria developed by the companies. And if they should be ours, we will have to believe, on the basis of printing, that such plays as *1 Henry VI*, *The Comedy of Errors*, *The Wise Man of West Chester*, the two-part *Hercules*, the two-part *Tamar Cham*, *Antony and Cleopatra*, *The Winter's Tale*, and *The Tempest* were failures; and on the basis of allusions, that most of the plays seen by thousands of playgoers on stages all over London for dozens of years were failures also.

There is another measure of popularity in terms of the commercial strategy of the Elizabethan companies, and in regard to this criterion, Shakespeare's play holds its own: namely, the participation in a new dramatic formula. *All's Well That Ends Well* is a comedy in the formula of domestic relations, preceded by or contemporaneous with such members as *Patient Grissil* (Admiral's men, 1599–1600), *The Golden Ass & Cupid and Psyche* (Admiral's men, 1599–1600), the two-part *Fair Constance of Rome* (Admiral's men, 1600–01), *How a Man May Choose a Good Wife from a Bad* (Worcester's men, 1600–02), *A Woman Killed with Kindness* (Worcester's men, 1602–03), *The Wise Woman of Hogsden* (Worcester's men, 1603–05), and the two-part *Honest Whore [and Patient Man]* (Prince's men, 1604–06). Even more telling of popularity, I believe, is the number of plays that Shakespeare's company staged in this formula in the wake of *All's Well That Ends Well*: *The Fair Maid of Bristow*, 1603–04; *The London Prodigal*, 1603–04; *A Yorkshire Tragedy*, 1605–06; and *The Miseries of Enforced Marriage*, 1606–07. The fact that the King's men acquired these plays after they had staged *All's Well That Ends Well* does not mean that Shakespeare's play was unsuccessful; rather, it means that playgoers continued to have an appetite for this kind of drama that the King's men fed with new offerings.

There are numerous parallels between *All's Well That Ends Well* and subsequent plays on domestic relations. For one, Bertram is a prodigal: "a foolish idle boy, but for all that very ruttish" (IV.iii.215–16); Drunkenness is his best virtue" (IV.iii.255); "for a cardecue he will sell the fee-simple of his salvation, the inheritance of it, and cut th' entail from all remainders, and a perpetual succession for it perpetually" (IV.iii.278–81). Enforced to marry, he rejects his wife: "I cannot love her, nor will strive to do't" (II.iii.145); "I will not bed her" (II.iii.270). This reaction is typical even of husbands who marry whom they choose but who later wish to be rid of their wives in order to consort with a whore. He humiliates his wife ("Here comes my clog" [II.v.53]) and turns her away with an impossible task ("When thou canst get the ring . . . and show me a child begotten of thy body that I am father to" [III.ii.57–59]). The King and the Countess, like parents and friends in these plays generally, are scandalized by the prodigal's actions and disinherit him. Parolles, a suitably parasitic companion for a dissolute young heir, encourages Bertram's waywardness. Helena, the patient wife, blames herself that her husband is cruel.

174

For many modern critics, Helena forfeits a comparison with the patient wife by following Bertram first to Paris and then to Florence, but the women in these plays are not necessarily passive. Mrs. Arthur (*How a Man May Choose a Good Wife from a Bad*) and Luce (*The London Prodigal*) come forward to testify at their husbands' murder trials. Anabell (*The Fair Maid of Bristow*) is the one who asks King Richard to provide a way for her husband to escape execution; and, when the King offers to let a substitute die in the prodigal's place, she disguises herself as a man and volunteers. Shakespeare augments the aggressiveness of the wife by incorporating another familiar person in these plays into the character of the heroine. In the pilgrimage, as well as in the device of the bed trick, Helena performs the function of the relative or friend who in disguise oversees the prodigal and protects him. These same critics say that the close of *All's Well That Ends Well* is unconvincing because Bertram converts under duress and without soul-searching. Yet in this kind of comedy, a prodigal always recognizes his error in a flash—when he is a beggar, or a prisoner on trial for his life. But, these critics continue, the ending is nonetheless tentative and conditional ("If she, my liege, can make me know this clearly" [V.iii.315]). I would answer that on the stages of Shakespeare's time, in the context of other plays treating domestic relations, the metaphor of redemption in a constancy such as Helena's was sufficiently festive to secure the happy ending.[9]

According to the lines of genre that I have drawn here, in which the plays with subjects from Rome and ancient Britain are histories (though of a tragical cast), Shakespeare supplied his company with only three tragedies: *Titus Andronicus, Hamlet,* and *Othello.* As a group, these plays show an interest in certain features of the revenge formula that had been popular on the Elizabethan stage at least since the debut of Thomas Kyd's *The Spanish Tragedy,* ca. 1587–88; the anonymous *Hamlet,* ca. 1588–89; and Marlowe's *The Jew of Malta,* ca. 1589–91. Shakespeare experiments in each play with the structure of the plot and the nobility of the revenger. *Titus Andronicus* is two revenge plays in one. It combines the delay of Titus, who (like Hieronimo) runs mad with grief, and the serial murders of Aaron and Tamora, who (like Barabas and Ithamore) are intent on killing as many enemies as the time of the drama allows. In *Hamlet*, Shakespeare controls the pace of revenge by giving Hamlet the mind and mischievous wit of a scholar. Hamlet delays because he dreads the consequences of an ill-considered act. He is therefore not tainted by the villain's decisiveness, and flights of angels sing him to his rest. *Othello* is a revenge within a revenge within a revenge. The evil Iago takes his revenge by turning Othello into a revenger without cause. Although Desdemona cries out from the grave that no one is guilty of her death, Othello, who murdered her in a villainous revenge, assumes the hero's role and avenges her murder by killing himself.

There is evidence that *Titus Andronicus* and *Hamlet* were very popular when they were first performed, and we have every reason to assume that the Chamberlain's and King's men revived them after the initial productions. Yet we have no evidence of subsequent runs. By the chance survival of a foreign visitor's diary and a draft of an account compiled for the Treasurer of the Chamber, however, we do know that *Othello* was revived, both in 1609–10 and 1612–13. No doubt, the King's men chose it in part because of its masterful theatrical qualities. But they also had a reason deriving from the principle of duplication in their commercial strategy. In the years after 1604–05, there was a succession of tragedies as well as a tragicomedy or two that repeated certain motifs present in Shakespeare's play. In such drama as *The Revenger's Tragedy*, *The Maid's Tragedy*, *Valentinian*, *The Second Maiden's Tragedy*, *Philaster*, and *A King and No King*—as in *Othello*—the center of tragic action moves from the battlefield into the bedroom. The crimes that provoke the tragedy are sexual ones: the Duke's assault on Vindice's beloved, the King's prostitution of Evadne, Valentinian's rape of Lucina, the Tyrant's siege of the Lady, Arethusa's supposed affair with Bellario, Arbaces's near-incest with Panthea, Cassio's alleged affair with Desdemona. In those cases where the crimes lead to acts of revenge, the revengers are contaminated by pride, false motives, and/or blood-lust. Like Desdemona, the good women are patient, obedient, and chaste. Like the

Desdemona of Othello's diseased imagination, the bad women are cunning whores. Not only five but also ten years after its maiden run, therefore, *Othello* was a still-current member of its genre.

Most theater historians of the nineteenth and early twentieth centuries attributed the success of Shakespeare's company to the nature of its fellowship and the quality of its drama. They saw the Burbages' invitation to the players to invest in the Globe and Blackfriars as a happy partnership, John Heminges as a benevolent manager, and Shakespeare as the supplier of the most excellent and therefore the most successful dramatic fare. In the last half-century, as theater historians uncover more information on the economics of the playhouse world, we are coming to realize that, whatever else the plays may have been, they were merchandise in a commercial enterprise. The purpose of the business was to attract customers, and the commercial strategy was to offer a large and changing repertory diverse in the age of the plays, the stories that were told, and the formulas that were used in the telling. The plays that the Chamberlain's men and King's men acquired, including those supplied by Shakespeare, were valuable in the ways that they exploited these features.

In one of the few instances in which a member of Shakespeare's company comments on the selection of plays for performance, we hear a concern for economics. Testifying before the Lord Chief Justice about the choice of plays for 7 February 1601, Augustine Phillips says that the Chamberlain's men had "determined to play some other play" than the one they were asked to perform on that Saturday afternoon because the play requested was "so old and so long out of use that they should have a small company at it" (*CSP, Dom,* V, 578). Given that the performance became embroiled in a conspiracy to commit treason, we may agree that Phillips speaks somewhat ingenuously when he explains to the judge that the players "were content to play" *Richard II* on learning that they were to make "40s. more than their ordinary." But we may agree also that he believes a motive of profit should—and will—exonerate the company.

APPENDIX

Note: I provide stationers' information on the plays through 1623, except for those by Jonson (through 1616) and Beaumont and Fletcher (through 1679). I provide information on continuations and revivals for all plays through June 1613.

The Alchemist. Benjamin Jonson. *BEPD* no. 303.
Repertory Date: 1609–10
Basis of Attribution: Naming of the company on the title-page of the text in the 1616 folio ("Acted in the yeere 1610. By the Kings MAIESTIES Seruants"); names of King's men in a cast list with the text in 1616, including Richard Burbage, John Heminges, William Ostler, John Underwood, and William Ecclestone.
Publication: S.R. 3 October 1610. Quarto, 1612; folio, 1616.
Continuation/Revival: Continuation, 1610–11, on the basis of a reference to a performance at Oxford in the Latin correspondence of Henry Jackson (*H&S*, IX, 224); Revival, 1612–13, according to a Chamber Account in 1612–13.

All's Well That Ends Well. William Shakespeare. *BEPD* no. 395.
Repertory Date: 1602–03; Wells and Taylor date it 1604–05.
Basis of Attribution: Authorship, by way of the First Folio.
Publication: S.R. 8 November 1623. Folio, 1623.
Continuation/Revival: None known.

Antony and Cleopatra. William Shakespeare. *BEPD* no. 405.
Repertory Date: 1606–07
Basis of Attribution: Authorship, by way of the First Folio.
Publication: S.R. 20 May 1608; 8 November 1623. Folio, 1623.
Continuation/Revival: None known.

As You Like It. William Shakespeare. *BEPD* no. 394.
Repertory Date: 1599–1600
Basis of Attribution: Authorship, by way of the First Folio.
Publication: S.R. 4 August [1600], "to be staid" (*BEPD*, I, 15); 8 November 1623. Folio, 1623.
Continuation/Revival: A conjectural revival in 1603–04, on the authority of a letter in the hands of the Pembroke family in 1865 (*Extracts from the Letters and Journals of William Cory,* ed. F. W. Cornish [London: 1897], 168).

A Bad Beginning Makes a Good Ending. John Ford? *BEPD* no. Θ173
Repertory Date: 1612–13
Basis of Attribution: Assignment to the company in a Chamber Account in 1612–13.
Publication: Humphrey Moseley entered a play in the Stationers' Register on 29 June 1660 that he called "An ill begining has a good end, & a bad begining may have a good end. a Comedy"; the title is bracketed with another, *The London Merchant,* and both are ascribed to "Iohn fforde" (*BEPD*, I, 69). John Warburton listed a play called *A Good Beginning May Have a Good End* by Ford in his inventory of playbooks (W. W. Greg, "The Bakings of Betsy" *The Library* 2 [1911], 247). Possibly Moseley and Warburton refer to this play.
Continuation/Revival: None known.

Bonduca. Francis Beaumont; John Fletcher. *BEPD* no. 655.
Repertory Date: 1610–11. The chronology is approximate, based on the careers of players named in the cast list. Robinson presumably joined the company in 1610–11; Ecclestone left the company in 1611 to play for two years with Lady Elizabeth's men; and Ostler died in 1614. Only in 1610–11 do the players' affiliations with the King's men overlap.
Basis of Attribution: A cast list published with the play in 1679 includes the names of such veteran players for the King's men as Richard Burbage and Henry Condell,

along with newcomers William Ostler, William Ecclestone, and Richard Robinson.

Publication: S.R. 4 September 1646; 30 January 1673. Folio, 1647, 1679.

Continuation/Revival: None known.

The Captain. Francis Beaumont; John Fletcher. *BEPD* no. 642.

Repertory Date: 1612–13. The chronology is approximate, based on the career of William Ostler, a player who is named in the cast list published with the text in 1679. Ostler joined the King's men in 1609–10, which is thus the earliest year to which the play may belong. I assign it to 1612–13 because the Chamber Account documents a performance in that year.

Basis of Attribution: Assignment to the company in a Chamber Account in 1612–13; a cast list published with the play in 1679 includes such veteran players as Richard Burbage and Henry Condell along with the newcomer William Ostler.

Publication: S.R. 4 September 1646; 30 January 1673. Folios, 1647, 1679.

Continuation/Revival: None known.

Cardenio. William Shakespeare; John Fletcher. *BEPD* no. Θ64.

Repertory Date: 1612–13

Basis of Attribution: Assignment to the company in Chamber Accounts of 20 May 1613 and 9 July 1613.

Publication: S.R. 9 September 1653, by Humphrey Moseley; in the entry the play is called "The History of Cardenio," and it is ascribed to "Mr Fletcher. & Shakespeare" (*BEPD*, I, 61). John Warburton uses the same title (W. W. Greg, "The Bakings of Betsy" *The Library* 2 [1911], 247).

Continuation/Revival: None known.

Catiline. Benjamin Jonson. *BEPD* no. 296.

Repertory Date: 1610–11

Basis of Attribution: Naming of the company on the title-page of the folio edition ("Acted in the yeere 1611. By the Kings

MAIESTIES Seruants"). There is also a cast list with the text in 1616, which names such veteran players as Richard Burbage and John Heminges; the recently acquired John Underwood, William Ostler, and William Ecclestone; and the newest member, Richard Robinson.

Publication: S.R. 10 June 1621. Quarto, 1611; folio, 1616.

Continuation/Revival: None known.

Cloth Breeches and Velvet Hose. Author unknown. *BEPD* no. Θ22.

Repertory Date: 1599–1600

Basis of Attribution: Naming of the company in the entry in the Stationers' Register on 27 May 1600 ("as yt is acted by my lord Chamberlens servant*es*" [*BEPD,* I, 15]); listing on the fly leaf of Register C with *A Larum for London* under the heading of "my lord chamberlens mens Plaies Entred" (*BEPD,* I, 15).

Publication: S.R. 27 May 1600.

Continuation/Revival: None known.

Comedy of Errors. William Shakespeare. BEPD no. 393.

Repertory Date: 1594–95

Basis of Attribution: Assignment to the company in the Revels Account of 1604–05; authorship, by way of Francis Meres's *Palladis Tamia* (1598) and the First Folio.

Publication: S.R. 8 November 1623. Folio, 1623.

Continuation/Revival: Revival, conjectured for 1597–98, on the basis of an allusion in "Satire V" of *Skialetheia* by Everard Guilpin, 1598 ("Perswade me to a play, I'le to the *Rose,* / Or *Curtaine,* one of *Plautus* Comedies, / Or the *Patheticke Spaniards* Tragedies" [ll. 28–30]). Revival, 1604–05, on the basis of the Revels Account of 1604–05, which specifies a performance at Court on Holy Innocents' Day.

Coriolanus. William Shakespeare. *BEPD* no. 401.

Repertory Date: 1607–08

Basis of Attribution: Authorship, by way of the First Folio.

Publication: S.R. 8 November 1623. Folio, 1623.
Continuation/Revival: None known.

Cymbeline. William Shakespeare. *BEPD* no. 406.
Repertory Date: 1609–10
Basis of Attribution: Authorship, by way of the First Folio.
Publication: S.R. 8 November 1623. Folio, 1623.
Continuation/Revival: Revival, 1610–11, on the basis of an entry in the diary (*Bocke of Plaies*) of Simon Forman, who saw the play and recorded a summary of most of the plot, but he does not date the entry or specify the playhouse he attended. Because of the similarity of this entry to those of *Macbeth*, *Richard the 2*, and *The Winter's Tale*, which Forman saw at the Globe in April and May of 1611, we assume that the performance of *Cymbeline* occurred in the same time period. Given the proximity to the alleged date of the play's entry into the repertory and the interruptions because of plague, the performance seen by Forman could as reasonably have been in a continuation of the maiden run as a revival.

The Devil's Charter. Barnabe Barnes. *BEPD* no. 254.
Repertory Date: 1606–07
Basis of Attribution: Naming of the company on the title-page of the quarto ("plaide . . . by his Maiesties Seruants").
Publication: S.R. 16 October 1607. Quarto, 1607 (two issues).
Continuation/Revival: None known.

Every Man in His Humor. Benjamin Jonson. *BEPD* no. 176.
Repertory Date: 1598–99
Basis of Attribution: Naming of the company on the title-page of the quarto in 1601 ("publickly acted by the right Honorable the Lord Chamberlaine his seruants"); assignment to the company in the Revels Account of 1604–05.
Publication: S.R. 4 August [1600], "to be staid" (*BEPD*, I, 15); S.R. 14 August 1600; S.R. 16 October 1609. Quarto, 1601; folio, 1616.

Continuation/Revival: A continuation into 1599–1600 conjectured on the basis of its popularity, the move to the Globe, and the debut of *Every Man out of His Humor*. Revival, 1604–05, according to the Revels Account of 1604–05, which specifies a performance at Court on Candlemas 1605 (2 February). A revival conjectured in 1611–12, in connection with a revision of the text in the wake of the success of *The Alchemist*.

Every Man out of His Humor. Benjamin Jonson. *BEPD* no. 163.
  Repertory Date: 1599–1600
  Basis of Attribution: Assignment to the company in the Revels Account, 1604–05; naming of the company on the title-page of the text in the 1616 folio ("Acted, in the yeere 1599. By the then Lord Chamberlaine his Seruants").
  Publication: S.R. 8 April 1600. Quarto, 1600 (three issues); folio, 1616.
  Continuation/Revival: Revival, 1604–05, according to the Revels Account of 1604–05, which specifies a performance at Court on 8 January 1605.

Fair Em. Author unknown. *BEPD* no. 113.
  Repertory Date: 1594–95
  Basis of Attribution: Its presence with *The Merry Devil of Edmonton* and *Mucedorus* in a volume marked "Shakespeare, Vol. I," allegedly acquired by David Garrick from the library of Charles II.
  Publication: Quartos, one undated [1593], another in 1631.
  Continuation/Revival: A revival conjectured for 1594–96. The play was old when it was acquired by the Chamberlain's men in 1594; therefore, its initial run with them was a revival. I assume that the company did not wait longer than two years to bring the play to the stage once the text had been acquired.

The Fair Maid of Bristow. Author unknown. *BEPD* no. 211.
  Repertory Date: 1603–04

Basis of Attribution: Naming of the company in the entry in the
Stationers' Register, which claims that this play was performed
"at Hampton Court by his ma*jestes* players" (*BEPD,* I, 20); the
title-page of the quarto repeats the reference to Hampton
Court, but not the name of the company, and adds that "the
King and Queenes most excellent Maiesties" were the audience.
Publication: S.R. 8 February 1605. Quarto, 1605.
Continuation/Revival: None known.

The Freeman's Honor. Wentworth Smith.
Repertory Date: 1600–01. Smith was busy writing plays for the
Admiral's men by April 1601 and for the Admiral's men and
Worcester's men in 1602–03; therefore, I date his work for the
Chamberlain's men before April 1601.
Basis of Attribution: Naming of the company in the dedicatory
epistle, which Smith wrote to Sir John Swinnerton for the
quarto of *The Hector of Germany, or the Palgrave, Prime
Elector* in 1615; Swinnerton, a former lord mayor, was a mem-
ber of the Company of Merchant Taylors; Smith says in the
epistle to Swinnerton that he had written a play "called the
Freemans Honour, acted by the Now-seruants of the Kings
Maiestie, to dignifie the worthy Companie of the
Marcha*n*taylors" (*STC* 22871).
Publication: None known.
Continuation/Revival: None known.

Gowrie. Author unknown.
Repertory Date: 1604–05
Basis of Attribution: A letter from John Chamberlain to Ralph
Winwood on 18 December 1604, in which Chamberlain gossips about the stir caused by recent performances, presumably
at the Globe: "The Tragedy of *Gowry,* with all the Action and
Actors hath been twice represented by the King's Players,
with exceeding Concourse of all sorts of People. But whether
the matter or manner be not well handled, or that it be
thought unfit that Princes should be played on the Stage in

their Life-time, I hear that some great Councellors are much displeased with it, and so 'tis thought shall be forbidden" (E. Sawyer, ed. *Memorials of Affairs of State in the Reigns of Queen Elizabeth and King James I,* 3 vols. [London, 1725], II, 41).
Publication: None known.
Continuation/Revival: None known.

Hamlet. Author unknown.
Repertory date: 1594–95
Basis of Attribution: *Henslowe's Diary,* 9 June 1594.
Publication: None known.
Continuation/Revival: A continuation into 1595–96 conjectured on the basis of an allusion in *Wits Miserie and the Worlds Madnesse* by Thomas Lodge. Since the play was old when the company acquired it in June 1594, the run that began at the Newington playhouse was itself a revival in the overall stage history of the play.

Hamlet. William Shakespeare. *BEPD* no. 197.
Repertory Date: 1600–01
Basis of Attribution: Naming of the company in the registration at Stationers' Hall, 26 July 1602 ("as yt was latelie Acted by the Lord Chamberleyn his servant*es*" [*BEPD,* I, 18]) and on the title-page of the quarto in 1603 ("acted by his Highness seruants"); authorship, by way of the title-page of the quarto in 1604/5 ("By William Shake-speare") and the First Folio.
Publication: S.R. 26 July 1602. Quartos in 1603, 1604/5, 1611, and one undated; folio, 1623.
Continuation/Revival: None known.

1 Henry IV. William Shakespeare. *BEPD* no. 145.
Repertory Date: 1596–97
Basis of Attribution: Authorship, by way of Meres's *Palladis Tamia* (1598), the title-page of the quarto in 1599 ("Newly corrected by W. Shake-speare"), and the First Folio.
Publication: S.R. 25 February 1598; 25 June 1603. Quartos in

1598 (two editions, one fragmentary), 1599, 1604, 1608, 1613, and 1622; folio, 1623.

Continuation/Revival: A continuation into 1597–98 conjectured, on the basis of popularity and contemporary allusions. Revival, 1612–13, according to a Chamber Account in 1612–13, if it is the play called "The Hotspurr."

2 Henry IV. William Shakespeare. *BEPD* no. 167.

Repertory Date: 1597–98

Basis of Attribution: Naming of the company on the title-page of the quarto in 1600 ("acted by the right honourable, the Lord Chamberlaine his seruants"); authorship, by way of the entry in the Stationers' Register ("Wrytten by mr Shakespere" [*BEPD*, I, 16]) and the First Folio.

Publication: S.R. 23 August 1600. Quarto, 1600 (two issues); folio, 1623.

Continuation/Revival: A continuation into 1598–99 conjectured, on the basis of its registration and printing in 1600 and its place in the serial leading up to *Henry V*. Revival, 1612–13, depending on the identity of "Sr Iohn Falstafe," which the King's men performed at Court according to a Chamber Account in 1612–13.

Henry V. William Shakespeare. *BEPD* no. 165.

Repertory Date: 1598–99

Basis of Attribution: Naming of the company on the title-page of the quarto in 1600 ("playd by the Right honorable the Lord Chamberlaine his seruants"); assignment to the company in the Revels Account of 1604–05; authorship, by way of the First Folio.

Publication: S.R. 4 August [1600], "to be staid" (*BEPD*, I, 15); 14 August 1600, transfer of "The historye of Henrye the vth with the battell of Agencourt" to Thomas Pavier (*BEPD*, I, 16). Quartos in 1600, 1602, and 1608 [1619]; folio, 1623.

Continuation/Revival: Continuation, 1599–1600, on the basis of its relative newness at the time the Globe opened in the summer of 1600. Revival, 1604–05, according to the Revels Account of 1604–05, which specifies a performance at Court on 7 January 1605.

1 Henry VI. William Shakespeare. *BEPD* no. 399.
Repertory date: 1594–96
Basis of Attribution: Authorship, by way of the First Folio.
Publication: 8 November 1623 (Greg follows tradition in giving the registration for the folio of "The thirde parte of Henry ye sixt" to this play [*BEPD*, II, 546]). Folio, 1623.
Continuation/Revival: A revival conjectured for 1594–96. The play was old when it was acquired by the Chamberlain's men in 1594; therefore, its initial run with them was a revival. I assume that the company did not wait longer than two years to bring the play to the stage once the text had been acquired.

2 Henry VI. William Shakespeare. *BEPD* no. 119.
Repertory Date: 1594–95
Basis of Attribution: Authorship, by way of the First Folio.
Publication: S.R. 12 March 1594, of "the firste parte of the Contention of the twoo famous houses of york and Lancaster" (*BEPD*, I, 10). Quartos in 1594, 1600, and 1619. *The Contention* is considered an abridged version of *2 Henry VI*.
Continuation/Revival: A revival conjectured for 1594–96. The play was old when it was acquired by the Chamberlain's men in 1594; therefore, its initial run with them was a revival. I assume that the company did not wait longer than two years to bring the play to the stage once the text had been acquired.

3 Henry VI. William Shakespeare. *BEPD* no. 138.
Repertory Date: 1594–95
Basis of Attribution: Authorship, by way of the First Folio.
Publication: S.R. 19 April 1602. 8 November 1623 (although the entry specifies "The thirde parte of Henry ye sixt," Greg attributes the registration to *1 Henry VI* [*BEPD*, II, 546). Quartos in 1595, 1600 (*The True Tragedy of Richard Duke of*

York, with an advertisement of Pembroke's men on the title-page), and 1619 (the second part of *The Contention*). *The True Tragedy* is considered an abridged version of *3 Henry VI.*
Continuation/Revival: A revival conjectured for 1594–96. The play was old when it was acquired by the Chamberlain's men in 1594; therefore, its initial run with them was a revival. I assume that the company did not wait longer than two years to bring the play to the stage once the text had been acquired.

Henry VIII. William Shakespeare. *BEPD* no. 400.
Repertory Date: 1612–13
Basis of Attribution: Accounts of the fire at the Globe, 29 June 1613 (Tuesday); the most specific of these in terms of company is a letter by Sir Henry Wotton dated 2 July 1613, in which Wotton says that the "King's players had a new play, called *All is True,*" which dramatized events from "the reign of Henry VIII," including "a masque at the Cardinal Wolsey's house" during which a shot was fired that ignited the roof of the playhouse (*The Life and Letters of Sir Henry Wotton,* ed. Logan Pearsall Smith, 2 vols. [Oxford: Clarendon Press, 1907], II, 32–33); authorship, by way of the First Folio.
Publication: S.R. 8 November 1623. Folio, 1623.
Continuation/Revival: None known.

Hester and Ahasuerus. Author unknown.
Repertory date: 1594–95
Basis of Attribution: *Henslowe's Diary,* 3 and 10 June 1594.
Publication: None known.
Continuation/Revival: None known.

Jeronimo. Author unknown, unless it is Thomas Kyd.
Repertory Date: 1602–03, arbitrarily, to coordinate with the theft of the play by the Children of Blackfriars.
Basis of Attribution: An allusion in the induction of *The Malcontent,* in which Condell justifies the acquisition of the play as revenge for the theft of their *Jeronimo* by the boys'

company at Blackfriars: "Why not Malevole in folio with us, as Jeronimo in decimosexto with them? They taught us a name for our play, we call it *One for another*" (ll. 75–77).

Publication: None known, unless *Jeronimo* was another text of *The Spanish Tragedy* or was one or both of the quartos that Edward Archer called "Hieronimo, both parts" in the catalogue of 1656.

Continuation/Revival: The King's men imply a revival by the Children of Blackfriars, 1602–03; if this play was Kyd's *Spanish Tragedy*, it was revived in 1592 by Strange's men and 1597 and 1601–02 by the Admiral's men.

Julius Caesar. William Shakespeare. *BEPD* no. 403.

Repertory Date: 1599–1600, according to Thomas Platter, a traveler from Basle, who spent about a month in England in the fall of 1599 and recorded subsequently in a diary that on 21 September he and his companions went to a "straw-thatched house [where they] saw the tragedy of the first Emperor Julius Caesar" (trans. Ernest Schanzer, "Thomas Platter's Observations on the Elizabethan Stage," *Notes and Queries* 201 [1956], 465–67).

Basis of Attribution: Authorship, by way of the First Folio; the identification of Platter's "straw-thatched house" as the Globe.

Publication: S.R. 8 November 1623. Folio, 1623.

Continuation/Revival: Revival, 1612–13, if it is the "Caesars Tragedye" specified in a Chamber Account in 1612–13.

King John. William Shakespeare. *BEPD* no. 398.

Repertory Date: 1596–97

Basis of Attribution: Authorship, by way of Francis Meres's *Palladis Tamia* (1598) and the First Folio.

Publication: Folio, 1623.

Continuation/Revival: None known; if there was a revival in 1610–11, that event might account for the publication of *The*

Troublesome Reign of King John in 1611 with a title-page naming authorship by "W. Sh."

King Lear. William Shakespeare. *BEPD* no. 265.
Repertory Date: 1605–06
Basis of Attribution: Naming of the company and playhouse in the entry in the Stationers' Register ("played . . . by his maiesties servantes playinge vsually at the globe on the Banksyde" [*BEPD,* I, 24]) and on the title-page of the quarto in 1608; authorship, by way of the registration (Mr William Shakespeare), the title-page of the quarto (M. William Shak-speare), and the First Folio.
Publication: S.R. 26 November 1607. Quartos, 1608, 1608 [1619]; folio, 1623.
Continuation/Revival: Continuation, 1606–07, on the basis of the date of the Court performance specified in the entry in the Stationers' Register.

A King and No King. Francis Beaumont; John Fletcher. *BEPD* no. 360.
Repertory Date: 1611–12
Basis of Attribution: Assignment to the company in the Revels Account of 1611–12, which specifies a performance on 26 December 1611; assignment to the company in a Chamber Account in 1612–13; naming of the company and playhouse on the title-page of the quarto in 1619 ("Acted at the Globe, by his Maiesties Seruants").
Publication: S.R. 7 August 1618; 1 March 1628; 29 May 1638; 25 January 1639. Quartos in 1619, 1625, 1631, 1639, 1655, 1661, and 1676; folio, 1679.
Continuation/Revival: Continuation into 1612–13, according to a Chamber Account in 1612–13.

The Knot of Fools. Author unknown.
Repertory Date: 1612–13
Basis of Attribution: Assignment to the company in a Chamber Account in 1612–13.

Publication: None known.
Continuation/Revival: None known.

A Larum for London. Author unknown. *BEPD* no. 192.
Repertory Date: 1599–1600
Basis of Attribution: Listing with *Cloth Breeches and Velvet Hose* on the flyleaf of Register C under the heading of "my lord chamberlens mens Plaies Entred" (*BEPD*, I, 15); naming of the company on the title-page of the quarto in 1602 ("playde by the right Honorable the Lord Charberlaine his Seruants").
Publication: S.R. 29 May 1600. Quarto, 1602.
Continuation/Revival: None known.

The London Prodigal. Author unknown. *BEPD* no. 222.
Repertory Date: 1603–04
Basis of Attribution: Naming of the company on the title-page of the quarto in 1605 ("plaide by the Kings Maiesties seruants").
Publication: Quarto, 1605.
Continuation/Revival: None known.

Love's Labor's Lost. William Shakespeare. *BEPD* no. 150.
Repertory date: 1594–95
Basis of Attribution: Assignment to the company in the Revels Account of 1604–05; authorship, by way of Francis Meres's *Palladis Tamia* (1598), the title-page of the quarto in 1598 ("By W. Shakespere"), and the First Folio.
Publication: S.R. 22 January 1607; S.R. 19 November 1607. Quarto, 1598; folio, 1623.
Continuation/Revival: A continuation into 1595–96 conjectured, on the basis of the debut of *Love's Labor's Won*. Revival, 1604–05, according to the Revels Account of 1604–05 and Walter Cope's letter to Robert Cecil dated 1604: "Burbage ys come, & sayes there is no new playe that the quene hath not seene, but they have revyved an olde one, cawled *Loves Labore*

lost, which for wytt and mirthe he sayes will please her excedingly. And thys ys apointed to be playd to morowe night at
my Lord of Sowthampton's . . . Burbage ys my messenger
ready attending your pleasure" (*The Third Report of the Royal
Commission on Historical Manuscripts* [London: HMSO,
1872], III, 148).

Love's Labor's Won. William Shakespeare.

Repertory Date: 1595–96

Basis of Attribution: Authorship, by way of Francis Meres in
Palladis Tamia (1598).

Publication: Quarto, date unknown; the title appears on a list of
inventory made by Christopher Hunt, an Oxford bookseller
in 1603 (T. W. Baldwin, *Shakespere's Love's Labor's Won*
[Carbondale, Ill.: Southern Illinois University Press, 1957).

Continuation/Revival: None known.

Macbeth. William Shakespeare. *BEPD* no. 404.

Repertory Date: 1605–06

Basis of Attribution: Plot summary by Simon Forman in his
diary, *Bocke of Plaies,* based on a performance he saw at the
Globe; authorship, by way of the First Folio.

Publication: S.R. 8 November 1623. Folio, 1623.

Continuation/Revival: Revival, 1610–11, according to Forman,
who dated the performance at the Globe on Saturday, 20
April 1610 (which Chambers corrected to 1611 because the
twentieth falls on a Saturday in that year but not in 1610).

The Maid's Tragedy. Francis Beaumont; John Fletcher. *BEPD* no. 357.

Repertory Date: 1610–11

Basis of Attribution: Naming of the company and playhouse on
the title-page of the quarto in 1619 ("Acted at the Blacke-
friers by the KINGS Maiesties Seruants"); assignment to the
company in a Chamber Account of 1612–13.

Publication: S.R. 28 April 1619, 27 October 1629, 29 May 1638, 25 January 1639. Quartos in 1619, 1622, 1630, 1638, 1641, 1650, undated, 1661; folio, 1679.

Continuation/Revival: Revival, 1612–13, according to a Chamber Account in 1612–13.

The Malcontent. John Marston; induction by John Webster. *BEPD* no. 203.

Repertory Date: 1603–04; G. K. Hunter theorizes that the Children of the Chapel Royal acquired the play new in 1602–03 and that the King's men took it over in 1603; he dates the acquisition after May because John Lowin, a player with others from the company in the induction, joined the company, after May 1603 (*The Malcontent* [London: Methuen, 1975], xli–xliv).

Basis of Attribution: Naming of the company on the title-page of the third quarto ("With the Additions played by the Kings Maiesties servants").

Publication: S.R. 5 July 1604. Quarto, 1604 (three editions).

Continuation/Revival: A continuation into 1604–05 conjectured on the basis of the plague closure in 1603–04 and expenses connected with the production.

Measure for Measure. William Shakespeare. *BEPD* no. 392.

Repertory Date: 1604–05; Wells and Taylor assign the composition to 1603.

Basis of Attribution: Assignment to the company in the Revels Account of 1604–05, in which the play is attributed to the King's men in a performance at Court on 26 December; authorship, by way of the First Folio.

Publication: S.R. 8 November 1623. Folio, 1623.

Continuation/Revival: None known.

The Merchant of Venice. William Shakespeare. *BEPD* no. 172.

Repertory Date: 1596–97

Basis of Attribution: Naming of the company on the title-page of the quarto in 1600 ("acted by the Lord Chamberlaine his Seruants"); assignment to the company in the Revels Account of 1604–05; authorship, by way of the title-page of the quarto in 1600 ("Written by William Shakespeare"), Francis Meres's *Palladis Tamia* (1598), and the First Folio.

Publication: S.R. 22 July 1598; S.R., 28 October 1600; S.R. 8 July 1619. Quartos in 1600 and 1600 [1619]; folio, 1623.

Continuation/Revival: Revival, 1604–05, according to the Revels Account of 1604–05, which specifies performances on Shrove Sunday (10 February) and Shrove Tuesday (12 February) 1605.

The Merry Devil of Edmonton. Author unknown. *BEPD* no. 264.

Repertory Date: 1602–03, on the basis of an allusion in *The Black Book* by T. M. [Thomas Middleton]. In a passage describing the devices used by a woman to deceive her husband, the narrator observes that she might get rid of her servant-chaperon by giving him "leave to see *The Merry Devil of Edmonton* or *A Woman Killed with Kindness,* when his mistress is going herself to the same murder" (A. H. Bullen, *The Works of Thomas Middleton,* 8 vols. 1885; [rpt. New York: AMS Press, 1964], VIII, 36). The allusion implies not only a currency with Heywood's play, for which Worcester's men bought apparel on 7 March 1603 (according to *Henslowe's Diary*), but also a proximity. Worcester's men were at the Rose in the spring of 1603 but moved to the Curtain after the summer. Presumably, therefore, *The Merry Devil of Edmonton* was in production sometime in March, April, or May of 1603 (W. A. Abrams, ed., *The Merry Devil of Edmonton,* 1608 [Durham: Duke University Press, 1942], 34).

Basis of Attribution: Naming of the company and playhouse on the title-page of the quarto in 1608 ("Acted, by his Maiesties Seruants, at the Globe, on the banke-side"); assignment to the company in a Chamber Account in 1612–13.

Publication: S.R. 22 October 1607. Quartos in 1608, 1612, and 1617.

Continuation/Revival: A continuation conjectured into 1603–04, due to the plague restraints of that year. Revival, 1612–13, according to a Chamber Account in 1612–13.

The Merry Wives of Windsor. William Shakespeare. *BEPD* no. 187.
Repertory Date: 1597–98
Basis of Attribution: Naming of the company on the title-page of the quarto in 1602 ("Acted by the right Honorable my Lord Chamberlaines seruants"); assignment to the company in the Revels Account of 1604–05; authorship, by way of the title-page of the quarto ("By William Shakespeare") and the First Folio.
Publication: S.R. 18 January 1602. Quartos in 1602 and 1619; folio, 1623.
Continuation/Revival: Revival, 1604–05, according to the Revels Account for 1604–05, which specifies a performance at Court on the Sunday following Allhallows (4 November 1604). Revival, 1612–13, depending on the identity of "Sr Iohn Falstafe," which the King's men performed at Court according to a Chamber Account in 1612–13.

A Midsummer Night's Dream. William Shakespeare. BEPD no. 170.
Repertory Date: 1595–96
Basis of Attribution: Naming of the company on the title-page of the quarto in 1600 ("publickely acted, by the Right honourable, the Lord Chamberlaine his seruants"); authorship, by way of the title-page claim of the quarto ("Written by William Shakespeare"), Meres's *Palladis Tamia* (1598), and the First Folio.
Publication: S.R. 8 October 1600. Quartos in 1600 and 1600 [1619]; folio, 1623.
Continuation/Revival: None known.

The Miseries of Enforced Marriage. George Wilkins. *BEPD* no. 249.
Repertory Date: 1606–07
Basis of Attribution: Naming of the company on the title-page

of the quarto in 1607 ("As it is is now playd by his Maiesties Seruants").

Publication: S.R. 31 July 1607. Quartos in 1607 and 1611.

Continuation/Revival: None known.

Mucedorus. Author unknown. *BEPD* no. 151.

Repertory Date: 1596–97; F. G. Fleay dates the play in 1588 and ascribes it to Thomas Lodge (*A Biographical Chronicle of the English Drama, 1559–1642,* 2 vols. 1890 [New York: B. Franklin, 1969], II, 49). The dependency of the narrative on the story of Musidorus's rescue of Pamela from the bear in Sidney's *Arcadia* (1590, 1593) makes 1591–96 a much more likely period of composition. I assign it to the offerings of 1596–97 because of its printing in 1598.

Basis of Attribution: Naming of the company and playhouse on the title-page of the quarto in 1610 ("By his Highnes Seruantes usually playing at the Globe").

Publication: Quartos in 1598, 1606, 1610, 1611, 1613, 1615, 1618, 1619, and 1621.

Continuation/Revival: Revival, 1605–06, on the basis of revisions in the text of the quarto in 1606 (Richard Thornberry, "A Seventeenth-Century Revival of *Mucedorus* in London before 1610," *Shakespeare Quarterly* 28 [1977]: 362–64). Revival, 1609–10, according to the title-page of the quarto in 1610.

Much Ado about Nothing. William Shakespeare. *BEPD* no. 168.

Repertory Date: 1598–99

Basis of Attribution: Naming of the company on the title-page of the quarto in 1600 ("publikely acted by the right honourable, the Lord Chamberlaine his seruants"); authorship, by way of an entry in the Stationers' Register on 23 August 1600 ("Wrytten by mr Shakespere" [*BEPD,* I, 16]) and by the First Folio.

Publication: S.R., 4 August [1600], "to be staid" (*BEPD,* I, 15); S.R. 23 August 1600. Quarto, 1600; folio, 1623.

Continuation/Revival: A continuation into 1599–1600 conjectured, on the basis of the move to the Globe and the registration in 1600. Revival, 1612–13, for two performances, according to Chamber Accounts in 1612–13.

The Nobleman. Cyril Tourneur. *BEPD* no. Θ33.
Repertory Date: 1611–12
Basis of Attribution: Assignment to the company in the Revels Account of 1611–12, which claims a presentation by the King's men at Court on Shrove Sunday (23 February); assignment to the company in a Chamber Account in 1612–13.
Publication: S.R. 15 February 1612. Humphrey Moseley entered the play in the Stationers' Register on 9 September 1653 with the alternate title, "Great man," and attributing it to Tourneur (*BEPD*, I, 61). John Warburton listed the play by the title "The Nobleman," calling it a tragicomedy by Tourneur; he had a separate entry by the alternate title, "The Great Man," calling this one a tragedy and leaving the attribution blank (W. W. Greg, "The Bakings of Betsy," *The Library* 2 [1911], 246).
Continuation/Revival: Continuation into 1612–13, according to a Chamber Account in 1612–13.

Oldcastle. Author unknown.
Repertory Date: 1599–1600
Basis of Attribution: On 8 March 1599 [1600] Rowland Whyte wrote to Sir Robert Sidney with details of the current visit of Louis Verreyken, a mediator appointed by Archduke Albert to negotiate a peace between England and Spain. According to Whyte, Verreyken had been entertained the previous Thursday (6 March) by the Lord Chamberlain: "vpon *Thursday* my Lord Chamberlain feasted hym, and made hym very great, and a delicate Dinner, and there in the After Noone his Plaiers acted, before *Vereiken*, Sir *John Old Castell*, to his great Contentment" (Arthur Collins, ed. *Letters and Memorials of State*, 3 vols. [London: T. Osborne, 1746], II, 175).

Publication: None known.
Continuation/Revival: None known.

Othello. William Shakespeare. *BEPD* no. 379.
   Repertory Date: 1604–05; Wells and Taylor date the composition of the play 1603.
   Basis of Attribution: Assignment to the company in the Revels Account of 1604–05, which attributes a performance by the King's men on 1 November 1604 at Whitehall; naming of the company and playhouses ("acted at the Globe, and at Blackfriers, by his Maiesties Seruants") on the title-page of the quarto in 1622; authorship, by way of the title-page of the quarto ("Written by William Shakespeare") and the First Folio.
   Publication: S.R. 6 October 1621. Quarto, 1622; folio, 1623.
   Continuation/Revival: Revival, 1609–10, according to an entry in the diary kept of the visit to England of Prince Lewis Frederick of Württemburg; on the date of 30 April 1610 the prince attended the Globe (*"alla au Globe"*) and saw a performance of *Othello* (*"l'histoire du More de Venise"* [qtd. in *England as Seen by Foreigners,* William Brenchley Rye (London: John Russell Smith, 1865), 61]). Continuation, based on a reference to a performance at Oxford in the fall of 1610 in the Latin correspondence of Henry Jackson (*H&S,* IX, 224). Revival, 1612–13, according to a Chamber Account in 1612–13.

Pericles. William Shakespeare. *BEPD* no. 284.
   Repertory Date: 1607–08
   Basis of Attribution: Naming of the dramatist, playhouse, and company on the title-page of the quarto in 1609 ("acted by his Maiesties Seruants at the Globe on the Banck-side. By William Shakespeare").
   Publication: S.R. 20 May 1608. Quartos in 1609 (two editions), 1611, and 1619.
   Continuation/Revival: A continuation into 1608–09 conjectured, on the basis of the interruption of the playing year by plague.

Philaster. Francis Beaumont; John Fletcher. *BEPD* no. 363.
Repertory Date: 1609–10
Basis of Attribution: Naming of the playhouse and company on the title-page of the quarto in 1620 ("Acted at the Globe by his Maiesties Seruants"); assignment to the company in a Chamber Account in 1612–13.
Publication: S.R. 10 January 1620. Quartos in 1620 and 1622.
Continuation/Revival: Revival, 1612–13, according to a Chamber Account in 1612–13, which cites two performances at Court in 1612–13.

The Revenger's Tragedy. Authorship uncertain. *BEPD* no. 253.
Repertory Date: 1605–06
Basis of Attribution: Naming of the company on the title-page of the quarto ("Acted, by the Kings Maiesties Seruants").
Publication: S.R. 7 October 1607. Quarto, 1607/8.
Continuation/Revival: None known.

Richard II. William Shakespeare. *BEPD* no. 141.
Repertory Date: 1595–96
Basis of Attribution: Naming of the company on the title-page of the quarto in 1597 ("publikely acted by the right Honourable the Lorde Chamberlaine his Seruants"); authorship, by way of the title-page of the quarto in 1598 ("By William Shake-speare"), Francis Meres's *Palladis Tamia* (1598), and the First Folio.
Publication: S.R. 29 August 1597; 25 June 1603. Quartos in 1597, 1598 (two editions), 1608, and 1615; folio, 1623.
Continuation/Revival: Revival, 1600–01, on the basis of testimony given in the Essex investigation by Sir Gelly Meyricke and a Chamberlain's player, Augustine Phillips (*CSP, Dom*, V, 575, 578). Revival, conjectured for 1607–08, on the basis of a quarto giving new information on the title-page and including the Parliament scene.

Richard the 2. Author unknown.

Repertory Date: 1610–11

Basis of Attribution: Simon Forman claims to have seen this play at the Globe on 30 April 1611, a Tuesday. In a section of his diary labeled *Bocke of Plaies,* he says that it dramatized the stabbing of Jack Straw, the duke of Gloucester's foiling of a treacherous stratagem by the duke of Ireland, King Richard's betrayal of Gloucester, John of Gaunt's plot against Richard, and Gaunt's execution of a soothsayer. These incidents do not occur together in any surviving playtexts. Therefore this play appears to be an altogether separate work from Shakespeare's *Richard II,* the anonymous *Woodstock,* and the anonymous *Jack Straw.*

Publication: None known.

Continuation/Revival: None known.

Richard III. William Shakespeare. *BEPD* no. 142.

Repertory Date: 1594–96

Basis of Attribution: Naming of the company on the title-page of the quarto in 1597 ("lately Acted by the Right honourable the Lord Chamberlaine his seruants"); authorship, by way of the title-page of the second quarto in 1598 ("By William Shake-speare") and the First Folio.

Publication: S.R. 20 October 1597; S.R. 25 June 1603. Quartos in 1597, 1598, 1602, 1605, 1612, and 1622; folio, 1623.

Continuation/Revival: A revival conjectured for 1594–96. The play was old when it was acquired by the Chamberlain's men in 1594; therefore, its initial run with them was a revival. I assume that the company did not wait longer than two years to bring the play to the stage once the text had been acquired.

Robin Goodfellow. Author unknown.

Repertory Date: 1603–04

Basis of Attribution: In a letter to John Chamberlain dated 15 January 1604, Dudley Carleton said that "On New Year's

night we had a play of Robin Goodfellow" (*Dudley Carleton to John Chamberlain, 1603–1624,* ed. Maurice Lee, Jr. [New Brunswick, N.J.: Rutgers University Press, 1972], 53); the only payment in the Chamber Accounts of 1603–04 to a company for a performance at Court on the night of New Year's, 1604, is to the King's men.
Publication: None known.
Continuation/Revival: None known.

Romeo and Juliet. William Shakespeare. *BEPD* no. 143.
Repertory Date: 1594–95
Basis of Attribution: Naming of the company on the title page of the quarto in 1597 ("plaid publiquely, by the right Honourable the L. of Hunsdon his Seruants"); authorship, by way of Francis Meres's *Palladis Tamia* (1598) and the First Folio.
Publication: S.R. 22 January 1607; S.R. 19 November 1607. Quartos in 1597, 1599, and 1609; folio, 1623.
Continuation/Revival: Revival, conjectured for 1597–98, on the basis of an allusion in "Satire X," *The Scourge of Villanie* by John Marston, 1598 ("pure *Juliat* and *Romio*" [l. 39]; "Curtaine *plaudeties*" [l. 45]); the poem is "Satire XI" in the edition in 1599.

Satiromastix. Thomas Dekker. *BEPD* no. 195.
Repertory Date: 1601–02 (Cyrus Hoy, *Introductions, Notes, and Commentaries to Texts in 'The Dramatic Works of Thomas Dekker' Edited by Fredson Bowers,* 4 vols. [Cambridge: Cambridge University Press, 1980], I, 181).
Basis of Attribution: Naming of the company on the title-page of the quarto in 1602 ("presented publikely, by the Right Honorable, the Lord Chamberlaine his Seruants; and priuately, by the Children of Paules").
Publication: S.R. 11 November 1601. Quarto, 1602.
Continuation/Revival: None known.

The Second Maiden's Tragedy. Author unknown. BEPD no. Θ87.

  Repertory Date: 1611–12

  Basis of Attribution: Marginalia in the manuscript of the play-book, which gives the names of two players, Richard Robinson and Robert Gough, both members of the King's men.

  Publication: Humphrey Moseley registered "The Maid's Tragedie. 2d. part" on 9 September 1653 (*BEPD*, I, 61), and John Warburton listed it among the plays in his library, using the title "Second Part Maiden's Tragedy" and assigning the play to Chapman (W. W. Greg, "The Bakings of Betsy," *The Library* 2 [1911], 246). Presumably Moseley and Warburton refer to this play.

  Continuation/Revival: None known.

Sejanus. Benjamin Jonson. *BEPD* no. 216.

  Repertory Date: 1603–04

  Basis of Attribution: Naming of the company on the title-page of the text in the folio ("Acted, in the yeere 1603. By the K. MAIESTIES SERVANTS").

  Publication: S.R. 2 November 1604; 6 August 1605; 3 October 1610. Quarto, 1605; folio, 1616.

  Continuation/Revival: None known.

The Spanish Maze. Author unknown.

  Repertory Date: 1604–05

  Basis of Attribution: Assignment to the company in the Revels Account of 1604–05, which calls the play "A Tragidye," and which claims that the King's men performed it at Court on Shrove Monday (11 February 1605).

  Publication: None known.

  Continuation/Revival: None known.

Stuhlweissenburg. Author unknown.

Repertory Date: 1602–03

Basis of Attribution: In the fall of 1602, Duke Philip Julius of Stettin-Pomerania visited London. One of his companions, his tutor and secretary Frederic Gerschow, kept a diary of some of their activities. Gerschow recorded visits to three playhouses, two of which have been identified as the Fortune and Blackfriars. At the third (unnamed) on 13 September, the duke's party went to a play "showing how Stuhl-Weissenburg was gained by the Turks, and then won again by the Christians" (Gottfried von Bülow, ed., *Transactions of the Royal Historical Society,* New Series [London: Longmans, 1892], VI, 7; see also *ES,* II, 367). The attribution is based on the conjecture that the foreign visitors, having been the newest public playhouse in London in 1602 (the Fortune), would have attended performances at the second newest one, the Globe.

Publication: None known.

Continuation/Revival: None known.

The Taming of the Shrew. William Shakespeare. *BEPD* no. 120.

Repertory date: 1594–95

Basis of Attribution: *Henslowe's Diary* 11 June 1594; authorship by way of the First Folio. H. J. Oliver explains the logic by which Henslowe's title becomes Shakespeare's play (*The Taming of the Shrew* [Oxford: Oxford University Press, 1984], 30–32). He says, essentially, that the Chamberlain's men would not have played *The Taming of a Shrew* if they had had access to *The Taming of the Shrew,* which they would have had if Shakespeare had joined the company by June 1594. This explanation is reasonable, but no evidence specifically identifies the entry in *Henslowe's Diary* ("the tamynge of A shrowe") as a reference to *The Taming of the Shrew.*

Publication: Folio, 1623.

Continuation/Revival: Continuation, from the run at Newington in June 1594 into the repertory of 1594–95; since the play was

NOTES

In the text, I cite documentary material from published editions, and these carry different styles of transcription. For the reader's convenience, I regularize and modernize these citations to some extent. I expand contractions and express peculiar Elizabethan scribal marks with italicized letters. I lower superscript letters but leave numbers and sums as is. I retain the spelling and capitalization of my source except for the substitution of "s" for "ſ." In citations from title-pages of quartos in W. W. Greg's *Bibliography of the English Printed Drama*, I delete hyphens that mark line-breaks on the title-page, italicize the normative title of the play, and use Roman type for other kinds of information. In the course of discussion in the text, I use conventional modern spelling for the play titles (i.e., *Upstart*, not *Vpstart*).

For the reader's convenience also, I cite the following standard references in the text using the abbreviations as specified:

> *APC: Acts of the Privy Council of England.* Ed. J. R. Dasent. 32 vols. London: HMSO, 1890–1907.
> *BEPD: A Bibliography of the English Printed Drama to the Restoration.* Ed. W. W. Greg. 4 vols. London: Bibliographical Society, 1939.
> *B&F: The Collected Works of Beaumont and Fletcher.* Ed. Fredson Bowers. 4 vols. Oxford: Oxford University Press, 1966–1979. I use this edition for all quotations from Beaumont and Fletcher's plays.
> *CSP, Dom: Calendar of State Papers, Domestic.* Ed. Mary Jane Everett Green. 12 vols. London: Longmans, 1856–1872.
> *Diary: Henslowe's Diary.* Ed. W. W. Greg. 2 vols. London: A. H. Bullen, 1904, 1908.
> *ES: The Elizabethan Stage.* E. K. Chambers. 4 vols. Oxford: Clarendon Press, 1923.
> *HD: Henslowe's Diary.* Eds. R. A. Foakes and R. T. Rickert. Cambridge: Cambridge University Press, 1961.
> *H&S: Ben Jonson.* Eds. C. H. Herford and Percy Simpson. 11 vols.

Oxford: Clarendon Press, 1925–1952. I use this edition for all quotations from Jonson's plays.

MSC: Malone Society *Collections.*

MSR: Malone Society *Reprints.*

Riverside: The Riverside Shakespeare. Gen. ed. G. Blakemore Evans. Boston: Houghton Mifflin, 1974. I use this edition for all quotations from Shakespeare's plays.

S.R.: Stationers' Register.

STC: A Short-Title Catalogue of Books Printed in England, Scotland, & Ireland, and of English Books Printed Abroad, 1475–1640. Comps. A. W. Pollard and G. R. Redgrave. London: Bibliographic Society, 1926.

WS: William Shakespeare: A Study of Facts and Problems. E. K. Chambers. 2 vols. Oxford: Clarendon Press, 1930.

Introduction

1. I accept the claims of ownership by the Chamberlain's and King's men on title-pages of quartos except in the cases of *The Famous Victories of Henry V* and *Alphonsus Emperor of Germany.* On the title-page of the first quarto (1598) *The Famous Victories of Henry V* is attributed to the Queen's men. That claim is probably right. There is no evidence to suggest the migration of the playbook to Shakespeare's company by 1617, at which time it was published with an attribution on the title-page of the quarto to the King's men. The company ownership of *Alphonsus Emperor of Germany* is more complicated. On the title-page of the first quarto (1654) the play is attributed to the King's men. Moreover, several documents locate a play named *Alphonso* in the company's repertory between 1630 and 1641 (G. E. Bentley, *The Jacobean and Caroline Stage,* 7 vols. [Oxford: Clarendon Press, 1941–1968], V, 1285–88). However, I do not find evidence that the company owned this play before Shakespeare's retirement. Neither George Peele, to whom the play is ascribed in the Stationers' Register, nor George Chapman, to whom it is ascribed on the title-page of the quarto, seems to

have traded with Shakespeare's company. The King's men did acquire some old Chapman plays in the 1630s; perhaps one of them was *Alphonsus Emperor of Germany* (known by then also as *Alphonso*).

Chapter 1

1. Edmond Malone, *The Plays and Poems of William Shakespeare in Ten Volumes* (London: H. Baldwin, 1790), I.2, 288.

2. J. P. Collier, *The Diary of Philip Henslowe* (London: Shakespeare Society, 1845), xiii. A subsequent citation is noted in the text.

3. F. G. Fleay, *A Chronicle History of the London Stage, 1559–1642* (rpt. New York: Burt Franklin, 1964), 94. Subsequent citations are noted in the text.

4. Bernard Beckerman, "Philip Henslowe," *The Theatrical Manager in England and America,* ed. Joseph W. Donohue, Jr. (Princeton: Princeton University Press, 1971), 43. A subsequent citation is noted in the text.

5. Bernard Beckerman, *Shakespeare at the Globe, 1599–1609* (New York: Macmillan, 1962), 5.

6. Neil Carson, *A Companion to Henslowe's Diary* (Cambridge: Cambridge University Press, 1988), 67.

7. Additional support for the argument that *The Love of a Grecian Lady* and *The Grecian Comedy* are continuations of *The Love of an English Lady* is the fact that the dates of their appearances, when collated (as in the excerpt from the play lists in October and November of 1594, at which time the title *The Grecian Comedy* takes over), fall into a pattern compatible with the frequency, spacing of performances, and diminishing receipts characteristic of single plays elsewhere in the lists. In the calculation of average receipts for these and other plays here, I round off to the nearest shilling.

8. Malone, I.2, 289, n. 1.

9. Foakes and Rickert summarize the suggestions that have been made (*HD,* xxxiii–xxxvi).

10. William Lambarde in *Perambulation of Kent* (1596 edition) refers

to two layers of prices in the galleries: "one pennie at the gate, another at the entrie of the Scaffolde, and the thirde for a quiet standing" (qtd. in *ES*, II, 359). For more on the relation of viewing areas and prices, see Ann Jennalie Cook, *The Privileged Playgoers of Shakespeare's London, 1576–1642* (Princeton: Princeton University Press, 1981), 150–52, 181–82; and Andrew Gurr, *Playgoing in Shakespeare's London* (Cambridge: Cambridge University Press, 1987), 15–18.

11. Samuel Keichel, a foreign visitor to London in 1585, remarked on the custom of double admission prices (*ES*, II, 358). For discussions of admission prices, see Cook, 190–95, and Alfred Harbage, *Shakespeare's Audience* (New York: Columbia University Press, 1941), 28–36.

12. *Stuart Royal Proclamations*, eds. James F. Larkin and Paul L. Hughes (Oxford: Clarendon Press, 1973), 14. Greg believed that there were no Sunday performances, and he corrected all of Henslowe's dates. Often there was a free Saturday or Monday nearby to which he could shift the offending Sunday performance, but not always. Theater historians have been curiously willing to believe Greg over Henslowe.

13. Greg also counted thirty-five, but he and I are not counting the same plays. I believe that the Admiral's men performed the first and second parts of *Godfrey of Bulloigne* ("Henslowe's Naming of Parts," *Notes and Queries* 30 [1983]: 157–60); Greg believed that the entries of the title represent a single playbook (*Diary*, II, 166). Further, I take Greg's suggestion about collapsing the three plays in the sample discussed above into a single stage run (Greg did not, in fact, take his own suggestion, as I do here [*Diary*, II, 170]).

14. I count the performance of "welche man" as a performance of *Longshanks;* Greg suggested that reading but did not embrace it (*Diary*, II, 178). I explain why I believe that *Longshanks* was a genuinely new play, discrete from *Edward I* by George Peele, in "Play Identifications: *The Wise Man of West Chester* and *John a Kent and John a Cumber; Longshanks* and *Edward I*," *Huntington Library Quarterly*, 47 (1984): 1–11.

15. Some of the data in *Henslowe's Diary* suggest a larger annual repertory. Strange's men offered twenty-four plays in eighteen weeks, and Sussex's men offered twelve in eight weeks. In 1599–1600 the Admiral's

men laid out cash for thirty-six new plays, along with which they must have scheduled at least a few continuations and perhaps a revival or two. But these accounts are deceptive. The Admiral's men usually scheduled more different plays at the start of a season than in later weeks. And in 1599–1600 the company was responding to the arrival of the Chamberlain's men across the street at the Globe as well as preparing for the imminent opening of the Fortune.

16. One of the details that users of the diary will interpret differently is the distinction between continuations and revivals when the performances of plays are widely separated. The treatment of *The Jew of Malta* is a good frame of reference for ambiguous cases. The interval of a year between performances (from 9 December 1594 to 9 January 1596) and the concentration of its performances in each run (June to December, 1594; January to June, 1596) suggest to me that the play was being revived in 1595–96, not continued. I consider *Belin Dun* in revival in 1595–96 and again in 1596–97 because its performances are widely separated: from 15 November 1594 to 11 July 1596; from 11 July 1596 to 31 March 1597. Nonetheless, given the isolated performance on 11 July 1596, another reader may reasonably consider the play a continuation. Other cases are the returns of *Long Meg of Westminster* to the stage at the start of the fall season in 1596–97, of *The Wise Man of West Chester* at the end of the spring season in 1596–97, and of *Doctor Faustus* at the beginning of the fall season in 1597–98. I consider all three to be revivals. I believe that the Admiral's men had retired each play but brought them back into production more quickly than they might have because of commercial conditions prevailing at the time.

17. Those plays and the number of performances are *The Wise Man of West Chester* (29), part one of *Seven Days of the Week* (22), *The Blind Beggar of Alexandria* (22), *A Knack to Know an Honest Man* (21), *Belin Dun* (16), *Crack Me This Nut* (16), *Alexander and Lodowick* (15), *The Grecian Comedy* (14, including those with an alternate title), *Chinon of England* (14), *Longshanks* (14), *Henry V* (13), *Valteger* (13), *The Comedy of Humors* (13, counting its continuation into the fall of 1597–98).

18. Beckerman, *Shakespeare at the Globe*, 8

19. The plays and numbers of months are *A Knack to Know an Honest*

Man (26), *The Wise Man of West Chester* (20), part one of *Seven Days of the Week* (19), *The Blind Beggar of Alexandria* (17), and *The Grecian Comedy* (13).

20. For the list by number of performances, these plays are *Doctor Faustus*, 24 performances over 29 months; *1 Tamburlaine*, 15 performances over 16 months; *The French Doctor*, 14 performances over 26 months; and *Jeronimo*, 13 performances over 10 months. For the list by months, substitute *The Siege of London* (12 performances over 20 months) for *Jeronimo*. If *Long Meg of Westminster* was being continued in the fall of 1596–97 instead of being revived, it should be counted in both lists (16 performances over 25 months).

21. In regard to these partial payments, Chambers believed that dramatists often took money from the Admiral's men without returning a product. There is some evidence, however, that the company received the parts of a play in installments as paid for. In a note dated 4 April 1600, Samuel Rowley instructed Henslowe to pay the bearer 40s. in earnest for five sheets of *The Conquest of the West Indies* and to "take the papers Into yo*u*r [Henslowe's] one hands" (*HD*, 294). Richard Hathway offered to sign an IOU for the money he had been paid on *The Conquest of Spain* if he could "haue his papars agayne" (*HD*, 295). I assume, therefore, that the company received *something* when it paid out money in earnest on a script that did not materialize, but clearly it did not receive what it had hoped to receive (a playable text).

22. For a discussion of revisions for revival, see my "*Henslowe's Diary* and the Economics of Play Revision for Revival, 1592–1603," *Theatre Research International* 10 (1985): 1–18.

23. *The Complete Works of Christopher Marlowe*, ed. Fredson Bowers, 2 vols. (London: Cambridge University Press, 1973), I. I use this edition for all quotations from Marlowe's plays.

24. In *The Real War of the Theaters*, R. B. Sharpe declared that the Chamberlain's men had no interest in the stories of knights, for their "audience . . . considered the romance bourgeois and old-fashioned" ([Boston: D. C. Heath, 1935], 48). He believed that even if a Burbage diary like Henslowe's were to be discovered, there would not be among

the titles "anything like equality with the Admiral's list in romance" (34). He asserted also that the company must have rejected biblical plays after the 1594 offering of *Hester and Ahasuerus* because in later years "we never hear of their presenting such material" (28). Sharpe's influence is evident in the statement recently of a noted theater historian, who claims that Shakespeare's company "left no sign of any wish to imitate . . . Alleyn trademarks" such as "[h]eroic plays in Oriental settings" and plays with devils (Andrew Gurr, "Intertextuality at Windsor," *Shakespeare Quarterly* 38 [1987]: 193). To his credit, even though he wished to differentiate and privilege the Chamberlain's men for the quality of their repertory, Sharpe did know—at a time when the idea was unthinkable—that the company's intention was to be *commercially* successful.

25. Beckerman, *Shakespeare at the Globe,* 18.

Chapter 2

1. Information here on the Swan and Boar's Head playhouses comes from *A London Life in the Brazen Age* by William Ingram (Cambridge: Harvard University Press, 1978) and *The Boar's Head Playhouse* by Herbert Berry (Washington, D.C.: Folger Books, 1986), respectively.

2. F. G. Fleay, *A Biographical Chronicle of the English Drama, 1559–1642,* 2 vols. 1891 (New York: Burt Franklin, 1969), II, 282.

3. *STC* 16677, 56.

4. "An Unrecorded Elizabethan Performance of *Titus Andronicus,*" *Shakespeare Survey 14* (1961): 108. As Ungerer points out, the companies named in 1594 on the title-page of the quarto of *Titus Andronicus* were either no longer "London" companies or no longer in business. The Admiral's men and Queen's men were in London in 1595–96, but there is no evidence that either company had acquired a text of this play. Except for a possible double ownership of *The Spanish Tragedy/Jeronimo,* I have not found an instance of two London companies' owning and performing the same playbook in competition with one another (I assume that Paul's Boys and the Chamberlain's men played *Satiromastix* in collusion in

1601–02, not in competition). Theater historians used to speak of performances in the provinces as a burden on companies. Due to the collections of records published by the Malone Society and the volumes in the project known as Records of Early English Drama, we have come to realize that companies traveled more often and more willingly than we had thought. The journey to Rutland, though difficult over winter roads, was not impossible to accomplish in the break between the company's performances at Court on 27 December and 11 January. From a commercial point of view, Christmastide was not a good time to be away from London, but we do not know the conditions and possible compensations of the invitation to travel. The company might have had quite an audience. According to Ungerer, Sir John entertained "as many as nine hundred visitors" over the twelve days of Christmas (103).

5. *The Diary of John Manningham of the Middle Temple 1602–1603,* ed. Robert P. Sorlien (Hanover, N.H.: The University Press of New England, 1976), 75.

6. *Skialetheia, or A Shadow of Truth, in Certaine Epigrams and Satyres,* ed. D. Allen Carroll (Chapel Hill: University of North Carolina Press, 1974). Carroll cites Stow's *Annals* on the fate of John Barrose.

7. *The Poems of John Marston,* ed. Arnold Davenport (Liverpool: Liverpool University Press, 1961). There is an allusion to "Montacutes," possibly to the Montagues in *Romeo and Juliet* in Guilpin's "Satire V" also. In a caricature of a soldier, Guilpin's satirist laughs at ". . . one in a muffler of Cad'z-beard, / . . . With him a troupe all in gold-dawbed sutes, / Looking like *Talbots, Percies, Montacutes*" (ll. 75, 77–78). "Montacutes," "Talbots," and "Percies" could be simply bywords for swaggering soldiers. But the references could also be to Shakespeare's *Romeo and Juliet, 1 Henry VI,* and either or both parts of *Henry IV.* Immediately after finishing the caricature of the soldier, the speaker looks ahead: "But see yonder, / One like the vnfrequented Theater / Walkes in darke silence" (ll. 83–85). The context of the allusion, therefore, is theatrical. These lines even suggest an allusion to *Hamlet* in the reference to "blacke fancies" and a "troubled breast" (ll. 86–87).

NOTES TO PAGES 65–74

8. Anne Barton discusses the disguised king as a dramatic motif in "The King Disguised: Shakespeare's *Henry V* and the Comical History" in *The Triple Bond: Plays, Mainly Shakespearean, in Performance,* ed. Joseph G. Price (University Park: Pennsylvania State University Press, 1975), 92–117.

9. Sharpe, 28.

10. *The Works of Thomas Nashe,* ed. Ronald B. McKerrow, 5 vols. (Oxford: Basil Blackwell, 1958), III, 315. I use this edition for all quotations from Nashe's works.

11. *A Warning for Fair Women,* ed. Charles D. Cannon (The Hague: Mouton, 1975), ll. 54–55, 56. I use this edition for all quotations from the play.

12. *Kemps Nine Daies Wonder,* intro. by Alexander Dyce (London: Camden Society, 1830), 22.

13. In two other plays on stage in 1594–1596, Shakespeare alludes to *The Jew of Malta.* In *Romeo and Juliet,* he invokes the scene in which Barabas waits in the street for his daughter Abigail to find the money hidden beneath the floor in an upper room of his house (now confiscated by nuns). Barabas sees movement at the window: "But stay, what starre shines yonder in the *East*? / The Loadstarre of my life, if *Abigaill*" (II.i.41–42). Romeo, having slipped into Juliet's garden, sees movement on the balcony above: "But soft, what light through yonder window breaks? / It is the east, and Juliet is the sun" (II.i.2–3). The death speech of Pyramus in *A Midsummer Night's Dream* (beginning "Thus die I") repeats key words from the final line of Barabas: "Dye, life, flye soule, tongue curse thy fill and dye" (V.v.89).

14. Gary Taylor, *Henry V* (Oxford: Clarendon Press, 1982), 4.

15. Hanspeter Born argues convincingly that *2 Henry VI* and *3 Henry VI* were composed by August 1592 and acquired as a pair by Pembroke's men ("The Date of *2, 3 Henry VI*," *Shakespeare Quarterly* 25 [1974]: 323–34).

16. Leslie Hotson, *Shakespeare versus Shallow* (London: Nonesuch Press, 1931).

17. Nicholas Rowe, *The Works of Mr. William Shakespeare*, 6 vols. (London: J. Tonson, 1709), I, viii–ix. A subsequent citation is given in the text.

18. T. W. Baldwin, *Shakespere's Love's Labor's Won* (Carbondale: Southern Illinois University Press, 1957), 30.

19. Wells and Taylor accept *Love's Labor's Won* into the Shakespeare canon in the Oxford *Complete Works*. Harold Metz settles the issue of the title masterfully in "*Wonne* is 'lost, quite lost,'" *Modern Language Studies* 16 (1986): 3–12. If *Love's Labor's Won* was not the narrative sequel to *Love's Labor's Lost*, audiences might not have been surprised. In 1594–95, the Admiral's men introduced a play called *A Knack to Know an Honest Man*. It seems intentionally to recall the title of *A Knack to Know a Knave*, yet it has nothing whatsoever to do with the earlier play.

20. Spencer had been a fellow of Jonson's in the company of Pembroke's, had been imprisoned with him at the Marshalsea over *The Isle of Dogs*, and had moved to the Admiral's men also in October 1597. Five years before, Spencer had had professional contact with some members of the Chamberlain's men, for he and several of them had been fellows in the Pembroke's troupe of 1592–93, at which time he had played in *3 Henry VI*. In 1598 he still lived in Hogge Lane, in the parish of St. Leonard Shoreditch where the Theatre and Curtain stood, and in the neighborhood of Holywell where the Burbages lived. We have the reaction of one of Jonson's professional associates to the duel: in a letter dated 26 September 1598, Philip Henslowe writes Edward Alleyn: "I haue loste one of my company w*hi*ch hurteth me greatley that is gabrell for he is slayen in [*f*] hoges den fylldes by the hands of benge<men> Jonson bricklayer" (*HD*, 286). Henslowe seems to express sorrow in the phrase "hurteth me greatley," but he follows with a line that may turn the whole passage into a request for Alleyn's business advice, given the player's loss: "I wold fayne haue alittell of your cownsell yf I cowld." What must Spencer's theatrical colleagues (and neighbors) in Shoreditch have thought? In *Satiromastix* Tucca seems to upbraid Horace with equal fervor for his epigrams, acting skills, and killing of a fellow player. Can this have been the Burbages' attitude? Whatever this incident may say about the emotional reactions of

Spencer's colleagues in the playhouse world, it does make clear that Dekker expected audiences to remember Jonson's duel.

Chapter 3

1. In essays in *Shakespeare's Playhouses* (New York: AMS Press, 1987), Herbert Berry discusses lawsuits connected with the property in Shoreditch ("A Handlist of Documents"), ownership of the property in Maid Lane ("The Globe: Documents and Ownership"), and the cost of the Globe ("A New Law Suit about the Globe"). I rely on these essays for information about the playhouse.

2. The records kept by Henslowe for the Admiral's men from 20 June to 20 December 1600 cannot be a full record of the company's expenditures. During this six-month period, there is only one payment for a playbook (20s. for *Fortune's Tennis*). There are a few payments in these months for apparel, alterations to texts, and general expenses, but the absence of payments for texts suggests that some of the company's business was going through agents other than Henslowe, perhaps senior members of the company. Thus the disparity between purchases of new plays in 1599–1600 and 1600–01 may not have been as great as it appears.

3. In recent years critics in the school of New Historicism have emphasized the fact that the players were called to explain themselves, implying that this revival illustrates the degree to which the drama in Shakespeare's time and that in the repertory of the Chamberlain's men in particular followed an agenda of political subversion. J. Leeds Barroll offers an alternative reading of the circumstances of the revival and its role in the Essex Rebellion in "A New History for Shakespeare and His Time," *Shakespeare Quarterly* 39 (1988): 441–64.

4. The first quotation here, of course, is from *As You Like It* (II.vii.139). The second is from *Every Man out of His Humor* (Prologue, l. 49). The third is from *A Larum for London* (Prologue, l. 1), cited from the J. S. Farmer edition for *Tudor Facsimile Texts* (1910), Microfiche,

Library of English Literature, #40023. I use this edition for all quotations from the play.

5. The idea that the sign of the Globe was Hercules with the world on his shoulders comes from George Steevens, in a note to *Hamlet,* II.ii.361, in the 1778 edition of *The Plays of William Shakespeare* (10 vols.). Malone repeated the note in 1790, and editors have routinely done so since. As Richard Dutton points out, the source of Steevens's information is not known, but it has good theatrical credentials, including the analogue of the sign of Dame Fortune at the Admiral's new playhouse (*"Hamlet, An Apology for Actors,* and the Sign of the Globe," *Shakespeare Survey 41* [1988]: 35–43).

6. Platter does not name the Curtain specifically, but he does say that the play was given not far from his inn, "in the suburb, at Bishopsgate," to the best of his recollection. This address would seem to fit the Curtain best. (Ernest Schanzer, "Thomas Platter's Observations on the Elizabethan Stage," *Notes and Queries* 201 [1956]: 465–67. I use Schanzer's translation of Platter here and subsequently.)

7. *STC* 12301. I use this text for quotations from Greene's prose work.

8. Sorlien, 48.

9. W. A. Abrams, ed., *The Merry Devil of Edmonton, 1608* (Durham: Duke University Press, 1942), Prologue, l. 15. I use this edition for all quotations from the play.

10. The answer that nineteenth-century theater historians would give to the question of a new text of *Hamlet* is that the quality of plays by Shakespeare was so superior that the Chamberlain's men would want his text for that reason alone. I do not know of any evidence that suggests a *company* replaced a text for artistic reasons. Why should it? New texts cost money, and playgoers seem not to have demanded literary masterpieces. Steven Urkowitz, who argues that the *Hamlet* quarto in 1603 is an early version of Q1604/5, is careful not to claim that Q1603 is a printing of the 1594 *Hamlet* ("'Well-sayd olde Mole': Burying three *Hamlet*s in Modern Editions," *Shakespeare Study Today: The Horace Howard Furness Memorial Lectures,* ed. Georgianna Ziegler [New York: AMS Press, 1986], 37–70.)

11. *The Shakespeare Apocrypha,* ed. C. F. Tucker Brooke (Oxford:

Clarendon, 1908). I use this edition for all quotations from the play.

12. Whyte's letter is transcribed in *Letters and Memorials of State,* ed. Arthur Collins, 3 vols. (London: T. Osborne, 1746), II, 175.

13. In "William Shakespeare, Richard James and the House of Cobham," Gary Taylor dates the revision to Falstaff in the Advent season of 1596–97, when Shakespeare's company was preparing a set of plays for the Court and when a lord Cobham was the Lord Chamberlain (*Review of English Studies,* New Series 38 [1987]: 334–54). Willem Schrickx has read Verreyken's papers in the archives in Brussels, and he finds no reference to the play at the dinner given by the Lord Chamberlain (*Foreign Envoys and Travelling Players in the Age of Shakespeare and Jonson* [Wetteren, Belgium: Universa, 1986], 8, 32). I am much indebted to Schrickx for a discussion of Anglo-Flemish relations at this time, but I do not agree with his assumption (along with Chambers) that the play referred to by Whyte was *1 Henry IV.*

14. *Troilus and Cressida* has been associated with the plays in the so-called Stage Quarrel, partly because of its nature as satire but partly also because of a quip in the second part of *Return from Parnassus* (Q1602), which claims that Shakespeare delivered the "purge" that finally got the best of Jonson. However, nothing in *Troilus and Cressida* seems to fit. There is a description of Ajax that lampoons the humors of the character, but this treatment is not really in the vein of personal attacks that we find in the characters of Crispinus and Demetrius in *Poetaster* and Horace in *Satiromastix.* Some critics believe that the trial and punishment in *Satiromastix* is the purge, but that imagery does not fit the action in this play either. If Shakespeare were joining the Stage Quarrel with *Troilus and Cressida,* the play should perhaps be dated in 1601–02. And, of course, it could not have had a curative effect unless it was brought to the stage.

15. Fredson Bowers, ed., *The Dramatic Works of Thomas Dekker,* 4 vols. (Cambridge: Cambridge University Press, 1953–1961), I. I use this edition for all quotations from the play.

16. Tucca alludes specifically to such very old plays as *Cambyses, Gammer Gurton's Needle,* and *Gorboduc.* I assume that most of the story subjects he mentions were to be found in current ballads as well as plays (including plays now lost from the Chamberlain's repertory). His coverage

is broad enough to include plays from more than one playhouse. Because of *Henslowe's Diary*, we can identify the Admiral's repertory offerings in his allusions the most easily. A sample of the names that call up Admiral's plays are Hieronimo, Damon and Pithias, Sir Tristram, Mother Redcap, Long Meg of Westminster, Alexander and Lodowick, Samson, Tamar Cham, and Tamburlaine.

Chapter 4

1. Larkin and Hughes, I, Proclamations #16, 26, 29.
2. J. Leeds Barroll, "The Chronology of Shakespeare's Jacobean Plays and the Dating of *Antony and Cleopatra*," *Essays on Shakespeare,* ed. Gordon Ross Smith (Philadelphia: University of Pennsylvania Press, 1965), 134. Barroll is not counting the summer months and the six weeks of Lent.
During this time of plague Shakespeare had more on his mind than commerce, for his brother died. The notice of burial on 31 December 1607 in the parish register of St. Saviour Southwark reads: "Edmond Shakespeare, a player: in the church." There is an additional parish record that Edmond's burial was accompanied by "a forenoone knell of the great bell, 20s." If he is the person baptised in Holy Trinity Church in Stratford-upon-Avon on 3 May 1580 (*Riverside,* 1828), Edmond Shakespeare was twenty-seven at his death. We do not know his company affiliation, but a burial entry in the parish register of St. Giles Cripplegate for 12 August 1607 gives us a glimpse into his private life: "Edward, sonne of Edward Shackspeere, Player: base borne." (Edwin Nungezer, *A Dictionary of Actors* [New Haven: Yale University Press, 1929], 315.)
3. G. K. Hunter, *The Malcontent* (London: Methuen, 1975), xli–xliv. A subsequent citation is given in the text.
4. Lowin was himself new to the King's men, but not to London playgoers; he had been a member of Worcester's men as recently as the spring of 1603.
5. In the induction, the players talk openly about their rights to the children's company's text. As Condell puts it, "Why not Malevole in folio with us, as Jeronimo in decimosexto with them? They taught us a name

for our play, we call it *One for another*" (John Marston, *The Malcontent*, ed. Barnard Harris [London: Ernest Benn, 1967], ll. 75–77). I use this edition for all quotations from this play.

6. *Extracts from the Letters and Journals of William Cory*, ed. F. W. Cornish (London: 1897), 168.

7. In New Variorum edition, Richard Knowles is noncommittal (*As You Like It* [New York: Modern Language Association, 1977], 633–34). In the Arden edition, Agnes Latham calls the performance "a tradition" (*As You Like It* [London: Methuen, 1975], lxxxvi).

8. Richard Thornberry, who calls attention to the revisions, does not suggest a more specific date for the revival than a period between April 1604 and 1606 ("A Seventeenth-Century Revival of *Mucedorus* in London before 1610," *Shakespeare Quarterly* 28 [1977]: 362–64). The revival could not have been in 1604–05 because the King's men gave *The Merchant of Venice* at Court on Shrove Sunday, according to the Revels Account. J. T. Murray attributed *Mucedorus* to the Shrove Sunday performance in 1606, apparently in reference to the advertisement of such a performance on the quarto in 1610 (*English Dramatic Companies*, 2 vols. 1910 [rpt. New York: Russell & Russell, 1963], I, 173, 178, n. 3).

9. Malone, I.2, 292–93.

10. In 1930 A. E. Stamp, at the time Deputy Keeper of the Public Records, provided facsimiles of the Revels documents in *The Disputed Revels Accounts* (Oxford: Shakespeare Association, 1930). He also reviewed the arguments once raised on the authenticity of the documents and supported their legitimacy.

11. *The Third Report of the Royal Commission on Historical Manuscripts* (London: HMSO, 1872), III.3, 148.

12. J. P. Collier, ed., *Early English Poetry, Ballads, and Popular Literature of the Middle Ages*, vol. 2 (London: Percy Society, 1840), 13. The story version from which I quote here and subsequently is in the fifth section of this edition, 12–15; the section carries the title-page, "The Mad Pranks and Merry Jests of Robin Goodfellow" and is dated 1841.

13. Alan C. Dessen, *Jonson's Moral Comedy* (Evanston: Northwestern University Press, 1971), 81.

14. *The Fair Maid of Bristow*, ed. Arthur Hobson Quinn, *Publications*

of the University of Pennsylvannia Series in Philology and Literature, 8.1 (1902), I.iii.92. I use this edition for all quotations from the play.

15. *The Shakespeare Apocrypha,* ed. C. F. Tucker Brooke (Oxford: Clarendon Press, 1908). I use this edition for all quotations from the play.

16. *The Shakespeare Apocrypha,* ed. C. F. Tucker Brooke (Oxford: Clarendon Press, 1908). I use this edition for all quotations from the play.

17. Barnabe Barnes, *The Devil's Charter,* ed. R. B. McKerrow (Louvain: A. Uystpruyst, 1904). I use this edition for all quotations from the play.

18. Cyril Tourneur, *The Revenger's Tragedy,* ed. R. A. Foakes (Cambridge: Harvard University Press, 1966). I use this edition for all quotations from the play.

19. Scott McMillin argues for an assignment of *Sir Thomas More* to the Prince's men (*The Elizabethan Theatre & The Book of Sir Thomas More* [Ithaca: Cornell University Press, 1987).

20. W. F. Arbuckle, "The 'Gowrie Conspiracy,'" *The Scottish Historical Review* 36 (1957): 7. For the official version of events, I rely on Arbuckle's narrative, 1–24; and for the public reaction to that version, I rely on the second part of Arbuckle's article, 89–110. For biographical information on the Ruthvens, I rely on Samuel Cowan's *The Gowrie Conspiracy and its Official Narrative* (London: Sampson Low, 1902).

21. E. Sawyer, ed., *Memorials of Affairs of State in the Reigns of Queen Elizabeth and King James I,* 3 vols. (London, 1725), II, 41.

22. It is worth noting that the children's company at Blackfriars presented several plays that offended King James, beginning with Marston's *The Dutch Courtesan* in 1604. In 1605–06, offensive drama cost the company the patronage of Queen Anne. I find it hard to believe that the King's men, so newly privileged by the distinction of their own patronage, would risk all with a play that openly insinuated the king's culpability in the Gowrie affair. Possibly, though, the use even of the official narrative seemed to some councilors to invite gossip about the king's motives.

23. Fleay's opinion is in *A Biographical Chronicle of the English Drama, 1559–1642,* 2 vols. 1891 (New York: Burt Franklin, 1969), II, 206–8; Maxwell's is in *Studies in the Shakespeare Apocrypha,* 1956 (rpt. New York: Greenwood Press, 1969), 169–71.

24. Roger Prior has discovered a number of cases in the Middlesex Sessions that indicate Wilkins's first-hand knowledge of such tavern behavior. It seems that by 1610 Wilkins was a victualler and innkeeper, probably also a whoremaster. One of the cases concerns the ruin of a young heir named Bonner. Several others are charges of physical violence against women; in one, he allegedly kicked a pregnant woman in the belly. See "The Life of George Wilkins," *Shakespeare Survey 25* (1972): 137–52, and "George Wilkins and the Young Heir," *Shakespeare Survey 29* (1976): 33–39.

Chapter 5

1. For information here on the lease of Blackfriars, I rely on *Shakespeare's Blackfriars Playhouse* by Irwin Smith (New York: New York University Press, 1964), 175–76; 243–47.

2. G. E. Bentley, "Shakespeare and the Blackfriars Theatre," *Shakespeare Survey 1* (1948): 46.

3. Each of these quartos carries a title-page on which *Pericles* is called a "much admired Play" (*BEPD* no. 284). Yet it is also called "LATE," and the reference to its performance is in the past tense: "As it hath been diuers and sundry times acted." If playing conditions had been normal, I would read this phrasing as proof that the play was retired, but I assume that schedules were so disrupted in 1608–09 that the companies hardly knew themselves from day to day what their offerings would be. Under these circumstances, I would not expect a stationer to know whether a playbook he had acquired was still receiving a few performances.

4. Qtd. in *England as Seen by Foreigners,* William Brenchley Rye (London: John Russell Smith, 1865), 61.

5. The title page might be as belated in its advertisement of performance as of additions, which in fact date back to Q1606. The Shrovetide performance may have been in 1605–06 also.

6. According to the Revels Account of 1611–12, the King's men joined with Queen Anne's men to perform *The Silver Age* on 12 January 1612 and *The Rape of Lucrece* on 13 January. Thomas Heywood,

at the time a player with and dramatist for Queen Anne's men, wrote both plays; I think it likely that Queen Anne's men owned the texts, not the King's men.

7. *The Second Maiden's Tragedy,* ed. Anne Lancashire (Manchester: Manchester University Press, 1978), 14–15. I use this edition for all quotations from the play.

8. *The Life and Letters of Sir Henry Wotton,* ed. Logan Pearsall Smith, 2 vols. (Oxford: Clarendon Press, 1907), II, 32–33.

9. Because Jonson changed the setting to London and Anglicized the characters' names, recent scholars date the revision after *The Alchemist* (Ralph Alan Cohen, "The Importance of Setting in the Revision of *Every Man in His Humour,*" *English Literary Renaissance* 8 [1978]: 184, n. 4).

10. Chambers identifies the "Falstafe" entry as a reference to *2 Henry IV* (*ES,* II, 217). I think it is more likely to have been *The Merry Wives of Windsor,* if for no other reason than the Revels Account of 1604–05, which shows the ability of the play to prompt a revival. However, due to the evidence of alternative titles used for *Philaster* and *Much Ado about Nothing,* it is possible that "The Hotspurr" and "Sr Iohn Falstafe," which were scheduled before different audiences, are also alternative titles and refer to the same play, *1 Henry IV.* No one has questioned that "Caesars Tragedye" is Shakespeare's *Julius Caesar,* but in the context of commercial duplication I must say that it is entirely possible that the King's men had more than one play on the life of this noble Roman.

11. Gurr, 169.

12. This wisdom apparently originates in *Historia Histrionica* (1699) by James Wright, who referred to Blackfriars and the Globe as the King's men's "Winter and Summer House" (qtd. in *William Shakespeare: A Textual Companion,* ed. Stanley Wells and Gary Taylor [Oxford: Oxford University Press, 1987], 90–91; Taylor points out that the seasonal change of playhouses may obtain in a period later than 1609–1613).

13. John H. Astington, "The Popularity of *Cupid's Revenge,*" *Studies in English Literature* 19 (1979): 217.

14. Lancashire, 5.

15. Richard Proudfoot, "Shakespeare and the New Dramatists of the

King's Men, 1606–1613," *Later Shakespeare* (New York: St. Martin's Press, 1967), 246.

16. Astington makes the case for success of the latter play in particular in "The Popularity of *Cupid's Revenge*," *Studies in English Literature* 19 (1979): 215–27.

17. Eugene Waith implies that by the phrase "familiar people" Fletcher means "gentlemen," that is, courtiers and noblemen. Waith considers the *"Imitation of manners in the familiar world"* to be a prime characteristic of Beaumont and Fletcher's tragicomedy, along with (2) *"Remoteness from the familiar world,"* (3) *"Intricacy of plot,"* (4) *"The improbable hypothesis,"* (5) *"The atmosphere of evil,"* (6) *"Protean characters,"* (7) *"'Lively touches of passion,'"* and (8) *"The language of emotion"* (*The Pattern of Tragicomedy in Beaumont and Fletcher* [New Haven: Yale University Press, 1952], 36–41). Waith uses *A King and No King* to discuss these features and to illustrate thereby the generic norm.

18. Smith, II, 33.

Conclusion

1. In "The Queen's Men and the London Theatre of 1583," Scott McMillin discusses political dimensions of the selection of companies for Court performances (*The Elizabethan Theatre* X, ed. C. E. McGee [Port Credit: P. D. Meany, 1988], 10–13).

2. Ingram, 150.

3. Greg, "The Date of *King Lear* and Shakespeare's Use of Earlier Versions of the Story," *The Library* 20 (1940): 384, 385. Pinciss, "Shakespeare, Her Majesty's Players and Pembroke's Men," *Shakespeare Survey* 27 (1974): 133.

4. Actually, there is no reason why the run of *King Leir* could not have been offered by the King's men at the Globe.

5. E. K. Chambers was much taken with the notion that the Chamberlain's men acquired *Woodstock* during the migration of plays in 1593–94; he believed that it was "so close" in story materials to

Shakespeare's *Richard II* "as to make it natural to regard it as having become a Chamberlain's play" (*ES*, IV, 43).

6. *Edward II* was printed again in 1598 and 1612, each time with an advertisement of Pembroke's men. There was such a company in 1596–97, but not, as far as we know, in 1612. In 1622, *Edward II* was printed yet again; some of the title-pages carry the name of Pembroke's men, but some carry an advertisement of the late Queen Anne's men at the Red Bull (i.e., of around 1606–1613). It is obvious to me that this play stayed in the hands of some player and/or company from 1593 to 1622, traveling from the bankrupt Pembroke's men in 1593 to the Queen's men sometime around 1606. But where was it from 1594 to 1605? I like to think that *Edward II* migrated to the Chamberlain's men from Pembroke's stock in 1594 and that the Chamberlain's men performed Marlowe's play either when Shakespeare was writing *Richard II* in 1594–95 or when his company brought his play into production in 1595–96. I would nominate Christopher Beeston as the player with whom the text traveled to Worcester's-Queen Anne's men.

7. As Robert Y. Turner puts it, the play is often accused of being "more of an age than for all time" ("Dramatic Conventions in *All's Well That Ends Well*," *Publications of the Modern Language Association* 75 [1960]: 497).

8. Beckerman, *Shakespeare at the Globe*, 15.

9. Peggy M. Simonds, describing the duality of marital and eschatological motifs in the play, makes this point much more fully in "Sacred and Sexual Motifs in *All's Well That Ends Well*," *Renaissance Quarterly* 42 (1989): 33–59.

INDEX

NOTE: Citations given within the text are not included in the index.

INDEX

in continuation, 140
parallels with other plays, 161–62
title-page advertisements, 142
King John, 60, 190
commercial value, 65, 71, 169
King John, The Troublesome Reign of,
71, 138–39, 191
company ownership, 8, 71
in revival, 169
title-page advertisements, 139
King Lear, 92, 107, 125, 191, 229
at Court, 107
commercial value, 129, 170
in continuation, 107
King Leir, 59, 107, 129, 170, 229
title-page advertisements, 170
King Sebastian of Portugal, 47, 49
King's men, 2, 3, 4, 7, 9, 12, 13, 18,
20, 54, 55, 59, 78, 103–33,
135–64, 165, 167, 170, 179, 180,
185, 187, 189, 194, 196, 198,
199, 202, 203, 205, 208, 212,
224, 226, 229 (*See also* the
Chamberlain's men and William
Shakespeare)
advertisement of the company,
108
anticipation of performances at
Blackfriars, 136
assertiveness, 132
commercial tactics, 177
at Blackfriars, 136
at Court, 168
comedies, 41–43, 112–19,
143–48, 174
duplicate plays, 129–32,
152–58, 176, 228
histories, 46, 125–29,
148–52
serials and sequels, 129,
152–58, 171
tragedies, 45, 119–25,
152–58, 176

tragicomedies, 158–63
Court payments, 104, 109, 132,
136, 137
employment of dramatists, 142
losses from fire at Globe, 164
on tour, 103, 138
patent, 103
patronage (*See* Patronage)
performances (*See also*
Performances)
with Queen Anne's men,
227–28
playhouses (*See* Playhouses)
repertory system, use of, 13, 136,
143, 177
continuations, 107–8,
137–40
new plays, 106–7, 137–40
revivals, 105, 109–11,
137–41, 142, 148, 176, 225
Knack to Know a Knave, A, 8, 22, 42,
52, 59, 220
Knack to Know an Honest Man, A, 10,
26, 37, 52, 215, 220
Knaves, The, 152
Knight of the Burning Pestle, The, 41,
112, 158
Knot of Fools, The, 143, 191
at Court, 140
Knowles, Richard, 225
Knutson, Roslyn L., 214, 216
Kyd, Thomas, 7, 11, 44, 66, 92, 175,
189

Lady Jane, two parts, 51, 94
Lambarde, William, 213
Lambeth Palace, 60
Lancashire, Anne B., 228
Langley, Francis, 14, 58, 71, 74, 169
Larkin, James F., 214, 224
Larum for London, A, 10, 81, 182,
192, 221
commercial value, 97–98